THE ALTAR

MEGAN GRACE

Table of Contents

Chapter 1

I slide out of the pew and crawl underneath, slipping away from Mother's sight while her focus is on the serpent that slithered from Elder Armsteine's left shoulder, then across the back of his neck, and finally perched on top of his right shoulder, the stout body curled in a circle and the broad head fanged at the man. I don't want to see another reenactment of what happened to Elder Barter the last time they did the snake ritual. The serpent wrapped tightly around Barter's neck and dug its fangs deep into the side of his cheek, the venom ran through his veins, turning the side of his face blue and purple. In less than five hours Elder Barter had passed away.

"He was the chosen one," Mother told me as I cried in bed that night, her fingers gently tugged at my hair as she racked her fingers through the knots. "You know what we say, the serpent chooses who will be the next sacrifice... Elder Barter was the chosen sacrifice." As I sat modestly in the pews this morning I couldn't take my eyes off of the wooden box where the serpent lay. I tried to ignore it but it was rather hard when you could hear it hissing throughout the sermon. I could hardly pay attention to what Reverend Finch was preaching about.

After three hours had passed, the time had come. Elder Armsteine carefully placed the box on a wooden pedestal and lifted the lid open and the serpent's head rose and began to search for the next chosen one. Elder Armsteine's eyes bulged with fear and amusement when the serpent turned around and stared up at him, its tongue hissed as Elder Armsteine sat on a wooden stool and Reverend Finch carefully placed the serpent on his shoulders. His breath quickened while the snake wrapped around him like a necklace.

I started to feel queasy and faint as I watched in horror. I should be used to this. It's a ritual that we do once a year as a sacrifice to the church for the sins of us all. It cleanses us and makes us pure again. But half of my fear wasn't about this ritual, it was also about the biggest ritual we have every five years. The sacrifice where Reverend Finch calls upon us younger girls and chooses one of us to be the next sacrifice for our savior. Even though it sure sounds the same, it's entirely different in every aspect. The snake ritual is to cleanse *our souls* and save us from *our sins*. The Sacrifice we have every five years is for our *Lord* and *Savior,* to feast upon one of us girls to keep *his spirit alive.* Even though it's a huge honor for one of us to be chosen it's still rather terrifying, for me at least. I don't know how the others feel about it. The last time I asked a girl, she just raised her chin high and said that it would be a great honor to be the chosen one. I try to keep how I feel tucked away from the others because they might tell on me, and then I would have to spend the next two days with Reverend Finch, listening to his gospels for hours on end, then he has you write a twenty page essay of why it is a great privilege for us girls to be chosen for the next sacrifice.

As the other girls can't wait to have that privilege, I feel that I'd rather not have it. Inside, I know that this is what I've got to do to honor my family, but a little bit in me feels like this is wrong... It's all wrong. Everything we do feels wrong, but I'm not sure why I feel this way? I do wonder if others truly feel the same or if it's just me that feels off. Either way, I need air... *fresh air.*

I silently slip through one of the tall wooden doors of the church and inhale the brisk air as the wind wraps around my face. It feels good to be finally out of that stuffy old church, rather hot too as we can't open the doors or windows for the breeze to come in, only when you're entering or leaving the church, then the doors must remain closed for the rest of the sermon.

"Are you feeling alright, Viola?" A small voice came from behind me. I turn to see Bonnie, standing in front of the church doors. She had a puzzled look with a hint of worry for me. Bonnie is the closest person to me. She doesn't give me strange looks and murmurs behind my back like the other girls do. I should've known better to think she wouldn't notice me and follow me out here. I don't want to get her in trouble.

I wave a dismissive hand. "I'm good, go back inside."

Bonnie's face dropped in relief, but instead of turning back inside, she walked down the entrance steps and stood beside me, stuffing her hands into her dress pockets. "I'd rather stay out here with you." Bonnie said, glancing around the woods that surrounded us.

I shook my head. "I don't want to get you in trouble. You should go back inside."

Bonnie ignored my response and walked over to an oak tree and plucked a yellow flower from the ground. She waved me over to come see. "A dandelion. The French call it, pissenlit. Which translates to, pee in the bed."

I giggled at her odd fact. She always knows the weirdest things. "And how do you know that?" I smile at her.

Bonnie looked down at me with her caramel eyes, they glistened in the sunlight that peeked through the trees. "I read it in a book. Here,"

She brushed my coily hair out of the way and tucked the dandelion stem behind my ear. She smiled down at me with fondness in her eyes.

"If I wear this to bed, will I pee in the bed?" I smirked.

Bonnie shrugged. "I don't know, maybe. The magic of the dandelion might possess you and make you wet yourself." We bellow out a laugh. She cracks me up.

"What are you two doing out here?" A stern voice came from behind us. We turn to see Mother with her hands gripping her hips while she squints her eyes into slits.

"Viola felt sick," Bonnie quickly replied. "I came to check on her."

"I'm feeling better now," I recoiled, bending my head down like a puppy does to their owner when they know they are in trouble.

Mother stared at us sharply. "Well, get back inside. You know what happens when you miss the sermon."

Bonnie and I nod and slide past Mother, giving her a weary smile. Bonnie and I took our seats. I sat next to Mother and Bonnie sat across the church with the other girls in rows. There we sat quietly for the next two hours as Reverend Finch went on and on about saving our savior and saving ourselves from the righteous spirits, and why Elder Armsteine is the chosen one. I drowned out most of it knowing better that Reverend Finch would test us on today's sermon for school tomorrow. But it was hard to focus when Elder Armsteine held a towel against his neck to keep the punctured snake bites from spilling blood on the wooden floors. His pale skin started to have a bluish tint and his veins popped out of his neck and cheek. I glanced back over to the hissing box, listening to the python thrashing the walls for a way out, wanting the taste of more blood.

It only felt minutes later when Mother eagerly tugged on my sleeve. I looked up at her as she towered over me. "Viola, get up this instant. It's time to go." She sneered at me and tapped an impatient foot on the floorboards.

I glanced around the church and noticed Reverend Finch and the Elders leaving through the church doors. I stood without a thought in mind and walked back out into the brisk breeze. I followed heel and toe with Mother and the others as the girls followed in suit with the adults. The girls were huddled, arms wrapped around each other as they trampled on the pathway back to the cottages. Bonnie was the only one who waited behind for me to catch up. I folded my arms across my chest staring down at the mossy ground. Bonnie slid beside me and I could feel her gaze on me until I looked up at her. She smiled, glancing at the flower behind my ear. "Yellow suits you." she said, fondly. I smiled and looked back down at the pebbled rocks that stuck out of the dirt and grass. Bonnie bumped her shoulder into mine. "Don't worry, it won't be you." She said with a calming voice.

She's talking about the ritual that's in six days. I haven't been able to sleep since Reverend Finch made the announcement eight days ago. I look at Bonnie, narrowing my eyes on her. "How do you know?"

She looked up past the trees and at the light blue sky that peeked through the swaying branches and shrugged. "Just a feeling, I guess."

Well, I'm going to need more than a feeling to know for sure. "How do you know it won't be you?" I asked, my curiosity getting the best of me.

Bonnie looked at me with a blank stare. "I don't."

I don't ask any more questions even though I do want to ask more. Such as, does that not scare you, knowing that you could be picked? Is she even scared? She looked more serene than I was. How can she do that? Pretending like our fate isn't going to be chosen for us. That it may be our last time on earth and our last time talking to each other. I am not ready for that...

Bonnie wrapped her arm around mine and we trampled through the woods until we made it back to our cottage. Bonnie and I were the last to enter and the others huddled by the bedroom door. They turned to look at us as we entered the room.

"What is that behind your ear?" Said Sally. A tall girl with long poker straight hair and plump cheeks. Her looks may be deceiving based upon her attitude. She reached over and snatched the flower from behind my ear and dangled it by the stem between her thumb and pointer finger like it was a filthy worm she didn't want to touch, and crinkled up her face.

"Eww, there are bugs in it," Another girl Joanne said, who stood beside Sally. Her golden locks were in thick coils and her ocean blue eyes glistened like the sea in the moonlight. The other girls made a disgusted face, not like they hadn't done their chores by working in the stables.

"Give it back," Bonnie said, sternly searing her eyes into hers.

Sally looked from me to Bonnie and giggled. "Oh, did your girlfriend pick this for you?" A devilish grin appeared on her rosy lips.

Bonnie and I stood in shock, as Sally dropped the flower and stomped on it with her stained white flats. Her grin faded as quickly as she expressed it and took a step back, clasping her hands in front of her. We glanced back to find Mother towering over us with fire in her eyes. "What do you girls think you're doing?" She snapped like a snake when they found their dinner.

When one of us gets in trouble, we all get in trouble. She says that we might not have started it but we sure did keep the fight going. Walk away, that's what the bigger person would do.

"Do you think this is how sisters treat each other?" Mother looked at every one of us and waited till we all shook our heads. "Now, go change out of your church clothes and come make dinner." Mother sneered and walked out the door, slamming it shut behind her.

The other girls broke out in laughter as they glared at me and Bonnie.

"We're not sisters." Sally sneered.

"Yes we are." I exclaimed. "Mother told us so."

"Mother isn't even our real mother, and that doesn't make us real sisters." Sally spat and walked off toward the bedrooms.

Mother is our chosen mother, same as us girls are our chosen sisters. We don't know what happened to our actual mothers but our chosen mother is all we have. We should honor that till death separates us. At least, that's what Reverend Finch says.

Bonnie squeezed my hand and followed suit with the others. I watched as she disappeared through a doorway before I knelt down and scooped up the mangled flower into my hands and entered through the doorway to the bedrooms. The other girls started taking off their dresses and putting on another dress. This one was black with long sleeves and the skirt draped down past our ankles. Our evening dress to wear to dinner. I slid the dandelion under my pillow for safekeeping until I could sneak a cup of water for it to sit in. The flower lost some leaves and was flattened but it was still as beautiful as it was before.

* * *

Later that evening I was stuck on peeling potatoes. Bonnie and I gave each other glances from across the table as she peeled the silk off the corn and tossed it in the garbage can beside her. We giggled as Madam Greta cursed under her breath because the soup didn't taste the way she liked it. Madam Greta is married to Elder Grimes who tends the crops and fields while we tend the gardens. She's a stern woman, but she knows how to let things slide. That is if you're on her good side.

Mother trotted over to the cabinet of dishes, grabbed a pile of plates and turned to face me.

"Viola, I'll finish the potatoes while you go and set up the tables." She said sternly like there would be no questions asked and I obeyed.

Walking out into the dining room with my arms full of heavy plates. Reverend Finch and the Elders were already seated at their table. They always insist on waiting inside for dinner to be done rather than being called in from outside. It makes Mother angry because she doesn't like to be rushed. But I can't blame them, that sun can be exhausting as it beats down on you. I placed the stack of dishes down on the table beside them and started one by one on placing their plates in front of them. The men didn't bat an eye at me as I slid next to them, making sure I quickly placed their plates down and slid back away. They don't like it if you take too long. Another reason why Mother prefers them to be waiting outside than in the cottage. They lose their patience quicker in here than out there. I try not to listen in on their conversations as I don't want to get in trouble. So I continued keeping my head down and eyes on the table as I set up the plates, silverware, napkins, and drinks and when I was finished I headed back into the kitchen to continue cooking. After the table is all set and dinner has been dished out, the girls and I take our seats at our table. Bonnie squeezed in next to me, and Reverend Finch started our feast with a prayer. After he signaled, we feasted. I always enjoyed the cabbage and potato soup with sweet corn, garlic bread, and freshly squeezed lemonade on the side. Easily one of my favorite meals to make. After us girls were finished we stayed seated until the adults were finished. It created a sense of respect but also boredom. Mother, who sat in the middle row with the other women, gave us a nod. Giving us the go to start cleaning up our table as the men seemed in full conversation that would probably last half of the night.

Since it is Sally, Joanne, Rebecca, and Tilley's day to do the dishes, I and the other girls head back to our bedroom and get into our nightgowns to wait for Mother's arrival to brush our hair. Each night Mother comes in and strokes a soft bristled hairbrush on each of our hairs for three minutes. Then we climb into bed and read aloud the affirmations before we go to sleep.

I sat on the edge of my bed and waited silently like the other girls, and waited for Sally, Joanne, Rebecca, and Tilley, to get in their nightgowns and sit at the ends of their beds for Mother too. When she finally arrives she shuts the door behind her and glides down to the step stool at the end of the room in front of a little mirror hung up on the wall. Mother kneeled on her knees and called for the first girl to get her hair brushed. "Viola," She called for me. I sat there stunned. Normally she goes from right to left. I'm always the last one. Why the sudden change?

The other girls snicker and murmur as I stand up and take my seat on the stool. Mother gave the girls a stern glare, immediately silencing them. She unraveled my braid and gently brushed through my hair. This part is always relaxing for me and Mother. It calms me and makes me sleepy. Mother stared deeply into my eyes through the mirror as she stroked through my knotted coils. Her eyes showed fondness as the edge of her lips curled up in the half smile she occasionally does. She smiles more with her eyes than with her lips. Affection is not her forte. "I would like you to come to the village with me tomorrow," Mother said practically in a whisper to not rile up the girls with jealousy and hatred that they already have for me. "Why does she get to go?" They would whisper to each other. "Why not me?"

"We need to pick up some flowers and vegetables for the ceremony." Mother added. I nodded without a word and she continued to silently brush my hair. After we're done she patted the top of my head with a firm hand and I dragged my body back to bed, curling up in the covers and ready to doze off into a deep slumber. But not until after we read our affirmations, of course. So I continue to watch Mother stroking through all of the girls' hair. I'm not the only one who's too sleepy to move as the other girls' lazily climb into their beds and lay there trying to keep their eyes from closing.

Mother gets up from the ground and looks at each one of us, pouting her bottom lip as we peek at her with half-closed eyes. Then she sighs and heads down the room, stopping at the door. "I can see that you girls are exhausted, so I'm not going to bother you to read tonight." She half smiled and the girls moaned in happiness as they buried themselves deeper into the pillows and sheets. "Just don't tell Reverend Finch, it'll be our little secret." She placed her finger on her lips and shut the door behind her. Secrets between us and Mother are the best. We're always told to tell the truth and never keep secrets from one another. But there's always got to be one bad Angel in the mix of many good ones. In this case, there are twelve...

Chapter 2

I stood and watched as the smoke pervaded the air and burned my lungs. Ash blew around me like snow falling from the atmosphere, coating my hair in a dry film. Flames crept up the wooden building until there was nothing else but fire. I was forced to watch in horror as my limbs were frozen stiff. The heat sweltered and burned my skin as it crept up my legs. I wanted to scream but when I opened my mouth, no sound came out.

Suddenly, something brushed my hand and held it firmly in its grasp. I wanted to look down to see who it was but my eyes stayed focused on the burning building. I squeezed my eyes shut as the flames grew up my stomach and stung my face, suffocating me until my body went numb.

Then I awoke in my bed with the blankets over my face. I pulled them down and gasped for air. Sweat soaked my hairline and my tongue felt like cotton. I glanced at the window beside my bed and the moonlight gleamed through the curtains, glowing up the room in a blue cast. I sat up and rubbed my eyes, confused about the dream I had. I never dreamt of anything like that before. What did it mean? I swallowed and my throat burned in agony, begging for something to cool it down. I glanced around the room and the others were sound asleep. I pulled my covers down and slowly stood up, the wooden floors creaking under my bare feet. I stopped at each creak and held my breath, listening to the rhythm of the girls' breathing. Sally shuffled in her sheets and turned to her side. I waited till I was certain she was asleep and continued to creep down the room toward the door. When I reached the door I grabbed the knob and slowly twisted it until it popped open. Carefully pushing the door open a crack, the hinges started to squeal as I slid out like a snake sliding through a crevice in the wall, and quietly closing the door behind me. I trotted from the cottage hallway and out through the yard to the other cottage from across ours where the dining and kitchen room are located. The moonlight gleamed down on me and chills went down my spine as the wind howled in the darkness. Besides the moonlight there were lamps that were lit next to the entrances of the cottage doors.

I stared at the flames that flickered in the glass, reminding me of my dream. The rich smell of smoke and the crackling of the burning wood. It was dark and dreary as I walked through the dining room. No sign of anyone else around, except when I abruptly stopped at the kitchen door. A slither of light came from underneath it. I contemplated turning back and forgetting the water when I remembered the dandelion under my pillow. It won't live for another day if I don't get it in water soon. Not sure why I'm fixated on keeping the flower alive when I know that it will likely die in a day or two, but maybe the water will help it live a little longer. It's worth the try.

I push an ear against the metal, listening intently for the sound of a living person inside. It was silent. I pushed the door open and peeked in, glancing around the small space. Not a person in sight. Maybe Madam Greta forgot to turn off the lights before she went off to bed? I'll be sure to turn them off before I leave. I walk in and head for the cupboard above the granite countertop. I grab a glass from the shelf and close the cupboard, nearly dropping the glass as I jump from the sight of Madam Greta hovering over me. Her lips were pursed and her arms folded across her broad chest. "Now, what are you doing up?" Greta said, sternly. Raising a bushy brow in curiosity.

"I- l needed water." I stuttered, not meaning to, but seeing the infuriated look on her face raised fear in me. Greta glanced down at the glass that I held up and held out a thick hand. I look down at her hand and quickly realize that she wanted the glass in mine. I gulped down saliva and gently handed the glass over, certain she would put it back on the shelf and demand me to go back to bed. But instead, she took the glass over to the refrigerator, poured water from a steel pitcher inside and handed it back to me with a slight smile.

"Thank you," I said, taking the glass and holding it firmly in my grasp.

"Very well then, get back to bed." Greta nodded and watched as I left the kitchen without a glance back. See, she's nice if you're on her good side. I must be on hers then.

When I made it back to my bedroom, I crept back to my bed and sat on the edge of it. I gulped down half the glass of water and placed it down on my nightstand. I reached under my pillow, pulled out the flattened dandelion, and draped it over the glass so only the stem sat in the water. Climbing back into bed and pulling up the sheets to my chin, I stared at the yellow flower until my heavy eyelids closed and I drifted back into a deep slumber.

Chapter 3

I tied the rubber band around the end of my braid and smoothed out my white cotton dress. It is my first time going to the village market. All the other girls except for me and Bonnie got to go. They always have stories about how it's never as we imagined it. They say it has stonewalls stacked high around the entrance and buildings that look centuries old and are built out of brick and stone. I never knew if I should believe them or not. I guess today I will have to see for myself.

Bonnie trotted in from outside and stood beside me. She watched as I slid on my, once were, white flats but now are a tinted brown from the dirt and mud that I trample through on a daily basis. I eyed myself in the mirror wondering if I looked suitable for the village or not.

"How do I look?" I ask Bonnie, shifting to the side to view the back of my dress. "Does my dress seem a bit frumpy, to you?"

"Your dress looks fine." Bonnie reassured me, looking me up and down. "You look good."

I give her a weak smile. My nerves are rushing through me from head to toe and I am so certain that Bonnie could see it on my face. She glances around the room and points to the dandelion that is clinging to the edge of the glass.

"Now *that* is frumpy." She chuckles as she walks over to it, bending down to have a closer look at the turning leaves. Half of the petals are dark brown while the other half is still a vibrant yellow.

I sat on the edge of the bed and shook my head. "No, *that* is drab."

Even though Bonnie loves to read books, she still gets a bit confused about what some words mean. We're not taught basic literature in class, so if you want to learn some new words you have to figure them out yourself.

Bonnie shrugged. "Still, it looks worse than your dress."

I snapped my head to look at her with wide eyes. "Hey you said my dress looked fine."

"Fine is a word that is between okay and not okay," Bonnie said matter-factly. "Besides everyone knows that fine means it is certainly *not fine*."

She's not helping my nerves right now. First impressions are important. You don't want to look bad, or in this case look *drab*. This is also my first time meeting people other than *my people*. So giving a good first impression is important to me. "Well, you better get used to it because you have the same dress as me." I state with a grin on my face.

Bonnie gives me a sly smile. "Yeah, but I can rock it better than you can. Besides, I did say you look good, didn't I?" She teased, cocking her head.

Mother entered the room with her arms folded across her chest. She was dressed in a long black sleeved dress that practically swept the floors as she glided through the bedroom. "Viola, we got to go. We have errands to run." She nodded towards the door... and I nodded back.

* * *

They lied. There was no stonewall entering the town but there were big brick and stone buildings that did look a century old. But probably not as old as they state it is. I walked beside Mother as she held a weaved basket with raw carrots that still had the stems draping over the edge. When you enter the market there are long lines of tents with tables of fruits and vegetables lying out in baskets as you walk down the stone pathway into the village. People stood behind the tables and hollered what they were selling to gather your attention. "Carrots," A man in a wickered hat and blue overalls hollered from in the distance as we approached his table. "Fresh carrots for only fifty cents each." Mother bought a dozen of them.

"Don't we have carrots at home?" I asked, remembering back to when we had to plant the seeds early in the morning before the morning rain starts.

"The soil has been going dry. We haven't been able to crop as much as we need." Mother stated as we walked down the stone pathway.

"Why is it going dry?" I drew in my eyebrows in confusion. We never had trouble with the soil going dry before. There has been plenty of rainfall. Maybe not enough to keep the soil damp though.

"Because there hasn't been enough rain." Mother broke off to the side, hovering over a stock of cabbages.

"Cabbage too?" I say bewildered. How could there not be enough cabbage? What about the cabbage stew? Mother nodded and picked up a stock and placed it in the basket. She dug into her dress pockets, pulled out a quarter and handed it over to a lady who stood behind the table. The lady thanked her and we carried on back down the pathway.

"Well, what can we do?" I asked Mother, looking at her with the hope that she would have the answers like she always does.

Mother glanced down at me with crescent eyes, her way of smiling without her lips. "Pray. Pray for rain. That's all we can do."

I nod, taking in what she has said. *Pray.* I will have to do that as soon as we get back home. The sun had fully risen and the warmth coated my face. We gathered herbs, fruits, and vegetables, and now we need to collect a couple dozen flowers for the ceremony which is now in five days. In four days is when Reverend Finch decides who will be the next chosen one. I didn't think my nerves could feel any stronger but as the days counted down to the ritual my nerves got so intense I had to stop and take a deep breath in to calm myself or else I would feel a sense of dizziness that I'm afraid will lead to faintness. I want to tell Bonnie about how I feel, but she will just tell me not to worry like she did a day ago. But I can't shake off the feeling that she could be wrong. Maybe Bonnie is right, I do need to stop troubling myself. Everything will be alright... Right?

Mother spotted the stands of flowers and dashed over to them. As I followed her from behind, my shoe snagged on a lifted stone beneath me and I plummeted to the ground, scraping my chin on a rock. People stopped and stared as I picked myself back up and touched my chin. The skin felt jagged and red tinted my fingers. I felt a wave of embarrassment while strangers stared at me from afar. It took them a moment to continue on as I brushed off the dirt on my skirt. I glanced over at Mother who stared intently at blood-red roses. A similar color as my fingers were stained. Good going, Viola. You made the perfect first impression of yourself. Clumsy and stupid. I rolled my eyes at myself and started over to Mother when a loud bell roared behind me, making me jump in my stance. I turn to see a tall stone building with a peak top where an enormous bell chanted across the village. It's similar to the church in the woods. Except only bigger and isn't made out of wooden planks.

I don't know what it was but something was calling me to it. It could just be the bell, but it felt more spiritual. Glancing at the stone staircase that led to two wooden doors. One of the doors was propped open. I have to go there. I climbed up the staircase and reached for the ajar door while glancing back at Mother who was in a conversation with the woman behind the flower stand before I entered the building. I was welcomed by the aroma of sage and lavender. Looking ahead of me there were rows and rows of pews from each side of the building, and in the center of them was a long walkway with thick brown carpeting. I walked down the pathway and towards a stoop that stepped up into a centerpiece of a wooden block in the center. An altar with two glass vases filled with white roses perched on each end of the tabletop. Above it hung a large wooden cross from the ceiling. The cross looked like the one that's at the peak of our church. Except this one was upside down. Instead of the top of the cross being longer and the bottom being shorter, this one was shorter at the top and longer at the bottom. Another odd thing with the cross was a statue of a long-haired man pinned up in the middle with a thorn crown around the top of his head and a dingy cloth wrapped around his waist. Ours don't have that. Who is he?

"Beautiful day, isn't it?" A deep voice came from behind me. I flinched before turning around to see an older man in a white robe with a long green scarf that draped over his shoulders sitting in a pew. The man stared up at the cross rather tentatively. He looked calm and at peace. A Reverend I assume. Reverend Finch wore similar clothing for his sermons. I glance up at the man on the cross before asking, "Who is he?"

The man looked bewildered at my question. "Why, that's Jesus Christ." He said calmly. "The Lord and Savior."

Jesus Christ? That isn't the name of our Lord and Savior. I never heard of that person before... "Why is he up there?" I pointed at the man hanging on the cross. "What happened to him?"

The Reverend cocked his head and gave me a weak smile. "He was nailed on the cross and died to save our sins."

I look at him, puzzled. "Why would he do that?"

"Because he loves us." He said matter of factly. "So we can have the choice to be a sinner or not."

I tilted my head to the side. "What's a sinner?" I remember hearing something similar in the sermons from Reverend Finch, but this seemed different. He doesn't talk about a man named Jesus.

The Reverend patted the auburn cushion beside him. "Come sit."

I was reluctant at first to obey his orders as I'm not supposed to be talking to strangers. But I figured I couldn't be in any more trouble than I already am for breaking off from Mother when I should be beside her at all times, and take a seat next to him. Making sure to leave a wide gap between us. For safety reasons, of course.

"A sinner is someone who does something bad," The Reverend said. "Someone who doesn't obey the law."

I nod, not quite understanding some of it. We should always obey our Lord's commands, but the law isn't a word I know of. "What kind of law?"

The Reverend inhaled before letting out a deep sigh. "I like to say that the Ten Commandments are all you need to follow. It teaches us to be a better person."

I went to ask him what the Ten Commandments were, but then the bell roared again. It's louder here than outside. Its ring vibrated the walls around us before coming to a standstill once more. The Reverend glanced up from the cross and then at me. "Do you go to church?"

I nodded, staring straight ahead.

"Well, what do you learn about?"

"The Lord," I say, fumbling with my fingers. "But I think he's different from yours."

The Reverend nodded in an attempt to understand but I knew he didn't. He doesn't seem to quite understand me. "Is your Lord named Gabriel by any chance?"

I looked at him with widened eyes from his correct question. "You know him too?" He nodded. "Oh yes, I know him well. He can be quite deceiving."

"Deceiving? What do you mean by that?" I asked. Deceiving is a word that I'm not quite fond of. I'm not sure what it means, but I'm assuming that it isn't a good thing by the frumpy expression on his face.

"Do you know the story about him?" The Reverend asked, skeptical of me.

I shook my head. I've heard stories of how he was chosen to be our savior, but is that even true? What can I truly believe these days?

"Well, Gabriel was an angel of God. The most beautiful angel that he created." The Reverend declared, straightening his posture. "He was given the name Satan when he disobeyed God and he got shunned into the underworld."

"He didn't follow the commandments?" I say, still not sure what the commandments even are, but yet again I assumed.

He slightly nodded his head. "He didn't like the rules that God had established. He wanted control and power over everything and everyone. But he wasn't doing it for good."

"So, he's not a good person?"

"Because of him, there is sin. That's why he can be deceiving. He might make you think that he is good but really, he's evil." We sat in silence for a while. *Evil.* Is that why we do the things we do? Does his Savior do snake rituals or sacrifices too? Or is that evil in disguise?

"Do you do rituals?" I asked, turning to him. Watching him intently.

He drew in his bushy eyebrows and frowned. "What kind of rituals are you talking about?"

I pondered if I should be telling him this? I should just go and find Mother, I'm sure she's wondering where I went by now. But my curiosity got the best of me. "Like snake rituals... Or sacrifices?"

His frown deepened and the creases around his eye crinkled as he eyed my appearance. "Where do you live?"

I stand up, now feeling uncomfortable. Why does he want to know? Mother says to never tell *anyone* anything about us, especially where we live. Why, is never a question I ever dared to ask. I start for the entrance doors but before I could distance myself from him, a thick hand clasped around my wrist and forced me to face him again. "You are one of the girls from the cult, aren't you?" He gasped, surprised.

The cult? What the hell is he talking about? "I- I don't know what you're talking about," I say trying to yank my wrist back, but the more I pull away the tighter his grip gets. Fear started to creep into me and I hoped he would let go. Why won't he let me go? And as if the Reverend read my mind he let go of my wrist and I ran down the pathway and out the door without looking back. What was that all about? What does he mean by the word cult? What did anything he say even mean?

A hand grasped my shoulder firmly and spun me around. Mother looked at me with fury in her eyes. "Where have you been?" She asked, glancing down at my busted chin. "What happened to you?"

I took a step back, touching my chin. "I tripped and fell, and I went to see if I could find a mirror in one of the buildings to see how it looked."

Mother narrowed her eyes at me as if she didn't believe me. I don't blame her, I don't believe myself either. I can be a terrible liar. I half expected her to yell at me for lying, but instead she grabbed my chin and lifted it up to get a better look at the wound, and sighed. "We better get you cleaned up, before it gets infected." I nodded and she took my hand and led me back down the stone pathway and back towards home...

Chapter 4

"The cult?" Bonnie said, narrowing her eyes at me in confusion. "Is that a bad thing?" I shrugged, not sure if it really was or not. Mother asked Bonnie to tend to my wound while she prepped for lunch. I just finished telling her what had happened back in town in the chapel with the peculiar Reverend and how odd it was how he had acted to my innocent question. He almost seemed scared for me. Like a sense of fear in his eyes that wasn't there before.

"By the way he acted, I'm going to assume that it is," I replied, watching Bonnie wringing out a ragged washcloth from a bowl of warm water.

She swept it over my wound and said, "and they do rituals?" Bonnie gently applied lavender oil to my wound. Lavender oil mixed with honey and olive oil and put in a jar makes the best ointment for cuts and scrapes. Mother makes it every spring when the bees start to pollinate and the lavender fields start to sprout.

I shook my head. "I'm not sure. He didn't give me an answer but he did start acting strange after I asked."

Bonnie nodded, gathering the things she used to tend to my wound and stood up, and started for the door until I grabbed her arm and gently guided her back with fear spreading across my face. "I think there is something seriously wrong here," I say so softly it's practically a whisper.

Bonnie squinted her eyes at me and shrugged my hand away. "Well, you need to keep it to yourself." She said sternly, turning on the ball of her heels and storming out the bedroom door. I was shocked by her sudden sternness at me. She never spoke to me with that tone before. She knows something is wrong here, she just won't admit it. But I will get her to admit it soon.

Mother

I barged into Reverend Finch's office without any notice of my presence, where he sat behind his desk grading the girls' essay papers. He peered over his spectacles, an expression of annoyance plastered across his face. "May I help you, Renée?" He said with displeasure in his tone. I became a sudden burden to him.

"We need to talk about that girl, Viola." I say, eagerly for him to listen. "She's trouble,"

Reverend Finch took off his spectacles and sighed. "You need to calm down, you are being frantic."

I stopped, realizing that I was pacing around the room. I inhaled deep breaths to calm my mind and body.

Finch stapled his fingertips together in front of him. Looking incredulous. "Alright, what happened in town?"

"She went into the church," I say, trying to control my tone from sounding pitchy and winded. My heart beating a mile a minute and I placed a firm hand against my chest to feel the fast rhythm slowly coming down to a gentle beat.

Finch glowered and leaned back in his chair. "Did she speak to anyone?"

I shrugged. "I don't know? All she said was she was trying to find a mirror to check a scrape on her chin because she fell. But she was lying to me. I know she was."

Finch rubbed his rather long hand down his overly round face. He said nothing but just closed his eyes to think.

I stomped my foot into the floor in defeat. "What if she said something to someone? What if she told the Reverend about us?"

"She didn't," Finch growled. I must be giving him a headache. Well, good. Because I have had one for over thirteen years. It's unfair how he puts all the responsibility on me to look after the girls, while he gets the easy route in life. I'm sick of it. I'm sick of worrying about getting caught. I would rather leave than stay and take the blame for all of this. But I can't leave. Otherwise I'm turning my back on my lord. He would never forgive me for abandoning my people and children. Sometimes, I just wish that Finch would choose me to be the next sacrifice. So I can get rid of this world and most importantly, to get rid of Finch and his dumbass laws.

"How do you know that she hadn't?" I fumed at him.

"Because we have taught the girls from a very young age to never speak to strangers. They wouldn't overstep our words."

"Well, what if she had? Viola is becoming suspicious. What if she had already told the Reverend or the girls?"

"They wouldn't believe her," Finch said, calmly. "They know their place here and they wouldn't disobey their savior."

I folded my arms across my chest and shook my head. "We need to do something about her. She *will* get us in trouble if we wait too long."

Finch rubbed his prickly chin and took a deep breath in. "Then you'll have to prepare her for the ritual." He looked up at me with contentment. I nodded without saying any more words. That's the most rational way to get rid of her for good. Before she gets the other girls suspicious. "Alright then, now will you mind? I have some papers to grade." Finch puts on his readers and continues shuffling papers around his desk. I turn on the heels of my shoes and exit through the office door, slamming it closed behind me. If I go down for this. I'm making sure he comes down with me...

Chapter 5

Bonnie hadn't spoken to me for two days straight. She hasn't been sitting next to me for breakfast, lunch or dinner. She hasn't even looked in my direction, avoiding eye contact at all costs. What did I do? Is it something I have said? Maybe it was. She did get rather stern with me that one evening when she was tending to my wound. Maybe I had frightened her with everything the Reverend had said to me. Either way, Bonnie had never avoided me before. I certainly wish that she wouldn't be avoiding me. Especially when in a short few hours Reverend Finch will be choosing which girl is the next sacrifice. I'm so nervous my hands were shaking while I was braiding my hair this morning. I also dropped several dishes and bumped into Madam Greta while she was carrying a pot of lukewarm water from the sink to the stove during breakfast this morning. She had enough of me and sent me outside with a large bucket in hand to water the garden instead. The sun crisped down onto my face, instantly making beads of sweat form along my hairline. As I lugged the bucket filled with fresh water from the stream in the forest, I frowned at our dying crops. Wondering if Elder Armsteine hadn't passed away two nights ago, the crops might have been flourishing as he was a natural at taming them.

Damn you serpent, I thought to myself as I tilted the bucket and poured generous amounts onto each buried plant. Carrot stems poked out of the dry soil, begging for water to quench their thirst. If it hadn't been for you I wouldn't have needed to go into town for vegetables. Something inside me was saying that it was the plan after all. To go into town, to discover the church and to speak with that Reverend. Maybe all of this was a plan? And I just need to listen. I turned around and jumped at the sight of Reverend Finch hovering over me with his arms folded across his chest. He deeply inhaled and glanced around the fields of nothing but dry grass and trees from the distance.

"It's a beautiful morning isn't it, Viola?" He said, looking down at me with sincerity in his dark eyes.

I nod. "Yes, it is a beautiful morning." I gripped the bucket handle a little too tight that my knuckles turned white and my fingernails punctured into my palms, resting crescent moons in my skin.

Reverend Finch smiled. "Well, let's hope it stays that way. Wouldn't want bad weather to ruin our ceremony today,"

"No, we wouldn't," I say, shaking my head in agreement. I don't know why but the way he is towering over me gave my chest a tight squeeze. No matter how many deep breaths I took it never fulfilled that lung striving for more air.

Reverend Finch didn't notice me trying to control my breathing or the fact that my face felt like it was burning up. I probably looked as red as a tomato. Unless he did notice just didn't say anything about it. But instead, he glanced down at the bucket in my hands and cocked his head. "Shouldn't you be inside prepping for breakfast?" He asked sternly, his smile fading into a deep frown.

"Madam Greta sent me outside to water the garden. She said I'm being too distracting." I respond, trying to control my tone from sounding small. It's hard to speak when it feels like someone is squeezing your vocal cords in their fists. My chest had become so tight it started to ache. Reverend Finch nodded, brushing his stippled chin with his long fingers.

"Very well then, finish up and come to breakfast." Reverend Finch walked past me, heading for the dining hall. Then he abruptly stopped in his tracks to face me again. "And no dilly-dallying, alright?"

"I won't, Reverend." I complied. He winked at me and then turned back for the hall. Once he was out of sight, I dropped the bucket and leaned onto my knees, trying to fulfill the need for air in my lungs. I never felt like this before. It's awful. It's-

"Are you alright, Vi?" A worried voice came from behind me. I stood up straight and glanced back to find Bonnie standing by the garden with her hands clasped in front of her.

"I'm fine," I simply say while picking up the bucket from the ground. I remembered what Bonnie said about the word fine. It's in between okay and not okay. Which is what some people say when they are certainly not okay.

"Well, you don't look fine," Bonnie stated, brushing a fallen coil from her face to behind her ear.

I take a few steps towards her so my face is an inch away from her. "Why do you care if I'm fine? You surely haven't cared for two days now." I raised my voice at her. Not meaning to but I still did. Bonnie was taken aback by my tone and further distanced herself from me. What does she expect me to say? I'm doing great, especially since you've been avoiding me. But don't worry. I forgive you. Certainly not...

"I- I didn't mean to avoid you," Bonnie stuttered, rubbing her arm like a chill breeze suddenly rushed through. "It's just," She continued. "We were always told that if one of us starts telling us false things. Then we must tell Reverend Finch about it. But I didn't want to get you in trouble,"

"So, you avoided me instead?" I say, narrowing my eyes at her. None of this is making any sense.

Bonnie shrugged. "I guess, I was worried that if I spoke to you then I would feel guilty for not telling anyone about it."

I throw down the bucket and take a step closer. "Don't you think it's a little odd that we can't talk to anyone other than *our* people? Or if we talk about anything from outside of here then we get in trouble?" Bonnie glanced around at the forest in the distance. She's trying to avoid eye contact with me because I know she thinks I'm right. I take another step closer. "Don't you ever get this feeling that something just isn't right here? Like the rituals for instance. One of us girls gets chosen to die and for what?"

"To save our souls," Bonnie interjected.

"Do you believe if one of us doesn't get sacrificed, then all of our souls would be taken? There are thousands of people outside from here and their souls haven't been taken." Bonnie kicked dirt with her toes. Not responding to me. I look her up and down in a judgmental manner. I'm judging the way she thinks and the way she's trying to avoid my eyes that bore into her skin. "I know you feel it and I know you believe me. You're just not *hearing* me, Bonnie." Bonnie slightly shook her head, straightened her posture and dropped her arms to her sides, standing taller than me.

"I came out here to tell you that breakfast is ready," Bonnie said in a terrible attempt to sound calm and collected. Then she turned on her heels and stomped back towards the hall without a look back. Leaving me alone in the middle of the smothering heat. I know she believes me. She's just not *hearing* me. And I know she doesn't want to either.

I continued the rest of the day doing my daily chores and tasks to prepare for the ritual. Like displaying roses in vases, setting out candles with matches and placing the silver dagger with a red velvet cloth overtop in the center of the altar.

Bonnie avoided me again but snuck glances in my direction. Probably to make sure I was okay without asking. I now sat at the end of my bed and waited for the others to get dressed in their red velvet gown that was specifically made for the choosing ritual. I fiddled with my fingers as the others chit-chatted which slowly died when Mother waltzed in with two sauce bowls in hand. One had a red substance, similar to paint, and the other had twelve roses with the stems cut off, stacked neatly in a circle. Mother places the bowls down in front of the stool and glances around the room at her children all in red. "Viola," She called out to me, bringing me back to my senses.

"Come." I obeyed and sat down on the stool in front of her. Mother dipped her finger into the red substance and imprinted dots along my cheekbones. I glanced down at Mother who also wore a red velvet gown, similar to the ones we wore.

"Why do we wear red?" I asked as she smeared the red paint on my lips.

She sighed, grabbing a rosebud. "It signifies the blood you give for your savior." I watched as she stood up and walked behind me, placed the rosebud on her lap, and undid my straggly braid.

"Do we wear red for the sacrifice too?"

Mother brushed through my hair, gathered it, and spun it into a low bun like herself. "No, we wear black. But the chosen one wears white to signify purity." She tucked the rosebud into the bun and gave my shoulder a tight squeeze. "Go sit down and wait for the others to be done."

After all eleven of the girls got their hair done with roses, we stood in two straight lines and waited until Mother came back into the room to walk out with us. The girls kept quiet as the nerves were settling in. Sally and Tilly were the first in line to help lead us girls over to the chapel. Bonnie and I were side by side in the center of the two lines. I fiddled with my fingers, staring down at the dark wooden floors. Bonnie nudged my side to get my attention. She stood straight with her head forward and her hands in front, identical to the others in line. I straightened myself and stared straight forward at a petite girl Marsha, her rose resting on top of her swirled bun.

The bedroom door swung open and Mother entered the room with red dots on her cheekbones like ours. She looked at each of us making sure we were all identical. When she was satisfied with how we looked, she nodded and guided us out the door and out into the chilly night air.

We headed across the fields and towards the woods when Marsha tripped over her foot and plummeted to the ground. I abruptly stopped and the others behind me ran into each other with groans. I pray that Mother didn't see that or we will all be in serious trouble. I glanced forward and saw Mother heading for the woods, not noticing our disruption. Thank goodness. The second line carried on towards the woods and Bonnie waved her hand telling us to hurry up. I bent down and helped Marsha up, brushing the dry grass off of her dress. She gave me a grateful smile and I nudged her forward. Six of us sprinted across the field and towards the woods. Sticks and rough grass prickled and stung our bare feet but we didn't have time to slow down.

We trudged forward until we came back in line with the others. Glancing forward Mother still hadn't noticed our falters and we quietly gasped for air. Bonnie gave me a congratulatory nod and we carried deeper into the eerie woods. The moonlight poked through the budding trees lighting up the pathway down by the chapel. I peeked out of line and saw torches lighting up the front of the entrance to church. A row of people stood along the pathway and Reverend Finch waited patiently at the door ahead. Women wore the same dark red velvet dress with the same hairstyle and face paint and the men wore a dark red button down with a rose poking out the chest pocket. Their faces were also painted but the dots were around the eyes and mouth, spiraling up their foreheads. Reverend Finch wore his usual white robe but instead of a long scarf around his shoulders, he had rose buds wrapped around his neck and draped down past his knees. As we got closer Reverend Finch outstretched his arms in a greeting. Mother joined the others in their lines as twelve of us stood in between, eyeing everyone that surrounded us. Reverend Finch plastered a wide smile as he bowed his head.

"Welcome, you beautiful young ladies," He spoke aloud. His voice carried through the trees and into a pit of darkness that surrounded us. "One of you will be greatly chosen to be the next sacrifice to save our souls." All eyes were on him now. I swallowed past a lump in my throat. Why do I feel this way? I know it's nerves but it won't go away. Reverend Finch recalled the set of orders we had to do for the choosing ritual. We have to bow down in a prayer form while Finch walks past us with his hand hovering above our heads. He will then stop in front of the next chosen girl and have them come forth to the altar. They take the dagger, slice their palms and drip eleven droplets of their blood into a bowl of purified water to signify the eleven girls who remain. The twelfth girl walks out of the chapel and gets sent back to their cottage to prepare for the following ceremony the next day. We nodded along until Finch finished his instructions and then moved to the side to motion for us to lead the way into the chapel for the ritual. We quietly entered the chapel and the pews were taken out to leave an open space for us girls and the adults to stand. The room was dimly lit with twelve candles that were placed in a circle where we would be kneeling in front of the altar in the center of the room. There were rose vases resting on the two sides as the bowl of purified water and dagger rested in the center. Reverend Finch waltzed over to us and spoke aloud. "You may kneel behind a candle in the center of the room." The two lines broke apart in two directions and Bonnie and I kneeled behind a candle right across from each other. We locked eyes as we waited for the adults to file in and stand quietly in rows as they would if the pews were there, and Reverend Finch stands in front of the altar.

Bonnie's dark eyes glistened in the candlelight and her caramel skin sparkled as the heat from the candle rose and formed sweat beads along her hairline. I can tell in her eyes that she feels guilty about our conversation earlier today. I sure do. I shouldn't have spoken to her like I did. She didn't deserve that. I get her wanting to believe there is nothing wrong here and that I shouldn't push my beliefs onto her like I did. I could be wrong about everything. After all, this *is* our home where we grew up. We know nothing else than what we were taught. But I can't shake that *I am* right. There is something wrong here. And I don't want to linger around to find out... I need to talk to Bonnie tonight. We need to get out of here, and soon.

Reverend Finch walked down from the altar and stood with his hands out. "You ladies may bow your heads and shut your eyes as you do in prayer." I took a deep breath in and bowed my head, closing my eyes. I could hear Finch's heavy steps as he trailed down the circle. "Tell me Savior, who would you like to join you?" He spoke from afar. Telling me that he's across the room. I clenched my jaw and squeezed my hands together to stop them from shaking. The warmth of the candle wrapped around my face and a bead of sweat slithered down my cheek, dripping down my chin. The unscented flame flickered through my eyelids, casting a shadow bouncing across my sight. "Tell me father, who is the *chosen one*!" Finch shouted, making me flinch from the sudden uproar. His steps drew closer and the vibration of the wooden floorboards became stronger. I can hear each girl suck in deep breaths as the Reverend hovered past them. Lilian, a petite, shy girl who stood behind me in line quivered as his heavy steps faltered in front of her. "Mhmm," Reverend Finch groaned. "Oh, I see now." I let out a breath of air through my lips as he came to a stop in front of Lillian. Then suddenly a heavy thud and strong vibration came in front of me. Then I knew I was screwed. "Viola," Reverend Finch called out. "You have been the *chosen one!*" My heart sank deep into my chest and tears welled from my eyes. Bonnie was wrong. It is me who got chosen.

Reverend Finch placed his sweaty palm on top of my head. "Child, come forth and pay your dues to our savior." He lifted his hand and took a step back. I opened my eyes and lifted my head. The others watched with widened eyes, suddenly aware that the ritual was truly happening. Bonnie's face flushed as she watched me stand and walk up to the altar. My hand shook as I reached out and pulled the velvet cloth, revealing the silver dagger that flickered in the light. I took the dagger in my hand and outstretched my other. Resting the sharpened blade on the center of my palm. I closed my eyes and focused on my rapid breathing. My heart drummed in my ears and my legs started to tingle. I took a deep breath in and dug the blade into my palm. A sharp sting and warm ooze trickled down my hand. I opened my eyes to see the dark red substance dripping down onto the wooden floors and formed a puddle of my blood next to my bare feet. I reached out my hand and watched as each droplet splashed into the bowl of water. The red swirled and the clear liquid turned into a hazy pink. With each drop it became darker and darker until the liquid turned a darker shade of red. I pulled my hand away, rested the stained dagger back down on the altar and turned around to face the crowd. The adults clapped their hands together as Reverend Finch guided me down from the altar and out the door.

I was welcomed with a chill breeze that dried up my sweaty face in seconds. I gasped for air as my chest started to collapse. Trampling on rocks and twigs with my steps making loud cracking noises that echoed through the forest. I walked alone back through the forest, across the fields and past the dining hall until I made it in front of my cabin.

Slamming the door behind me, I snatched the rose out of my hair and threw it across the room. I tousled the bun loose until my coily hair draped over my shoulders. I tugged on my nightgown and flinched as my hand seared with pain. I looked down at my blood-soaked hand. I'm now realizing the throbbing sensation that started to pain me. Tears welled up in my eyes and made my vision blurry.

A thud came from behind me and made me jump as I whipped my head around to see a disoriented Bonnie. I wiped my eyes with my sleeve and sniffled my soggy nose. Bonnie stood with her hands behind her back and her eyebrows drawn in. What does she want? I started to think but as if she read my mind she replied with eagerness in her tone.

"Where would we go?" She asked, taking a step forward.

I cocked my head and narrowed my bloodshot eyes. "What do you mean?"

"You said you wanted to leave. Where would we go?" She replied, a curl fell loose in her bun and swept across her face.

I shrugged. "I don't know? Somewhere better than here."

"What if there is nowhere better than here?" She asked, discerned.

I wiped my nose and sniffed. "I'm sure there is." I slouched down onto my bed and my heart rate started to slow back down almost to my normal rhythm. Bonnie rushed down to my bed and stood in front of me.

She folded her arms across her chest. "Then tell me," She said. "Tell me there is something wrong here and there are better places than here."

What is she talking about? I *have* been telling her. I've been telling her for days now. Like I said, she doesn't want to *hear* me but maybe now she's ready to listen. I look up at her with confidence in my eyes. "I *know* there is." And as if what I had been saying finally soaked into her brain. Then she nodded with contentment.

"Okay, I trust you."

A smile grew on my face on the satisfaction of finally leaving this place and leaving it with her by my side. But we can't leave tonight as the others started to file through the door and instantly change into their nightgowns. We'll have to leave tomorrow before the ceremony. For now, we need to get a good night's rest. As Bonnie helped patch up my hand, I kept getting glances and murmurs from the others who started getting cozy in their beds. I ignored them and carried on. Climbing into bed and waited until Bonnie climbed into hers. She gave me a nod and we slouched deeper into our sheets. I stared at the now welted dandelion and closed my eyes. Mother won't be in for hair brushing tonight. And I eventually drifted off to sleep with the thought of leaving this place and never coming back.

Chapter 6

I woke from the sudden disturbance of the bedroom door slamming shut. Mother waltzed down the room and stood in front of my bed. She yanked the covers off me and the sudden coldness sent chills down my spine. "Get up," She demanded, towering over me. "You have preparations to attend too."

I lifted my head and watched as she rummaged through the closet of dresses. I sat up in bed and glanced around the room. The other girls must have left to do chores because it was just me in bed. What time is it? It must be the afternoon as the sun has already risen bright in the sky. Or at least, from what I can tell from the sun shining through the window. I looked at Mother, puzzled. "Preparations for what?" I yawned, scratching my oddly itchy cheeks.

"For the ceremony, of course." Mother replied, shuffling through dresses. Oh yeah, the ceremony. How could I forget? I woke several times in the night with the sudden remembrance of the ceremony that was meant for me the very next day. If I don't leave tonight. Then I'm done for. And I'm afraid that if they catch me, they will do much worse than the ritual. They always warned us that something very bad would happen if we snuck out of our bedrooms at night. That is why I was mortified when Madam Greta caught me in the kitchen a few nights ago. Luckily, I am on her good side... Mother turned to me, tossed a white-washed dress on the end of the bed and pointed to my face. "Go wash that paint off before you get a rash." She noticed my itching and most likely, red cheeks. I watched as she stomped to the door and stopped, turning on her heels sharply to face me. "Get dressed and meet me in the dining hall quickly."

When the door slammed shut I sat up in bed and rubbed my face to help awaken me. Once I felt more alive I sighed and tugged off my nightgown. My bandaged hand stung in sharp pain when I tugged on the white-washed dress and yanked the skirt down until it draped past my shins. Looking in the mirror now, I stared at the red paint that smeared down my cheeks. The dots were still visibly there as it seems it has stained my skin. I continued with combing my knotted hair with my fingers and weaved it into a braid.

Now heading across the lawn towards the wash house, I entered a dimly lit room with a shower in one corner and a sink and toilet in the other corner. Three girls each week get to take a quick shower as Reverend Finch says that saving water that we can consume is far better than wasting water on cleaning. This week was Marsha, Rebecca, and Joanne's week to shower. Mine isn't for another two weeks, which I won't be here for. I stood in front of the sink with a raggedy washcloth and turned on the spout. The water flowed down into the bowl as I wet the cloth and scrubbed my face. Glancing into the dusty mirror I noticed the red wasn't washing off. Only a red hue tinted my cheeks and lips. I continued to scrub harder but it was no use. It won't come off. I wonder if the other girl's faces are stained red too. I didn't notice if Mother's face was red because I was only half awake at the time. I'm sure Mother has a remedy to get it off. She always has a remedy prepared for any cause. As I headed back outside to the lawn, I noticed a few of the girls were tending to the garden. Two were watering with a bucket of water from the stream, two more were planting seeds and one was digging up the little carrots that refused to grow any larger than an inch of a stubby finger. They glanced back at me with wonder as I walked into the dining hall.

Mother, Madam Greta, Madam Valerie, and Bonnie sat at a table in the center of the room, rummaging through a box of fabrics and sewing supplies. Bonnie looked up from the needles and thread with a gloomy grin. She still hasn't taken the news lightly. I would be upset if I had to help prepare for Bonnie's sacrifice too.

"Come, stand here." Mother ushered me like I am wasting her precious time. She pointed at the center of the room for me to stand.

Madam Valerie, who's a long-faced older woman with ashy gray hair, bent down beside me and tugged on my skirt. She squinted her eyes and pursed her lips in disdain. She always looks irritated at all times. I'm starting to think it is just her face. "What size is she?" Madam Valerie pondered, glancing over to Mother.

Mother laid out a white satin square of material on the table and smoothed it out with her hands. "She's an eight."

"An eight?" Madam Valerie said flabbergasted. "Shouldn't she be a size ten by now?" Mother looked up with irritancy. "She's petite,"

"I'll say," Madam Valerie agreed. She stood up from her knees and headed over to the table to gather material. She stared down at a roll of pearly-white satin material and raised an eyebrow. "What do you think?" She asked Mother.

Mother pointed at the material and nodded. "I think this is it."

"With this thread?" Bonnie asked, holding out a roll of thread that was almost the exact match to the material. Mother nodded and Madam Greta clasped her hands together with excitement. "Good, then that's settled."

"What's settled?" I said, still standing in the middle of the room with a deer-in-the-headlights look. Everyone looked at me like they forgot that I was standing right here.

"This is the material we're using to make your ceremony dress." Mother sighed, walking towards the dining door.

"You do remember what happened last night, don't you?" Madam Valerie snapped, her eyes severing into mine. Of course, I remember. How could I ever forget? Bonnie looked down and fiddled with the thread and needle. I nodded and Madam Valerie shook her head in disappointment and turned to face Mother as she reached for the door.

"I'm going to get the rest of the sewing supplies," Mother said, turning to face Madam Greta. "While I do that you can start measuring her." Madam Greta nodded, grabbed the measuring roll off the table and headed for me.

After what felt like an eternity of standing up straight and holding out my arms, the dress was officially complete. The dress looked the same as my many other white dresses but this one did have more of a nightgown look to it than the others. It also had a light smoother feel while the others felt thick and rough. The sleeve length was longer and the skirt went past my ankles. How am I supposed to walk in this dress if I keep tramping on it?

"It looks lovely on you," Madam Greta complimented me as I looked down at it. "Do you like it?"

"She better like it," Madam Valerie snapped, looking me up and down. "We spent four hours on it."

I gave a small smile to Madam Greta. "I like it, thank you." Thanking them for making me a dress that I'm going to be sacrificed in is not something to be thankful for. But still to save me from a scolding, I did as so.

Mother waltzed into the room from the kitchen and flicked her hand at me. "Go get changed before you dirty up the dress." She demanded. Bonnie walked over to me and handed the dress I wore earlier to me and I headed for the door. After changing I laid out the dress on my bed for tonight and tugged on my old dress, and headed back out the door. The sun dawned and the once fluffy white clouds were now pink and orange from the hue of the sun. As I headed for the dining hall for dinner, Mr. Berkshire grabbed my elbow and yanked me back from entering the dining hall. "What do you think you're doing?" His wrinkled eyes and scruffy beard towered over me as I looked up at him with pleading eyes to let me go.

"I- I'm going to dinner, sir." I stuttered, taking a step back. His grip was firm and tight and he refused to let me go.

"Do you know nothing child?" He scolded as he leaned his face closer to mine. His breath smelled of tobacco and hay. "You are to not be fed anything because you can only have the blood of our savior tonight at the altar." The blood of our savior? What does he mean by that? But instead of questioning him I just gave him a simple nod. But before I could turn away, he swung me around and shoved me to the ground. I pushed myself up onto my hands and stared up at him with bewilderment. "Now go back to your room and wait there until the ceremony!" He shouted, turned sharply on the ball of his heels and slammed the door shut behind him. I slowly got up on my feet and headed back to the bedrooms again. Tears uncontrollably welled up in my eyes before I could stop them. If I'm not even prepared for a sacrifice then how am I going to be prepared for the world outside of here?

Chapter 7

Bonnie

I snuck out the dining hall door with a biscuit filled with apple jam that oozed out into the center of my palm. There's no need for Vi to have to starve the whole day. Especially if it is her last meal. Reverend Finch said for a sacrifice you can only have the savior's blood in your system as a way for them to be as one. I don't completely understand how it works but that's what Vi has to do. It seems quite unfair. That's why we're leaving. That's also why I'm sneaking out to speak to her about when we're leaving and how. I sprint across the yard and dash into the bedroom cottage. I knocked on the bedroom door before I entered. Viola sat at the end of her bed, wiping her pink eyes. She was crying.

"Are you okay, Vi?" I asked, latching the door behind me. Viola wiped her stuffy nose with her sleeve and sighed.

"Yes, I'm okay." She responded with a gloomy smile. She won't have to worry about everything anymore. We're leaving soon. I nodded and held out the apple biscuit. She looked down at it with a somber expression. "I'm not supposed to be eating anything," She responded.

"Yes, but that's because you're supposed to drink the savior's blood at the altar tonight." I stated. "But since you're not going to be there to do so, you can have this." I held the biscuit closer to her. "You need to eat something for energy." Viola finally took the biscuit and took a small bite out of it, resting it on her lap for later.

I sat down beside her. "When should we leave?" I asked, drowning in her emerald green eyes. She has such pretty eyes. Prettier than my mud water ones. Viola thinks otherwise. She thinks they are the perfect earthy brown that glistens in every lighting.

Viola shrugged. "I'm thinking tonight when it's dark. It will be harder for them to see us at night."

I nodded, liking that idea. But how are we going to sneak out when the ceremony starts right at sunset? All eyes will be on her. "But what about the ceremony tonight?" I say, pondering on my thoughts. "How can we leave when everyone has their eye on you until then?"

Viola shifted towards me. "You might have to start a distraction, so the ceremony will have to be pushed back. Once the attention is off of us then we will leave."

It's easier said than done. "What kind of distraction should I cause?" I asked, cocking my head.

"Umm," Viola hummed, squinting her eyes as if that would help with her thoughts. "Do something with the altar."

"Like, light it on fire with the candles?" I blurted out the first thought that came to mind. I mean, it would work.

"That would work," Viola said, nodding her head. "But that wasn't what I was thinking of." "Oh, then what were you thinking of?"

Vi shrugged. "There's supposed to be a dagger for the ceremony tonight. Maybe take it and hide it somewhere they will never find."

That plan sounds better. Less risky of burning down the church and starting a forest fire. I nod with a comforting smile. "Okay, I will see what I can do."

As the sun had dawned and the moon had risen, the preparations for the ceremony had begun. The adults got dressed in their black gowns and button-downs, and I had my black dress that dangled down to my shins, making sure I was the first to be done while the others scrambled to get dressed. Breaking off from the girls who were doing their hair, the braids along the sides of their heads trailed down into a low bun. I snuck out the bedroom door and ran for the fields. Dashing through the pastures and towards the eerie forest. Without a glance back I ran into the dark woods with fear as the trees crackled and the wind howled in rage from the gray clouds that filled the night sky.

"Beautiful night for a ceremony," Reverend Finch had said earlier that evening when he walked me to the bedrooms to prepare for tonight. The gray clouds moved quickly through the skies and the wind pushed me around like I was just a feather floating in the air. "Don't you think, Bonnie?" He glanced down at me with a thick eyebrow raised. His eyes examined me.

"Yes, it is." I say in a lie. The night couldn't get any worse. Thunder roared around us and made me jump from the sudden surprise. Yes, it could get worse.

Reverend Finch patted my back. "I know this can't be easy for you," He said, stopping in front of the cottage door. "I know how close you and Viola are. Just know that she is doing this for *us*." He sympathized, placing a firm hand on my shoulder. "For *you*. Alright?" I nodded with a slight smile and watched as he walked away and towards the adult cabins. He has no idea how close me and Vi are. But maybe they do. Maybe that's the reason he chose Vi to be the sacrifice? I don't believe that he *heard* the savior's voice. No one ever has. He just picks and chooses who he wants and that is Viola. Maybe they saw how reluctant she has been with everything here. In our *chosen family*. I have always wondered where our *real* families are at. Our birth family.

Maybe we don't have one and that's why we're here. Either way, I am leaving this family for good.

As gravel began to crunch under my feet, I knew I was on the right pathway to the chapel. As the light started to appear just like yesterday with the torch flames rising high in the wind. My heart started to race in fear of getting caught. I don't know what they will do to me if they catch me sabotaging the ceremony. Nothing good I assume. I stood in front of the little white church that stood high in the middle of the forest. I glanced around me making sure that I was the only one here. When I saw no one but the shadows of oak trees, I entered the church doors wary of who might be inside. I peeked through the doors and nothing but silence filled the air. I locked eyes on the altar and started towards it. Climbing up the wooden steps with a thud, I peered down on the altar with eagerness. Nothing but two candles perched on the red cloth that lay on the table. I looked around for the dagger but couldn't find it. The elders haven't brought in the supplies yet. The dagger and the "savior's blood" is supposed to be here. What am I going to do? Then I looked up the lit candles that warmed my skin from afar. I guess I'll have to go back to my original plan. I knocked the candles over with my hands and the white wax trailed down the glass and onto the red cloth. The flames flickered back and forth searching for something to consume. It finally found the red cloth and burned into it. The flames trailed across like a serpent slithering across the ground. I stepped down from the altar and watched as the flames grew higher and higher until the altar was engulfed in fire. The smoke rose with vigor as it coated the high ceiling above. I choked back smoke as I turned away and ran out the door. Coughing with each step I took, I trailed back down the pathway and towards the cottages. Back to Vi.

Chapter 8

I stared at myself in the mirror with anxiousness in my eyes. I needed to know if Bonnie had fulfilled our plan. Did she find the dagger? Did she hide it yet? Not only am I worried about her getting caught, I'm also scared about running away later tonight. But Mother intruded the bedroom to gently brush through my hair with the soft bristled brush. She twisted my coils to enhance my curls and lay them resting on my shoulders. Mother glanced at me in the mirror and sighed, gathering my long mane to the center of my back.

"You're doing good for us, you know that?" She raised her eyebrows, expecting a response from me.

I nodded with a smile. "Yes, I know. It's an honor." I say, knowing very well I'm just saying what she wants to hear. She couldn't care less what I think anyway. Mother pressed her lips together and squinted her eyes as if she were trying to detect my lie.

"You're a terrible liar." She blurted out, making her way to my bed. She brought roses that intertwined together into a circle. The thorns were cut off thankfully, so they wouldn't dig into my skull. I stood there stiffly as she placed the rose crown on top of my head, looking at me through the mirror. I stared at my reflection, face flushed as I realized that all of this was real and I was dressed for my death. How did I come to this? I was just a young girl doing my daily chores with the cooking and gardening, going to church every Sunday and writing essays of the savior. And yet, here I stood dressed in a long pearly-white gown with rouge painted cheeks and a rose crown just to be sent off to my sacrifice. I don't know how to feel other than being scared for my and Bonnie's life. I don't know what to think...

A bang came from behind us, making us jump. We spun around to see who barged in so abruptly. Bonnie stood in the doorway, gasping for air as if she just ran a twenty mile race around the property. She pointed anxiously out the door with her pointer finger.

"The- the ch- church is- is on-," Bonnie heaved for oxygen, leaning on her knees.

Mother put her hands on her hips and stomped her foot onto the wooden floorboards. "Spit it out girl!" She demanded, her face turning a rouge from anger.

Bonnie took a deep breath in. "The church is on fire." You've got to be joking. Taking the dagger was too hard to handle, she had to go and burn the whole church down instead?

Mother's eyes widened with a fearful look plastered on her face. "Did you tell the Reverend?" She said, stomping towards her.

Bonnie nodded, still gasping for air. "Yes, but he said to gather you and meet him down in the forest." For the first time in my life, I watched as Mother sprinted out the door with such eagerness in her stride. I have never seen her run in my entire life. I didn't think she had it in her.

Bonnie watched until Mother was long gone to stand straight up and sigh, no longer gasping for breath. What a great performance, really. I cocked my head and placed a hand on my hip bone. "You couldn't have just taken the dagger from the altar?" I said with annoyance in my tone.

Bonnie rolled her eyes. "I would have if it was there. The elders haven't set anything out yet."

"You couldn't have thought of a different way?"

Bonnie copied my stance and tapped her foot. "You want to get out of here or not?" Fair point. Still she could've done something less destructive. Something that won't burn the whole forest down with it. "So what should we do?" "Bonnie asked wearily, like things were now getting serious. "Should we just leave or do we have time to gather food first?"

I shrugged. "I don't know?" I didn't tell her that I hadn't thought that far into the plan because I didn't think it would happen. But now that we're here, panic started to settle in me. I take a deep breath to subside it. "Depends on how much time we have until they figure us out."

"You think they could figure it out?" Bonnie said, drawing in her eyebrows. And as in the most perfect timing ever, yelling came from outside. Bonnie dashed outside the door and raced back in, slamming the door shut. "They're coming," Bonnie panicked. "How could they possibly have figured us out already?"

My eyes widened in horror. I didn't think they would figure it out. They are not dumb but they're not that smart either. How in the hell did they figure it out? Bonnie glanced around the room and settled on the window beside my bed that headed towards the forests behind us.

"You need to get out of here," Bonnie said eagerly marching for the window. She unlatched the lock and slid it open. "You can escape from the window."

I took a step back, bewildered. "What about you? You are coming with me-,"

"I can't," Bonnie interjected. "There won't be any time for me to escape. They're right outside the door and I can hold them off for a while. I can say that I don't know where you went." The yelling grew louder as they got closer.

I shook my head dismissively. "That wasn't part of the plan."

"There is no plan, Vi." Bonnie stepped closer to me and placed a soft but firm hand on my arm. "I will be fine. I know how to handle them. Now go, before it's too late." Bonnie pushed me towards the window. I placed my hands onto the windowsill but before I started to climb out, I turned to face her and pulled her in for an embrace. Our heartbeats were rapidly rising but the motion of our hearts pounding as one started to drop until we both matched the same slow pace. Once I pulled away, mine picked up pace again and the thumping grew louder as I climbed out the window and planted my feet down on the dried, crunchy grass. A pound came from inside the cottage door. When I spun around to face Bonnie, she had already closed the window and locked it from inside. I could see her standing in front of the window. I so desperately wanted her to look back at me one last time but she never did. She disappeared from the window and yelling came from inside soon after.

Without a thought in mind, I dashed into the woods. The rose crown blew off and was left abandoned on the ground behind me. My bare feet stabbed in pain as I stepped on twigs and rocks underneath. Moments later shouting came from behind and I quickened my pace, weaving through the trees with only the moonlight guiding my way. Owls howled and cicadas buzzed into the night sky. The wind huffed and pushed me into a giant oak tree, scraping my sleeve on the bark and tearing a rigged hole down my arm. I yelped as the bark dug into my skin. Pulling myself up and onto my feet I looked down at the jagged slice and from what I could see was a dark substance slithering down to my wrist. Blood. Hollering came from behind me and I started farther down into the woods until they grew fainter and fainter the deeper I went until I couldn't hear them anymore.

I didn't know how long I was running for with only the sound of tree limbs clattering in the wind keeping me company. A loud rush came from somewhere up ahead. Following the sound to where the trees broke off and my feet flattened on rough surface. A road I figured as the surface carried down both sides and disappeared the farther I could see. The roads have to lead me somewhere, right? It just depends on how far it will go to get somewhere. A crack came from the woods making me jump and run down the road. A sudden sharp stab stung through my right foot, making me trip and fall from the pain. I landed on my side with a shriek as hard pebbles dug into my skin. I bit my tongue and sat up, looking down at my foot. A red substance stained the pavement. I drew in my knee and looked under my foot with a gasp. A silver slender object drenched in my warm blood stuck out the center of my foot. I wondered if I could carry on but the searing pain that spread through my foot, stopped my train of thought. I need to get it out. Tears streamed down my face and I started to regret it as I knew how much this was going to hurt. I wrapped my fingers around the ball of the bloody object and took deep breaths to calm my nerves. 1, 2...3. I pulled the object and it started sliding. The pain grew stronger than before. I cried as I yanked it out until it was in my shaky grasp. Looking down at it with tears pouring out my eyes, I can get a better look at it now. The object was round and long with a pointed end that blood dripped off and onto the ground with a splatter. I threw it towards the woods and closed my eyes, trying to focus on my breathing and not the throbbing pain growing up my ankle. The ground started to rumble and a trudging noise came from in front of me. I opened my eyes to a large truck moving towards me from down the road. I remember seeing one in a book once. The truck had a long box connected to the back to transport belongings. I believe I read it was a semi-truck but the truck was blue and silver. The one that headed towards me was red and silver though. Normally the box has a name plastered on the company brand that it ships for but this one did not. It was just plain white. The truck started to slow as it came down the road. Now realizing that the truck was coming right next to me. I pushed myself to my feet and started down the other way, limping and groaning as my foot seared with pain. The truck came to a halt beside me and the glass window went down. A man with high cheekbones and a scruffy white beard with a trucker hat that sat lazily on the top of his head.

"Hey darlin'," His voice rang with a deep southern accent as he looked me up and down. His eyebrows drew in with a tone of worry. "Is your foot bleedin'?" I stopped and glanced behind me.

A trail of my footprint in dark red painted the pavement. I turned back and began to walk, ignoring what the man had said. I'm not supposed to speak to strangers. That's what Reverend Finch and Mother had said since we were little. But I no longer belong to Reverend Finch nor Mother and I don't need to follow their rules anymore. And yet there I was with my mouth firmly shut, not looking in the man's direction as he spoke aloud to me with concern.

"Can I take you somewhere? To your parents' house or the hospital?" He questioned, watching me limp past his truck. He moved the truck forward. The truck huffed out air as he drew on his brakes. "There's a diner a few miles from here. I can take you there." He said, practically shouting at me now. I still ignored him and carried on. I can make it to the diner myself. "You can call someone to pick you up there? Or I can get you something to eat. Are you hungry, darlin'?" As if what he said had opened a part of my mind that suddenly realized that I was starving. My stomach grumbled at the thought of food and some water as I started to feel dizzy. But that might also be from the lack of blood that has disgorged from my body. Either way, food will help. I haven't eaten since Bonnie snuck in a biscuit for me... I miss her. She would know what to do.

I stopped and looked up at the man. He gave me a weary smile and waved his hand. "Hop in, if you can." He mumbled as he unlatched the door and pushed it open for me. I gripped the door handle and stepped up on the bottom step. It took me a moment to climb into the truck without applying pressure on my foot but once I was in I planted myself onto the cushioned seat and swung the door shut. "A little high up, huh?" He giggled and pushed on the pedal and the truck started forward again. A *little high* is an understatement for how tall I was sitting. I felt like I was in a tower looking upon the forest. Okay, maybe not quite like that but it sure felt like it. The man glanced at me and to my foot before focusing his gaze onto the road. "What happened to your foot?" The man questioned again as he flicked a switch that made the truck lights brighter. The lights raised to the leaves of the trees and I almost spotted an owl but it quickly flew away back into the darkness of the forest. I focused on the trees that swayed in the wind. The branches rammed into one another as they stood close together. "Did you step on something?" The man now prying for answers, flicked the switch again and the lights dimmed back onto the road as a small vehicle drove past. Once the car was out of sight he flicked the switch again and a flock of crows frightened and confused, soared off into the dark night sky.

The man tapped my shoulder with his stubby pointer finger. I flinched my shoulder away as I peered up at him, wondering why he cared so much for me to answer him. The man sensed my uneasiness and quickly placed his hand back on the steering wheel. "Didn't mean to scare ya," He glanced at me with a weary grin. "You know, what people say about truckers isn't true. We're all not bad people."

I narrowed my eyes on him. "What do people say?" I never heard anything about truckers. I only know about their trucks and what they do for a living.

He shrugged. "Well, I don't want to tell ya because I don't want to scare ya, but they just say some unkind things about us. Which isn't true. Well, not always. Some truckers are bad news but I'm not one of them.

I have a granddaughter that's about your age," He added as if knowing that he has a granddaughter would make me see him as a good person. But his mentioning my age made me feel more uneasy. How would he know my age if I hadn't told him?

"How do you know what age I am?" I asked wearily, searching his wrinkly face for answers.

The man bellowed a righteous laugh. "I don't, but I can tell by your height and appearance. You both have that young look to ya that speak the same age."

That makes sense, I guess. Bonnie looks to be around my age but she may seem older as she is an inch taller than me. I glanced out the front windshield, the road ahead curved around some trees alongside the pavement. I look back at him with wonder. "How old do you think I am?"

He smirked at how fun the guessing game was. He stroked his beard with his hand, pondering on the question. "Well, my granddaughter is eleven but you do have a bit more structure to ya' face. So I would say around twelve and fourteen, maybe?" He glanced at me expectantly for my answer to see if he was right.

I gave him a courteous smile with my eyes wide in surprise that he'd gotten it somewhat right. "I'm thirteen," I say in amazement.

He giggled. "I told ya, it's all in the appearance." I nodded, glancing back at the tree lines. "How old do you think I look?" The man said playfully. "It's a bit harder to tell as we get older. Eventually we all look the same at the end."

I looked up at him, searching his face. He has deep-set wrinkles along his eyes and forehead, and his beard is white with gray stubbles. He looks around Reverend Finch's age but he is a bit wrinklier than him. Probably from hard labor. Most of the elders who tend to the crops and fields look older than Reverend Finch even though they are younger than him. Finch doesn't do much, that's why he looks younger. I squint my eyes as if that'll help me see him better. But it just makes him a tad bit blurry. "I say around fifty-seven and sixty."

The man looked at me impressed by my answer. "Not bad, I'm fifty-nine."

An uncontrollable grin grew on my face as I turned away, looking back into the forest. We sat in silence for a while as I watched the long road that never seemed to come to an end. "What's your granddaughter's name?"

A warm smile spreads across his face as if the thought of her filled him with joy. "Her name is Wendy. I miss her a bit because I haven't seen her in a while."

"Why haven't you seen her?" I asked, glancing up at him.

"Because of work," He said with a sour face as if he just tasted something bad. "I've been traveling across states to deliver packages to companies. I have to deliver a couple more before I can start heading back home. But the first thing I'm going to do when I get back is to see Wendy. I normally buy her something every trip I'm on, this time I've gotten her a stuffed horse." He pointed behind our seats. A few paper bags were in the back assuming that the horse was in one of them.

"That's nice of you." I said. I never got gifts from anyone before. One time we were given a rubber balloon to play with, but that was only because Sally begged Mother to buy her some. Sally always gets what she wants. But my favorite gift was the dandelion Bonnie gave me a few days ago. I would've brought it with me but the petals fell off and were scattered on the nightstand. Hopefully one day I can give Bonnie a gift too...

The man smiled. "I'm Patrick, by the way."

"I'm... Viola." I hesitated, not sure if I should give him my real name. But he seemed nice enough. Besides, I don't need to listen to the rules that Reverend Finch and Mother instructed me to follow. I'm no longer with them...

"Well, now that we know each other a bit more, do you mind telling me what has happened to your foot? Did you tramp on something?" Patrick probed.

I shrugged, looking down at my bloodied foot. It still stings but the aching has subsided. "I'm not sure what it was?"

Patrick nodded. "I have a pretty good idea of what it was. What did it look like?"

I took a deep breath in, trying to reimagine it. "Umm, it was long and it came to a point at the end,"

"Was it made out of steel?" Said Patrick, itching his beard.

I nodded slightly. "I think so?" I'm not too sure if it was or not. I don't even know what steel is.

"A-huh," Patrick nodded. "You stepped on a nail."

"A nail? What's a nail?" I mumbled but Patrick understood me.

"A nail is something that holds things together, like wood and such. Nails are used in a lot of things such as our houses and decorating places." Patrick glanced down at my foot and scrunched his nose as if the sight of blood grossed him out. "The nail mustn't have been that long since it didn't go through the top of your foot. I should take you to the hospital to get a tetanus shot,"

I looked at him so quickly that the back of my neck made a popping sound. I can't go to the hospital or else the others will find me. "A tetanus shot?"

"It's a vaccine that helps bacteria from rusty nails to keep it from getting infected. By the way you are bleeding out like that, I would say you should get one. The doctors will bandage ya' foot up too."

I glanced up ahead and lights started to come from afar, letting me know that we were almost to town. "Are they going to ask me for a parent?"

"Well yeah, they're probably gonna ask for your parents' contact information so they can let them know where ya' are." Patrick narrowed his eyes on me. Now he's trying to read my face.

Nerves started pumping through my veins. I need to go. I can't go back or I will be dead. I shook my head. "I-I don't want to go to the hospital,"

"Well, I think you should." Patrick swerved barely dodging a deep pothole. "You could lose your foot if it gets infected."

I remember him mentioning the diner. I will have to run away from there. "I'm hungry," I said quickly. "Can we get something to eat first?"

Patrick sighed. "The hospital has food,—"

"But maybe we could go to that diner you have mentioned instead." I interrupted, boring my pleading eyes into his. He looked into mine with a frown of pity. "I'm sure the food is better there than at the hospital."

"Well, of course it is. Nothing can beat diner food." Patrick stated, slowing down the brakes as we entered town. The town had an old western style to it, buildings were made from thick dark wood with neon signs flashing their logos. I've seen Western styles from history books about the old Wild West, this is how I would imagine it. The only building that stood out of place was a short red building with large windows wrapped around the building and a flashing open sign in one of the windows. "Tanya's Diner", flashed a red sign out front that stretched up high to the sky. I prayed Patrick would pull into the parking lot, and as if my prayers had been heard and answered he pulled the semi into a parking space up front. He pulled the lever in the center forward and glanced down at the bloody mess that tinted his navy carpet. "I suggest ya' wait here as I go and order some food, alright?" He gave me a weary smile as I nodded my head. He popped his door open and hopped out, closing it shut behind him. I watched him with eagerness as he swung the glass doors open and headed inside.

Chapter 9

Patrick

I was greeted as I entered the retro building. The red and white checkered flooring and leather booths immediately caught my eye as I walked up to the counter. It's an unusual building to have in the Deep South in the center of town but that's what I like about it. It's different from a matching town. A woman with afro black hair and plump lips stood behind the bar and leaned her forearms against it. She smiled and a dimple appeared from both sides of her peachy cheeks.

"Good evening, Patrick." Tanya said rather cheerfully. "You want the usual?"

I traveled through this town five times in the last six months and I always made sure to stop at Tanya's Diner for a thick cheeseburger with sauerkraut. Each time Tanya makes a mental note of it and without a word, she brings me my meal with a heartfelt smile. She's normally scrambling around the diner gathering people's orders and refilling drinks but this time she stood quietly behind the bar waiting for her eight customers to finish their meals to tidy up. It's late so business is slow as she is going to be closing in an hour soon. I return a weakened smile usually from sleep deprivation from traveling for eleven hours nonstop every day and I continue to drive eleven more the next day for the next two weeks, and also from the pity I felt for that little girl, Viola. For a kid her age to run away in the middle of the night, something terrifying must've happened back at home. Abuse would be the regular cause for running away which is likely her case but she doesn't have bruises from physical contact except for that scab on her chin which to me looked like a scrape from face planting something. The ground perhaps? Wendy has gotten several scrapes and scabs from so. Her arm looked torn up as well, her sleeve from her dress split down her arm but I couldn't make out if her arm was hurt or not. She may have bruises underneath her silk gown, that I don't even think little girls wear anymore. My daughter never wore silky dresses at that age. She wore graphic t-shirts of ponies and her favorite kids shows with shorts or jeans. Which she continued to wear until she hit fifteen and started experimenting with different styles of clothing. Now she's thirty-three years old and wears nothing but suites and pencil skirts as she's now a family law attorney. The way Viola seemed terrified when I mentioned taking her to the hospital proves that it's a family situation, probably scared that they're going to contact her parents. Something pretty bad must've happened or will happen.

I shook my head. "No not this time, Tanya."

Tanya's smile faded and the corners of her mouth turned upside down. "Is everything alright, Pat?" She asked with sincerity in her tone.

I glanced behind Tanya and landed on a glass plate with a lid perched atop a wooden cake stand. A half-sliced apple pie was inside. It looked so delicious with the apple sauce oozing out the side daringly for me to taste.

"Actually, can I take a slice of pie to go please?" I nodded behind her.

Tanya straightened up and grabbed a small to-go box from behind the counter. "You didn't answer my question." Tanya stated, lifting the glass lid and setting it to the side. Grabbing the pie slicer. She sliced a generous piece and plopped it into the styrofoam box. She glanced back at me with an eyebrow arched.

I sighed, slouching over the countertop. "I found a little girl along the side of the road, a couple of miles from town." I say, rubbing my face with my hand. The exhaustion is kicking in. I just need to take that girl to the hospital. When I can trust leaving her with someone then I can get a room at the local motel and pass the hell out. "I think she ran away from home," I added, watching as Tanya closed the lid to the little white box and walked over to me and placed it on the counter beside me.

Tanya narrowed her eyes. "How do you know she ran away?"

"Because why would a little girl run away when it's pitch dark out without any shoes?" I say, digging into my jeans pocket to get my wallet. "Besides, she was pretty banged up and had gotten a nail through the foot."

Tanya scrunched her face from the thought of how painful that must feel. "How's she doing now?" She asked, shifting from one foot to the other.

"I think better," I opened my wallet, pulled out a ten-dollar bill and handed it to Tanya. Her pies are homemade and for only six bucks. I only have a ten and a twenty in my wallet, most of my cash has been used for hotdogs and drinks from gas stations. I need to make a mental note to go to the ATM to withdraw some smaller bucks in the morning. "She's waiting out in the truck."

Tanya shifted to the side, peering beside me and at the truck. The moonlight casted a shadow into the truck and could see nothing but the darkness within. Tanya looked back at me with wonder. "Where are you taking her? You know you can't take her home with you, right." Tanya grinned at me.

I smirked, nodding my head. "Yes, I know that." Even though Wendy would have a blast hanging out with someone her own age. She's been begging her parents for a sibling for months now, complaining about how lonely she is even though she comes over daily to hang out with us. We may or may not buy Wendy new toys weekly to help keep her entertained. But I'm not sure if I want Wendy to be around that girl, Viola. I can't judge her from her past and obvious issues, but something just seems off with her. I wouldn't wanna risk anything happening to them both. "I'm gonna take her to the hospital, get her checked out. Not sure what I'll do from there..." I say shoving my wallet back into my pocket.

"Well, don't forget to call the cops when you get there." Tanya noted, walking up to the cash register and popping the bottom drawer open. "You're gonna need them there."

I raised my hand to stop Tanya in her tracks as she went to grab a dollar from the register. "Keep the change," I say as I grabbed the to-go box and headed for the door.

"Thanks for coming, Pat." She hollered at me. "Have a good night."

I glance at her with a smile. "Same goes for you."

The brisk breeze blew with such vigor as the storm moved closer to town, nearly blowing my hat off and into the wind. I walked around my truck to the driver's seat and swung the driver's side door open. Without realizing until I climbed in and shut the door that the little girl, Viola was gone...

Chapter 10

Looking back, the town that shone bright in the darkness looked like stars twinkling from above. The storm-filled clouds hovered above the town, thunder rumbling from afar as I kept walking down the dirt road that led to endless fields of nothingness. I walked on the dead grass beside the rocky road as the hard pebbles and piles of crushed dirt seeped deep into my wound. My foot was crying in agony as the pain swelled up to my knee. The dried grass is more gentle even though it spiked through my footsteps making a crunching sound with each step. I ignored the aching and carried on down the road.

A rumbling noise came from behind me, my mind telling me that it was just the storm but my instincts were telling me to look behind me. Glancing back I saw a semi truck trudging towards me, the same truck that picked me up and brought me to this town. I can't have him take me to the hospital or the others will find me. I can't go back to counting my hours to my death. I won't allow it...

I veered off the road and climbed over a wooden post as a fence guarded off the flat field. I ran farther away from the road without looking back. The truck's engine huffed as it carried back down the road. I ran until my legs wouldn't allow me to run any further. I glanced around my surroundings, gasping for oxygen. Nothing but endless fields of grass surrounded me. No town. No lights. No road, not even a car, just grass that carried on for miles and miles away. I carried on walking, forcing my tired legs to keep going until I spotted a dirt hill. I sighed with exhaustion and started up it. At the top I peered down a field, searching for anything to hold me over for the night as I rested.

Suddenly when I was about to cry from disappointment and discomfort, I saw a dark building standing tall from down below. I trudged down the hill with relief that there was a place out here in the middle of nowhere where I could rest my heavy eyes and tired limbs for the night. As I got closer to the building I could see that it was made from dark wood that looked distressed from the weather. The one side of the building was a lighter shade of wood like someone had patched it up with newer wood. The roof came to a peak at the top and the doors were large with a latch in the center to keep it sealed shut. As I stopped in front of the door, shuffling and huffing noises came from inside. The thought of turning back came to mind but what other choice do I have? Who knows how far the next opportunity will come? I'm afraid if I travel further my body will just shut down and I'll pass out in the middle of a field with rain crashing down upon me.

Thunder roared over me as a heavy cloud moved above, the stars vanishing in the thick clouds in seconds. I dash up to the door and slide the latch to the side, the door pops open and more tousling comes from within. I took a deep breath in and swung one of the wooden doors open. From inside was a lantern that sat on a wooden box in the center of the floor, the flame flickered and dimly lit up the room. I slowly walked in making sure my steps were as light as a feather to not spook whatever was inside. I stopped in front of the lantern and bent down to pick it up when a huff of air blew in my right ear making me jump back and I bit my tongue to keep from screaming. I saw a black shadow move on the wall and it shuffled away from me. Whatever it was, I sure spooked it like it did me. Its frame was large with a long snout and pointy ears, its height hovering above me and it snorted out its nose. I bent down again and grabbed the lantern and held it above my head to see what was in front of me. The four-legged creature's head turned towards me, its eyes were dark and it was a pale brown with a white stripe going down its snout. It's a horse, a very large one. It stood behind a wooden door with only enough room to lay.

"Hey there," I whispered, slowly stepping closer to it. I held out my hand and its round snout pressed up against my palm, sniffing heavily at my scent. Another shuffle came from behind me. Whirling around and holding the lantern out came another horse in the light but this one was as dark as a shadow. Only its eyes glistening in the light were visible to the eye. It peered down at me with its ears moving back and forth as it analyzed me, wondering who I was. I showed the lantern around the room, rope and tassels hung up on the walls with ribbons and trophies that were displayed on a shelf above. Buckets, mane brushes and blankets are stacked in the corner of the room. In the back corner was a staircase that led up into another space where hay bales were stacked neatly against the walls. This will have to do. I will head back out in the morning before anyone wakes up. Assuming that there is somebody who owns this barn. Who else will take care of the horses? Certainly, not themselves. I went back down the steps and pulled the barn door tightly closed, making sure it wouldn't pop back open from the wind. I grabbed a thick wooly blanket from the other end of the barn and headed back up the stairs. I placed the lantern on the clunky wooden floorboards and wrapped myself tightly in the blanket to keep warm. I laid down next to hay bales while using my forearm as a pillow. As soon as my eyes closed I fell into a deep slumber that drowned out the storm's rage that made the ceiling creek and crackle as the lantern blew out from the wind that came through the cracks of the wooden walls.

Chapter 11

Smoke evaporating onto my skin, my cheeks burning from the heat. As I listened to the popping and crackling of the fire consuming the little white building, footsteps came from behind me. The footsteps crunched from the dried grass and it grew louder as they came closer, then they carried to my left ear and abruptly stopped. I listened to them intently. Their breath shuttered as they released the air through their mouths. Then a small shaky hand weaved their fingers through mine and firmly clasped my left hand. I tried to turn my head to see who it was but I was still frozen. I couldn't move any part of my body except for my eyes. Then suddenly a palm was placed on the small of my back and I was pushed forward. I stumbled and fell to the ground, bashing my forehead onto the orange dirt...

I abruptly awakened to an older man kicking my dirty feet with his big boot. He towered over me, his eyes crinkled as he squinted down at me. His thick white hair stuck out the sides of his cap and his thick brown jacket broadened his figure and made him look like a giant man. I quickly sat up and crawled back into a hay bale, looking up at him with pleading eyes. The man raised a bushy eyebrow, revealing deep wrinkles along his forehead. He looked about in his sixties, maybe seventies from the deep set wrinkles that didn't disappear when he relaxed his face and by his blotchy, damaged skin from the sun.

"Who are you and why are you here?" His voice was deep and rugged with a tempered tone. I stared up at him and was too afraid to speak. So I didn't say a word. The man sighed and folded his arms across his chest with a wide stance. He waited for my response but it never came. "Well? I would like to know who's been using my barn as a motel." My breath quivered and my mouth gaped open in shock. The man rubbed his eyes with his thumb and pointer finger, already exhausted from the morning. It must've been early because there was a blue haze that came from the opened barn doors. "Well, are you injured?" He asked, nodding toward the steps. I glanced over the direction and my eyes grew wide. Bloody footprints stained the light wooden floors that trailed to where I layed. "You left a trail of bloody footprints on my wooden floors." He looked at me expectantly, tapping his foot against the floorboards. I inhaled deeply and tried to keep myself from stuttering out of fear.

"I-I stepped on a nail," I say, remembering what the truck driver, Patrick, had told me.

The man took a long sigh and glanced around the barn with his hands on his hips. "Alright, show me." The man said, crouching down in front of me.

I cocked my head. "What?"

He looked at me and his forest-green eyes bore into mine. "I have to see how bad it is." he simply replied.

I straightened my posture trying to come off dominant enough for him to let me go. But I probably looked more like a foolish child than I thought. "I won't go to the hospital," I say sternly, clearly unsettled with the idea. I spent half the night trying to get away from a man who insisted on taking me there. I don't want to do it all over again.

The man seemed to think I am funny because all he did was let out a bellowing laugh. "I don't think you got much of a choice." I was taken aback by his tone and started to feel anxious. He nodded to my foot and I reluctantly pulled back the wooly blanket. Blood and dirt coated my foot and ankle in a dry film. The once deep red is now a dark brown with a rouge tint almost a charcoal color. He nodded, sucking in air between his teeth. "Yep, you got it good." He grabbed my swollen ankle and made me flinch from the sudden stab of pain. He loosened his grip when he noticed my discomfort and examined the wound. "Looks to me like it was a big one. Might take some time to heal. I can take you to the hospital and contact who-"

I yank my ankle free and push my back deeper into the hay while shaking my head. "I am *not* going to the hospital."

The man stood up with a huff. "Alright, but Jodi will say otherwise."

Who is Jodi and why would I care what she says? *No one* can persuade me to voluntarily go to the hospital. You would have to drag me by my hair while I kick and scream for me to go. I'm not planning on staying long enough for that. Without any time to react the man walked up to me grabbed my elbow with a firm grip and pulled me up onto my feet in a rush. My foot seared with pain and I bit my bottom lip to keep from screaming in agony. I pulled my arm away and the man narrowed his eyes on me.

"Can you walk alright?"

I flattened my skirt down and glared up at him. "I walked here, didn't I?"

The man pursed his lips in a satisfied smirk. "Very well then. Follow me." He nodded before walking down the creaky old staircase down to the barn. I lamely followed suit, limping and sinking my teeth deeper into my lip as the pain swelled up into my ankle. As I figured it out the horses were drawn from their stables and sunken hoof prints stamped the dry soil and trailed out into the open pastures. I squinted my eyes as the sun rose above the trees and the rays blasted my face in warmth. Chills slithered down my spine from the chilled morning air that embraced me as I walked beside the rugged man up towards the hill where I came from the night before. The man took my arm and held it up to inspect my injury from the rigged tree branch. "Got ya self good there too."

I pulled my arm back and looked down at the soiled grass. The ground was damp from the rain last night. I figured it would be muddy but there were no muddy patches in the ground to tell otherwise. "It was from a tree." I finally said.

The man glanced around the pastures and nodded his head. "Ahh, I see. And your chin?" He asked, tapping his chin with a thick, stubby finger.

"I tripped and fell on cement."

"Ahh," He breathed again with another nod. "I sliced my finger with a rusted nail once."

I squinted up at him. The sun peeked out from behind his head. "How did that happen?"

He sighed. "Well, I was taking down old boards from the barn and one of them had a rusted nail sticking out of it. I hadn't noticed until my ring finger slipped and sliced open." I made a sour expression and he laughed with a nod. "Yeah, that was my expression as well. Anyway, it bled a lot and my wife Jodi kept telling me that I should go to the hospital before it gets infected. But I don't like the doctors much, never have." The corner of his lips turned upward and the wrinkles around his eyes deepened. I guess I know who Jodi is now. He continued on with his rant. "I thought that soaking my finger in rubbing alcohol would do the trick. Oh boy was I wrong. The next morning I had to be rushed to the emergency room because my finger got deeply infected and it hurt like hell..." he trailed off, waiting for me to ask him what happened. Probably to get me to engage with him more. Probably to help me feel like I could trust him. It's hard to trust someone when the people you trusted most ended up being the ones you should've ran away from a long time ago.

I still enlightened him and asked him the question he was looking for. "Did they fix it? Your finger?"

He shrugged, stifling back a wide grin. "If chopping the finger off is fixing it? Then yes, they did." He slid his right hand out of his coat pocket and held it up for me to see. There was nothing but a stub from where his knuckle began. I flinched at the sudden sight and he chuckled as he shoved his hand back into his coat pocket. I understand what he's getting at but still the fear of going to the hospital and seeing Reverend Finch and Mother walking through the doors to pick me up, just to take me to my death still sends shivers down my spine every time I think of it. Still, I don't want my foot to get chopped off. But would that really be as bad as death? We strolled down the field, or more like limping down it and I didn't remember if this is how far I had to walk to get to the barn last night? It was pretty dark. I couldn't really tell. To me, the entire night felt like it would never end. The relief I felt when I lay down that night, finally taking a moment to just breathe was one of the best feelings I have ever felt. I limped silently beside the man when I took a step forward and my right foot sunk deep into the earthy grass and made me fall onto my knees with a jolt of force. The man bent down and grabbed my arm and pulled me back up and onto my feet with such ease like I was just a feather he plucked from the ground...

"Yeah, you've gotta be careful walking through the pastures. Those damn horses always dig their hoofs into the soil." He shook his head in a disapproving manner, like he's disappointed in the horses for putting sunken holes into his grass. He must have trampled into them enough times to warn me about them. The thick grass hides it like a blanket draped overtop. We carried on down the hill and made sure to keep an eye out for more sunken holes hidden underneath the grass. "My name is Carl." He said suddenly.

I sighed, considering if he should know mine or not. I suppose he should since he is helping me and all. "My name is Viola." I kept my eyes on the ground still in search of holes in disguise.

Carl inhaled the muggy air in and sighed. "I suppose you aren't going to tell me why you're out here all alone."

I kept quiet. Like I have said, I can't trust anyone. How do I know he isn't going to take me back to Mother and them? He is not going to want me to stay here and intervene in his and Jodi's life. I'm not sure where I will go? But I surely can't stay here. I have considered just running away now but he will probably catch me in an instant and bring me back here. Maybe after he helps me with my foot. Then I will go.

Carl sighed again and stopped in his tracks. "We're here."

I stopped and stared at the tall white house that was in the distance. It looked old with the white paint chipping off the walls but it still looked lively with the large pots with purple and pink flowers along the large wrap-around porch where two rocking chairs swayed in the wind and a tall weeping willow tree planted beside the house. Its long vines swayed in the breeze as it blew softly around us. A rusted red truck parked next to the house which only added to the style of it. My jaw fell open from the sight of the house that perched on a small hill in the middle of the pastures. I couldn't help but admire it from afar. I have never seen a place as large and quite pretty as this one is.

"Beautiful ain't?" Carl said as he too, admired it from afar. Then he nodded and started down the hill. "Come on, let's go meet Mrs Granger."

I followed suit and went down the hill. The house grew larger as I stopped at the porch and glanced up at the dark roof that came to a peak at the top.

"Jodi! Will you come out here please!" Carl shouted, propping his boot on the porch steps and readjusted his hat on his head. Moments later an older woman with gray hair that twisted up into a bun with rosy cheeks, walked out the screen door with a creak and a slam as she stepped towards Carl. The woman reminded me of Mother but only if she was older and with a few wrinkles around her eyes and mouth. She gazed at Carl with a bewildered look as she dried her hands on a floral towel. I stood as still as possible hoping she wouldn't notice me, but her gaze fell onto me and drew in her eyebrows as she looked from my face and down to my bloody foot.

"Who is she and why is she bleeding?" Jodi nodded towards me, looking back at Carl expectantly for answers. Her gaze was cold and empty which sent a sensation of chills down my spine. She scares me more than Mother ever has.

Carl glanced back at my worried face and gave me a reassuring smile, but that still didn't stop the chills from raining down upon my back. "I found her sleeping in the barn," Carl informed his wife. "She got a nail through the foot. Well, luckily not completely through. But still, she needs our help."

Jodi examined me with pursed lips. "Where are your parents, little girl?" She demanded, placing her hands on her hips. It seemed like Mother was asking me that question herself.

Carl shook his head. "It's no use. She won't say."

"Why did you bring her here then?" Jodi turned to Carl. "You should be taking her to the police station or to the hospital,"

"Well," Carl sighed, climbing up the steps. "I was hoping that you could check her foot out." His size towered over her like the weeping willow that towered over the porch. "She refuses to go to the hospital," He whispered to Jodi as she glared up at him.

"It doesn't matter if I look at her foot or not!" Jodi raised her tone, folding her arms across her chest. "If she stepped on a rusted nail, then she will need to get a tetanus shot."

"I know," Carl breathed. "But if you look at it first then maybe she will feel more at ease for us to take her to the hospital."

I narrowed my eyes at them wondering why they are talking about me like I'm not even here. Like I have told him before, I will *not* be going to the hospital. I shifted my stance off of my wounded foot as the pressure started to cause more discomfort from my toes to my ankle. Jodi's eyes shot back at me and let out a long sigh. "Come inside."

Chapter 12

The inside was just as stunning as the outside. The walls were a beige with pictures of horses and fields of trees. A wooden bench in the walkway with dried muddy boots on a worn woven rug. A gold frame stood out by the front door with younger Carl and Jodi. Carl wore a black suit with a bow tie and slicked back hair and Jodi wore a white laced gown with flowers, and a twisted bun like she wears now. While she held a bouquet of deep red roses in her hands. Her cheeks and lips were plump and tinted red, similar to the liquid that Mother put on my cheeks and lips for the ritual that is still stained on my skin. That stuff does not want to come off. Maybe it is my past holding onto me and won't let go? Eventually my past is going to have to say goodbye. I will have to say goodbye.

Jodi led the way to the sun lit kitchen where colorful flowers painted the walls and plain wood cabinets faltered atop the oven and sink. A large window above the sink shows out into the green pastures with the sun shining from above. I wonder why their house is so decorated with pictures and colors? I never had my walls painted a dark or light color. Neither was the kitchen. Just plain white walls and dusty plain cabinets. The others would show disapproval of Jodi and Carl's home. Material things aren't what you need. It's what you want, and you shouldn't want anything as the Savior has given you everything. At least, that's what Finch says...

My bare feet slapped hard onto the stone flooring. The roughness of the stone picked at my dry heels as I walked to the corner of the room breaking off from Carl. Jodi opened a cupboard above the stove and pulled out a clear glass bottle and two white cotton balls. She brought them over to the round wooden table in the center of the room and gently set them down. Carl pulled out a rickety wooden chair and patted the back with his large hand for me to sit down. I obeyed and quietly slid into the chair and planted my feet on the ground to keep the chair steady. One leg seemed shorter than the others, making me sit on a slant. I wonder if Carl had made the table and chairs himself? The engraved flowers look delicately sketched into the wooden table. It was a dark oak but the engraved flowers were light like there was a hidden color underneath the dark surface. Carl pulled out a chair for Jodi and she lowered herself into it while she unscrewed the cap from the oblong glass and kept it tucked into her palm as she grabbed a cotton ball and carefully poured the clear liquid onto it. The stench was strong and burned my nostrils as I took a ragged breath. Rubbing alcohol. This isn't going to feel too good. Jodi bent down and picked up my leg from the ankle and rested my foot on her lap. She gently swiped the damp cotton ball on the wound and I gritted my teeth from the burning sensation that spread up to my ankle. I appreciate her gentleness but it still doesn't help it from feeling like my foot is in a pit of fire that is torching my skin. It feels nothing like the dream I had thirty-minutes ago. I kept my focus on Carl watching as he opened a cupboard and drew out a drinking glass. He took it to the sink and filled it halfway with water. He carried it over to the table and placed it beside me, giving me a small smile as he stepped back and folded his arms across his chest. He observed Jodi wiping the cotton over the wound. I grabbed the glass with a shaky hand and gulped down the lukewarm water that submerged my dry insides and made me feel fresh and cool.

"Were you out there all night?" Jodi questioned as she dropped the dark brown cotton ball on the table and drenched the other with more alcohol. Continuing to dabbing and wiping the white fuzz now a tinted red. "Alone?" She added, looking up past her thin eyebrows at me. I set the

glass back down and slowly nodded my head without saying a word. Jodi let out a long sigh and I expected her to ask why, but instead she pulled my foot off her lap and gathered the cotton balls into a hand and carried them to a cupboard that opened into a trash can, dumping the remnants of the dirt and blood into it. She turned around and faltered her gaze onto me. "Why don't you go and get yourself cleaned up in the bathroom." She said softly, nodding to the hallway. "It's down the hall, the last door to the right." She looked at me expectantly and I glanced at Carl who agreed with a nod. I stood up and shuffled out of the kitchen. I stopped in the hallway and stood up against the wall next to the kitchen. I know they are going to talk about me and I have a pretty good idea what it will be about.

A cupboard to a cabinet slammed shut. "You are going to take her to the hospital." Jodi demanded Carl.

Carl sighed, scooting the tilting chair back against the table scraping on the floors with a *screech*. "She doesn't want to go to the hospital, Jodi." Carl protested.

Jodi slammed something down on the countertop. I can tell she's giving him a sharp look with pursed lips, similar to the look Mother would give us disobedient girls. "I don't care what she wants. She's a child who carelessly ran away and ended up here, on our property. She does as we say. You either take her to the hospital or I'm calling the police."

Without refraining myself I stepped out from the wall and stood in the doorway, shaking my head. "You can't do that."

Carl and Jodi snapped their heads at me with narrowing eyes. Jodi folded her arms across her chest and tapped her foot on the floor. "And why is that?" She asked tersely, raising her thin brows.

I take a deep breath in, trying to calm my nerves down. My right hand started to shake from the sudden adrenaline rush. I grip the seam of my dress tightly to keep it steady. "Be-cause," I stuttered in a breath. "Then *they* will know where I am."

Carl drew in his eyebrows in confusion. He shook his head not understanding why. "Who are *they*?"

I peer down at the gray and red floors, my body stiff as a board. "Reverend Finch and Mother." I say lower than expected, practically in a whisper. My voice was soft and quiet and my eyes darted around each brick that was intricately placed in a row that trailed across the room. I never realized how much I coward down by only saying their names. They're not even in the room with me and I feel a gut wrenching pain in my abdomen from the fear I feel when they are around. Maybe it's because I know I'm not supposed to be giving strangers their names like they taught me. It's not like they can give me a rational punishment later. I'm no longer with them, they can no longer hurt or yell at me... right? Carl looked down then his eyes went wide like he suddenly understood everything. He looked back to me and pointed a stubby finger in my direction.

"You're one of the girls from the cult up north, right?"

There's that word again. *Cult.* What does that even mean? Before I could even ask what he meant, Jodi chimed in with the same confused expression that Carl had seconds ago. "What the hell are you talking about?" She said with a southern twinge to the word hell. I hadn't noticed her accent until now. It's definitely not as strong as Carl's accent. "There is no cult up north,"

Carl turned to Jodi, nodding his head. "Oh yes, there is. Seaney told me about them."

Jodi made a *pssh* through her lips in disagreement and rolled her eyes. "How would Seaney know? He is dumber than a box of rocks. He doesn't know nothin' about up north." Carl took a step closer to Jodi, still nodding his head. I couldn't help but feel embarrassed that I'm just standing in the doorway while they argue about some person named Seaney. Who even is Seaney?

"I'm telling you that Seaney got a call about some group of people with a bunch of little girls living on a farm a few miles north. They had built themselves a church and cabins." Carl shifted his stance and folded his arms, leaning against the counter behind him. "He was all freaked out too. Said they wore all matching black dresses and button down shirts,"

Jodi smacked her arms down to her sides. "Then why didn't Seaney do something about it?" She questioned, now leaning against the counter like Carl is. I still stood awkwardly straight with my hands clenched to the seams of my skirt. So tight my fingernails stung my palms even through the material.

"No one owned the fields and they weren't causing any harm. Seaney said he couldn't do anything unless they do something against their regulations." Carl glanced at Jodi, shaking his head. "I'm not too sure how that works."

Jodi looked back at me and I froze, not breathing or blinking just me staring back at her. I can't help but see such a resemblance between her and Mother. They look nothing alike but they do at the same time. I can't explain it. Maybe it's their demeanor? Their attitude? The look they give when they're angry or inspecting you for the truth? Either way, both of them make my gut wrench when they pierce their hollow eyes at me. "This is the last time I am going to ask you this. You decide whether you want to answer truthfully or not." She took a deep breath through her nostrils inhaling the sweet scent of cinnamon and vanilla that was in the aroma. "Why did you run away?"

I exhaled a shaky breath. "I was the chosen sacrifice. But I didn't want to die."

Jodi clenched her jaw and the fire that burned in her eyes started to settle down into ash. "And why can't we call the cops?"

"Because, they are already gone." That and I don't want them to know where I am. If they call the police, then they will instantly know where I am and they will come for me. I'm afraid of what they will do to me if they find me. One thing I know about them is that they have no mercy for anyone who steps in their way.

Chapter 13

I bobbed up and down in my seat as the squeaky tires crushed the gravel along the road. Who thought it would be a smart idea to use pebbles of stone as a base for a road? A road that rubber wheels ride on, crunching each stone deeper into the dirt and tires. As surprised as I am of how the stone pebbles don't bust a hole in the wheels, I am more shocked that this rustic piece of metal still works. The once dark red paint is now an orangey-brown. I could tell it was once red from the splotchy patches along the truck showing through the rust. When Jodi inserted the key into the keyhole and jiggled it a bit until it turned in place and the engine spat on. Jodi cursed under her breath angrily saying,

"Damn it, you piece of tin shit." And "When will Carl replace this pile of garbage for a new one?" And she pulled out onto the bumpy road.

For a while nothing was around except for large pastures of grass and dirt, some empty and unkempt and others with horses eating from the green fields and their babies prancing behind their mothers to keep up with their long strides. Not knowing where I was but I do know where I am going... to the hospital. Jodi had insisted I go and even though the thought of running away came to mind as we trampled through the stoned pathway towards the truck with Carl striding closely behind to make sure I wouldn't run away. But my body didn't urge me to do so. Where would I have gone? There's nowhere I could go. I was lucky enough to find a place to rest before the storm rushed by last night, and from the sight of seeing just fields of nothingness tells me there would have been nowhere for me to go when the next night is drawn near. I would have been stuck sleeping out in the open grass with ants crawling all around me without knowing how much further I would have to walk the next morning. I suppose that would have been a chance I was willing to take to save my life from the only few people I have known since birth. I sure hope I don't end up being forced back to them...

Jodi smoothed out her flyaways from her loose bun and glared at me with her simmering gaze, which she has done a few times since we left the property of her home. I have ignored her by keeping my eyes out the dusty windows. This time she had parted her lips like she had something to say but then quickly pursed them shut, carefully thinking on the words she wanted to say before parting them again.

"I hope you understand that you're only staying with us temporarily until we know what to do with you." Jodi said, sternly. She barely moved in her seat as the front tire sank into a pothole on the side of the road before rolling through and back down the straight path. Meanwhile I looked like a fish out of water. I nearly thumped my head onto the roof. I held myself down by gripping the handle on the side of the door.

I nod. "I understand." A cut stung into my gut from how insincere she spoke. I can't be upset with her though, she doesn't even know me and neither do I. I'm just a girl who showed up on her doorstep and now she feels reliable for where I end up. Maybe leaving would be a better option than staying? I don't want to stay somewhere I was not invited.

Jodi stared at the road ahead, gripping the steering wheel a bit too tightly her knuckles turned white. "You're going to be doing chores while you are with us. Don't think you are free loading here." She glanced down at my bloody foot. The wound began to bleed again from the stoned pebbles stabbing into my puncture wound. I am sure she is not thrilled by the blood that trickled

down my foot and dripped onto the split carpeting. It shouldn't be bothering her that much since there are dark spots and dried up mud along the tan carpeting. The carpet peeling in on the corners from too much usage of such an old vehicle. Jodi sighed looking back to the road. "You will be helping me with the house chores until your foot heals. Then you will be helping Carl out in the fields."

I look at her with eyebrows drawn in. "With what?" Back at what used to be my home, we girls were only allowed to do the cottage chores and help tend the gardens. But we were never allowed to help out in the fields. "It is a man's job." Reverend Finch said, after I questioned him one morning while I stood and watched the Elders out in the fields trying to get an old tractor they had found along the side of the road to start running again. They had gotten it fixed and working by sunset. They were quite proud of themselves as they are with most of the things they fix. But I always wondered what it would be like to work in the fields. Hot, I would imagine.

Jodi shrugs. "Helping Carl finish the projects that he has started but never finished." The corners of her mouth twitched upward almost in a half grin. Then she sagged her mouth again like she had just noticed that moment of weakness. That glimpse of fondness escaping her mind. I can tell Jodi showing affection doesn't come naturally to her, and neither for me too. Maybe Jodi and I are more similar than we think we are? "He tends to do that." Jodi said, cautiously watching the road, like a horse will suddenly appear out of thin air and run out in front of us. Maybe it has happened before? "You will also help with the horses." I nodded, drawing my eyes back onto the road. Ahead were faint buildings the size of ants perched up on a hill. That must be the town where Jodi's taking me to. I'm surprised by how many towns are within a short range of each other. Unlike the last town that trucker Patrick took me to, this one had a sign that we shortly passed by that read in big bold black lettering, **"Welcome To Mayors Town"**, with a large clementine fruit beside it. I wonder what clementines have to do with the town?

I bobbed in silence as the buildings grew larger and larger until we passed by them in a rush. The buildings were small and crammed together but each one was painted a different color. I glanced at them as we drove past. Red, orange, white, yellow, blue, a sky blue, and a pale pink caught my attention and I watched them shrink away in the side mirrors as we headed down a pathway through town. People roamed the streets heading into buildings and back out of them. A woman and her small child patiently waited at the end of the road to cross the street. They held hands as the child smiled down at a toy his mother must've bought him. Instead of stopping to let them cross the street, Jodi drove past without any mind of them. My head moved with them and I kept my gaze on the woman and child who now crossed the street before snapping my head back in front of me. Mother told me it was rude to stare at strangers. But I think it was more so we wouldn't bring attention to ourselves. Not like it was hard when we all wore similar clothing anyway. Carl made me realize how much strangers do notice us. More than I ever thought. Who else knows about us and is calling us a cult? *Us*, isn't a word for me anymore. There is no more *us*, just *me...*

Jodi turned the steering wheel to the right and a large building emerged in the front window. It was tan with a flat roof and windows aligned in a row. A sign flashed in bold lettering above the entrance reading, **Mayors Towns Hospital & Emergency Room.** It didn't take long for Jodi to find a spot for the truck because no one was there. Big hospital for such a small town. Jodi took the keys out of the keyhole and shoved them into her shoulder purse before turning her upper body towards me with raised eyebrows.

"If anyone asks who you are, you say that you are my niece and I am your aunt. Do you understand?" Her forehead creased into thin lines as she raised her brows higher, waiting for my response. I nodded and she let out a sigh she was holding and nodded, reassuring herself that everything will be fine. She grabbed her purse and clutched it tightly in her hands and inhaled deeply before exiting the truck.

* * *

I sat in a white room on a big high chair with plastic paper that crinkled when I shifted in my seat. It slowly agitated Jodi who tapped a short nail on her thick brown purse. Shelves and a counter were next to me with jars filled with small white cotton balls and a long white stick with fluff at the ends, and a plastic bottle with a clear gel liquid stood next to the jars by the end of the counter. I suddenly became very aware of my appearance. Of my white, silk gown with tears in the arms and the frayed edges at the bottom of the skirt. Of my wild golden hair that coiled with frizz and knotted in the back from never getting it brushed since yesterday. Of the blood and dirt stains going up my ankles and knees and my sliced arm, and my scabbed chin. With all the new wounds, I started to forget my old ones. I stared down at my palm and traced my thumb along the cut caused from the knife at the choosing ritual. The stinging is gone now and a thin layer of skin overlapped the cut, healing it from the inside-out. I try to keep my hand partly closed so the wound won't split back open and cause more pain. Then I jump from a sudden knock on the door. Jodi straightened her posture and placed her hand on top of the other and smiled as a tall older man with thin hair and a white coat draped around his shoulders. He held a clipboard that he looked up from with a broad smile plastered across his face.

"Hello, I'm Doctor Bernard." He exclaimed as he rolled a backless chair in front of me and sat down. The clipboard balanced on his lap. A hickory and oak scent wafted up my nose and permeated my nostrils with a sweetness of honey. The scent reminded me of when me and Bonnie would run through the forest to collect sticks and logs for a bonfire that we never had before. The oak trees permeated around us as the wind ruffled the leaves. Bonnie had shown me a log hanging from a branch with little honeybees swarming around it. She taught me about honeycombs and honeybees and how they make a nest for the queen bee to nest in as they gather pollen from flowers to create honey. We stood and watched for what felt like hours seeing bees come in and out of their nest and fly around to find a spot to land their honey. We later had gotten yelled at for taking too long and were sent to bed early before the bonfire had even started. Hearing the chants and giggles from the others outside the cottage made us feel slightly jealous that they got to stay up late and have fun. But we never regretted the time we had that evening and watching the honeybees at work for their queen. We had our own fun that night.

"I must say, I was a little surprised to hear that Jodi has a niece." Doctor Bernard said, bringing me out of my head and back to reality. He smiled at me and glanced behind him at Jodi.

Jodi shrugged with a curtsy smile. "Not everyone knows me as well as they think they do, I suppose."

Doctor Bernard nodded in response. "That is quite alright. Not everyone needs to know everything about someone's life." He turned back to me and looked down at his clipboard. "I see here that you, Viola, got a nail in the foot?" He glanced up from his clipboard and looked at my dirty feet. His eyes raised to my scarred palm that I traced with my thumb. I clasped my hands together not wanting him to question me on where I have gotten the scar from. He took the mental note and looked at me with a wide smile. "I can see that you have other injuries as well." He nodded to my sliced forearm. His smile contorted as he pondered something in his head. "How exactly did you get these injuries?"

Panic jumped inside my chest. Jodi never told me what to say about how I have gotten my wounds. What am I supposed to say? My eyes flickered to Jodi that caught a glimpse of my panic and said, "Oh you know children. They run through the pastures barefoot and not watch where they are stepping." Jodi chuckles but stops to a serious tone. She realizes it's not that funny of a story. Because it's not. Even though that's not entirely how any of this had happened, I continued to play along. Like how I had to play along my entire life, back with the group. I've become so used to pretending that none of this fazes me anymore.

Doctor Bernard nodded. "And what about her arm?"

"I tripped and scraped my arm into a tree branch that stuck out." I said gingerly. "When I tramped on the nail." I added, making sure what I said was clear as Doctor Bernard just looked at me without any sign of understanding. I don't think he is buying it. I'm not sure what there is to buy? Accidents do happen, like mine.

"Alrighty then," Doctor Bernard finally said, rolling his chair across the room to put the clipboard down on the counter. "We will give you a tetanus shot for the foot. And for that arm, it doesn't look deep enough for stitches. We'll just put some glue on it to seal it shut." He smiled and rolled up closer to me. "And do not fear, it won't hurt."

"Thank you, Doctor." Jodi says kindly, more kindly than she has ever spoken to me.

"My pleasure," Doctor Bernard stood up and walked over to the door. "My nurse will be in with the supplies." He rested his hand on the doorknob and turned back to look at me. "Oh and I heard Jodi sews some nice dresses. I can tell." He looked me up and down still with weary eyes but the smile fools his expression. "Well, before it got torn up a bit."

Jodi smiled gingerly and glanced at my dress with slight disgust. I'm sure she's thinking how her dresses are made better than the ones Greta, Valerie and Mother made for me. Doctor Bernard closed the heavy door behind him, leaving me and Jodi alone in silence.

Chapter 14

Back at the house I followed Jodi up the rickety staircase and to a bedroom door. She said she had some clothes I could borrow, until they find me someplace else to go. Neither of us knows what to do with me. There's nowhere for me to go and no place to call home. Even though the

group was the last place I would call home. I entered the bedroom with tan walls and a tapestry of the pastures with the barn hung up over the slim bed, similar to the one that I and the girls had back at the group. My toes brushed the round woven rug under my bare feet in the center of the room. The auburn and green thread weaved delicately together in a circle and the soft bristles tickled the balls of my feet. Well, my left foot because the other is wrapped with a bandage.

"You will be sleeping in here." Jodi stated, walking over to the little closet across from the bed. "I will make the bed later." Jodi slid the closet door open and reached in, soon pulling out a little yellow dress with a white underskirt sewn underneath. She carried it towards me and put it up against my body, eyeing it on me. "What size are you?" She asked as she slid the dress off the hanger.

I squinted my eyes trying to recall what size I am. I remembered Mother mentioning to Greta and Valerie that I'm a size eight, I believe. Then Valerie said I was too small for my age, petite actually. "I'm an eight, I think?"

Jodi narrowed her eyes on me. "You're tall but quite thin. Did those people feed you often?" *Those people* are a new term for them. One that I could get used to hearing other than calling them a *cult*. Whatever that means, I still don't know. I nodded my head knowing very well that they hadn't fed me the other day for the ritual. They wouldn't even allow me to drink a glass of water. Luckily, Bonnie cared enough to bring me a biscuit with jam. But that was hours ago and I still haven't eaten anything since then.

Jodi laid out the dress on the bare mattress of the bed and turned to me with folded hands. "Well, I assume you're hungry. I'll have Carl cook you something quick to eat." She pointed to the dress. "Put it on while I gather my sewing kit. I'll have to make some adjustments later." Jodi brushed past me and stood in the center door frame, giving me one last glance before shutting the door behind me. I walked towards the dress and traced my dainty fingers along the yellow material. It was soft with a hint of gold in the yellow. It reminded me of the dandelion flower that Bonnie had given me as a gift to stay calm. I blinked back tears that welled in the corners of my eyes and tried to ignore the lonely gut feeling of not being able to see Bonnie. Maybe she will run away and we somehow cross paths with each other again? She can't possibly want to stay with the group after everything they had put her through. Could she? I like to think she wouldn't...

I pulled up the skirt of my dress and tugged it over my head, dropping the once white satin dress on the floor. I gently took the yellow dress in my hands and slid it over my body until it draped loosely on me. The skirt draped over my hips and went down to my knees. The short sleeves covered my bare shoulders. The neckline went up to my collarbones and white lace trimmed the edges of the sleeves and skirt. It felt softer on my body than it did with my touch. I wonder why Jodi made this dress. She doesn't have any children... unless she did. If so, what had happened to her?

A knock on the door made me jump in my stance and shortly thereafter Jodi emerged through the door. She carried in a small tin box that had a picture of a sugar cookie on the front of the lid. She stopped in her stride when she saw me awkwardly standing in the dress. She examined me. I could see pain in her dreary eyes as she gave me a thin smile and let out a deep sigh.

"It looks good on you." She said, striding towards me. She placed the tin box down on the rug and bent down onto her knees. She grabbed the loose material around the waist and cinched it tighter with her fingers. "A bit large, but that's nothing a few pins and thread couldn't fix. Now stand still." I once again found myself standing straight with my arms out like a bird soaring through the sky as Jodi pinned the loose material together. I looked down at her focused face and now realized more of her features. Her small blue and green colored eyes were dimly lit like a candle that's about to run out of wax to burn. Her thin lips were chapped and the color of a pink peony. Her cheeks were tinted red like a freshly bloomed rose. I wonder what's behind that mask she wears? Behind her stern and high willed attitude. Is this who she truly is or is this only the part she wants me to see? But I can tell she's really someone that's kind and caring. I catch that when her guard breaks down like she did when she saw me in this dress. I could see it pained her seeing me wear it, but the small smile she expressed showed that she appreciated me wearing it. I know I shouldn't think much about it, especially if I'm not planning on staying for long but I can't help myself from wanting to know who she truly is...

"Why do you have this dress?" I say bluntly, not realizing what I said till after I had already said it. My curiosity is getting the best of me.

Jodi took the pin from between her lips and pinned it through the seam of the dress. She took a deep breath in. "What do you mean?"

I know that wasn't really a question because she knew very well what I had meant. I glanced around the room. "Whose room did this belong to?" Once again my curiosity got the best of me. I wished I would have taken my question back as soon as Jodi snapped her head up at me with fire in her eyes. They weren't dimly lit anymore. I could see flames rage in her dark eyes and smoke nearly coming out of her ears.

"Didn't your people teach you not to meddle into someone else's business?" She fumed, squinting her eyes at me. I bit down on my bottom lip and nodded. Of course Mother taught me that. She would punish us if we didn't mind our own.

"Never question the adults and never get into their business." Mother would tell us girls. If we did we would get a palm to the cheek and sent immediately to our beds. We would be stuck there for hours until Mother came to get us the very next morning. I guess running away from the group made me forget I couldn't just do that to the group, but to any other adult either. How could I have been so foolish?

Jodi stared at me, waiting for a response. I gulped down saliva and continued nodding my head. "Yes, they did teach me that." I say slowly, not wanting to provoke her anymore than she already is.

"Then stop meddling into mine." Jodi tugged on the dress to get me to move closer in her direction and snatched a few more pins from the tin box to put between her lips. "Now hold still and be quiet."

Chapter 15

"I would've had you in that dress earlier," Jodi mentioned as we walked down the staircase towards the kitchen. "But I didn't want you to get blood on my rugs." The dress was perfectly hemmed to fit me. Jodi also ran a brush through the bird's nest on top of my head. My hair is now smooth but a bit frizzy from my coiled hair that entwined at the very ends. Jodi's black boots that stopped at the ankles and had a slight heel at the bottom, clunked on the wooden floors as she stepped off the last step and headed for the kitchen. She glided in her stride like a swan floating through a river with such smoothness, elegance and grace. I'm certain Jodi would be a swan if we humans reincarnated into any animal species of some kind. I think a swan is fitting for her...

We were greeted by Carl as we entered the kitchen and he motioned to a plate of stacked squared bread with sliced strawberries, blueberries and a thick brown syrup drizzled over top, on the table beside him.

"Made ya some French toast." Carl twanged as a toothpick stuck out between his thin lips. Strands of his hair fell into his eyes as he washed a frying pan in the kitchen sink.

"French toast?" I said gingerly, slowly sitting down in the wobbly wooden chair that stood in front of the plate of toast.

"You never had it before?" Carl questioned as he dried the frying pan with a towel and shoved it into a bottom cupboard. I shook my head and picked up the fork that was beside the plate on the table. I then stabbed the pointy end into the soggy bread and lifted a piece to my eyes, watching the brown ooze drizzle down onto the plate. "That's maple syrup," Carl leaned his back against the countertop with his arms folded across his chest. His eyes narrowed as he watched me carefully bite and chew the piece of toast. The French toast was crunchy around the edges and gooey in the center. The sugary maple syrup flooded my taste buds with the sour taste of the strawberries and the sweet blueberries. I hadn't noticed but my eyes were wide and a slight grin crept up my face. Carl smiled and nodded his head. "It's good, huh?"

I swallowed and dug my fork in for another piece. "Yes, it is. Thank you."

Jodi mumbled with annoyance as she scrubbed the stovetop with a wet rag. The thick white substance clinged onto the brown surface, refusing to scrub off. She tossed the rag down on the stove and turned to Carl. "Is it so hard to clean up the mess after you make it, Carl?" She said sternly, shooting him a piercing look. Carl sighed and Jodi proceeded to pick up the rag and scrub harder than before.

"Jodi," said Carl, taking a few steps towards her. Jodi scrubbed and scrubbed but the substance still stayed strong on the stovetop. Carl reached out and touched her elbow and she whipped her head and glared at him. "I think we should talk."

"About what?" Jodi lowered her voice and glanced back at me. I quickly looked away and stared down at my plate. Carl nudged his head towards the hallway. Jodi put the rag down on the counter and they walked out the room together. Their voices muffled through the walls as I finished my toast. I didn't care to ease into their conversation this time. If I want to stay, which I really do, I have to prove it by putting in the work and helping Jodi and Carl as much as I can so they will let me stay. And that starts by helping around in the kitchen. I take my plate over to the sink and turn on the water. The lukewarm water splattered my arms as I scrubbed the plate with soap and a sponge until it was shiny white again. I set it over on the side sink to let it dry because I don't know where everything goes. I assume I will learn over time. I took the rag that Jodi had and rinsed it under hot water. The heat stung my hands but I ignored it as I carried the rag over to the stovetop and held it down on the white substance that I assume was a part of making the French toast. I held it there for a few minutes until it moistened and scrubbed completely off. Returning the rag back over to the sink for a rinse. I continued to wipe off the counters and table top before setting it back down on the counter beside the sink where Jodi had left it. I looked out the kitchen window and out past the green pastures that shined as the sun blazed down onto it. I suddenly felt gravitated to march outside and lay in the pastures as I got showered by the sun's rays. And that's what I did. Before I turned the knob and swung the front door open, I heard Carl and Jodi bickering in a room with a lumpy couch and a chair that didn't suit the decor that was estranged around the room. Horse photos framed on the walls and little ceramic horses propped onto the side tables next to the couch. A sewing machine on a table and a chair in the corner of the room. A large portrait of Carl and Jodi hung above the fireplace mantle. I crept up to the doorframe and listened in on them as I watched the white lace curtains flow in the air as wind blew through an opened window.

"I think we should get the belongings out of the attic." Carl's voice twanged.

"What belongings?" Jodi said casually as her footsteps clunked on the hard wooden floors. "Don't pretend like you forgot,"

Jodi's footsteps abruptly stopped and she seethed. "Why would I ever want to bring those down?"

"Because it will give Viola something else to wear while she's here." Carl says. "She can't wear the same dress every day."

"They're not *her* clothes." Jodi quipped as she paced the room again. Her steps clunked harder this time.

"She never even got to wear them, Jodi. And they're not doing any good collecting dust up there." Carl said with a sympathetic tone of voice. The room fell in silence and I took that as a sign to leave...

Outside the wind blew with warmth and the sun sweltered my fair skin as I stepped off the porch and walked out to the middle of the pastures. I found a small patch of flat grass and I sunk into the ground with every fiber in my body as the grass tickled against my cheek. My muscles relaxed and for once I felt nothing but peacefulness as I breathed in the earthy breeze. And there I lay for what felt like an eternity, watching the sun gradually dawning and the little birds soaring high in the sky, and off to their cozy nests for the night.

Chapter 16

Grass crunched beside my ear and I opened my eyes to Carl peering down at me with narrowed eyes and thinned lips. "Ya sure do come out here often." Carl twanged his thick southern accent. For the past several days I have helped Jodi with the cleaning and cooking while having to listen to her snicker when I don't do something the way she likes. Her temper has risen a lot more since I've been wearing the clothes that were boxed in the attic. I can tell by the way she looks at me in them that it brings her a sadness I have never seen before. She hides the pain behind her anger to disguise it as something else, but I know there is more to her than just her temper. I just haven't seen it yet. I refuse to ask Carl what these clothes meant to her and I bite my tongue to keep the peace, but it doesn't stop me from wondering what it means to her.

I squint up at Carl and say, "I finished my chores." I defend myself even though I probably don't have to. It's not like he had asked me why I am out here in the first place.

Carl nodded. "I know. I can tell that house chores ain't as fun for you, huh?"

House chores are all I know. Except I do miss attending to the gardens that Jodi doesn't have. I don't mind the chores I do now, but it is all the same as before. Cut up the vegetables and skin the potatoes. Grab the sponge and scrub the dirt and grime off the plates and tables. Grab the broom and sweep the floors. It's always the same. I shrugged. "I guess."

Carl peered out past the fields as I stared up at him, wondering why he would ask me that. It's not like I have been complaining or anything. Carl sighed with his arms folded across his chest. "How about I tell Jodi I need extra help with the horses and stables and I would like for you to come help?" He looked down at me with a glimmer in his eyes. "If you're foot ain't bothering ya?"

I haven't noticed any aching in my foot or arm in the couple of days I have been here. It's almost as if it was never there at all. I sit upright in the grass and smile up at him. I have watched him everyday outside the kitchen window, hauling haystacks and letting the horses roam freely in the fields. I always wondered what it would be like to tend the horses and pastures. It had to be more fun than being on your hands and knees scrubbing the textured floors with a hand brush and a bucket of soapy water. I vigorously shook my head. "No, my foot doesn't hurt at all."

Carl grinned. "Good, then I'll get ya up at five in the morning tomorrow." And as if morning couldn't come faster. I was sitting on the edge of my bed, watching Jodi in her tightly wrapped robe with hair that stuck up in all directions from a night of restless sleep. She entered the room with navy blue bottoms, similar to the ones Carl wears except these ones are several sizes smaller and the edge of the pant legs were wide at the bottom. I cover my mouth with my hand to hide my yawn as I blinked vigorously to clear my vision from the blurry morning eyesight. Birds chirped outside the bedroom window where a ray of blue light streamed inside along the cracked windowsill. Jodi held up the pants by the waistband and cleared her throat. "These are jeans. They should be the right size for you. If not, then I will have to find another pair up in the attic somewhere."

I drew in my eyebrows as I stared at the two legged pants. "Jeans?"

Jodi nodded. "Yes, jeans." She analyzed my face as she cocked her head. "You surely don't think you would be wearing nothing but dresses out in that filthy barn? It's bad enough you've got grass stains on the back of them from lying out in the yard every evening."

I shook my head. "No, I just didn't know they were called jeans. That is all." My mouth spread into a thinned smile as I hoped she wouldn't take what I said as a snarky comment. I barely know what is rude or not anymore as it seems every single word that comes out my mouth is a way to get snapped at by Jodi herself.

Jodi tossed me the jeans and opened the closet doors. "Put on the pants as I search for a top for you to wear." She rummaged through the racks of dresses that she had hung up yesterday morning as I cleaned up the kitchen after breakfast. I stood up and slipped my bare legs in the

pant holes one by one and pulled them up past my waist. They were loose in the legs and wide around the waist even when I buttoned the buttons in the front. I looked up at Jodi when she turned around with a plain gray t-shirt in her hands. She looked at the jeans and sighed. "Well, you've got time to grow in them." She tossed me the shirt and walked towards the door. "Put that on while I go find something to tighten the waist."

I stared at the new girl in the mirror and admired her as her peachy cheeks tainted through her porcelain skin. She's vaguely familiar but different at the same time. So different I don't even recognize myself anymore. My braid trailing down my neck was the same but the serene face and the light that twinkled in my eyes was something I have never experienced before. I looked down at my spotless clothes. You never noticed how much you hate something until you try something new. That for me was dresses. I always hated them but they were all I ever wore. Not anymore…

Jodi entered the room with a strand of yellow yarn in one hand and a pair of brown, embroidered blue flowered cowboy boots in the other hand. She kneeled down in front of me and dropped the boots down onto the floor with a thud. "I don't have a belt for you but yarn will do, until I go to town to run some errands. I will have to pick you up a belt your size." I raised my arms out to the side while she put the yarn through the belt loops around my waist and tied it into a bow in the front. "Not sure how I will find a belt your size." Jodi muttered as she tucked my shirt into the jeans. "You are nothing but skin and bone after all." She grabbed the boots and placed them in front of me. She stood up straight and marched for the door, turning back to look at me. "Put on the boots and head outside to the barn. Carl is already out there waiting." She turned and walked out the door, keeping it ajar as her footsteps faltered down the hallway. The sound of a door closing shut creaked through the cracks. Leaving me in the dimly lit room with only the oil lamp on the nightstand and the sound of the birds singing their morning chorus…

Chapter 17

The next few weeks were continuous work out at the barn. Moving haystacks up to the attic of the barn and feeding the horses while learning how to file down their hooves and changing their horseshoes. I also have been assisting Carl with taking down the broken wood planks to the side of the barn wall and hammering the nails into the fresh boards as fast as possible. We're trying to prepare the barn and horses for the upcoming winter weather. The wind has become crisper and the sun is dawning earlier than expected, making us worried that winter is approaching early this year. We still have necessities to deal with. Carl tells me to pray for us to finish our chores before the harsh winter arrives. I haven't prayed since I left the group two months ago. I have been rather scared too. Scared that I might pray to the spirit I was told to. The spirit that Reverend Finch prays to. The wrong spirit. When I asked Jodi who she prays to every night before bed, she told me that she prays to God.

"Always pray to God." she told me before shooing me off to bed. I stared at the metal cross that hung above my bed frame for far too long before climbing under my covers for the night. The light blue sky that glows before the sun awakens, shined through the crack of my window when my eyelids drew heavy and I finally drifted to sleep. Moments later, I awoke to the sound of shoes scuffling across my room. I rolled over and squinted my eyes to see clearly. Jodi rummaged through my closet, pushing aside the dresses and shirts that don't meet her standards, before she pulled out a dandelion colored skirt that flowed through the air as she tossed it onto the end of the bed. She also pulled out a white lace top still on the wire hanger and carried it over to me. "Are we going somewhere?" I asked, rubbing my eyes awake. I assumed by the ankle length skirt and the blue blouse Jodi wore that we are going somewhere.

"We're going to church." Jodi confirmed as she laid the top over the skirt.

I sat up in bed with a nervous look spreading across my face. "B-but-," I stuttered, swallowing hard to get the saliva to pass through my dry throat. "I haven't been to church since I left."

She looked at me serenely while slightly shaking her head. Her tightly wrapped bun stayed in a knot on the back of her head. Sleek and sturdy with no flyaways in sight. "Oh honey, that was never a church." Jodi moved swiftly to the door before turning back with a tight smile. "We leave in an hour. Be ready at the door by seven." The door clicked shut while my heartbeat drummed into my ears. By the way Jodi acts towards the group, the Cult as she puts it, the church she goes to can't be like the one I've always known. Right? I guess I will find out...

* * *

The gravel pathway leading upward a hill crunched under my shoes, leaving foot shaped imprints between the tiny pebbles. Speeding up my pace to stay close behind Carl and Jodi while they made a plan on how to introduce me to the expected strangers inside the church. I scanned my surroundings. The trees danced with the breeze and the orange and brown leaves chattering a song, before letting go of their branch and floating away. They eventually land in their chosen spot before a gust of wind stirs them up again. Floating to their new place to rest. Similar to reality. I let go of my branch and was guided to my new place. I'm waiting for the gust of wind to guide me to a new location. But I like where I am now. Hopefully, the wind never blows...

"-Viola," A voice brought me back to my senses, shortly realizing that the voice belonged to Jodi. I jogged to catch up to her. Jodi looked down at me with raised eyebrows. "Do you remember what we told Doctor Bernard?" She asked, examining my face. Sometimes I think she is trying to read my mind. I scrunched my nose and tried to remember. It's been five weeks since I saw Doctor Bernard. I remember telling him that I was her niece. I nodded and refrained what Jodi had told me that day. Jodi nodded along. "That's right. So if anyone asks you, say that you are my niece and you will be staying with us for a while."

"What if they ask why I'm staying with you?" I questioned.

Jodi looked ahead with a smile and waved to an older man at the end of the pathway. Her smile strained as she got closer to the bald headed man. When the man turned his back to her, she slacked her face and inhaled the oak and maple tree scent before saying, "Then you tell them to mind their own."

As the end of the pathway neared, a tall red and brown bricked building appeared from behind the trees. The shingled roof came to a peak and a cross was perched high on top. The sun shining behind it made the cross glow in a yellow sheen. The one thing that I have noticed about churches is that they are all different from the others. Some are more simple like a white wooden box with a peaked roof. Others are more like stacked stone with a large bell hanging from the roof. And others are like this one, stacked with bricks and a simple cross on top. It's quite fascinating seeing the different ways that people can make them, and all for similar reasons. A high pitched squeal startled me from admiring the building and made me stumble backwards. My shoe brushed a large rock making my ankle bend inwards and start plummeting to the ground. But luckily, Carl has fast reflexes and grabbed my arm in time before I hit the ground. He pulled me upright and I smoothed down my skirt trying not to feel embarrassed from my clumsiness. I glance up at Carl with a grateful smile. He returned the gesture by nodding his head before redirecting his attention at the woman who had startled me. This woman looked around Jodi's age but her pinned up hair and her floral sleeved dress made her look older than she really was. She squealed as she pulled Jodi in for a tight hug.

"Oh boy, have I missed you." The woman chippered with a deep southern accent. She pulled away and beamed a bright smile at her. The woman seemed happy to see her, but Jodi on the other hand looked annoyed by the sight of her. She held a tight smile with dull eyes as the woman rambled on about how her husband started renovating their little house and praised her two children making the lead roles in the school play. Hansel and Gretel. Whatever that is about. Me and Carl stood stiffly behind as we waited for the woman to finish her one sided conversation. The woman must've said something humorous because she batted Jodi's hand as she giggled away, but Jodi kept her straight smile. Although Jodi is looking right at the woman's face, I'm certain that she's not even seeing her at all. Like she's gone into a world where the woman isn't there. "Anyway," the woman sucked in a deep breath and cocked her head with a peachy smile. "Where have y'all been lately?"

Jodi finally blinked her eyes. The woman must've brought her back from her secret escape and she shook her head. "Oh we have been busy." Jodi said shortly as I know how much she hates people nosing into her business. I learned that the hard way.

The woman furrowed her brow and huffed out air between her pastel lips. "Too busy for God? That mustn't be true."

Jodi squinted her eyes a bit, still holding that tight smile. "It is true, Mary. You see, my sister has become ill and I have been taking care of my niece for the past couple weeks."

Mary, peered behind her and looked me in the eyes. Her eyes squinted and her eyebrows drew in. The once wide smile now turned into a deep frown and her hand rose to her chest as if Jodi had told her a tragedy. "Why, bless your pea pickin' heart." She twanged, bending her knees a bit to get to my level. I glanced down at her pearly white shoes and watched the spiked heels dig deep into the gravel. "You must be missing your mother?" She said somberly, slightly nodding her head as her bright blue eyes pierced into mine. I looked at her blankly, not really understanding what to do or say. But before I could decide, Carl intervened with a hand on my shoulder.

"I'm not too sure about that, Mary." Carl replied with a sly grin. "I think she's been enjoying herself with all the chores we've done around the barn and house. We have been keeping her really busy."

Mary looked back at me blankly, still waiting for an answer from me. I quickly nodded and said, "Yes, really busy."

Mary's eyes looked from one eye to the other. The skin around her eyes crinkled with a smile. "Well, that's good. Can't live in a house for free." She gave me a final nod and stood up, turning her attention back to Jodi. "Although I must say, Jodi. I recall you telling me you were an only child?"

Jodi's tight smile turned into a deep frown and her eyes shot daggers at Mary. "Well, if you weren't blabbering about yourself all the damn time, then you would've known I mentioned that I was my *mother's* only child. My father has two."

Mary slightly nodded. I can tell she's forcing a smile now as her cheeks slackened and her eyes dimmed. She took a deep controlled breath. "I see. Well, I must skedaddle inside. My family is already inside." Mary glanced over to the wide church doors that were propped open. Strangers huddled through the doors to be the first ones to their seats. Jodi nodded with a pleasant smile.

"You do that." Mary glanced back at Jodi, Carl and I.

"It was nice seeing you all again." Her eyes faltered on me before she raised her heels out of the gravel and marched up towards the church doors. Soon disappearing through them. Jodi pivoted herself around to face us. She forcefully blew out of her nose.

"Ready to go inside?" Before we could respond, Jodi marched to the open doors without a glance back...

As soon as you cross through the wooden doors the smell of mahogany and honeysuckle fills your nostrils with the rich woody and a sweet scent. Pews aligned across two sides of the room, leaving the center open for the pathway to the altar. I gasped as we walked in a line down the aisle, looking up to the ceiling that caved into a peak with tree logs as beams going across in a row with two giant crystal chandeliers. They twisted and twinkled when a gust of wind blew in through the doors. I had never seen a chapel this extraordinary before. The older chapel back with the group looked nothing like this. It was small and crammed with seats and the ceiling was bare and empty. Reverend Finch stood on a stool behind the altar which was a wooden table with candelabras on the corners. The altar at this church is a long oak table with a lace rug draped over top with two candelabras on each side of the altar, and a metal cross hung on the front for all to see. This place also was cool which I assumed meant they had air conditioning unlike the other chapel that was always sweltering in the summer and freezing in the winter. It's all the same but very different...

Jodi scanned the space for an open seat and when she spotted one she dashed over to it before suddenly stopping in her tracks. I scanned ahead to see Mary and the bald man from earlier are sitting next to the open seats. A boy and a girl looked around my age, sat next to them. They whisper undefined words to each other. I looked back at Jodi who sighed and rolled her eyes before sliding into the empty seat next to them. Planting herself down on the red velvet cushions. The bald man whom I assume is Mary's husband, smiled broadly at Jodi and Carl and nodded his head in a greeting. Jodi and Carl both gave him a courtesy smile before redirecting their attention to the front of the room where a thin man stood behind the altar wearing nothing but a white robe. The Reverend raised his hands to gather his audience's attention before starting the ceremony.

There I sat only half listening to what the Reverend was preaching and not understanding anything he said. But the words that jumped out to me were the words the Reverend had mentioned to me back in the village. That God gave us a man named Jesus Christ who died on the cross to save our sins and to give us everlasting life. Heaven wasn't something that Reverend Finch mentions only that our Lord, *their* Lord now, died to save their souls and they will go to a place where he will be. Remembering back to the choosing ceremony, how I got chosen to save my people's souls and give them redemption to their lives. How I didn't want to die for them says more than I ever knew. I knew it wasn't true. I knew there were people that believed in different things than what I was brought up to believe. If it were true, then I wouldn't be here today and I wouldn't have found Carl and Jodi. They wouldn't have found me. I wouldn't have put Bonnie's life at risk if I wasn't certain I was right. How I hope she's doing fine with me gone. I hope she escaped shortly after I did. I shouldn't have left her like I did even if it meant sacrificing myself like I was chosen to do. I look at the cross that stood tall behind the altar and pray to God that she is well and to help guide her towards me. I hope that I will see her again, someday soon...

When the Reverend closed out his sermon I knew what would be next. The snake ritual. I wasn't sure if they did that or not but I wasn't going to sit around to find out. I turned to Jodi and leaned forward to whisper in her ear. "I have to go to the restroom. Where is it?" Jodi told me the directions to the restrooms and I nodded. I quickly walked out the same way we came in, down the aisle and towards the entrance doors. I stopped at the entrance, facing the now closed doors and looked to my left. There was a single door that was shut. I reached for the handle, when it suddenly turned and the door flung open. It almost knocked into me. I took a step back and saw the same girl that sat next to Mary and her husband. It must be her daughter, she had mentioned who had gotten the Gretel character in their school play. She had blonde, wavy hair that draped across her shoulders and a navy blue dress with silver stars printed across the top. She flattened her skirt down and glanced up at me. Her bright blue eyes widened when she noticed me staring at her and stepped aside.

"Oh, I'm sorry. Do you need the restroom?" Her voice was soft and her pinky lips parted into a pleasant smile. I nodded with a shy grin. The girl went to walk down the aisle when she turned back, cocking her head at me. "You're Jodi's niece, right?" She asked, looking at me narrowly.

I cleared my throat. "Yes, I am."

The girl nodded. "My mother Mary, had told me. I'm Isabelle," She reached out a flattened hand for me to shake. I accepted the gesture and introduced myself as well. She drew in her eyebrows as I mentioned my name. "Viola? What a unique name." She narrowed her eyes like she was pondering whether my name was acceptable as a good name or bad. A grin grew on her face and she nodded her head again. "I like it. You surely don't hear it often." When she let out a giggle it sounded squeaky like a mouse. I giggled as well but I wasn't sure why. "I sure haven't met anyone else named it before." Though I haven't met many people to find out anyway.

"Neither have I met anyone named Isabelle before." I added because it was true. She's the first person I have ever heard named it.

Isabelle waved a dismissive hand. "I know five from school." She said flatly, glancing back down the aisle. She looked back at me with a sweet smile. "Well, I better get back to my seat before my mother questions where I am. It was nice to meet you, Viola." Isabelle started back down the aisle before I could tell her the same. Before I entered the restroom I couldn't help but think how peculiar that girl was...

Back at the house I changed into my t-shirt and jeans before helping with the daily chores. I never want to go back to dresses now that I have been wearing pants, but I know Jodi will make me wear one every Sunday morning for church. The church was fine. When I left the restroom everyone was leaving the chapel. Carl and Jodi were waiting outside for me as they had already made it past the doorway. I asked Carl while we headed back down the pathway if they had done the snake ritual. Carl bunched up his face before responding, *No?* He never cared to ask what the ritual was, assuming he could tell by the title. My body sagged in relief after that. I knew it was never a normal thing to do.

Now I'm helping Jodi with the after dinner dishes. She washes while I dry and put them away into their belonged spots. We haven't spoken since we got back to the house. Which is just the same as everyday. I can tell she thinks more than she speaks. The crease between her eyebrows becomes deeper and deeper as her eyes daze off into the abyss. Sometimes I wonder what goes on inside her head? Jodi hands me a plate and clears her throat.

"Did you meet Isabelle today?" She asks me while scrubbing a soapy sponge over a speckled glass. I nod and put a plate into the top cupboard, stacking it onto the identical ones.

"I did. Doesn't she seem a bit *peculiar* to you?"

Jodi rinses the glass under the steamy faucet before handing it to me to dry. She shook her head. "That whole family is peculiar."

"Who's peculiar?" Carl asked as he entered the kitchen with an iron horseshoe in his dirty hand. The iron didn't shine in the kitchen light from all the dirt and sand that was packed on it.

"The Jones's." Jodi replied, glancing over to him.

"Yeah. That family is an odd bunch." Carl dropped the horseshoe onto the kitchen table with a *clank*. A chunk of dried dirt broke off and sprinkled the table top with brown specks. Jodi whipped her head around and glared at the dirty horseshoe like it was another thing on the list that annoyed her. She inhaled a deep ragged breath.

"Why is that in my kitchen?" She asked, sternly. She handed me another glass to dry with a shaky hand. Her blood is boiling now.

"I figured Viola would want it." Carl said, bringing his attention towards me. "It's a lucky horseshoe. You hang it up above your door to bring good luck into your home." He pointed a finger towards the front door. "There's one hanging right up there."

I glanced down at the horseshoe and gave him a grateful smile. "I love it, thank you." Carl was pleased with my acceptance.

"I can hang it up for you later."

Jodi huffed and turned off the faucet. She walked over to the table with a wet cloth in hand. "Well, can you remove it from my kitchen? You're getting dirt on the table." Carl looked at me and rolled his eyes. When Jodi heard me faintly giggle at Carl she shot me a warning look that immediately stopped the giggles from boiling up inside me. Carl grabbed the horseshoe off the table and said,

"I was going to wash it before I hang it up."

Jodi roughly scrubbed the table and shook her head dismissively. "No. You can clean it at the outside faucet. You ain't clogging up my drains with mud."

An uncontrollable smile rose on my face and placed the towel down on the counter shortly before joining Carl outside. These two are a peculiar pair. But a peculiar pair I won't ever want to be apart from.

Chapter 18

I, Viola Granger, officially became a part of Carl and Jodi's quaint, little family on September sixteenth as of four years ago. Four years ago we celebrated my first birthday. Which was really my fourteenth birthday but the group I was raised in didn't believe in holidays other than the ritual, the ceremony and their lord's birthday, which was always celebrated on the same day each year. I finally got to see what a birthday was like. We had flan which is now a yearly tradition for each holiday of the year because it tastes sweet and delicious. Then Jodi gave me a gift, a gold necklace with a V pendant for my name. I never took it off since she clasped it around my neck that day. I do think it's weird that regular people need their initials on things for the world to see, but it's the first gift that I ever received. I never want to take it off.

For the next three years was the same as the others. The traditional ways of chores around the house and the barn stables as well as the new additions to the farm. Pack of twelve sheep and six chickens. Carl figured since he'd inherited pastures that ranged from miles and miles away which he never even used, except for the two horses. Hazel and

Coal. Why not put a few more animals on the farm? Especially now that he has me to help tend to them.

Carl told me the house and land was inherited from his ancestors and great grandfathers, who then passed it down to Carl's father and then lastly to Carl. The land goes to the first born son of each generation. Carl is the oldest sibling to his younger brother, Joel. I found it hard to believe he has a sibling as I always assumed he and Jodi were the only children to their parents. Carl never mentioned Joel until the day he told me about the history of his farm. His ancestors were settlers who bought the land when they came on a boat from France. They built the house that still stands from each generation keeping up on it throughout the decades. I continued to ask what happened to Joel since he's never mentioned him in the last few years I have lived with him. He told me after his father passed and he inherited the house and land that Joel wanted for himself. Of course as it was written in the will that Carl receives the land because of the history, he and Joel had gotten into an ugly fight and they parted ways from each other. Neither of them have spoken in the last eighteen years. Carl began to tell me he doesn't resent his little brother and also doesn't blame him for being upset about the situation. But the greediness and anger got in the way of their relationship, and instead of being siblings, they're strangers instead. Carl figured when Joel needs him or wants to apologize then he will call him. Carl wants to respect his peace and boundaries. If Joel wants to talk with him then he will talk...

Another year goes by and I start towards my bedroom door as I glanced up at the horseshoe nailed above it. The morning sun rays shining through my window and the birds chirping a graceful song. The lambs cried for their mothers and the rooster yelled out. My boots clunked down the wooden staircase and thudded as I reached the bottom floorboards and made my way towards the kitchen. I can hear

Carl and Jodi's voices as they strike up a conversation. The kitchen was spotless as per usual and Carl and Jodi sat at the table where a plate of flan rests in front of my seat. Carl and Jodi drew wide smiles as Jodi stood up from her seat and walked towards me with arms stretched out wide.

"Happy birthday, Viola." She sang as she held me in her embrace for a moment. A smile rose on my face with happiness to be celebrating yet another birthday with the people I love most.

Carl chewed on a thin toothpick and smiled when I looked at him. "So, how does it feel to be eighteen?"

I shrugged. "The same, I suppose."

Carl nodded and leaned back in his seat. "I remembered when I turned eighteen, my father gave me his old-broken-down truck. I couldn't wait to fix it up and drive Jodi to wherever she demanded to go." He chuckled. Jodi glared at him with a playful grin. He stood up from his chair and walked to Jodi's side, wrapping his arm around her frail waist. "Your assertiveness is what I love most about you." He said with a smirk before planting his lips on her cheek. Jodi rolled her eyes and quickly shooed him away with a hand. She walked over to the cupboards and slid open the utensil drawer and returned with a fork in hand, placing it beside my plate of flan. I gave her a grateful smile and picked up my fork and stuck it in the jelly flan. My taste buds overflowed with the sweetly flavored dessert. Flan is easily my favorite dessert. The taste of vanilla and the salty caramel will always make my mouth water and will forever cease to satisfy me. Jodi grabbed a glass out of the cupboard and filled it with icy water.

"I heard that the church is having line dancing for the teenagers later today?" Jodi placed the glass in front of me. "Are you and Isabelle planning on going?"

I nodded with a mouthful of flan. Isabelle had asked me yesterday after church service if I would go with her. I had agreed then but now I am having some doubts about going at all. I have never been to a gathering before and neither do I know how to line dance. Isabelle told me it's easy and she will be by my side at all times to help teach me how to dance. She's quite assertive and doesn't take no for an answer. It can't be that hard to learn. Right? Carl returned to the table with a slice of flan and a fork, he huffed out air through his mouth while he lowered himself into his chair. He hasn't said anything but I know his back has been bothering him by the slight grunting and huffing he does whenever he sits or is carrying hay down from the barn attic. He's aging and the farm work is not getting any easier for him. I'm glad I'm here to help him. Carl glanced over at me, probably making sure I didn't notice his huffing. I just give him a weary smile before returning to my flan without a word. Carl sliced a piece of flan in half with his fork and scooped it into his mouth. He slowly chewed and swallowed down the remaining piece in his mouth.

"I think it's good to go meet other people your age." He retorts, slicing another piece of flan. "It's good to socialize and talk to them about whatever yer' teenagers talk about nowadays."

I shook my head in disagreement. "Why do I need to do that when I have you two? Also I do have Isabelle." Isabelle has been my only friend for the past five years. We aren't close like I am with Bonnie... or *was* with her. A day never goes by when I ain't wondering where she is now or what she is thinking about. Is she thinking about me too? It is a thought I had for a while and still don't know the answers to...

Carl nodded. "Well, I guess that is right." I know I'm right, is a response that I had to bite back from saying aloud. I carried my empty plate and fork to the kitchen sink, grabbed the soapy sponge that lay in the clean sink and was ready to wash my plate when Jodi snatched the sponge from my hand and shooed me away and out the kitchen.

"I'll clean the rest of the kitchen up." She said, "You need to get the farm chores done before you have to leave later." I accepted my fate without complaints and headed outdoors and towards the barn, where the horses are inside their stables.

Chapter 19

Jodi

As much as I hate to admit it, I grew quite fond of Viola. She has been a huge help around the farm and doing the daily chores and with the cooking as well. That is the reason why I kept her. That and the fact Carl now sees her as a daughter more than a girl we both barely knew. Now we know who she is. Maybe not as well as we hoped by the way she quickly changes subjects

when I ask her questions about her past. I understand why she doesn't want to talk about her past, she wants to start over. Begin a new life with new people and new possibilities. From what she has been through, I don't blame her. I would want to, if I was in her shoes. But that is now all in the past and it should stay there forever...

I remember telling Carl several times after Viola showed up at our front door step. Do not get too close to that girl because she is not staying here. I knew he wasn't going to listen to me. He never does. And he does have a familiar way to get what he wants. His stubbornness is always winning in fights. He could have gotten it from his mother. That old prude was always stubbornly vile since the day I first met her. She never liked me much, but the money Carl and I earned from her death was worth dealing with her audacity for several years. It was like a paycheck for working hard on not losing my shit on her. Though the amount is small, I would have preferred much more. Just her not being here, nagging me anymore is more than money could ever pay. Though the money is a nice bonus... or Carl has been spending too much time around me that my assertiveness and hard headed attitude has rubbed off on him. I knew the day he brought Viola home that she was never going to leave. Five years later, she still hasn't.

Seeing Carl with her, seeing how happy they are together, has always caused a pain that never subsides when I look away. It lingers and stays there in the center of my chest, swelling up and never shrinking. Guilt is what causes the pain.

The guilt from what had happened to her. It wasn't my fault, neither was it Carl's fault. She was a stillborn because of my age. The doctor said that placenta ages faster in older women and it makes it difficult for the baby to get the oxygen and nutrients she needs. It's not my fault, what they kept telling me but I never believed them. I was forty-three years of age and my placenta aged quicker than it should. I always doubted wanting a child. I never felt the need to have one. But something had changed for me when I was in my late thirties.

I was out shopping at the grocery store when I spotted a woman, a mother, and her son. He looked around two years of age. He was stomping his foot with balled up fists as his mother reprimanded him about his bad behavior. He squished his face and drew out a pouty lip that quivered in a sob. I remember thinking how grateful I was that I didn't have to deal with that, but then something happened, something that changed the gears in my brain to stop and shifted the other direction. Grinding around and around in a way that it has never done before. The mother knelt down and wrapped her arms tightly around her son in an embrace as she closed her eyes and hummed a sweet song. Over the rainbow from The Wizard of Oz. The boy's face relaxed and his small hands lifted up and clasped around her neck, lowering his head to her shoulder. They held each other tightly, until the humming song ended and they broke the embrace, the mother wiped away his tears with her thumbs and smiled softly at him as he wiped his runny nose with his hand. He gave her a weak smile before the mother stood up, took the boy's hand and they walked down the aisle.

In that moment I knew that is what I wanted more than anything in the whole world. The endless love and bond between a mother and child. The connection they shared with each other is an amazing thing to have. I had it for seven months before my world turned around and never went back. Carl and I tried to conceive for several years. Going back and forth between doctors and changing my diet to help improve my eggs for fertility. After three years went by with no luck, I accepted my fate, that it was too late for me. As if the lord had seen how hard I have worked and how much I truly wanted to be a mother, he granted me the gift a month later. Carl and I were ecstatic with joy. We could barely contain our excitement. Our hearts were full of love for this little baby that wasn't even the size of a raspberry yet.

The months went by and we later found out that our little blessing was going to be a girl. I immediately sewed as much clothing as I could make until my fingertips were raw from threading and embroidering my soon to be daughter's clothing. I even felt her moving inside of me, kicking to get out. When a few more months went by I prepared for her arrival, but then something happened. Something tragic.

I noticed her movements dwindling as the weeks went by. I figured she was getting large and was running out of space to move. Eventually, she just stopped one random afternoon. That day I went into early labor.

It didn't last long when the nurses couldn't find a heartbeat. The doctor rushed me into the surgical room. On September Sixteenth of seventeen years ago, our daughter was born. I could never get the image of her out of my mind. Her pale and bluish skin, her thick auburn hair. Her lifeless body ingrained in my mind. Sometimes I still see her when I close my eyes. Like I'm right back there, in that bright white room with doctors and nurses scattering around the room trying to do anything to bring her back to life... it was all pointless. Everything I did and went through was pointless.

After the burial a week later, I went to my room, took off my black velvet dress and heels and curled up inside my covers and I never left. I never left to eat, I never slept. I just stared at the blank ceiling until my body eventually gave up and needed to recharge after my battery was completely empty. It took a year to finally get back to my daily routine again, before I was pregnant. Back to the old life I used to be fond of. I know something inside of me is broken and I know it always will be... now I am on my porch soaking in the chill breeze that called for autumn. Soon winter will be here. Winter always comes early here. I always say we have late summers and early winters. There's only a few weeks of autumn before the snow comes raging down on us. I cross my arms over my chest to keep warm as I watch Carl warm up the engine to the rusted truck that parked down the pebbled driveway. The front door to the house opened and emerged Viola in wide legged bell bottoms, brown boots that peeked out from under the bottom of the pants, and a checkered flannel that was tied into a knot in the front. Her breast lengthed hair was styled in her usual braid that trailed down along her spine, the braid swayed as she moved swiftly down the porch steps. The church dance had started five minutes ago. She's in no rush as she moved down the driveway, the stone pebbles crunching under her boots.

"Have fun!" I called out. Viola turned around and gave me a weary smile, her nerves already getting the best of her. She's shy when she meets new people, not until she gets to know them. Then all of that introverted behavior is gone and she becomes the most annoying person you will ever know. But I wouldn't change her for anything less. She is mine and I am hers, and I am damn sure glad she is the one who gets to annoy me.

Viola now dashing to the car as Carl sat inside, waiting for her arrival. She opens the creaky door to the passenger side and climbs in, slamming it shut. That is the only way to get it to latch shut. I stepped carefully down the porch steps and stopped at the bottom. The strands of my hair broke free from my bun and rapidly blew around in the breeze. I waved goodbye with a smile as the truck rolled out of the driveway and down the dirt trail that leads to the rustic town. I watched the truck stir up dirt from the wheels and swirled in the wind until the truck was no longer visible to see. I started to head back inside to attend to the endless chores that awaited my arrival. As I climbed up the porch steps, I heard a branch crunch from the forest that was a mile from the house. Trees aligned the property, creating a natural fence that blocked off people outside from seeing our house. The forest was deep but if you kept walking straight you would get to the roadway that led into town. I stopped in my tracks and whipped my head to the side, scanning the tree line for any sign of movement nearby. But there was nothing there. Luckily, Carl and Viola gathered the animals into the barn for the night to keep the lambs from staggering away from their mothers and to keep away the predators that feast at night. I figured it was a fox or coyote coming to check if the animals were out as bait. I turn back to the house and go inside, locking the door behind me...

Things work in mysterious ways. Everything that Carl and I have gone through has shown us how much we truly love one another. Through thick and thin. The lord knew who we needed in our life and he brought her to us... He brought me my Viola.

Chapter 20

Viola

I stared at the square building that stood beside the church. It was just constructed to be able to hold dinners and dances like tonight's. The church figured to have a line dancing party for the teens as a treat for the new building. Burnt red brick stacked higher than the church itself. The door to the building opened and Isabelle emerged in an oversized flannel that flowed in the wind like a cape behind her, revealing a white tank top underneath. Her jeans flared out by the feet and had ripped holes at the knees. She sashayed in her leather boots, dashing through the grass and towards me.

"She spotted you," Carl smirked when I glanced back at him with a, don't make me go, expression on my face. "There's no turning back now." I inhaled deeply before swinging the passenger door open and climbed out into the raging wind. Carl hollered for me to have fun before I slammed it shut behind me. I walked over to Isabelle with a weary smile as she had a pearly white smile that went from ear to ear. She fiddled with her two braids that lay past her shoulders. She cocked her head at me as we walked through the grass and towards the building.

"There's no need to be nervous." She grinned at me, flipping her braids behind her. I quickly shook my head. "I'm not nervous."

Isabelle raised an eyebrow and hummed a, *mhmm*, clearly not believing me. I stuffed my hands into my jean pockets and rolled my eyes at her. "I'm not," I protested. "I just don't know how to line dance. That is all."

Isabelle waved a dismissive hand. "Oh it's easy, just copy what I'm doing. The best thing about line dancing is that all you need to do is move your legs. So, just keep moving your legs." Isabelle trotted to the door and swung it open. Music blared out of the doorway with a song I don't know. I've only heard a few country songs from Carl playing them as we worked out in the barn. Dolly Parton was the main singer that we listened to while we worked. Carl always knew each lyric from every song she had sung...

Isabelle held the door open for me, gesturing for me to enter with a hand in a courtesy manner. I entered and immediately was flooded with familiar faces from church, only from Isabelle introducing me to a few of her school friends from throughout the years. Some people were scattered around the dance floor, chatting with one another while the rest danced in the center of the room. They stomped to the beat and clapped as they spun around. Some held hands and wove their arms together while everyone kicked in unison to the music. They all had broad smiles that beamed throughout the crowd. It seemed like fun until I remembered that I can't dance and I know Isabelle will drag me out to the center stage to dance with the others while I look foolish for not knowing the choreography. Isabelle stood beside me and nodded her head to a group of friends of hers by the drinks station. We weaved through the crowd and when we reached the group, a boy with fiery red hair that coiled in short locks on top of his head, handed her a drink with a freckled smile. She accepted the drink and took a sip, grabbing a full cup from off the table and handed it to me. I gingerly took it, looking at the red substance with weariness.

"It's just fruit punch, V'." Isabelle clarified with a grin stretching out onto her face. I take a sip of the cherry juice. V' is her nickname for me. It's different from Vi', which only one person has ever called me. Bonnie.

"So Isabelle, are you planning on dancing tonight?" A girl with icy blue eyes asked, bringing her cup to her lips to hide a playful grin.

Isabelle flashed her teeth. "Oh you know I will, Crystal." She replied before taking another sip of her punch. The crowd stomped behind me, signaling their finality as the song ended. Some people broke apart to get a drink while others stood in the center waiting for another song to start. I was so focused on the crowd that I hadn't even heard Isabelle chatting with her friends. Before I could focus on what they were talking about, another song kicked on and the crowd started to tap their boots on the hard cement floors. Isabelle gasped, catching my attention. I turned to see her beaming while she put her drink down on the table. She snatched my cup from out of my hand and placed it next to hers.

"I love this song!" She shouted over the music and took my hand into hers. "Come on, dance with me!" Before I could protest, she dragged me out to the center of the stage. She glided through the room as she danced to the chipper song, glancing at me with a smile that could light up the world if there was nothing but darkness. She nudged me to follow her as she kicked the air with the toe of her boot. I moved rigidly, intently watching her feet as I tried to copy her movements. I delayed a few movements in between the song but I kept moving, like Isabelle had told me. Isabelle moved with so much confidence in her stride that even if she messed up I wouldn't have noticed it. And it was as if my surroundings had slowed and Isabelle's braids bounced wildly and her arms lightly floating through the air. I stared in admiration of her confidence and the way she giggled with purity and excitement. She danced like nobody else was around as if she was in her own world where nobody could judge her or tear down her happiness. And as if someone pressed the play button, everyone no longer danced slowly and the music blasted my eardrums in a final burst of instrumental choir before the song abruptly ended. Isabelle heaved in air through her mouth as she turned to me with a cheerful smile.

"See, it wasn't that bad." She giggled, nudging my arm with her fist. "You did great for only a beginner."

I rolled my eyes with a smile that naturally appeared. "Yeah right. I felt like I got all of it wrong."

Isabelle nodded. "Oh you definitely got some steps wrong, but not as much as I did the first time I started line dancing." I chuckled at her response and started walking back to the table for a drink when a slow paced song came on and Isabelle grabbed my wrist and tugged me towards her. She grabbed my right hand and held it out while she placed her left hand on my shoulder, pulling my body closer to hers as we swayed side to side. Isabelle glanced around the room,

looking for something, or someone. I watched her eyes scan the crowd, her sapphire and emerald eyes faltering on a boy with shoulder length hair and a hooked nose that took up most of his face. He blankly stared at us as Isabelle looked up at me.

"Sorry, I just didn't want to dance with him." She whispered as if he could hear her from all the way across the room with blaring speakers all around us.

I narrowed my eyes on her. "Who is he?" I don't remember her mentioning him before. I'm certain she never had.

"His name is Ralph." Isabelle said with disgust as if mentioning his name grossed her out. Yeah, she has never mentioned Ralph to me. I feel like that is a name I would remember. She continued on to explain more. "He's this guy that has had a massive crush on me, ever since first grade. If he saw me alone, he would have asked me to dance with him... I don't want to dance with him." She glanced back at him to see if he was still watching, which he was. I look back to get a better look at him. He's tall but has a bit of fat on him. He had soft features that made him look almost angelic and kind. I look back at Isabelle who gave him a smug face.

"He seems nice." I say, regretting my words the second Isabelle shot me a look. The look was similar to Jodi's but only colder. A shiver ran down my spine as her pupils thinned like the serpent that looked at Elder Barter the second its head popped out of the wooden box.

"He's a sexist asshole." Isabelle sneered. "He thinks just because his parents have a traditional marriage, everyone should have a traditional marriage. You know, one where the man works and the woman cooks and cleans the house all the while taking care of her children and husband." She narrowed her eyes at Ralph, swearing under her breath at him...

Carl and Jodi have a traditional marriage, but it works for them. They seem happy together. Jodi has never spoken ill of her marriage. Though they do come from a past where that was normal for them to have, I suppose. Jodi has told me one random day to always listen to the lord and my intuition. It knows my life's path that I'm supposed to follow. That's what led her to Carl and to me, and their long journey through life. Though I can tell life hadn't been easy for her by the deep wrinkles around her sorrowful eyes that had cried far too many times. And yet, she still says that she wouldn't have it any other way. The happiest moments are far more important to start her life completely over...

I drew in my eyebrows at Isabelle in confusion. "You don't have to be with him just because he asked you." Unlike the past, women do have a choice to decide what journey they want to take in *their* life.

"I know that." Isabelle looked at me, her disdain for Ralph still showing through her face. She glanced down at her boots as we took slow strides throughout the dance floor. "My mother wants me to marry him. She says that Ralph comes from a wealthy family and if someone with wealth wants to be with me, then I should let them."

"And you don't want that." I say not as a question but as a statement. Isabelle has always been the independent type. She never asked for help with anything, she always did it herself and with pride. She never wants attention from boys unlike the other girls in church who would bat their eyes with a sweet smile that showed interest in them. The last time a boy had even talked to Isabelle, she walked away mid conversation, which she never spoke once to, and flipped him a finger over her shoulder when the boy shouted out to her. She never told me what the conversation was about because she wasn't even listening to a word he was saying. She knew the type of boy he was, so she didn't waste her time with him...

Isabelle shot daggers through her eyes and said with a temper, "of course not." "Then what do you want?" I asked, calmly.

She shrugged. "I don't know, I guess I just want to travel the world. Maybe, become a journalist." I cocked my head at her response. "A journalist?"

A smile arose on Isabelle's face. "Yeah, a traveling journalist who interviews locals and writes unique perspectives on places and cultures. I think it's quite fascinating, don't you? To be able to travel across the globe and write about non-typical tourist destinations, and to just see the world in person."

Isabelle looked to me for acceptance of her dream and even though I might not find it as interesting as she does, I will still choose to support her in anything she wants to achieve. I know what it's like to be told what to do and how to do it with my past self. How it felt not being able to control my life. I was told I was the chosen sacrifice by the people I believed in most, and if I hadn't listened to my intuition and I never left. Then I wouldn't be here today to be able to help guide Isabelle to listen to herself and not what others say to her. I don't want someone to make her feel the way I felt five years ago. Isabelle stared at me for a response I could tell she hoped would be acceptable. I inhaled a deep breath before responding. "I think, if it is something you are passionate about and you are sure you want to do, then I think it is worth a try." Isabelle's eyes lit up and her shoulders un-tensed. She pulled me close to her and wrapped her arms around me in an embrace and laid her head on my shoulder, relaxing her body against mine. I held her tightly as we swayed to the music. For once, I never wanted the night to end...

Chapter 21

The chill breeze smothered me as the sun stayed hidden beneath the gray cotton-ball clouds that clumped together along the horizon. Hazel bore her hooves into the wilted grass, halting up on the tip of a hill. She breathed heavily through her nose and her hair flowed majestically in the wind. Carl halted beside me, staring down the hill at the sheep and lambs that played. The lambs pranced around their mothers as they ate what was left of the fresh grass. Thunder roared amongst the clouds, a raging storm was approaching and the animals needed to be put in the barn for safety before it hit. I glanced behind me looking at the house from afar. It was as small as a seed with storm clouds hovering above. We normally don't let the sheep out this far from home but with the grass dying and the stock of hay running low, there was no other choice but to let them venture out into the pastures. Even if it is further from home.

"Storm's close," Carl says, looking up at the gloomy sky. "We need to be quick before it hits us again."

A week after the party at the church, a high wind and rain storm rushed through with only little warning signs. It came faster than we expected. Carl and I were caught drenched in the rain as we gathered the animals into the barn. Shortly after we got the barn locked up, the wind blew stronger than ever and caused part of the roof to fall off. With a gaping hole in the ceiling and the thick droplets of water coming through, Carl and I put out a ladder and climbed up to the top of the roof and nailed a flat board to give coverage until we could fix it when the storm had passed.

After that, it was a miserable night. As Carl and I rushed to get the lambs into the barn, herding them with our horses like a shepherd guiding them to their homes, when I noticed a dark figure standing between the trees from the corner of my eye. I look over to only see swaying trees and brown leaves descending from above. I don't think much of it. Coyotes and foxes have been spotted around here since we brought the chickens home.

The wind blasted my eardrums making a warped sound from within. I watch as Carl climbs down off of Coal with a wince from his lower back, and opens the barn doors. The sheep huddled inside and into a large stall that Carl and I had built for them. The chickens clucked in their nests in another stall. I climbed down Hazel and led her by the reins to her stall. I take off her saddle and drape it onto the stall door, soon latching it before leaving the barn. Carl shuts the doors and latches the chain around the door handles to keep the doors from blowing open from the wind.

The rest of the night was spent indoors by the warm fireplace playing a game of Scrabble as the wind raged and the rain poured heavily down on the house. Thinking the storm would stop by morning, it hadn't. The rain subsided for the afternoon but the wind raged worse than before. Branches broke off the trees and lay among the fields. I looked outside my bedroom window scanning the pastures of the mess that will be cleaned when the storm passes. But my eyes landed on the swinging doors to the barn that flapped open and closed. The chain that clasped the doors closed was lying broken on the damp grass. A head of a chicken peeked out the door before scurrying back inside when the wind blew strong. "Shit," I bluntly say as I dash over to my bedroom door, slipping on my boots before dashing down the staircase.

"What's wrong?" Jodi and Carl asked in unison as Jodi dished out breakfast by the stove and Carl came marching down the stairs behind me. I didn't have time to respond as my lungs filled up with crisp air and my heart pounding inside my chest. I ran across the field and towards the barn. The wind blew strong and the sun stayed hidden beneath the grey clouds. I stretched my arm out as I reached the barn, grabbing one of the doors and started pushing it shut.

Bernadette, a frail hen who was smaller than her sisters, flapped her wings as she jumped back and away from my boot that I stretched out in front of her to keep her indoors. I leaned my body against the door as the wind pushed into me. I tried reaching my arm out to grab the other door as it flapped in the breeze away from me, but I couldn't reach. Carl came up beside me and grabbed a strong hold onto the door and pushed it shut. I kept my back to the door as Carl bent down and grabbed the chain.

"It's broken!" I shouted through the wind. It's so strong I could barely hear myself through it. He wrapped the chain around the door handles and tied it in a knot. I nod my head. "That works too!" I practically say to myself. Carl patted my back with a thick calloused hand and we walked back to the house. But something caught my attention from the corner of my eye. The similar dark shadow I thought I saw the other day, but this time when I turned to look, it didn'tdisappear. It in fact, stood out amongst the tree line and stared directly into my soul. Chills slithered down my spine as I stared at the figure cloaked in red. My heart sank to the pit of my stomach and bile arose in my throat. I recognized the blood red cloak with the wide hood. Everyone wears it at the sacrifice ceremony as you lay down on the altar and wait until a dagger is driven into your heart. The color is a symbol for the savior's blood that you drink before the ceremony starts. They are all his children filled with the same blood as his. The figure was hidden beneath the hood of his cloak but I can tell it was a man. He had broad shoulders and a tall stance. I hadn't noticed how long I was staring at him for until Carl came down the porch steps with a rifle in hand, dissuading the stranger in the woods to leave.

"Get the fuck off my property!" Carl raged, lifting the rifle up to point the end at the man. The man turned slowly around, lingering his gaze upon mine and strides away. Soon disappearing back into the forest of trees. Carl lowered the rifle and looked me in the eyes. I could only see flames and darkness in his once bright ones. But something stayed hidden beneath those flames. Something sorrowful that shone through. That same feeling reflected inside me. At that moment I knew what was next to come, and he knew too.

Chapter 22

I didn't sleep that night. My eyes were closed but my consciousness was awake. My mind frantically spun around and my body ached, causing me to toss and turn until I completely gave up and climbed out of bed. I watched the trees swaying in the wind from my bedroom window. Scanning the tree line for any sudden movement, any sign that proved that my past has come back to haunt me. *They had found me,* my mind kept repeating. *But how did they find me?* I also asked myself until the sun arose from the horizon and the birds had awakened, singing their soft melodies in their cozy nests. I don't understand why they cared to find me? Why haven't they forgotten me? After all the years I've spent creating myself a new and better life, forgetting the one they ruined for me. They came back to destroy this one too. But, I won't let them. I'll be damned to let them come and destroy the life I had built for myself...

When I hear the sound of chatter and the smell of burnt coffee in the morning. I get up from the windowsill and march downstairs to pour myself a cup of hot coffee. I'm not a coffee drinker but I do enjoy the occasional cup or two, especially on sleepless mornings like today. Carl and Jodi sat at the table with mugs full of black coffee to the brim.

Jodi was wrapped snugly in her white fuzzy robe with her hair pinned up in her usual bun, and Carl who usually changes into his work clothes as soon as he awakens, was still dressed in his black t-shirt and checkered pajama pants. His hair was tousled and his eyes were swollen from lack of sleep. Were they up all night too? I wondered as I drank my coffee standing, poured myself a second and joined them at the table. We drank our coffee in silence. We listened to the creaking and cracking of the house settling in the wind. The ever long storm has finally passed our town and only the soft breeze was left behind. I watched Carl take a long sip of coffee as he stared blankly down at the scratches in the table top. In one smooth motion he set his mug down and wiped a wide hand over his mouth. His eyes may look blank but I could tell he is pondering on something he wants to tell me. But I didn't pry to know, I just silently drank my second cup of coffee and rested my tired eyes...

"I was thinking, you should go live with my brother Joel." Carl blurted out. I shot my eyes open and gave him a puzzling look.

"What?" I say. Carl looks up at me tightly from lack of sleep and weary of my reaction.

Carl continued on. "He lives a few hours from here, and he runs a diner where you could work at—"

I put up an interjecting hand and narrowed my eyes at him. "You're telling me, I should go live with your brother whom you haven't talked to or have seen in several decades? And how many hours are you talking about?"

Carl pondered, then said. "Like, five hours."

My mouth dropped open and I started waving a dismissive hand. "No, absolutely not."

"Viola," Jodi said with assertiveness in her tone. She clutched her empty mug with both hands and displayed a hard look that couldn't hide the sadness that portrayed in her eyes. She's just as upset about this as I am. But I continued to shake my head in disapproval.

"I am not leaving you to live with someone I don't even know. And five hours is way too far." I declared.

Carl shortly inhales through his nose and nods his head. "I understand you may not want to live with him because you don't know him, but that is why you should. If *they* have found you, then that means they've never left." Carl took my hand, holding it tightly in his with a pleading gaze for me to listen and understand what he is saying. "I don't know how they found you, but there is no way they can find Joel. Especially since I haven't spoken to him long before you arrived."

I looked down at his hand that held mine. Thinking this may be the last time he could. I blink back tears that formed in my eyes. I pull my hand away from his grasp and lean back into my seat. "How do you even know if he would agree to this? I thought you left each other on bad terms."

"We did, but I called him this morning." Carl said, leaning back into his seat. "I told him everything he needed to know, and surprisingly he agreed to let you live with him."

I glanced around the kitchen in disbelief on how he could decide what I will be doing with my life without my knowledge or agreement. "So, that's it then. He just agreed to let some person he doesn't even know live with him because you asked him to."

Carl interjected with the point of a thick calloused finger. "Under one condition, of course. Joel wants you to work at the diner while you stay with him."

I stared down at the trees painted on my mug. The winter snow falling down onto them and a small doe tilting down and burying her snout into the snow covered ground. The painting takes me back to the winters here on the farm. I stare out my window every morning to find deers prancing amongst the tree line and birds nestling in their nests, some snuggling up together as the snow falls down from the sky. Owls hooting when the sun goes down two hours earlier than in the summer. I'm going to miss these days here on the farm...

Jodi cleared her throat. "We figured just to be safe from *them* finding you by your name, that you should go by the name Morgan."

I look up at her with wide eyes. "You want me to change my name?"

"Not legally. Just when you announce yourself to others or on paper work. In case they've been tracking you by using your name."

"It doesn't have to be permanent. Just for a little while to make sure you're in the clear from them." Carl interjected. They waited for my response but I never gave them any. I just stared down at the mug I turned slowly around in my hands, watching the deer and birds change around each corner. Jodi took a deep breath in and dragged it out past her lips. She leaned across the table and reached a lanky hand onto my forearm.

"I chose the name Morgan for you, after our daughter who passed." Jodi's eyes softened and tears pooled in her swollen eyes. "I have always loved you as a daughter." Jodi tilted her head to meet my gaze. Wet and salty substance slithered down my cheeks, dripping down onto the table and creating a small puddle of tears. Jodi gave me a hearty smile. "You will always be my daughter, no matter what."

The urge of grief and anger overwhelmed me until I couldn't hold it in anymore. I pounced into Jodi's arms and we both uncontrollably sobbed as we held tightly onto each other, until we had no more tears left to cry.

Chapter 23

It all happened so fast. Packing my bags and carrying them out to the truck, where we all sat in silence as Carl drove us to the train station. The train is the only way to the city, except for driving of course. I know how to drive thanks to Carl for teaching me through the backroads and the fields. But I still don't have my license. It had never been a priority for me, until now. Carl would have driven himself to the city, but the worry of *them* following from behind and knowing where I will soon live, changed his mindset. They bought me a train ticket I currently held softly between my fingertips, being sure not to crinkle the paper or fold in the edges. No one spoke, no one glanced at each other. We just stared straight forward at the open road, and listened to the squeaking sounds of the front tires that were rusted from within and needed a good cleaning I know it will never get.

The station was filled with loved ones returning home or going home. Carl led us through the crowd, using my two duffel bags to get strangers to move out of the pathway to the train doors. Over the years I had gained more clothing and some accessories. Jodi insisted I take a duffel bag full of sheets and blankets for my new bed. She said Joel lived alone and most likely had one pair of bedding just for him. If he only has one bed then where will I sleep? A question I still hadn't asked. I'll find out when I get there…

Carl placed my bags down next to the open doors. The train looked to be vintage but it was kept up on throughout the years. So it looked brand new. The glossy black shone in the sunlight, glistening from the sparkles in the paint. Exhaust arose from the chimney as the horn blared from the front, signaling it was time to board. I face Jodi, tears welling up in her eyes. I lunged into her, wrapping my arms tightly around her shoulders. She held me firmly for a moment before patting my backside and pulling away. She forced a soft smile to appear. I turned to Carl, bracing myself for a burly hug as he bent downward and scooped me up, holding me for two heartbeats.

"Have a safe trip," said Carl with a tight smile. "Make sure to get off last so Joel will know it's you, alright?" Carl told Joel my features over the phone, but I'm not uniquely different from any other woman. To make sure Joel knows it's me, he asked me to board off last. My seat is in the back of the train anyway. Carl doesn't know what Joel looks like now, but he did say he has pale features with dirty-blonde hair and emerald green eyes… I nodded and picked up my bags, swinging the long strap onto my shoulder and the other hanging from my forearm as I held the ticket out with my hand, letting the conductor analyze the ticket to let me on board. He handed back the ticket with a smile, nudging me to the back of the train. I glance back out the door, giving one last look at Carl and Jodi never knowing when will be the last time I get the chance to. Jodi wrapped an arm around Carl's waist and they both waved with a smile. I waved before turning back and going through the last doorway to the seating area. I lunged my weighted bag to the end of the hallway, stopping at my seat. I dropped my bag onto the floor with a sigh of relief. The tension in my shoulder dissipated, feeling weightless again. I fold in my ticket and stuff it in the back pocket of my jeans. I stuff my bag up in the top compartment above my seat. I sat down and let out a heavy sigh. I can't believe I'm doing this. This is what my life has come to. Leaving the only people I learned to love and trust to live with a man I have never met. Why do I always have to leave someone I love behind? First Bonnie, Isabelle, and now Carl and Jodi. I never even got to say goodbye to Isabelle. I wonder what Jodi will tell her when I don't show up to Sunday church with the rest of them. Probably what they told them before when Mary asked why I was still with them after a month of meeting me. I finally went home after Jodi's sister was healed after her battle with a mysterious five year illness that kept her bedridden in the hospital. Mary is very gullible. But Isabelle never questioned it. I think she was happy to make a new friend rather than care about why I was there. I hope she chooses to follow her dreams and passion, despite what her mother wants for her...

The train wailed and loud chugging sounds came from underneath. The train started slowly moving forward. I squeeze my eyes shut and don't open them until the train picks up speed and I know for sure it has left the station. I didn't want to look out the window at Carl and Jodi, because I knew it would be too hard to look away. My throat started to burn and my eyes started to soil. I force the saliva to pass the lump in my throat and I wipe my eyes with the back of my hands....

The next five hours were a blur. Keeping my eyes closed for the entire trip and never opening them until I felt the tracks starting to slow before coming to a halt. I opened my eyes to see passengers boarding off the train. Strangers grabbed their bags from up tops and stood in a single file line. I watched the line dwindle down to just one person walking out the doors, leaving me in silence as I stayed seated in my seat. I glanced out the wide window to see a tall man with shaggy blonde hair that reached the lower back of his neck and fair skin that was a bit tan from the sun. He stood waiting by the front door to the train, his eyes darting around his surroundings. He was the only person left in the station. I sighed and reluctantly stood up from my seat and stretched out my back from sitting for five hours straight. I grabbed my luggage and slowly carried them out the doorway. I could see the man's face better in the luminous orange glow from the sun setting from behind me. The man, who I assumed is Joel, had a rounder face than Carl's and a sharper jawline with piercing emerald eyes that searched my face for the first time. He looked to be in his mid forties with slight wrinkles around the corner of his eyes and the grey stubble that slightly grew around his chin. He looked put together, wearing a grey shirt underneath a navy jean jacket and clean jeans. He didn't look like the farming type like Carl is. To think Joel wanted the house and land to use for the same purpose Carl is using, seems a bit odd of him. Even if I don't know him yet. I slumped my bag onto the cement ground and caught my breath.

"Morgan?" Joel asked, raising a thick brow. His voice was deeper than I expected with a slight grumble in his letter G's. I almost corrected him before remembering that is my new name. I wonder if he does know my real name? He slightly shook his head as he waited for my response. I nodded.

"Yes. You're Joel?" I'm not sure why I asked, it's obvious that he was. I didn't want to say nothing at all. Even though saying nothing is better than saying something that makes you look stupid...

"Yeah." Joel said, bending down and effortlessly grabbing my bag. He backed away as if in a hurry to get going, and nodded his head towards a direction that led to the parking garage beside the station. "My car's this way." He took off through the station and I rushed to follow suit. He's tall and lean almost like Carl is. They look the same height but Carl is broader than he is, Joel doesn't have as much muscle mass. Carl works on a ranch, lifting haystacks and a lot of manual labor. Joel owns a diner. I don't think there is much heavy lifting in waitering, except for delivery plates of food. He weaved through crowds of people and made it to the parking garage. We passed at least thirty cars before arriving at Joel's. His car was a truck, similar to Carl's but taken care of more kindly than his. There's no rust or peeling paint, it's a shining navy blue with sparkles mixed in the paint. The window shields aren't scratched, and there are no indents on the side of the door or the back bumpers. It doesn't look like a truck that has been through endless work with loading and unloading necessities for the farm. It's a truck that's just been used for driving. He tossed my luggage in the bed of the truck and drew out his keys from his pocket, inserted it into the key fob on the side of his door and turned it until he heard a *click*. He swung the door open and pushed the button on the inside to unlock the passenger door. Swinging it open, I climbed in and in silence he drove out of the parking garage and into the busy streets of the city.

The drive felt longer than it was. The awkward silence filled the space, only the squeaking sound of the wiper blades was heard as the rain sprinkled down onto the windshield. I heard it rains more in the city than in the flat lands. Less airflow from the buildings which caused it to be hotter, raising heat into the clouds until it can't hold any more causing it to overflow down onto us. The clear droplets slithered down the glass zigzagging until it disappeared into the crevice of the window. Joel turned onto a street that was tucked in between buildings that were in a row on both sides of the road. Vehicles parked in front of the buildings only left one spot open in front of a lit up building with a large bold red sign that read, **CRUEGERS**. Two large windows viewed the inside of wooden tables and chairs with people eating off of silver platters. Warm lighting shown through the gloomy haze. Joel turned off the engine and pulled the keys out of the fob. He pointed upwards to a brick building above the, I assume diner....

"That's the apartment, up there." Joel explained, letting out a tired sigh.

"Above the diner?"

Joel nodded, unamused by the question. "Yeah, a lot of the Victorian buildings have apartments above their businesses." I glance down the street at the tall buildings, taking note that they are Victorian buildings. Some shops looked freshly painted with colors that range from brown to a sky blue. Each building had its own sense of style. While some other buildings look abandoned with the brick above chipping in chunks and the washed-out paint peeling off in strips. I wonder why some of those buildings haven't been occupied yet?

The slam of a door broke me from my thoughts and I looked around as Joel was nowhere to be seen. I stepped out into the pouring rain, sprinting toward the front door that belonged to the diner. It had a plastic material that draped over the entrance. It was covered in green and red stripes and fringed along the edges. Joel emerged from the wet haze with my duffel bag in hand. He nudged to the glass door behind me and swung it open, he led the way through the diner. The warmth of the air defrosted my icy face. Strings of lights hung around the room, illuminating the space with a warm glow. Tables full of people scattered around and a long bar table with stools were placed in the corner with shelves full of bottles and glasses behind it. Strangers at tables gave a greeting nod to Joel. Some strangers struck up a conversation with him as soon as they saw him. I looked at two broad men sitting at the bar with a large glass in hand. One made eye contact with me, his eyes sagged from drunkenness and scratched his grey, straw beard. I looked away and Joel led me to the back door and into a white steamy room. Chefs in white aprons attended to orders, moving fast but swiftly through the kitchen with eagerness to get orders made and served in time. A man with a white t-shirt and jeans, turned to Joel with a broad smile when he spotted him.

"There he is!" He hollered, wiping his hands on his stained apron. "I missed you this morning. I figured you were trying to get out of work." The three chefs behind him laughed as they dished out food onto silver plates.

Joel gave him a playful look. "I had to run some errands across town."

The man pointed to me. "Is she one of them?" He smiled politely at me and gave a gentle nod. I return the gesture in a weak manner. I don't know this guy yet. I'm also in a space I have never been in before. Isabelle said that's when my introverted side comes out. But I could never be so

outspoken like she is. I get a sense of fear that she seems to be immune too...

Joel glanced at me for a second before responding. "I had to pick up my niece Morgan, from the station today."

The man nodded. "Ah, I see. Is she staying with you for a couple days?"

"Somethin' like that." Joel said with a hint of southern twang escaping his tongue.

"Well, let me introduce myself." The man stepped forward to be only a few inches away from me. "I'm Cameron but you can just call me Cam." He held out a blistered hand, probably from hot surfaces touching his skin.

I shake his hand and repeat his name so it will stick into my brain. "Cam."

"Alright," Joel sighed, breaking up our greeting. "I need to get her situated in the apartment. Do you think you can handle things down here for a bit longer?"

"Of course." Cam said, backing off towards the kitchen. "It might cost you extra though." He chuckled, resuming back to his cooking.

Joel playfully shook his head before leading me to a staircase behind a pantry. The auburn walls were bare with only white trimmings to decorate them. The staircase led to a bare wooden door at the top. Joel took out his keys from his pocket, turning the doorknob shortly after. He carried my bag through a narrow hallway and at the end of the hall was an open room with a small white kitchen on the right, a narrow living room in the center of the space, and two doors to the left. Which I assume leads to a bedroom and a bathroom. The walls were a beige and only two pictures were hung up behind a dingy sofa. One was a simple photograph of the eiffel tower that probably came with the frame itself. The other was a photograph of an older woman with soft facial features and bright green eyes, an older man with sharp facial features and dark blue eyes that stood beside her, and one each side of them were a younger Carl and Joel. They both look identical to them now, just a bit younger then. Carl is broader with sharp pointed features just like his father. And Joel is more lean with softer features, just like his mother. As they posed beside their parents, their smiles were wide and pearly and their eyes were as bright as the stars in the dark sky. Behind them was the house on the field. This must've been before Carl and Joel cut ties with each other. Before their parents had passed away. I wonder how close they were before anger and jealousy overran their relationship?... Joel dropped the luggage with a loud *thunk*, from the hardwood floors. He looked over to the left and pointed to the second door.

"That's my room, the other is the bathroom." He then pointed over to the sofa. It was an ugly bright red with unmatching cushions that are darker than the rest. Like he replaced the matching cushions for these ones and didn't realize they were the wrong shade, and instead of replacing them with the right color, he just said, "fuck it" and left them be. "That's where you'll be sleepin'." Joel twanged, looking back at my unamused face. I don't mean to express ungratefulness, but going from a cozy bed with an actual mattress to a dingy old couch that has seen more things than I have in the last decade, isn't something I feel rather grateful for. I try to look less uncomfortable by the thought of sleeping on the couch, but I can tell it's not working by the way Joel rolled his eyes. Then he walked over to the couch, bending down and taking the cushions off to find a strap in between the cushions and pulled out a foldable box spring and mattress and laid it out. The mattress was a bright white and has never looked used before. My face relaxed and I let out an uncontrollable sigh. Joel walked towards the kitchen island and dropped his keys in a small, blue floral china bowl and looked at me with raised eyebrows. "You think you're going to be alright up here alone for the night?" Joel asked, with a bit of a huff. I can't tell if I'm annoying him or if he just lacks patience? Either way, I quickly nodded. The faster I agree with him the faster he will leave me be. With how fast everything has been, I need a bit of time to myself to think through the endless thoughts, and to try and calm my nerves down a bit. He pinched his lips in a thin line and nodded, glancing around the room before looking back at me. "Alright. I'll show you around the diner tomorrow morning before we open. Just make yourself at home." He moved towards the door. I gave him a final nod before he walked out the apartment door and left me alone with only my thoughts keeping me company...

Chapter 24

Cedar burned in the hot flames that absorbed the pale building whole. Why do I keep coming here? "It's a sign," a voice responds beside me. A voice that sounds so familiar but so different at the same time. The person that held my hand, leaned in close to my left ear. Their breath wavered, warmth smothering my cheek, making goosebumps patch my arms. "Listen to it." Their voices echoed in the air. I didn't try to move because I knew my body would be too stiff to. Instead I took in my surroundings. The sky was pitch black and only the twinkling of stars painted the night. Trees surrounding the small white building that was now engulfed in flames. Only the peak of the roof was visible, a cross perched above. A church. Before I could look further, suddenly everything went dark...

I awoke to the smell of eggs and bacon. The small pull-out bed creaked and cracked as I rolled over onto my back. My spine was stiff and sore from the thin as a cracker mattress that was so called a bed. I would have been more comfortable if I slept on a wooden board than this stone rock. I peered my eyesight at the kitchen in front of me. Joel stood his back towards me, hovering over the stove as sizzling sounds came from in front of it. Two plates of bacon were left on the countertop, steam rose from them and evaporated into the ceiling above, giving a sign that they were freshly cooked. A *click* came from the burner and Joel spun around with a sizzling frying pan in one hand and a spatula in the other. He hovered the pan over the plates and dished the pebbled yellow meat onto each plate.

"I hope you prefer scrambled." Said Joel, glancing up at me. I squinted my eyes, shielding them from the overly bright light above and sat myself up onto my elbows. I silently nodded, wiping a hand across my face.

"Carl likes to make them that way." I said ruggedly. I cleared the phlegm out of my throat before pulling off the covers and standing from the, almost touching the ground mattress. It's almost as close to the ground as an ant is. The middle of the mattress sank in, leaving you in a bent position for the entire night.

"Does he now," Joel said, placing the pan and spatula back down onto the stove to cool. "I thought I was the only one who made them this way." He cocked his head and narrowed his eyes before taking his plate and turning to sit down at a two seater table in the very corner of the room. Sarcasm once again. I barely knew him but I could already tell that he will be a difficult person to be around. I rolled my eyes and walked over to grab my plate. I sat down on the other side of the table where a glass of orange juice was placed. Joel thumped a red bottle with a white lid down in the center of the table. The label read, **Heinz Tomato Ketchup**. I watched Joel scoop plain eggs onto his fork and devoured it into his mouth. I assume he doesn't like the eggs and ketchup combination, but I do. I drizzled a bit of ketchup on top of my eggs. He watched with slight disgust as I stirred my eggs in the sauce and took a bite. I swallowed and blankly looked up at him...

"You don't like ketchup?" I asked before shoveling another fork full of eggs into my mouth. The acidic taste of tomatoes stung my taste buds. I think eggs are rather plain alone. The ketchup gives it a flavorful taste that it can't give itself.

Joel shrugged. "Not really. I figured you might've." He said with a mouthful of crunchy bacon. I then remembered how Jodi would make a delicious meatloaf and ketchup was the main ingredient. Oh, how I am going to miss her and her scrumptious food. I narrowed my eyes. "Do you like meatloaf?"

Joel stared at me with a blank expression. He shoveled the last remaining eggs and bacon into his mouth and quickly stood up from his seat. I watched him, puzzled as to what I might have said wrong. He placed his plate into the sink and marched for the front door without a glance back. He swung the door open and before he left he looked at me.

"Get dressed and meet me downstairs at twenty." Without waiting for a response, he dashed out the door, slamming it shut behind him. I looked down at my full plate of food and glanced at the little round clock above the table. It read, **6:34**. I sighed already knowing that today is going to be a brutally long day...

...

I got dressed and did my hair, the usual braid that trailed down my spine. The ends coiled as I tied it off with a hair tie and flattened down my frizzy edges with water. Knowing that it won't hold for long and once it dries the frizz and ringlets will come back like a lion's mane. I try not to worry about it too much. I trotted downstairs and into the steamy kitchen where the chefs were preparing more orders like before. Cam spotted me from the corner of his eye and he turned to me with a goofy grin, one I assume he always displays.

"Good morning, princess." He chippered, while the other chefs chuckled. "I bet you ain't used to getting up this early, huh?" He kneaded dough with his palms with a skilled touch from someone who's been kneading dough far too many years.

Actually, Carl used to wake me every morning before the sun rose. He'd say that is the best time to work before the sun comes up and bakes you half to death. It is currently the middle of autumn where the mornings are freezing and the days are chilly. I highly doubt we could bake half to death when it is below fifty-degrees! I shake my head. "I get up earlier than this."

Cam raises his eyebrows in surprise. "Okay, I see you. Well, Joel is out at the bar." Cam nodded to the swinging door that headed out to the diner. "I'm sure he will find something for you to do." He gave me one last smile before getting back to work. I walked through the swinging door and

into the diner where there were already people seated at tables and waiting for their breakfast to be served. Joel was standing behind the bar cracking open a bottle of beer and chatting with an older man that seated himself on a low barstool. Jodi told me the people who drink alcohol first thing in the morning are low life people that hate the world. But I was used to it. The elders back in the group used to drink wine and alcohol for breakfast everyday except for the sacred days, when we had church service. Reverend Finch made it a rule to not drink on those days. Not after one of the elders showed up drunk and made a fool out of himself during service, to the point where he had to be escorted back to his room where they locked him inside for the rest of the day without any food or water, to teach him a lesson about getting drunk before service. The elder learned his lesson until five months later when he showed up drunk once again during church service. Reverend Finch searched his room and found out that he was stealing alcohol from the kitchen and hoarding the empty bottles in his closet. Ever since that day, we had never seen the elder again. Almost like he vanished into thin air. No one ever mentioned him. Almost like he had never been born at all. No one dared to ask questions. We didn't know if we would be next.

Now thinking about what might have happened to him, sends chills down my spine...

I stood by the bar and patiently waited for their conversation to end. I didn't dare to listen in on what they were discussing. A habit that hadn't left since I did. "It is rude to intervene in people's conversations." Mother's voice echoed through my head. I pushed her frail body off a cliff in my mind. A never ending cliff that will keep her falling for eternity and never finding the end. Similar to the trail they keep following that ends with me. I'm falling but no matter how long, I never find an ending. Joel glanced over to me and pointed his pointer finger up. A signal to wait a minute or two. I did, of course. I looked at the dark painted walls thinking that if it was a lighter shade of color it would brighten the diner up. Maybe that is the point, to keep the place dimly lit. Also, what kind of diner has a bar? Joel walked over to me and handed me something black.

"Wear this." he said as I took it from him. I straightened it out. It was a square material with pockets on the front and two long strings on the sides. I narrowed my eyes on him. He sighed. "It's an apron. You wear it around your waist." He turned around and walked away towards the front entrance. I followed suit as I wrapped the apron across my waist, tying a little bow in the back. A cabinet was placed next to the door entrance. Joel opened a door and revealed long menus stacked on top of another inside the cabinet. "When a person comes in, you ask them how many will be seated at a table." Joel explained, grabbing one of the menus. "Then you grab as many menus as they need," he lifted up the book. "and you guide them to an empty table where you will be serving them. Got it?" I silently nodded along. He returned the menu back into the cabinet and shut the door. Then he opened another cabinet and took out a small square tablet of empty paper with a pen clipped to the side. He continued. "Then when they are ready to order, you write the name of the food down and take it to Cam in the kitchen."

"Then I serve it to them when it's ready." I said, wanting to get this introduction over with. Joel stared at me expressionless. Probably mad I interrupted him. "I have stepped foot into a restaurant before." I added. Taking the tablet and stuffing it into my apron's pocket.

"Glad we are on the same page, then." He walked past me and headed for the bar before turning back one last time. "I'm going to be attending the bar. Just, do your job. Alright?"

I raised my eyebrows and brought two fingers to my forehead and swooped them out in a salute. "Ey, ey captain." I rolled my eyes and turned away from him, retrieving back over to the entrance stands where I stood in silence waiting for the customers' arrival...

When I said that today is going to be a, *Brutally long day,* I meant it, and it in fact was. I spent most of the whole day on my feet. Just a normal day for me as I never had a break from attending the farm. I answered questions strangers asked about me suddenly working at the diner. "Oh, I didn't know Joel had a niece." Was the basic response to my telling of how I knew Joel. "How long will you be here for?" Was another. Which I replied with a shoulder shrug and a goofy grin. "For as long as Joel needs me here." Sometimes I have gotten the, *I don't believe you* glare at my obvious lies. Lying wasn't allowed back in the group. As if the adults weren't lying about everything they had preached about. It's easy to become a liar when my whole existence was nothing *but a lie.* But sometimes lying is what keeps you safe from dangerous situations and people... ignoring the questions that were continually asked by what felt like the whole town, I finally had my last table to serve.

The sun dawned and the alcoholics came out. Most I assumed weren't alcoholics by ordering one or two drinks before leaving, but others came in a bit tipsy or hadn't left the barstools since the afternoon. This particular customer that I served at the last table in the back was a group of five men. Some wore leather jackets and a few wore basic jean jackets which had a serpent head patch sewn onto the backsides of them. The snake head coiled and with its jaw opened wide revealing sharp spiked teeth that pointed to a spear. Ready to inject its fangs into their next victim and give out its deathly venom, and a deep red tongue with slits that used to taste flesh. Its eyes were a bright yellow with red and orange flames coming from within. Intimidating, is what they were going for. Instead to me it looks peculiar and quite, stupid. The only intimidating part about them would be their broad shoulders and their rocks for arms. One of them could easily knock Joel out with just a slap across the cheek...

I could feel their gaze all over me as I stood stiffly still while writing down their food orders. Most customers idly stare at their menus as I jot down their orders or they fidget with their cups on the table. Doing everything not to awkwardly stare at me. These guys stared at me tauntingly as I caught some of their protruding eyes looking me up and down. Some idling at my breasts.

As I walked back to the kitchen to drop off the note to Cam I glanced over at Joel, looking for any indications that I shouldn't be near these gang of men. But instead all I saw was Joel chatting up a conversation with the same man that's been sitting on the barstool for hours and taking his time sipping his beer as he nodded along to what Joel was intently saying. Not paying any mind to the men that now bellowed laughter at their table. Within minutes empty beer bottles gathered at the table beside the group of men, taking up space on another table so theirs won't be cluttered. I gathered the bottles in my arms while I ignored their stares and grins once more. I'm too exhausted for this shit. I took the empty bottles to the kitchen and dumped them into the sink to be cleaned. Joel likes to reuse the bottles instead of tossing them into the trash. Supposedly, it saves him money. I don't question it, unless I want more smartass comments from him. Cam rang the bell that indicated there's plates to be served. I gather the steamy plates two at a time onto my hands and carry them carefully over to the men. At first the men were in too deep of a conversation to notice I was there. I thanked God they haven't noticed me yet and I set down the plates in front of them. Recalling who ordered what from the top of my head. But I spoke too soon. I grabbed another two plates and I sat them down onto the table. The men eyed me with malicious grins plastered onto their faces. A man with a thick beard cleared his throat.

"Well, aren't you a pretty young lady?" He said with a deep voice. The other pack of men bellowed a laugh. The man next to him with a scraggly mustache licked his lips as his gaze fell over me. Over my body. It's not like I was wearing something scandalous. I wore my usual t-shirt tucked into my bell bottom jeans with boots. The shirt wasn't tight, it was loose and the collar came up to my neck. Jodi would murder me if I wore something that didn't cover up my chest. If I wear a flannel, I have to put on a high-necked tank top underneath. I never questioned her reasons to cover-up because I knew they were good ones. She always tried to look out for me...

"You new here?" The man asked, bringing me back to my senses. "I think I would remember seeing you around." A perky smile arose on his face and revealed a set of yellow tinted teeth. Ignoring them, I walked back over to the kitchen and grabbed the final plate. I took a deep breath in before walking back out to their table. The last plate belonged to of course, the man that was speaking to me that I so generously ignored. I could tell that my lack of response angered him by the way his smile dropped and his eyes glowed red. Metaphorically speaking, they did to me. I reached my arm over the table and placed his plate down in front of him. As I began to pull my arm away, the man's thick calloused hand clasped around my wrist. My wrist looked so small compared to his large hand. His hands were so large I was sure he could grab my entire face with one. Knowing too well to pull my arm away that it won't budge against his strength. I looked into his devilish eyes that seared into mine.

"It's rude to ignore a man when they ask you a question." His tone raised. And for a split second the man no longer looked like himself. Instead it was Reverend Finch. His dark hair slicked back into a side part, his eyes looked like deep pits in the lighting, his sunken cheeks that made him look like a skeleton, and his thin lips spread into a devilish grin. I thought I had forgotten what he looked like all this time, but it turned out I remembered everything about him. A muffled voice came into my ear. I forced myself to blink and when I did, Reverend Finch was replaced with the same man as before. Then all of my senses came back and suddenly I could recognize the voice. Joel came up from behind me and asked the man if everything was alright. The man quickly let go of my wrist and I pulled my arm away, stumbling back a few steps. The man plastered a fake grin before responding, still staring at me.

"Yes, everything's great."

Joel nodded and stepped back, grabbing me by the elbow for stability. I hadn't noticed that I was wobbling in my stance. He probably thought I was going to pass out, but I didn't feel faint in the slightest. I was aware of everything. Too aware. I felt eyes on me from every corner. But nobody was there. But I knew they were there, ghostly stares at me with crooked smiles that wordlessly said, *"I found you."* Adrenaline pumping through my veins, my hands started to shake uncontrollably. Joel nodded.

"That's good to hear. Enjoy your meals." He smiled before pulling me around and walking me into the kitchen. He placed his palms onto my shoulders with bent knees to meet my gaze into oblivion. When he raised his eyebrows, his forehead creased into crinkled lines.

"Are you okay?" He asked apprehensively, glancing down at my shaking hands. I couldn't muster a word, as if my tongue was cut out.

All I could do was slowly nod my head. Joel guided me to the staircase that leads to the apartment. "Why don't you go upstairs for the night. I'll finish down here." I nodded once more before clumsily walking up the staircase. Upstairs was chilly compared to downstairs. Goosebumps formed on my skin as I undressed into a t-shirt and checkered pajama pants. I climbed underneath my blankets and stared up at the pale ceiling, knowing that I won't get any sleep tonight as my mind raced like a car on a race track, going around and around, and never seeming to run out of gas...

Chapter 25

The week went by faster than expected. The same boring routine of catering filled up my weekly schedule. Joel and I had never had a single conversation since I arrived other than the ketchup on eggs mishap and Joel mustering a word to me every morning. "Good morning," in almost a forced chipper tone. The gang of men hadn't come back since the day I served them. I wondered if Joel told them something that would draw them away from here? I doubt it. They could throw him through a wall if he ever looked at them oddly, let alone say something offensive. I hope they never come back... well, hope is a useless word anyway.

I grabbed two steamy plates of steak and French fries for a couple sitting in front of the window. I placed them down in front of them with a weak smile that they returned with thank yous' before I walked away, when I made sure that they didn't need anything else of course. The little bell above the door dinged when a group of young boys came in. They looked to be around my age with a bit more height than me. I unconsciously counted four of them before I walked over to the cabinets to grab the menus. I still let the boy in front with dark brown hair and hazel eyes tell me there are four of them because that's the *polite thing to do*, in Joel's words. I nodded with a smile as I guided them to a table in the far left corner where two chairs and a long booth were. The hazel eyed boy wore a plain dress shirt that rolled up on the sleeves and dark trousers with dress boots. He dressed differently than his friends who were dressed in regular t-shirts and jeans. His short comb over hair made him look preppy like he came from a line of richness. He smiled at me politely while his eyes scanned over me with pleasantness. I clenched my teeth as flashbacks from the gang that looked at me similar to him, though his eyes were softer and didn't linger around my chest. Unlike the other men who stared hard with stoned eyes and malicious intent. The boys chatted with each other as they sat in their seats and I placed the menus in front of them. None of them except for the one who eyed me, seemed to not notice me at all. Which was nice. I'm someone who would rather hide in the shadows of a crowd of people than be in the light with them. I take their drink orders and leave to the kitchen to prepare them. I placed the drinks on a tray and carried them out to the dining room.

As I entered the room I felt the room shift. The aura was different than before. My eyes scanned the room to see what it was and they landed on the five leather jacket men that sat in the same spot as the last time they were here. They were in a deep conversation as they took off their jackets, making themselves comfortable. A sign that they aren't planning on leaving anytime soon. I look over to the bar where Joel normally stands throughout the days but for once in his life he was not there. Coming to think of it, I haven't spoken to him since this morning. Where has he been? I considered turning around and going back into the kitchen but the brunette boy locked eyes with me, raising an eyebrow in confusion. I told myself that everything would be alright. The diner was packed with people eating their afternoon meals. If the men tried anything with me everyone would see. They wouldn't risk getting caught... would they? I walked quickly past their table and to the boy's table. I hand them each their drinks with a shaky hand.

"Are you alright?" The brunette boy asked, looking down at my hand. I nodded while glancing around the diner for any sign of Joel. He's still nowhere to be found.

"Well, we're ready to order." The boy said. I looked at each boy who stared at me and waited for any indication to rack off what they wanted. I flipped open my tiny notebook, clicking the end of the pen. I jotted down their orders and ended with a small smile and a " it'll be out shortly", before walking off towards the kitchen. But before I could get to the kitchen door, a gravelly familiar voice stopped me in my tracks.

"I'm ready to order!" The man in the serpent jacket hollered out to me. "It's rude not to attend to customers." He said matter-of-factly. I took in a deep breath before slowly letting it out through my mouth, grinding my teeth out of irritation at the men that decided to come back to taunt me and of the fact that I don't know where the hell Joel was. For once he's not around analyzing me and telling me what I'm doing wrong. I guess he can be unpredictable sometimes. I slowly turn on my heels and march up to their table. Their maliced grins were plastered on their faces and their eyes shot a look of amusement at my demeanor, which was stiff and rigid and my expression was blank. I flipped open my notebook and stared at an empty page while I waited for their response. After I got their orders I marched back into the kitchen and handed Cam the notes. He read them with widened eyes.

"Big orders, huh?" He retorted, pinning up the notes on a string with several clips along it. The other chefs scanned the notes and quickly began making the orders. They take their jobs quite seriously back here, especially when they try to beat the lunch and dinner rush. Try being the only server here, I think to myself on a daily basis. The four chefs, including Cam, start getting stressed out about how much food they have to make in under an hour. To think that a diner so small gets a large amount of customers a day is wild. I guess Joel's diner is the best in the entire city. Cam turned back to me and cocked his head to the side. "You alright?"

"Where's Joel?" I glanced around the kitchen with bewilderment to where his presence was.

Cam wiped his hands on a stained rag that hung out of his apron pocket. "I believe he went to run some errands," Cam replied, stuffing the rag back into his pocket. "Why? Is everything alright, Morgan?"

I huffed out air through my mouth. "The men are back."

"The men?" Cam was puzzled. "You need to specify, 'cause a lot of men come and go."

I placed my palms onto my hips and sighed. "The group of men that have the serpent on the backs of their jackets."

"Oh," Cam rubbed his brow with a stubby hand. "Yeah, they come here once in a while."

"Well, I don't like them." I interjected with a shake of my head. "They taunt me."

"If you want me to serve them, I can." Cam offered. And as if it was planned, a chef carrying a large pot of boiling water, misplaced the stove and dropped it onto the floor with a loud *clunk.*

"Shit!" He cried out, hopping on his feet to keep from the steaming water that soaked the kitchen floor to seep into his sneakers and burn his feet. The two other chefs rushed over to start cleaning up the mess while cursing under their breaths.

The chef, Charles, walked over to the man and smacked him over the back of his head with a greasy palm. "You dumbass! Now we have to start over!"

Cam wiped a hand over his face and let out a long sigh. His expression was blank but I could see the annoyance and anger in his chocolate colored eyes. I shook my head and waved a dismissive hand in the air. "No, it's fine. They seem to be behaving right now anyway." I say glancing at the door and regretting that I have no choice but to serve them. I look back at Cam. "Just let me know when Joel gets back."

Cam nodded. "Gotcha." He turned around and looked at the man that dropped the pot, who was wiping his sweaty forehead with a rag while looking down at the mess he made. Two chefs scrambled to mop up the mess. Cam waved his hands out to the side and shook his head. "What the hell, James." His tone was low and calm which is what makes him scarier than the one man shouting. "Don't just stand there and weep. Help them clean up the mess you've made."

Like I said, the men behaved while I refilled their drinks and served them their meals. Only a snicker and a grin from them as I walked past them to serve other customers. The boys chatted with one another throughout eating their lunch. The brunette boy stole glances at me that I ignored, keeping myself busy enough so he wouldn't stop to talk to me. He seemed nice and well mannered but something about him displeased me in a way I couldn't quite explain. Like a part of my brain said to stay away from him while the other part was curious about him. It is all conflicting in a way. I took empty plates to the deep sink, my shoes sticking to the floors from dried up soap suds. The chef James didn't wring out the mop enough and added too much soap to the bucket when he cleaned up his mistake, and yet again he made another mistake. Charles gave him an ear load about mistake number two and he told him that after closing, he will be cleaning the entire kitchen until it is to Charles's perfection. Cam says Charles takes his job very seriously. I say he just loves to boss people around. I think I'm more accurate than Cam is.

I head out to the diner and glance at nearby tables to see if I need to take empty plates from people. The boys still had food on their plates, so I'll give them a few minutes to finish. But of course the gang of men cleaned their plates off and left no crumbs or sauces behind. I blew out my cheeks before composing myself to walk over to their table. As I stood in front of their table I asked if that would be all. They gave confirming nods with their usual maliced grins. I grabbed the first plate to the right and I expected for them to gather their plates to the center of the table for me to take but instead they had me reach across the table to gather their plates. One by one the men took their time with their eyes feeling me up and down as I bent over to take a plate. The last plate was from the man that grabbed me the last time. I moved to his side and reached over him to grab his plate and as I did, the man placed a hand on the small of my back and slid it down to caress the back of my thigh with a devilish smile and heaping red eyes. Like a lion to its prey. Without any time to think clearly, I did the first thing that came to my mind. Rage consumed my entire body. And with a plate in my right hand, I twisted my hips and swung my arm like a baseball player swinging to hit the ball with the center of their bat. The plate clashed with his face and broke into pieces like a brick smashing into a glass window. Shards flew in the air, sparking into the lights. The man fell back and his chair broke from underneath him. Everyone in the diner quickly stood up from their seats and scooted forward to get a better view as their eyes were wide open and mouths gaping holes. The man was no longer smiling as he sat up with a hand over his face and he yelled in agony. I stood stunned as his friends rushed over to him and brought him up onto his feet. He removed his hand from his face and red painted his skin like a canvas. His nose was crooked to one side and his lip was sliced in half above. Blood oozed down his face and neck, disappearing under the neckline of his shirt. He stood staring at the bloody mess on his hand with widened eyes. He looked at me with murderous eyes. I knew right then and there that I was going to be killed by this man. That was until Joel appeared from what felt like thin air and pulled me away by the arm, and stood in between me and the burly man. Their lips seemed to move but all I could hear was a high pitched ringing in both of my ears. Shock had taken over me, and realizing I still hugged a stack of plates with my left arm. I let them clash to the floor making more of a mess than there already was, and I stumbled back into the kitchen. Cam emerged in front of me reaching out to me with silent words. I pushed him away from me and I kept walking until I reached the exit door and stood in the alleyway of the diner's building.

Chapter 26

I place a shaky hand on my chest, feeling the thumping of my heartbeat. The rhythm was fast and unsteady. I inhaled deeply through my nose and slowly out through my mouth until my heartbeat slowed and became steady. I take in my surroundings hoping to clear my racing thoughts. The air was brisk in the breeze but felt sharp to the touch on my bare skin. A green dumpster with a black lid rested down the shady alleyway. A trash bag with a slit down the side spilled out the front of the dumpster with the lid collapsed on top. Soda cans dumped out of the open slit and blew around on the speckled concrete. I huffed out of frustration from the mess that I now have to clean. I picked up cans and shoved them through the slit of the bag. Once I gathered them I lifted the lid to the dumpster with one hand and moved the trash bag away from the edge, pushing it down as hard as I could until the lid closed with only a sliver of the insides visible. I brushed my hands together and turned back towards the door when a tall and lean figure appeared from the corner of my eye. I stepped back with clenched fists as the preppy boy from inside stood in front of the alleyway with his hands tucked in his trouser pockets. His eyebrows drew in and his eyes squinted even though the sun was hidden behind the greying clouds that waited to fill up with enough moisture to burst out in heavy rain again.

"I didn't mean to spook you." The boy said with a forced chuckle in hopes of lightening up the mood.

"Then why are you standing there like a creep?" The words left my mouth before I could register them in my brain. I bit my tongue out of embarrassment while I held my ground. He *was* being a creep. A sly smile slowly crept up on his face and his eyes lit up in amusement.

"I apologize, I just wanted to see how you are doing."

"Why? You don't know me." The words ran out with no stopping them. Apparently my mouth has taken complete control over me.

The boy nodded. "That is true," he took a few steps forward, entering the alley space with me. "But I couldn't help but ask anyway. My mother raised me with empathy."

"Did your mother also tell you that staring is rude?" I said, taking a step forward. "That goggling your eyes at a girl is bad manners?"

He shrugged. "Only to girls I think are pretty."

Confident is one word for him, arrogant is another. I narrowed my eyes on him. "And, how often is that?"

He shook his head with a serious expression as he took another few steps forward. "Not very often."

I clenched my teeth and folded my arms across my chest. The wind is getting stronger and icier. I glanced up at the clouds that moved quickly across the sky. A sign that another storm is brewing. "Look, I just wanted to check on you." The boy said, stepping closer to me. We now stood a few inches away from each other. I took a couple steps back to make it more. I appreciate his kindness to me, but I would rather be alone. I've dealt with enough men for the day, or so the rest of the week. I forced a smile but only a little grin appeared.

"Thanks, but I'm fine." I glanced to the kitchen door, a signal that I'm done with this conversation. Whatever this was, I am ready to go inside and up to my awful bed and wallow in silence. "I should get back inside." I pointed to the door and slowly creeped towards it and tried not to seem too eager to get rid of him. But he caught on and started backing away.

"I get it, you've had enough with guys right now." He threw up his hands in a surrender to his game of *catching the girl*. "Maybe we'll talk tomorrow, then." His question is not meant to be a question at all. He *will* be here tomorrow, whether I like it or not. I opened my mouth but nothing came out. I'm not sure what I'm supposed to say to that other than nodding. A big grin plastered his face and raised his brows. "I'll see you tomorrow...?" He narrowed his eyes and pointed a limply pointer finger at me indicating that he wanted my name.

"Vi- Morgan." I stuttered. My cheeks heated up out of embarrassment of my almost slip-up. I'm still not used to my new name. How could you when you were only called one name your entire life.

"Morgan?"

I quickly nodded. "Yep, Morgan. That's my name."

"Alright," he chuckled. "My name is Dean." He placed a hand to his chest. Without saying any other words Dean backed away and gave a farewell nod before turning on the ball of his heels and trotting away and soon disappearing from the alleyway.

I stood in the center of the alleyway, puzzled as to what I had gotten myself into. I squeezed my eyes shut and rubbed my temples with my fingers. I bashed a man's face in with a plate, and now I'm meeting with another man who clearly has a crush on me sometime tomorrow. How did I get here? If it wasn't for that man in the woods on that stormy day then I wouldn't have left Carl and Jodi and end up with Carl's younger brother Joel. I wouldn't be working here at this diner and bar and I wouldn't have gotten myself into these situations. Now I have to mentally prepare myself for getting murdered by Joel for the destruction of his diner that I have caused. I haven't been here long to know that Joel's customers mean more to him than anything else in his life. It was quite obvious the first day working here. My body will probably be stuffed into a duffel bag and thrown into the closest lake where my body will deteriorate in the muggy water and become food for all the freshwater fish that swims the lakes. All the while, Joel will be sued or worse, getting tortured to death from the devilish gangs of crooks for what I've done to their mate. What they will do with his body, I will never know. Probably just leave it in the middle of a dark alleyway or throw it into the nearest dumpster to become one with the trash. The endless possibilities are overwhelming...

After a few minutes of overthinking, I finally headed for the door. I took one last deep breath, placing a hand on the metal doorknob and exhaling as I entered into the brightly white kitchen where no one was around. I walked up to the swinging door to the diner, pressing an ear against its brass painted wood. I could only hear the sound of muffled talking and a sudden outrage of another voice. Joel is likely trying to talk his way out of a lawsuit and brutal death while the man that bled out is cursing at him and is probably one step closer to punching Joel's face in. I backed away from the door and decided that it's best if I didn't go anywhere near the man and his group of gangsters, and instead headed upstairs to that stone bed to sleep my sorrows away.

* * *

I awakened from a beeping sound. An ongoing *beep beep beep*, that lasted for a long three beeps before stopping to silence. Then about twelve seconds later another three obnoxious beeps followed. It continued three times until I finally climbed out of bed and trusted my instincts to guide me to the kitchen as my eyes remained closed. Shuffling my bare feet across the room, my toes bumped into the bottom cupboard and I forced the lids to lift open enough to let my eyes adjust to the lighting above. The beeping continued until my eyes cleared and I could see the navy blue microwave in front of me. I pushed a skinny finger on the **Off** button silencing the enraging sound. I swore for a second, I could still hear the beeps that engraved into my brain and slowly chipped at the thin ice I've been on since yesterday evening. I thought getting some sleep would help me feel better, but all it did was make me feel worse. The dull aching in the lower back of my spine sure doesn't help either. I pulled open the microwave door to reveal a plastic bowl with the leftover lasagna we got from the premade refrigerator selection of the grocery store that we made two nights ago for dinner. Just what I want for breakfast. I grabbed the plastic container that seared my fingertips and placed it on the granite countertop. Joel obviously doesn't know not to heat up food in a plastic container otherwise he will come back to melted plastic in his food... a creaking sound came from behind me and as I turned around. Joel emerged from the bathroom door. His shaggy hair was slicked back and damp and he wore his usual flannel with jeans and boots. He moved towards me, rolling up his sleeves to reveal his pale forearms. It doesn't surprise me that his skin is fair, it's not like he can get much sun from inside the diner. I noticed my tan was getting fairer and fairer everyday since living here. I was always paler than the other girls back in the group. Too pale that the other girls would pick on me for it. Saying that I looked sickly or that if a bird shit on my head it would just blend right in with my skin. Another way of saying that I looked like shit. But Bonnie never judged me for being pale. She used to compliment me on it. Saying that I looked as pretty as the glistening snow that fell in the winter. Bonnie's favorite season was winter. She would lay out on the dead grass as the snow fell from the sky and melted on her rosy cheeks.

She would say that it's peaceful, and when the snow covers the ground in a blanket and the icicles hang from the trees, that it's simply the most beautiful thing she has ever seen. Getting that compliment was special because I knew how fond she was of snow... God, I miss her.

"Mornin'," said Joel with a small smile. He strode towards the fridge and swung open the door, soon grabbing a carton of milk. He grabbed a glass from a cupboard and poured himself half a glass. Why just half, I will never know. I watched as he chugged the whole glass and then put his glass in the sink. He looked over to the lasagna sizzling beside me and pointed with a stubby finger. "Are you hungry?"

"No," I say blankly. "And you're not supposed to put tupperware in the microwave."

Joel raised a brow as he grabbed a plate out of a cupboard. "Huh?"

"The tupperware," I explained, motioning a firm hand to the container that the mushy lasagna was rotting in. "It will melt in the microwave. Stop doing it." I walked out of the kitchen and towards my so-called room without walls, and took a seat at the bottom of the bed. Joel pressed his lips together and nodded.

"Good to know." He took a fork out of a drawer and dished himself some steamy lasagna. He brought the plate to the island and took a bite. I could hear the mushing chomps of wet noodles coming from inside his mouth. I closed my eyes and inhaled deeply trying to regain some of my sanity so I don't burst out in rage. I looked back at Joel who seemed to mind his own as he ate his breakfast. I expected him to yell at me and tell me how he will get sued for the damage that I have caused and that he will have to close his diner for good. Instead, he's acting like nothing has happened at all. I shifted my position on the bed and cleared my throat.

"So, what happened to that guy?" I apprehensively asked. "Is he going to sue or something?"

Joel stabbed his fork into a noodle and shook his head, and said a nonchalant, "No." before shoveling a limp noodle into his mouth.

"Then, what's going to happen?"

Joel shook his head again. "Nothings going to happen."

I drew in my eyebrows, confused. "But, I broke that man's nose."

Joel nodded and shoveled another noodle in his mouth. "Yeah and with one of my plates." He pointed up a finger. "Which by the way, you are going to pay out of your weekly allowance to afford another set."

I slowly nodded. "Okay, but what about that man and his gang? Will he be coming back?"

Joel set his now empty plate to the side and sighed. "Look, all I did was threaten him. He won't be coming back."

That can't just be all. No, that seems too easy. "What did you say to him?"

Joel glanced up to the ceiling and squinted his eyes, trying to recall his exact words. "I said something along the lines of, if you call the police then I will tell them about what you did one night at the pub."

"What did he do?" I asked, wanting to know what could have happened to scare him off so easily.

"A friend told me that a gang was smuggling illegal drugs into a pub one night."

I cocked my head. "How did you know it was them?"

Joel shrugged. "I just assumed. They're the only gang well known around here. It was only a matter of time before they got themselves in some sort of trouble."

I sat there, motionless, shocked. That was it. I wasn't going to be murdered and stuffed into a duffel bag and thrown into a lake. Thank God. I was terrified for my and Joel's life... that man did deserve it though. I'm glad I broke his nose and whatever else that was hit by the thick glass plate. Maybe, he had learned his lesson and won't be putting his unwanted hands on another woman. I hope that my face flashes into his mind, haunting him from touching another girl again... Joel set his plate in the sink and walked towards the door.

"I'm heading down." He turned towards me and looked me up and down. He can see that I am still in my pajamas and my hair probably looks like a bird made a nest on the top of my head. "Be down at twenty." He left. Leaving me alone as always.

The self control I had to do to not crawl back into bed and finally get a good sleep after knowing that everything will be alright, was immaculate. All of the years of controlling to be honest, quiet, waking up early in the wee mornings, and be a "proper young lady" that some of the elders would say in the group, has paid off for days like today. Forcing myself to undress and climb into the shower. Spending half of my twenty minutes under the warming water. The other half was of course, getting dressed, hair braided, getting a small snack to eat, and just taking an overall moment to myself. Something I haven't done in over a decade. Little moments to myself were when Bonnie and I would wander the forests, pointing out every little insect and plant we would see. Bonnie would tell me all the names of the plants, trees, and insects. She was the only girl that chose to purposefully read the geographical books. She says that she finds it interesting...

"Why shouldn't we want to learn about nature and the living creatures that make the earth?" She would say with eyes full of warmth and wonder. "Earth is our homeland. Might as well learn a little bit about it." She would take me to the creek that ran through the forest, weaving around the trees and bushes. Showing me the tadpoles that swam through the water, and holding toads in her hands to show me their fascinating bodies and eyes. She finds them more fascinating than I ever did. But watching the joy light up in her eyes and the wide smile of excitement and love she gives to all the creatures she encountered, was far more enjoyable to me than the things we saw. Bonnie guided me through the forest to an opening of trees and a field of nothing but yellow flowers peppering the landscape from ahead. It was the prettiest place I have ever seen. It looked like a painting with the endless vivid yellow flowers up pastures from miles and miles away, and the sunny light blue sky with large pearly white clouds painted in various places. We raced out to the center of the field and lied down in the bed of flowers. I watched as the clouds drifted amongst the sky and sheltered the beaming sun making the world around us dimmer before peering back out and filling us with warmth. There was a perfect breeze brushing past our cheeks and swaying the trees from afar. Bonnie reached beside us and picked the little yellow flower with her two fingers and held it up to the sky so it glowed a yellow tinted aura.

"The scientific name for these flowers are Ranunculus acris." Bonnie said matter-of-factly. Her eyes examined the flower with fondness, swearing that I even saw a twinkle in her eye. "The other name that most people call these is, Meadow Buttercups. They are more like weeds than flowers, but still give off that pretty appearance." I examined the flower. Its five round edge petals were a vibrant yellow that gave a very contrasted glow. The center had almost a dandelion appearance with a powdery texture for the pollen. It was a little flower but it was still so lovely! "Here," Bonnie took my hand and held it up and hovered the flower against my palm. "Do you see it glowing?"

I squinted my eyes and looked closely. And yes, there was a faint yellow glow that shined ever so slightly onto my palm.

"Yes, I do see it." I respond, drawing in my eyebrows. "What makes it glow?"

"The glow is of layers of air situated just beneath the surface. These layers reflect light like mirrors do and contribute to the glowing appearance." Bonnie explained like she was reading straight from a book. Her mind never ceases to amaze me. "It's beautiful, isn't it?"

I turned my head to look at her, watching her gazing up at the flower with fondness in her eyes, and she held a soft smile that could heal my heart if it was broken. The only beauty I see is hers. Not only is she beautiful from the outside but from inside as well. Her kind heart is truly wonderful and her gentle way of caring for others is admirable. She's truly one of a kind. At that moment I hoped she would turn her head to look at me with her chocolate brown gaze, but instead she dropped the flower into the grass and rested her hands on her stomach. She gazed up at the clouds that slowly drifted over us. I looked back at the sky and closed my eyes, listening to the breeze blowing by and the trees clattering to the sound of the wind. Soaking in this relaxing moment with her. Finally feeling like I could just breathe. It all felt like a dream. But like every dream, they all come to an end...

* * *

Half of the day was spent on the usual tasks. Serving, cleaning, and catering to the customers, some that I see almost everyday. Joel kept himself busy behind the bar attending to the same scruffy older man who comes in to get nothing but beers and a basket of deep-fried-pickles. I wonder if Joel ever checked up on the man, or maybe had told him that everyday drinking is a sign of alcoholism. It's not like he arrives two days a week to drink. No, this is *everyday* drinking. I wonder what his life story is that led him to this routine. A loss of a spouse or loved one? An illness like depression or PTSD from a tragic event in his life? The gold wedding band that he wore everyday and never seems to take off, gives me an indication that it might be the first one. Or rather both, really. Either way, I hope that he takes care of himself.

"Morgan," Joel called out to me from behind the bar. I was suddenly aware that I was leaning my back against the wall by the kitchen door and was staring down at the floor in a daze. I looked at him with eyebrows raised and wide eyed. He cracked a bottle with a beer opener and nodded toward the front door. I zoned out so far that I never heard the little bell above the door chime. I walked towards the front door ready to greet the customer with a courtesy smile when I noticed the customer was tall and lean with dark hair and dressed in a button-down and trousers. He was looking out the door window when he turned suddenly towards me, hearing the sound of the heels of my boots clunking across the floor. He gave me a wide smile and his eyes seemed to light up.

"Morgan," he said cheerfully. "You do remember me telling you that I would come back sometime today, right?" He questioned probably from my weary facial expression. I hadn't seen him all day and I had figured he decided not to show. It is now evening. A part of me was a little bit sad that he hadn't shown earlier, but another part was a bit relieved when I thought he wasn't coming. Now my emotions are a bit conflicted about being surprised and I think happy that he's now here. I'm not used to being tuned into my emotions, but it's all rather confusing.

"Dean," I nodded, folding my arms across my chest. "Yeah, I do."

His shoulder slackened not realizing how stiff he was before. His hands were in his trouser pockets and he sighed with relief. "Oh good. I couldn't tell by the expression on your face." He chuckled nervously. "You didn't seem too thrilled to see me."

I quickly shook my head. "Oh no, I'm just a bit surprised you actually showed up." I gave him a small smile.

His smile grew even wider that the corner of his eyes crinkled. "Well, I am a man of my word."

"Who's this?" A voice came up from behind me. I turned to see Joel standing with his arms folded and a rag draping over his left shoulder. He arched a brow, looking at the both of us out of curiosity. A grin grew on his face.

"I'm Dean Forester." Dean leaned over and held out a flat hand to the side for Joel to shake.

"Joel Granger." Joel courteously shook Dean's hand, and later returned it to its last position. "Your father owns Forester Motors." It wasn't a question because he surely knew he was right.

Dean nodded his head. "Yes, my father has spoken about your diner before. He said the food was delicious. I should know because I had already eaten here before, and I must say that he is right."

Joel slightly shook his head dismissively, and his grin soon turned into a bright smile. "All the credit goes to the chefs."

Dean chuckled. "Well, they are great at their jobs."

I felt suddenly aware of my presence. I just awkwardly stood between them as they bantered with one another. I suddenly felt the urge to just walk away and leave them be, but I didn't want to seem rude as Dean is here to speak with me. Not Joel. I couldn't help but clear my throat to disrupt them from their conversation. They both glanced at me with smiles before saying something.

"Well," said Joel, reading my discern expression. "What brings you here?" The question was to Dean, not me. Otherwise I would say that my old past has come back to haunt me and I had to leave the only true family that I ever had to live with a man I never knew and tirelessly work at his diner and bar and getting felt up by disgusting men, and now I'm talking to a boy that clearly has an interest in me while I feel conflicted on how I feel about all of it... I inhale deeply through my nose and out through my mouth. Dean opened his mouth to respond while glancing back at me.

"I actually wanted to ask Morgan out." Dean cleared his throat. "Like on a date." He added. I could tell he's a bit uncomfortable asking this question in front of Joel. I thought I saw a bit of sweat beads forming along his hairline.

"Oh," Joel nodded. "Why don't you take her out now." I turned to Joel with widened eyes. Is he being serious? I didn't even agree to anything yet.

"Oh no, I meant some day when she's not working." Dean explained with a similar expression as mine.

Joel shook his head. "She's never not working."

Dean turned to me. "Only if you want to of course."

I waved a dismissive hand. "It's fine, we can go now." I said before my brain could catch up to my mouth. The people pleasing is ingrained into my brain, and no matter how hard I try to relent from the urges, I always continue to lose anyway. I took off my apron and jabbed it into Joel's chest without thinking. Joel took it and gave an amused smile. He must be loving this, embarrassing me as he always does.

"Great," Dean chippered and held the front door open with a chime from the bell, waiting for me to exit first.

As I did so, Joel shouted, "Have fun!" Dean and I marched down the sidewalk to his car.

* * *

We sat in silence as Dean drove through the busy city streets, nearly stopping every two miles from a traffic light or traffic itself. I kept my gaze out the window and my hands clamped to my lap, never looking over in his direction. This is by far one of the weirdest things that could have ever happened to me. I felt a little strange being in a car with a boy I just met not even twenty-four hours ago, and a bit of anger for Joel not knowing how to ever keep his mouth shut. If it wasn't for him, I wouldn't be in this awkward situation right now... Dean cleared his throat.

"I didn't have anything planned for today because I didn't expect to be taking you out now." He gave a weary chuckle. "Funny how you could get yourself into odd situations, huh." It wasn't really a question, but I still nodded in agreement. "So, what do you want to do?" Dean asked, glancing back at me. "Want to go anywhere?"

I shook my head. "I don't know what's around here or anything else."

"Ah," Dean replied with a head nod. "Just moved here?"

"A couple weeks ago," I responded, keeping my eyes forward. I stared at the back of a small truck with peeling white paint and a dented bumper. It almost reminded me of Carl and his rusty old truck. It sends a painful feeling into my gut. I wonder if he's alright.

"You live with Joel?" Asked Dean, breaking my trail of thoughts. The pain in my gut immediately subsided and I forced my eyes to look away from the truck and planted them onto Dean.

"Yep," I accentuated the *'pah'*, in the P, while deeply inhaling. "Joel's my uncle."

Dean drew in his bushy eyebrows and gave a, huh? "I didn't know Joel had a niece. I mean, I barely know him but my father has spoken to him a few times before, and he never mentioned anything about having any siblings."

"Well, he has a brother." I said, now fidgeting with my un-pampered nails. I haven't gotten around to doing any pampering with myself since I've gotten here. But my nails are long overdue for a trim.

"Oh, do they talk much?" Dean already assumed the answer to his question, but I guess he wanted me to clarify before he made any assumptions.

I gave him a subtle, "no," before changing the subject so he wouldn't question me more about why I am here. "Where do you like to go to eat?" Not sure why I questioned him about food as I am not really hungry. But it felt like a topic he would enjoy discussing. A smile rose on his face and his eyes lit up. He seemed excited that I had asked him that question, as I figured he would be. "Well that would be *The Sushi Bar.*"

Chapter 27

The next six weeks were a blur in itself. The main topic that happened was that Dean and I had gone on an "official date" and it must have went so well, that now he's been showing up at the diner almost daily to see me, and has made the upstairs telephone ring more than I have ever heard before. I assume we are now an "official couple". I'm still not too sure how to feel about all of this. But I can tell Dean is starting to grow on me. Which does feel good...

Then there was the usual waitress chores and surprisingly, I got to get to know Joel a bit more. He told me how he used to date this woman, Cheryll, for eight years before they decided to break it off because they had a different vision on what their future would've looked like. Now Cheryll is married to a man from the church they used to go to and they had a son two years ago. Joel actually seems happy for her. He said that some people just aren't meant to be together, but that shouldn't change how you view them. I'm glad they both seem happy with their new lives. And I'm glad Joel is finally feeling more comfortable around me to be telling me important stories from his past. Still never caring enough to ask me about my past though. Maybe he could sense I would rather not talk about it? Which is true. How could you start enjoying your new life when you won't stop talking about your old one...

Now it is a special day as it is Cam's birthday! Joel decided to tell the community to come and celebrate his birthday with a surprise party. He told Cam we were going to be closing the diner today to relax and celebrate his special day. Cam thinks we invited him over for dinner and some cake after, but he doesn't know we have decorated the diner with balloons and party streamers that went across the ceiling with some fairy lights that lit the room with a soft glow. Dean and I helped with the meal prep. Making many sorts of finger foods and drinks for the party. People flooded the doors and made themselves comfortable, some seating themselves at a table and others sprang up conversations with one another. Joel of course, handed out alcoholic beverages from behind the bar while I handed out food for the people who were hungry.

When Cam arrived we all shouted, "Surprise!" With glee, as I watched the emotions on his face shifting from frightened, to shocked, and then to happiness all in a matter of seconds. It must be an overwhelming feeling to have so many people love and support you enough to spend their day celebrating with you. Cam radiated nothing but happiness the entire day as he spoke with each person in the room. Then we all sang along to, "Happy birthday to you!" As he blew out his candles and dug into his cake.

I stood in the corner of the room and watched everyone laugh and smile as they all chatted together. It was a warming feeling that felt similar to the day Carl and Jodi clarified my birthday. They sang to me on my first birthday with them when I blew out a single candle that was deep into my flan. I caressed my fingers over the V symbol necklace that had been clasped to my neck since the day I received it as my birthday gift. It's round and dainty but it sparkles as brightly as the stars in the night sky. I caught myself smiling over the fond memories of those special occasions...

"What are you smiling about?" I jumped from the sudden voice that came from beside me. I hadn't realized Dean was standing against the wall next to me. He smiled wide at my sudden wince from fright.

An uncontrollable smile went across my face and I pointed a finger up at him. "You have got to stop sneaking up on me like that." Dean chuckled and took a step forward, wrapping his arms across my shoulders.

"I'm sorry. I promise I won't do it again." He knew his promise was a joke because there *will* be another time. I closed my eyes as we embraced in a hug, shifting from side to side on the balls of our shoes. He moved his mouth closer to my ear and whispered. "Do you want to head upstairs?" Warm air evaporated over my chilly cheek and sent chills slithering down my spine. We pulled away from each other and he smiled wearily as he glanced around the room. "These events could get a little overstimulating for me." He added and he sunk his fists into his pockets.

I narrowed my eyes. "Doesn't your father always have parties going on?" Dean's father owns one of the largest car dealerships in the city. I remember Dean telling me that there is always an event planned down at the dealership and his father would force him to go. I wouldn't think parties would be overwhelming for him, as it seems that there is always one going on for him. But I don't really know too much about him anyway.

Dean nodded. "Sometimes. But I don't always go."

"Ahh," I say as I nod along. "Well, okay then. But I will warn you that I don't exactly have a living room to lounge in." I guided him through the kitchen door and up the staircase.

He cocked his head in confusion. "What do you mean?"

I grin at him from over my shoulder. "I mean that it is more like my bedroom than a living room." Dean doesn't say anything else and he watches me climb the staircase and turn the knob to the apartment door. I stepped to the side to invite him in and closed the door from behind. Dean glanced around the apartment and soon landed his eyes onto the unfoldable mattress from straight ahead. Dean nodded with a grin.

"Ahh, I see what you mean." He sat down at the end of the bed and scrunched up his face. "Not as comfortable as it looks."

"Unfortunately." I sighed, standing behind the kitchen island. I glanced at a cupboard that holds our glasses. "Do you want something to drink?"

Dean took in a deep breath and shook his head. "No, I'm good. It just feels good to have a space to breathe." He chuckled, seeming a bit nervous. But I'm not sure why?

I moved from behind the island and sat down next to him. "If you really wanted space to breathe, then you could have just gone outside."

He nodded, pressing his lips into a thin line. "You're right. I could have." We sat in silence, taking in our surroundings. He took in the apartment, scanning his eyes alongside the dark walls while I scanned him. At his loose button-down that untucked from his pants. His smooth dark hair that was perfectly held in a combover with his straight sides. His jawline was sharp and his nose slanted into a peak at the end. His lips were smooth and plumped unscathed from the frosty breeze. My lips start peeling off the second I step foot outside in the brisk winds. No matter how much chapstick I smear on nothing helps me from the winter weather that started towing in on us. Dean felt my gaze and looked over at me. His eyes were a dark green like the leaves on a tall tree that relished the spring sun. He smiled softly at me as his sharp eyes drifted down my face and stopped at my lips. Dean and I never had our first kiss. It was something I never wanted to rush into. I wanted it to naturally happen when the time feels right. Now at this exact moment, I couldn't tell if it was the right time. But I felt myself slowly lean forward and planted his soft lips onto mine. A weird feeling went through my stomach. A feeling that some would say are butterflies. But really, it was more of a sickening feeling of a ball of nerves... At that moment, I knew we were officially a couple.

Chapter 28

"What's that from?" Dean pointed to my palm as I combed out my frizzy hair with my fingers. We were at The Sushi Bar which I thought was a metaphor for his favorite restaurant but no, it is actually called that. My hair frizzed out of my braid from the treacherous wind outside. I am trying hard to detangle the nest that the rats' tried to make on my head. I was unaware that the scar left on my palm was visible. The cut closed but a faint white scar stayed behind. I quickly closed my palm and gave a weary smile.

"It's nothing, I just cut my palm on a nail from the farm I used to care for." I told Dean some facts about my past that I may have restructured to sound less complicated. At least, in my eyes it seems that way.

"Ouch," Dean gave a pained expression. "That had gotta hurt. Deep too, if it left a scar that large." I just gave a nod while a waitress delivered our sushi bowls. Seaweed with carrots, wasabi, avocados, shrimp, all on a bed of rice. There is an actual sushi bar. All you can eat. But I have been feeling off these past couple of weeks and didn't feel too hungry. So I ordered something premade that was served in a smaller bowl.

Since that night with Dean, our relationship got closer than expected. I didn't feel as weary around him and I haven't felt conflicted about being with him really. I guess that's a good sign. But I will say that his arrogance and comments can be off putting. But it doesn't faze me anymore. I'm far used to it by now. All thanks to my so-called Mother who had said backhanded compliments for my entire existence. But the other little things he says or does are sweet, I guess. Our relationship must be close now that he's taking me to a gathering at his parent's house. He wants me to meet his parents, which I assume is a big deal for us as Joel had made a comment about it being a bit too early. But I'm not completely sure what he means by that. Why is it such a big deal anyway? It's not like I'm going to meet the Queen of England or something. Another metaphor I picked up from Isabelle in the past when her mother would make a comment on what she would wear to church.

"Why does she care what I wear?" Isabelle would say, with a sarcastic tone. "It's not like I'm meeting the Queen of England or something." That was usually her go to moto. I wonder if she ever told her mother what she really wanted for her future?

"Have you decided on what to wear for dinner?" Asked Dean, who had already eaten half of his bowl of rice mix. I looked at him with what I assume is the *deer in headlights look*, and gave a little, "Mhm?" to his question as he had gotten me off guard. Dean narrowed his eyes on me. Probably wondering where my mind had been this entire time. "For dinner with my parents."

I narrowed my eyes on him as well. "I thought it was a gathering. Like a party or something."

Dean nodded before swallowing a spoonful of rice and shrimp. "It is. But it's dinner with my family. My cousins and aunts and uncles are showing up for dinner."

"Oh." I say before finally answering his first question. "Yes, I did. I'm going to wear that navy blue top with some jeans I showed you the other day." Dean had taken me out shopping for some dressier clothing as I mainly just had flannels and jeans in my bag. They were the only things I could fit into my duffel bag before I left. I'm not the dressy type of person anyways.

"Oh." Dean almost looked disappointed. I had only found a navy shirt with fringes around the arms and a v-cut neckline, and Dean had found me a reddish-orange dress that went down to my knees with a flowy skirt and sheer sleeves with also a v-neckline. "I was hoping you could wear that dress I had bought you instead. My mother would like it better on you anyway." Another sly comment that I didn't ask for. I can't blame him though. By the way he dresses daily, I wouldn't doubt his family dresses in over the top dresses and expensive suits for just casual everyday attire. Don't get me wrong, the dress does look great on me but I'm not sure if I feel comfortable wearing it to dinner. I feel more confident in something that gives coverage to my legs like pants do. It almost makes me feel like I went back in time to the days when I had no choice but to wear dresses daily. I don't like the memories they give me. But if Dean prefers me to wear it to his dinner, then I will do it. He wants me to make a good first impression on his mother more than anything else. What harm will it do for just one night? I gave him a simple nod.

"Okay, whatever you want." Dean watched me mush my food around with a fork while I stared down at the table with no thoughts in mind. He placed his spoon down and reached a long hand over the table and grabbed my wrist gently. I gazed up at him and he gave me a small smile.

"Not that the other outfit doesn't look good on you. Because it does. I just want to make a good impression on my mother, " Dean stopped and hesitated, glancing around the room for a choice of words to jump out in front of his face. Then he looked back at me softly, and continued his train of thoughts carefully. "She can be a little bit hard to please. I just, really want her to like you. Alright?" His words sank deep into my brain and a jolt of nervousness flooded my stomach. Now I am more nervous to meet his mother than ever. The idea she might not like me is scarier than it sounds, but I have got to control myself. I'm sure she will like me anyway. God, I sure hope she does. I placed my other hand on top of his and gave a weary smile.

"I know, it's okay." I padded the top of his hand before we continued with our lunch. I had gotten halfway through my sushi bowl before an awful taste of, what I assume is old ocean water, permeated my nose and taste buds. My stomach tossed and turned before a thick sensation came through my stomach, up to my chest and into my throat before my eyes started to water like a waterfall splashing down into a pool of water. Dean glanced up at me and furrowed his brows.

"Are you okay?"

I didn't dare open my mouth or bile would just flood out. So instead I dropped what was in my hands, shook my head, quickly stood up, and raced to the restrooms somewhere in the restaurant. Luckily there was a large sign that read, **Restrooms,** in a bright neon green color. I hurled my body into the door and scanned the room for an open stall, of which there was one open at the end. As soon as I made it inside the thick bile poured out through my mouth and splashed into the toilet. I couldn't count how many times I hurled over the toilet, but it was enough to empty my stomach dry. There goes my breakfast and lunch all in one go. When I was certain that I was done, I wiped my mouth with a piece of toilet paper and flushed the toilet as it was an ugly sight for anyone to see. I walked over to the sink and placed my hands onto the tan countertop, heaving in breaths of air through my mouth. I might not have been taught much about human anatomy, but I surely knew what this meant. I felt it deep into my soul, and I certainly was not prepared for any of it. I knew what was about to come...

Chapter 29

I knew Dean's parents were rich, but not filthy rich! Dean pulled up through the driveway and came across a bricked fencing that went around the large property. Bright red and tan bricks stacked high above from my peripheral. No one can look in and no one can climb over into their property. A metal gate that is shaped into long thorn roses from top to bottom, and a surveillance camera perched on top of a passcode padlock. The camera lens shifts zooming into the car window detecting whoever is inside. The driver's side window was already winded down the second we hit the pebbled passageway to the property line. Dean leaned half out of the window and typed in a short code, making sure that his back blocked the view from the coding pad. Like I would mesmerize the code and break into their house to take whatever catches my eye tonight. I'm not a thief. I wouldn't ever do such a thing. But apparently he doesn't think so. After he pushed in the mysterious code, the rose gate made a loud crusted clanking sound before slowly moving away from the car, inviting us into the Foresters' bundle abode. We rode through the pathway where trees lined around the property. It looked like a forest full of vibrant trees and flowers that were hand planted into the rich soil making it look like a dream that came to life. A dream of a forest of lilies, dandelions, buttercups, and daisies that flourished the pasture with magnolias, oak trees, and copper trees that went on from acres away. Everything was well preserved like a landscaper arrives a couple times a week to keep everything fresh and clean. For how far their pastures go, they probably have several landscapers to keep up with this. As we got closer to the house, a dog jumped out from behind a tree barking at our sudden approach. A border collie with long black and speckled white fur followed the car with loud barks that sounded in alarm.

"That is, Samuel," Dean pointed out to the raging dog. His teeth fanged with fury and his eyes were blackened into his coloring, making him look like a demon summoned from the depths of hell. "He's my mother's favorite son." He gave a slight chuckle that disrupted into a sigh, like her affection for Samuel is insulting to her real son. I peered at the dog from out my window as we slowly drove past him.

"He looks angry." I say, giving Samuel one last glance before returning back to what is in front of me. A long zigzagging stone pathway that went up a little hill and obscured what's ahead.

Dean waved a dismissive hand. "Nah, he's welcoming us." I just nodded to his response, obviously not believing him. I don't think Samuel wants me here. I haven't met him yet and it seems like I'm the least fond person to him right now.

As we drove up the hillside from the top of the peak emerged the sight of the Forrester Manor. And it was in fact a manor. A tall brick mansion that was two stories high with a tall peak from the rooftop above that made it look three stories taller than it was. Probably a large walk-in attic that could be converted into another master bedroom up there. The manor was a dark red with dark auburn bricking with dark brown shutters that decorated the large windows. A thick stone staircase led up to a patio that walked along the front half of the building with a peaked roof to sit under and with five black rocking chairs that stood along the patio in a half circle. White and black Range Rovers parked in a corner next to a building that looked to be another home than a parking garage. The garage door was slid open and revealed two other Range Rovers and a cherry-red Convertible parked in a line on one half of the garage and the other half was stacked high against the walls with large metal tool boxes, a shiny vintage jukebox in the corner, and an oversized flat-screen-tv displayed on a back wall. Carl would have a heart attack if he saw this garage. He would either love it so much that he wouldn't ever want to leave, or he would have hated it and say something along the lines of, "Stupid Richies, always wasting their damn fortune on extreme shit. I can show you what one handheld toolbox can do." But Carl wasn't the mechanical type where he fixes cars for a hobby. I could see Dean's father is the exact type of guy to have that hobby. Dean drove up next to a white Range Rover and put the car in park, soon shutting off the engine. We sat in silence as we both stared at the astonishing manor that Dean gets to live in everyday from the window. I turned to him with widened eyes and a gaping mouth as he looked at me with narrowing eyes like my reaction is a bit strange to him.

"What?" He asked, nonchalantly. He shifted uncomfortably in his seat.

"Your father bought all of this from just owning a dealership?" I asked, glancing around my surroundings.

A grin spread across Dean's lips and he gave a slight chuckle. "You seem surprised."

"Shocked, is more like it." I responded automatically, bringing my lost attention back to him. Dean shook his head, his grin is now a beaming smile.

"No, my father inherited this property and place from my grandfather." Dean explained as he checked his hair in the rear view mirror. He ran his fingers through it to lay down the flyaways from the wind. He went on. "My grandfathers were all mechanical engineers who fixed cars, planes or trains for high end companies for years. My father decided that he wanted to be an engineer for cars as he had always had an eye for them. After years of designing them he went and got his business degree to open his own dealership to sell the cars he designed. Now he just sells cars, but he still fixes some up from time to time as more of a hobby instead."

"One expensive hobby," I thought to myself, but the bellowed laugh that came from Dean was a sign that I had accidentally said it aloud.

Dean nodded, "Expensive, indeed."

We sat in silence just staring at the enchanting mansion in front of us. I could tell Dean isn't too thrilled to be here with me. I think he's worried his family might not like me or the news we are going to slap in their faces, which isn't ideal for meeting your boyfriend's family for the first time. I'm not even sure if they knew Dean was dating anyone. I try to ignore the aching feeling of nervousness in my stomach and take in short but reassuring breaths through my nose and out through my mouth. Dean's long and lanky hand wrapped firmly around mine. He gave a reassuring squeeze and asked me a question I didn't know if what I felt was true.

"Are you ready to head in?" He raised his eyebrows and flicked a smile, unsure about if he himself was ready.

I plastered on a wide smile and nodded. "Of course."

A woman dressed in an apron with her hair tied up into a long black ponytail, led us into the grand foyer. May, was the woman's name. She is their live-in house maid who keeps this palace nice and shiny. All the while, catering guests or whatever else the Forester's need her to do really. Dean taught me the basics of what I will need to remember for tonight. Everyone's names and professions. As much as I know about May is that she has been a housemaid for ten years and she absolutely loves her job. I don't blame her, she gets the weekends off to do whatever she wants while she gets a free-ish palace to live in and food to eat. I would love this job too. Well, except for the endless cleaning. You hate at least one aspect of your job. Her appearance looks to be in her mid-thirties but her mannerisms are telling me much older. She holds herself with a type of maturity and self awareness that radiates around her like an aura. It might actually be her aura, I don't know. I'm not a clairvoyant, so I wouldn't know. The grand foyer was enchanting. The marble floors shined with a glossy finish and the wraparound staircase was large with thick oak carving railings of a forest landscape. Fitting I would say, with a thick dark green rug that trailed up the steps with such cleanliness it looked like it was never used. Coming to think of it, the whole house was spotless like nobody even lives here. May has done a great job with this place. No wonder she's been working here for ten years. May's boots clunked on the marble floors as she walked past a round table from the center of the foyer with fresh flowers of wisterias and... dandelions. The sudden yellow flowers flooded my brain with memories. It made me wonder what am I really here for?

I should be with her... with Bonnie. I should have never left her. I should have stayed or found a way to take her with me. She stayed to distract Mother and the elders. It had worked and it got me further into the woods before being chased by them. But, what if we planned to leave sooner rather than later? Would it have worked? Would Bonnie and I be here right now if we did leave sooner? I would never be in this predicament if we had gotten away together. I'm afraid that I made a grave mistake...

We followed May through the hallway and into the dining room where there was a long table with thick wooden chairs that gathered along the slender length of the table. The table itself had taken up the space in the whole room, only a glass cabinet filled with wine glasses and fresh bottles fit in a nook in the corner, and a large portrait of the mansion itself hung on the back wall in front of me. Only a young woman with long dark brown hair and olive skin sat in one of the chairs with her petite nose in a book. I cocked my head to read the spine, it read *Dracula Bram Stoker*, in bold red lettering. Dean thanked May and held my hand to guide me to the other side of the table from the undisturbed woman. He pulled out a chair for me to sit. I gave him a smile and sat down, taking shallow but controlled breaths to help ease my mind, where a siren blared into my ears to alert me that I shouldn't be here. I should have never agreed to be with Dean. I should leave and never speak to him again. But that is only a temporary thought as I am now stuck with him forever, unfortunately. Dean sat down in a chair beside me and cleared his throat to get the woman's attention. She looked to be around Dean's age. Maybe two years older. Her structured face was similar to Dean's but her darker hair and skin was different than his. Maybe she is a cousin of his? Dean did say his aunts, uncles and cousins will be here tonight for dinner. When the woman raised her head out from her intriguing book, her eyes flashed a piercing emerald green around her pupils. Those same eyes were exactly like Dean's eyes but only a bit brighter and much rounder than his. He mentioned having five cousins, three girls and two boys. Whom must she be then?

"Still have your nose in a book, I see." Dean flashed a playful smile, but she didn't do the same. She seemed rather annoyed by his remark or maybe she's just annoyed by his interruption to her reading. Either way, she doesn't seem too thrilled to be here. I could say the same. She flashed her eyes from me to him and stayed on him. She snickered.

"It's a requirement for class." She closes her book with a sigh and sets it down onto her lap, away from eyesight. "I have to write an essay on it." That's right, Dean has a cousin who's in college to be a literature professor. But what is her name again? Dean turned his upper half towards me.

"Tabitha always has a book in hand." Dean exclaimed, gesturing towards her. He told me she is a huge book nerd. She wanted to go to college for literature but her family told her that if she wants to do something like that, then she will go to be a professor as she won't get a job any other way. Tabitha's parents are both professors at an elite college. They talked her into being one as well. "Ever since she was young." Dean continued, he looked from me to Tabitha and back to me. He bellowed a laugh to himself before speaking, like whatever he was thinking was funny to him. "I remember her carrying around the Llama Llama books when she was three. Don't you remember that, Tabs?" He turned to her. Her lips spread into a sly grin. She nodded.

"Shockingly, I do. I also remember you tearing one of them into tiny little pieces, as well." She bore her eyes into him. I could tell she still holds a grudge for his mischievous behavior that must've happened decades ago. A chuckle escaped from inside me as I silently looked from one to the other.

"What's so funny?" A deep voice came from behind me. It was so sudden that I slightly flinched in my seat. No one seemed to notice me and continued to look at the man that emerged into my viewpoint. He swiftly moved towards the other side of the table to sit down next to Tabitha. He was an older man, looked to be in his mid fifties with graying dark hair and prominent sharp features that stuck out when you glanced over at him. He had high cheekbones and a pointy long nose with a mustache that curved slightly on the ends. Tabitha's sharp features and large eyes resembled his, making it known that he is her father. All I know about him is that he is a professor in, I'm not sure what major, but in something smart I'm sure. He has two daughters and a wife who is Dean's mother's sister. I'm pretty sure most of Dean's aunts and uncles are related to his mother. There will be three aunts and uncles with their children here soon. I wonder where Dean's parents are? The man glanced over at us with a praising smile. Dean responded to his question.

"Nothing much. Just reminiscing about the past, that's all." Dean smirked at Tabitha who gave him a graving look and then glanced over at me. Her look was almost like she was expecting me to say something, but I'm not sure what exactly. Dean got the message and turned back to me. "This is my uncle, Arthur and his daughter, Tabitha." Dean motioned over to them with a flat hand. He moved the hand around my back and rested it beside my right hip bone. "This is my girlfriend, Morgan." He announced. Arthur kept his smile and nodded to me. His gaze trailed off above me and his smile grew wider.

"There you are," Arthur said gleefully. It took me a second to realize that he was speaking to a woman who had just entered the room behind me. She was tall and lean and seemed to be a bit younger than Arthur, but it was obvious that the woman was his wife by the look she gave him. A look of fondness and appreciation for her husband. She had dark brunette hair like Dean and Tabitha but her features were less sharp and more soft. Her overall appearance looked more related to Dean than to her daughter Tabitha, who has taken over her father's appearance more. She had her hair pulled up in a twisted low bun and her lips pigmented red as brightly as cherries. We exchanged glances and smiles, then she turned to Dean to ask him how college search is going. Dean hadn't told me anything about going to college and what for. I guess we never got to that subject yet. I listen intently to Dean's response.

"I'm still searching." Is all Dean says, clearly not wanting to talk about it anymore. That's probably why we never spoke about it, he doesn't want to either. "Not that it matters much anyway. *You know who* doesn't agree with my choices."

The woman shook her head disapprovingly. "Don't say that. Your father is happy that you want to take over his business. Why wouldn't he be?"

Dean sighed. "Because he would rather me go to be an engineer like his father had. He doesn't want me to take over his business."

"Why wouldn't he?" Tabitha interjected, confused. "Wouldn't most fathers want their sons to?"

Dean shrugged, propping his elbows on the table. His body tenses as he looks around at us. "Because he's controlling. He doesn't think I have what it takes for the company. He's probably worried that I'm going to change so much that he doesn't want me to."

Arthur shook his head as he rolled his eyes. Arthur seems to disapprove of Dean's father. I wonder if they get along with him or if they resent each other? "Dean, if you think you could change the business for the better, then do it. He will regret not keeping his company with his bloodline in the future."

Dean nodded. "I do think that. I'm not going to change my mind because of him." Dean sounds so sure about what he wants whether his family agrees with him or not. Ambitious and stubborn, two of the few things I like about Dean. Maybe less on stubbornness and more on ambition, though. Dean's aunt interjects.

"Either way, I could put in a good word for you at our school, if you'll like."

Dean nods to her and gives her an appreciative smile. "Thanks, Aunt Ophelia."

Ophelia nodded and as their conversation broke down, people started flooding into the room behind me. They all silently took their seats and waited for the dinner to start. I glance around at all of them, suddenly feeling like the black swan in a room of white swans. I decided to keep my gaze down and my mouth shut for the rest of the evening. Wanting no attention attracted to me.

As we ate together, lemon salmon and herbed rice with a side of coke soda as the older adults drank a deep red wine with silence filling the air. The wine almost looked like blood that was freshly poured from someone's body. The Dracula book that Tabitha was reading earlier flashed into my mind. I wouldn't doubt if they are all secretly vampires. Only vampires live in castles with maids and a chef. I don't believe in that fantasy stuff, but these people are making me think otherwise. Dean's parents sat silently at the end of the table. His mother Meredith and father Spencer, glanced at the people that shoveled their mouths full of salmon and rice. Meredith has smooth porcelain skin that makes her look years younger than she really is. A vampire. Only vampires don't age. Her hair was down to her waist and shined an auburn haze in the light. Her facial features matched Deans, including her eyeshade. While Spencer on the other hand looked foreign and out of place. He had deep-set wrinkles that went along his forehead and around his eyes, which only made him look older than he actually was. I don't think he is a vampire. Maybe it's only on Meredith's side. Her sisters all looked ageless sitting next to their graying husbands. Spencer has all gray hair, short on the sides but slicked back on top just like Dean's. His eyes glistened a shade of blue when the light caught them at the right angle. He sat down with his fork next to his plate and turned to face his son, suddenly striking up a conversation. Unfortunately, the conversation was about me.

"So Dean, why don't you introduce us to that lovely lady next to you." Spencer smiled, gesturing toward me. So much for keeping attention off of me. It only lasted halfway through our dinner.

Dean swallowed food in his mouth with a gulp and turned to face me. "Everybody, this is my girlfriend Morgan. Morgan, this is everybody."

I didn't know what to do, so I just gave a forced smile and continued with my meal, praying that the conversation would move forward to someone else. My prayer wasn't answered.

"So Morgan," Spencer started, cocking his head at me. "Are you planning on going to school for anything?"

I just shook my head as to not knowing what to say. School was never in my mind. Surviving from a cult who wants to crucify me has taken up most of my brain power lately. Lately, as in for five years. School was never an option for me and it never will be. "Umm, no." I finally say. All eyes are on me now and I absolutely hate it. "I never put much thought into it."

"How couldn't you?" A man with scraggly red hair eyed me from across the table. Bertram was his name. He's married to Meredith's second sister Francine. There was no denying that Francine was her sister. She looked almost identical to both of her sisters. The only feature that looked different from her sisters was her pointy nose that curved in on the tip. She is beautiful, there's no denying that, but the man that wore a matching wedding band to her ring was not. She is clearly way out of his league. His eyes were far too close together and they slanted down in the corner of his eyelids. His mouth was always in a slight frown and his eyebrows furrowed as he looked around at the people in the room. I could see most of the appeal to his appearance but only when he sits by himself. Next to her, all of his bad features came out. Definitely not a vampire either. Like I said, just Meredith's side...

Francine elbowed Bertram in the arm and gave him a scolding look. "Don't say that." Bertram looked at her and then to me and once again, furrowed his brows.

"But how couldn't she? Why wouldn't she want a career?"

Meredith cleared her throat. Salmon stabbed on the end of her fork, hovering over her lips as she spoke. "Why would she need a career when she has my son." She shoves the fork into her mouth and chews rather hard for a meat that is naturally tender. Her eyes were sharp as she glared at me, shooting daggers into mine. I haven't even spoken a word to her yet and she already hates me. So much for wearing this hideous dress that Dean insisted she would like. I'm not sure what she completely meant by her remark but I ignored her gaze and opened my mouth ready to defend myself, somehow.

"I-"

"You do have a high school diploma right?" Bertram interrupted and his pale eyes staring eagerly at me. I could feel my cheeks burning and my heart started to pound into my chest. Bertram sat back into his seat and somehow narrowed his eyes more than they naturally were. "Did you ever complete high school?" Who does he think he is, detective Bertram? Last time I checked he was a citywide architect. They don't interrogate complete strangers. I froze in my seat, not knowing what to say as their eager eyes examined me for a response. Unless the hellish teaching that Reverend Finch made us learn for years counts as school? Then no. I have never been to school before. Let alone graduating from school. I wonder what I really am going to do in my life? I have no reputation or a high school diploma. I don't even know what you learn in real school. The only choice I do have is to marry someone who can go to college. But, is that what I really want? A marriage? As if Dean could read my mind he turned the attention away from me by asking one of his cousins how football season is going. His one cousin Dagwood plays football for his high school team. He's been traveling around cities to play against other football teams. So far his team has won every game... Meanwhile I just stared down at my half eaten salmon and rice. My appetite suddenly vanished from the embarrassment I now feel from Dean's family. I want nothing more than to stand up and leave. To never talk to Dean and his family again. But the only thing keeping me here is the fetus that is living inside of me that is forever going to be a part of his family.

Chapter 30

I gather the girls' things while counting each belongings. Two backpacks full of two lunchboxes, two tin tumblers with two bendy straws peeking out of the top of the lid which of course are both the same shade of periwinkle to keep from arguing about wanting the same color bottle, two granola bars for the ride there, and one stuffed monkey for little miss Merritt. Whom she sat by the front door, taking her good ol' time tugging on her rainbow printed rain boots. Vivian's feet thudded on the floorboards upstairs as she raced against the clock. Daylight savings time was Sunday morning in which we forgot to set the clocks an hour ahead, making us an hour late for school the next day. Sundays are family dinner days with Dean's parents. Sundays are also my dreaded days. So daylight savings time was not on my mind.

I helped Merritt with her backpack straps and handed her, her tumbler with a wrapped granola bar balancing on top of the lid and her stuffed monkey Charlotte, which always comes along the rides to school every morning. I finally got Merritt to leave Charlotte with me when she goes to school. Finally breaking the attachment barrier with her and her damn monkey. It's like a security blanket that Vivian used to have. She took it everywhere we went. To the grocery store, to school, to family dinners, and even to the park. The amount of times I had to rewash her purple flowered blanket is too many times to even keep count. But on Vivian's seventh birthday, she suddenly didn't want anything to do with her blanket. She packed it away along with her baby clothes and old keepsake toys that are now up in the musty attic. Left there alone in the dark for who knows how long. But Merritt still takes Charlotte everywhere she goes, just not into school. Not after Charlotte went missing in the school a month ago. Merritt had me and her teacher searching everywhere for that goddamn monkey for over an hour. We weren't allowed to leave, to try again tomorrow until we safely secured Charlotte back into her arms where she carried it around her elbow for the rest of the day. After that mishap, I sat down and had a long talk with Merritt about leaving Charlotte safely with me until she gets back from school. There were tears, of course. It must be hard for a five year old to give up her security monkey for just a few hours a day. To get Merritt to agree with me, all I had to do was make it sound like it was all her idea. Not mine. If she remotely felt like it *was my idea* then she would refuse to leave Charlotte and continue to carry her into school everyday for the rest of her life. God, I hope she doesn't carry around that damn monkey for the rest of her life...

Vivian's mismatched-sock feet padded down the staircase in a hurry. Her feet slipped across the wooden flooring like Bambi walking on ice. I chuckled as I watched her dash around the house, doing who knows what an eight-year-old needs to be doing before school? Especially, since I'm holding everything she needs for school in my two hands. She disappeared in the mudroom beside the kitchen doorway. After a minute of silence from her way, I called out to her.

"Hurry up, Vivian!" I said louder than expected. I tuned my tone down a bit, taking deep breaths to soothe my patience that's slowly dwindling as the clock keeps ticking. "We have got to go."

"In a minute!" Vivian shouts back with heaving breaths. Probably tired from the amount of running she has done in a little over an hour. I glanced over to the grandfather clock that stood against the dining room wall. It now strikes nine-thirty. I let out a heavy sigh and looked down at Merritt who was standing patiently by the front door with her cup held tightly tucked under one arm and her monkey drooping over her second arm. Her emerald green eyes flicked up to mine and her smile was as warm as sunshine peeking through the clouds on a dreary day. Her eyes resemble Meredith's, Dean's mother. Her whole appearance resembles her really. She has her soft facial features and her long auburn hair that went halfway down her spine. Meredith's genes are strong with Merritt being her mini me and all. That's probably why I chose to name her Merritt, because even since a newborn she resembled Meredith the most. But Vivian resembles more of me. She has my high cheekbones but soft round face, my river blue eyes and small lips, and my frizzy blonde hair that can only grow to the small of my back. But each child resembles Dean and I perfectly. They were a match made in heaven. I was not expecting to have Merritt at all. She was our surprise baby.

Dean and I were considering *possibly* having another baby when Vivian was one. But only later on. Then Vivian started *the terrible twos*, which changed our plans on expecting a second baby entirely. When I finally became content with only raising one child, Merritt decided it was her time to shine, and when I found out I was pregnant I was filled with nothing but joyful tears. I didn't expect to be so excited for a second baby but I so deeply was. Dean on the other hand wasn't too thrilled about the news. I could tell Vivian was enough for him to handle. I figured that all he needed was time. And time was all it took. When

Merritt started to move and kick from inside of me that made it feel real for the both of us. That she was real. The same feeling we had with Vivian. And since then Dean has been filled with excitement every day. Now that the girls' are older Dean has been working more hours and he's rarely home. The baby and toddler faze was more of his thing. It was mine too, but it always has been. Now he's a little more distant with the girls but he always tries to make an effort to always support them in school projects and even at home. Either way, two kids weren't planned but I wouldn't change it for the world...

I gave Merritt an annoyed expression for Vivian taking what felt like eternity to leave the house. We both giggled and turned towards the front door. I unlocked it and swung it open, holding the screen door open for Merritt to walk out of and towards the black and white Range Rover that was parked in front of the, *too small to park a car in the garage,* where only Dean's lawn mower and outdoor essentials are in. The Range Rover was a pregnancy gift from Dean's parents. They said that we would need a bigger car before the baby arrives but I truly believe that she didn't want us to look poorly for her family's reputation. The dealership owner's son is driving around an old three-seater truck with his wife and daughter in it. They would look better in a brand new Range Rover. *Richer*, I should say. But why should I be complaining? It's a *brand new car.* And as much as I hate to say that Meredith was right, we did need a bigger car. Especially now than before. Besides the car is the only thing she gifted me or the girls. She doesn't give much presents to them because she says that she doesn't want to spoil them too much. It's totally not because she doesn't like the woman who birthed them...

I turned my head to shout over my shoulder. "Well, I'll be in the car! So, hurry up." But as the words carried through the air Vivian hopped out of the mudroom on one foot as she tugged on her floral printed boots with one hand and carried the other boot with the other.

"Hold on," she said irritably, tugging the ball of her heel into a boot. "I couldn't find my other matching boots." I looked down at her one striped sock on one foot and the polka-dotted sock on the other. I chuckled.

"Couldn't find matching socks either?" Vivian stopped and glanced down at her feet, like she just now noticed her mis-matching pair of socks. She rolled her eyes before tugging on her other boot. I handed her her belongings and she finally marched out of the door. It only took twenty-minutes to leave but as I stepped out into the spring mist and locked the door with my spare key that jingled on a chain of others, I let out a restraining sigh before heading to the car...

When we arrived at school, Vivian unbuckled her seatbelt and climbed out of the car. She grunted when I wished her a good day at school while rolling her eyes and slamming the door shut behind her. I promise she loves me. She's just not a morning person, never has been. Even as a baby I had to wake her up for a feeding and a change of nappy because if I didn't, then she would stay asleep for hours. Merritt on the other hand is completely opposite. She prefers to wake bright and early rather than sleep-in in the mornings. That is why she was standing by the door waiting on Vivian. Merritt's school is down the block from Vivian's. I watched as Vivian waved to us behind her and entered the tall brick building. When I'm sure she's safe, I put the car in drive and drove off down the block. There's no cars waiting in front of the schools because the children are already in school. It is now ten o'clock and school had started a little over an hour ago. But hey, better late than never, right? As I drove I glanced up at the rearview mirror. Merritt munched on her chocolate chip granola bar while looking out the window from in her booster seat. Next to her was Charlotte the monkey, strapped into the middle seat. I glared at that damn monkey from the mirror with disdain. I know it's just a stuffed monkey but I can feel its eyes burning into mine. That monkey has brought on so many tantrums since the day Merritt received it from no one other than Meredith. Charlotte loves to play hide and never come back out. Once she goes missing, she might as well be lost forever. But she somehow manages to be found after hours or even weeks without any trace of where she was originally hiding. The amount of sleepless nights because of that damn monkey has built up so much resentment that will never break down. I hate that thing with a passion...

When I'm in front of Merritt's school, I put the car in park and watch as she unbuckles her seatbelt, places the empty granola wrapper on Charlotte's seat and climbs out of the car. She heaves her heavy backpack onto her shoulders and turns to face me.

"Take care of Charlotte for me. Okay?" Her *okay* was a tiny plea for me to not let Charlotte out of my site. Even when I'm childless for a few hours, there is always someone for me to look after. *Something* is more accurate for that thing. It is only a thing with a person's name. I nod with a smile.

"Okay, I promise." When Merritt was sure I would keep my word, she gave me a small smile and shut the door. I watched as she ran towards her school doors, trampling up the steps and soon disappearing into the building. Leaving me *and* Charlotte alone in nothing but silence.

As I drove back home after stopping at the grocery store to pick up ingredients for dinners for the busy week. I like to keep quick and easy recipes in a notebook inside one of the kitchen drawers for simple dinners that I can get done in a hurry if I had to. Simple dinners are my go to for the week, mainly out of boredom. I hate cooking. I prefer serving them rather than making the meal itself. That simple thought brought back short memories from when I worked for Joel as a waitress. I quit after I moved in with Dean shortly after our marriage was finalized. Dean worked two jobs while in college for business to support his newly wife and daughter. I couldn't work at the time as I didn't have anyone to watch Vivian for a few hours a day. Dean also didn't like the idea of his wife working to help pay for the mortgage. He grew up "old fashioned" where the husband provides for his family financially and the wife takes care of the household and children. As I don't have any true school experience nor a diploma, I couldn't help with the money anyway. As much as I would have liked to go to college like Dean did, I surely wouldn't pass as I don't even know basic skills for school anyway. When I told Joel about my pregnancy he didn't have any sort of reaction really. He never mentioned it or asked any questions, not until Dean and I sat down with his parents and Joel, that's when he seemed interested. When Dean's parents told us that we should marry before the baby arrives because that's the old way of things. The way that Joel's parents did when they were expecting Carl. So it wasn't a surprise when he agreed with Dean's parents, and I didn't have any life plans in mind, I agreed as well. I'm not sure if I ever regretted my decision. Maybe once or twice but now that life has gone on, I feel content with the little family that Dean and I created. I almost rarely get second thoughts anymore. Almost...

I take my keys out of the ignition and hop out of the car. I opened the backseat where I stacked my grocery bags down on the floor. As I hooked the bags around my left arm I glanced at the monkey that was still buckled safely in its seat. I watched with amusement as I slammed the door in its face, shortly before locking the car with two short *beep beeps.* Charlotte will be safer staying buckled to her seat. She can't disappear from me if she's locked inside and has never been touched since Merritt strapped her in. I am not risking losing that damn monkey again. If I had, Merritt would simply hate me. It will have to do until I have to pick her up from school in the afternoon.

I trudge to the bright red front door to my three bedroom house. The house is small with little space for a kitchen, dining room, living room, bathroom, and three bedrooms that were separated from the girls' bedroom upstairs and Dean's and my room downstairs on the right. It was cheap, which was great for newlyweds expecting a child. It's small but cozy in almost a cottage house kind of way. It's deserted on the end of a dead end street where the neighbors are two blocks up from ours. I never met them but I do know that most of the neighborhood is filled with retired people who are older than Carl and Jodi. It's nice in a way because none of them cares enough to walk down to our house to get to know us. I like not having to fake a friendship that I know will never last. Nothing lasts forever. I would know.

I unlocked the door and heave the groceries in and collapsed my arms on the kitchen floor. The tendons in my arms relaxed with a burning sensation that lasted for a few moments before dissipating and making them feel like jelly. I haven't done hard labor other than hauling a basket filled to the brim with dirty laundry around the house or carrying a few pound babies around my hip for years. I'm not in shape anymore for manual labor. Just thinking about working on Carl's farm like I had eight years ago, makes my body ache in pain. I flick on the flat screen tv that hung up against the living room wall and left on whatever station was playing as I unloaded the groceries away into the refrigerator and cupboards. I don't really watch the tv, I just use it as background noise while I work around the house. Sometimes the silence of an empty house can be too consuming for me to enjoy. The quieter the place around me is, the louder my thoughts get. The local news station played wordlessly behind me. I only grasped a few words that the anchors were saying but not much to raise awareness of anything. Not until the familiar names ran through my eardrums and soon registered in my brain. I stood up straight and watched the news anchors speak.

"Tragic news has emerged about a local couple who lost their lives due to a gas leak that occurred one fateful night." The woman had a somber expression, her eyes flickering down as she continued on. "Carl and Jodi Granger were found deceased in their beds, and authorities have indicated that the gas stove downstairs had not been fully turned off, leading to the accumulation of harmful fumes through their home. This incident serves as a poignant reminder of the importance of safety precautions when using gas appliances." The channel soon switched to the weather station. I stood there in a daze. In disbelief of what I had just heard. My ears started to squeal a high pitched ringing that wouldn't subside. I took a step forward to balance myself when my boot crunched something hard from under my soles. I looked down to see a carton of eggs faced down onto the floor. The yellow yolk separated from out of the broken shell and slithered across my floor. I hadn't noticed that I dropped the carton of eggs during the news report. I couldn't wrap my head around the giant mess I had just made. This can not be happening. There has to be a mistake. Jodi wouldn't be too stupid to leave the stove on when she does nothing but cook off of it everyday. She wouldn't have forgotten about it. No, there has to be another explanation. There just has to be. And as my mind raced and my ears felt like they were going to bleed, I pivoted on the ball of my feet and marched out of the house. My right shoe slightly slipped across the floor from the oily yolk that is now tracked through my clean house. I slammed the front door shut and hopped into my car, soon racing down the street like my life depended on it.

* * *

I trudged through the diner and into the steamy kitchen. My face immediately sweltered from the heat that arose in the air. Cam looked at my sudden appearance with widened eyes. He hasn't seen me in over five years when my life became too chaotic to visit him. He looks the same with just a few wrinkles around his eyes but not much to notice. I didn't greet him as I didn't have time. I didn't want to have time. I marched up the staircase to the apartment I once lived in. As I approached the door I pounded my fist three times on the splintered wood. I heard sudden movements from inside and a slight mumble came through. Then the door opened and emerged Joel who had looked like he had taken a beating to the face. His eyes were sunken in and tinted a shade of red in the whites of them. His pupils are dilated and they searched me for any indication that I knew what was going on. His cheeks sheened redness and his lips were pale and swollen. He clenched his phone in his fist and his shoulders were tense with rage. Even though his body looked angry, I could see the pain in his face. I stepped inside and unknowingly wrapped my arms around his chest and held him tightly. His shoulders slacked as he let out a heavy sigh shortly before weeping into my shoulder.

Later I sat down beside Joel at his kitchen table as we sipped our freshly brewed tea. Joel narrowed his eyes down at his mug that had a small child's handprint stamped in blue on a white surface. The back of the mug said, **Best Uncle Ever!** In splotchy lettering. Vivian had made it for him for his birthday one year. She has always referred to him as her Uncle Joel. I never minded it, neither has he. It makes them feel close in a way that I always loved to see. Joel usually comes to visit twice every two weeks but not lately as he has been busier than ever with the diner. People randomly started moving to the city one year which made his diner a hotspot for guests to come and enjoy some freshly cooked meals. I'm glad to see his diner is thriving more than it was eight years ago. He deserves it... losing his brother on the other side, he does not deserve that. Even though they weren't close, I could tell how much his brother's death had made an impact on him, and in such a short time. No matter how often they spoke, he had still lost his family. His only family that is. But he hasn't lost us, and I will always make sure that he doesn't....

Joel sighed and opened his mouth, preparing to tell me something. "I had just scheduled their funeral for this Thursday at the church they attend at." He said matter-of-factly. I just silently nodded as he went on. "I figured their friends from there would like to attend their funeral as well. I'm going to head down there Wednesday afternoon and spend a few days in a motel to get everything with the farm and house figured out." He looked to me for acceptance, but I'm not his mother. I can't force him not to go, not that I wouldn't want him to go anyway. He needs to go for closure. I get it, he needs to figure out what to do with the farm that has been in his family for generations. I'm not sure what he's going to decide to do with it. I'm not sure if he knows either. He probably thought it would be decades before death would happen for his family. I thought so too... I felt his gaze on me and I looked up from the table and into his foreign eyes. They were swollen and wet from the tears he just shed. Mine probably don't look any different. I tugged a wavering smile to appear on my face and nodded.

"I think that's a good idea."

He could read my face and he knew what else I was thinking. "I would have loved for you to come with me, but I'm not too sure if it would be the smartest decision. With the cult and all. Which I highly doubt they're a problem anymore." That word, *cult,* is still something I'm not used to hearing from people. I agree with them, but it's still strange to hear what others used to think about the people I was raised by. It almost sounds and feels fake to me. I push past the word and place a cradled hand over his.

"I know, and I'm okay with you going without me. I mean, they don't know about you. I think you will be safe." The words, *you will be safe,* shot out of my mouth before I could register it from my brain. Joel narrowed his eyes on me.

"I will be safe." He says almost in a matter of minutes. "What do you mean by that?" I closed my eyes and inhaled a deep breath before sitting back further into my chair. "You don't think they have something to do with this, do you?" I looked down at the table and slowly nodded my head. Joel leaned back into his chair with his eyebrows furrowed.

"I mean," I start, biting at my bottom lip. "They might have? It just seems strange to me that the report is saying that Jodi left the stove on and that's how there was a gas leak." I looked at Joel whose face was hard and stern as he bit at the inside of his cheek. "Jodi wouldn't do something like that. I know she wouldn't. She would check the stove several times a day to make sure it was off. She's paranoid about things like that, Joel." I shake my head. "It just doesn't make any sense."

Joel pondered on my words. I could see them twisting around in his brain like a corkscrew. He relaxed his facial muscles and turned his upper half towards me. "So, you think that the cult killed them by breaking into their house in the middle of the night, and by turning their stove on? But why?"

I shrugged, not really knowing the answer to his question. "Maybe they knew I left? Maybe to try and bring me back?"

Joel raised a thick brow. "Do you truly believe that after all these years, they are still trying to find you?"

I pondered on that question for a moment. I *know* they are. I know them and I know that they wouldn't let anyone get away. I was the one who got away and now they want me back. I nodded my head. "I do *truly believe* that they are. They found me after five years of searching. Why couldn't they find me now?"

Joel wiped his face with a long hand and sighed. His eyes searched the room for answers, somehow. "But why? Why-" I placed my hand flat down on the table to get his attention. He looked at me, his glossy eyes sparkling in the lighting above. So full of wonder and sorrow.

"Because I was the one who got away. They will come for me. It's only a matter of time before they do."

Merritt climbed into her booster seat and looked beside her. Her face lit up with joy and a bright smile when she saw Charlotte sitting buckled into her seat. Just where she had left her. Merritt's school ends thirty minutes before Vivian's school. We only have two options. We go walking around to the nearest store until then or we sit and wait in the school's parking lot and listen to the radio. I feel mentally and physically drained from the morning I had. I'm not up to walking and pretending to be normal around a crowd of strangers. I force a smile to appear on my face as I look at Merritt from over my shoulder. I decide to act like nothing's wrong. The girls' don't know anything about Carl and Jodi and neither does Dean. I never mentioned them because I never had too. It's also a way to move on with my life rather than remembering them through words that will forever be in the air, and I will never be able to take them back. Now I will never mention them ever. It was easier to remember them as alive and well. But now all of my memories have changed. I will now remember them as the News Anchor had reported them five hours ago.

"Buckle up, Merritt." I tell her with a hoarse voice, probably from the amount of crying I did this morning. I haven't cried like that ever. I turn back to the wheel and wait to hear that *click* from the seat belt locking into place before driving up the road and pulling into an empty parking spot in front of the school doors. A few parents were seated inside their cars in a row, some bobbing their heads on the radio and others chatting with their younger children in the back seat. I watched Merritt through the front mirror as she unbuckled Charlotte and held her tightly in her arms. We silently listened to whatever song was playing on the radio for what felt like an eternity, when really it was only twenty-eight minutes. Children with their large backpacks hanging floppy from behind them started flooding out of the school doors. Each child ran to their parents' car with eagerness to leave school for the day. I spotted

Vivian walking out the doors with two girls beside her. She talked to them as they walked towards the parking lot and stopped before waving goodbye to each other. Vivian never talks about her friends from school. So I wouldn't know any of their names or who their parents are. She can be private about some things and chatty about other things. It really just depends on her mood for the day. She marched towards the car and swung open the backseat door. She tossed her backpack onto the floor and climbed in. She sighed before turning to me.

"There's a parent- teacher conference tomorrow evening that you and Dad have to attend too." Vivian informed me as she buckled her seat belt. "My teacher says so." Vivian's teacher is the typical snobby, rude teacher who acts like she hates her job. Vivian said that she can be really nice to her students but she can get stern with a few that act up in class. It also just depends on her mood for the day. A parent-teacher conference is basically just meeting up with the teachers to talk about how well your child is doing in school and whether they need a tutor for more one-on-one teaching. Vivian's teachers always say the same things about her. That she's really smart and a fast learner, and there is no worries on if she's failing or not. Which is great but it always ends up to be a waste of time. We mainly just stand around and talk to other parents and plan what the next school fundraiser or class party will be. I never give my input because I don't want to participate with the fundraisers or class parties, but I always somehow get dragged into them anyway. I usually get stuck with paying for all of the desserts or decorations, but they do make Vivian happy to have something fun to do for school instead of just the same ol' boring classes. So I guess I will continue to participate in them no matter how much I and my wallet hate them. Vivian raised an eyebrow at me, waiting for my response. I just smiled and nodded. "Okay, I will be sure to tell your father later." I say shortly before backing out of the parking lot and heading back home.

When we arrived home I forgot about the mess I made in the kitchen when I entered through the front door. The groceries are still in bags and egg yolk smeared across the floor as the carton lies open down onto the floor. Vivian walked over to the mess and slowly turned to me with a puzzled expression on her face. I waved a dismissive hand at the girls' and told them to put their bags upstairs while I cleaned up the kitchen. They didn't pry for answers and gladly did as they were told. After the kitchen was cleaned up, I started on dinner. Garlic chicken with a baked potato and a salad on the side. It's simple but a delicious meal for dinner. As I dished out the food onto plates, Dean came walking in through the mudroom's door. He had a newspaper in hand as he silently took a seat in his usual spot on the end of the dining table. He unfolded the paper and began reading without saying a single word to me. That's how he usually comes home. Walks in without saying "Hello" or asking how my day has been, and just sits down to read the newspaper as he waits for dinner to be served. The house feels more empty when he's in it. Not like it used to feel a few years back. He would come home with a huge smile on his face, happy to see me and Vivian as she ran into his arms for a hug. He would wrap his arms around my stomach from behind and would softly kiss my cheek and ask me how my day went. I would ask him the same question and we would strike up a conversation during dinner. Now it's just dead silence with only the padded footsteps from upstairs when the girls' prepare to come down for dinner. I looked at Dean waiting for him to glance up from his paper but he never did. I sighed before setting down his plate in front of him.

"There's a parent-teacher conference tomorrow evening at Vivian's school." I informed him as his eyes trailed along the fine print on the white sheet of paper. I continued after there was no response from him. "You have to be there. So don't plan to work late tomorrow. Alright?"

Dean tends to "accidentally" work later than usual when we made plans the day before. He would always say that it was a coincidence or wrong timing for something to come up at work. I think he just lies so he won't have to attend to the plans because he simply doesn't want to. But I make sure the word gets around.

Dean mumbled. "Mhmm. I always go to those meetings." His gaze stayed on the newspaper and never flicked upward to give me a confirming look. I continued to set the table and call down the girls' for dinner. The rest of the evening was quiet as I made sure that the girls' did their homework and got ready for bed. I brushed out the girls' damp hair when they climbed out of the bath. Just like my mother always did for us girls every night before bed. I pecked them goodnight on their cheeks and tucked them cozily into their blankets before retreating to my bedroom to get myself ready for bed. Dean was already asleep when I changed into pajamas and washed my face, soon tucking myself under the covers and stared up at the dimly lit ceiling. My mind raced around in circles and before I could comprehend what went on today, I slowly drifted away into a deep sleep.

Chapter 31

Tuesday morning was the same as yesterday. Get the girls to school, come back home to clean and do the endless pile of laundry that seems to take hours to complete, and head back out to pick up the girls from school. I prepared dinner and as I had told Dean yesterday evening, he arrived back home on time and helped me get the girls ready to take them to their grandparents house for an hour to go to the school conference this evening. Meredith had graciously agreed to watching the girls for an hour, but only if we *will* be gone for an hour. Any longer than that and I would be messing up her evening routine. I didn't even know she had an evening routine, but alright. I promised her that it won't take long and we will probably be getting the girls out of her hair faster than an hour anyway. Now we stood in the corner of the green and blue classroom as we silently waited for the other parents to arrive for the meeting. We were the first ones to arrive and now we get the punishment of waiting until the room fills up with eager parents to get this meeting over with. Dean excused himself from me to head towards the bathrooms, leaving me to wait alone. As Ms. Springfield, Vivian's teacher, strode into the room with a clipboard in hand, the room fell silent and waited for her to excuse one of us parents to come speak with her alone. She looked up from her clipboard at me and inhaled a deep breath.

"Mrs. Forester, since you were here first I will speak with you now." She led me out of the classroom and into the hall. Her long black ponytail swayed side to side as she took clunky steps in her heels. She's older than me but not by much. Her sunken eyes were her most prominent feature of her face other than her plump cherry lips that she smacked every time she began to speak. I glanced around the hallway for any sight of Dean, but it was just an empty space with no one other than me and her to fill it. As if she read my mind she turned to me with a raised brow. "Will Mr. Forester be attending this meeting?" She asked with a sharp tone of disapproval that he wasn't by my side. I almost wanted to agree with her disapproval but I knew that Dean was in the bathroom and not at work.

I nodded. "Yes, he's using the restroom. I'm sure he will be joining shortly."

Ms. Springfield eyed me from head to toe before nodding and turning back to an open door in the hallway. She led me inside to a brightly painted room with yellow walling and white popcorn ceiling. She gestured for me to sit in one of the chairs in front of her desk as she lowered herself into a chair behind it with a huff. "I would like to speak about how Vivian is doing in class." She began adjusting papers on her clipboard with pursed lips. She eyed a paper and looked at me with what I thought was a courtesy smile, but the corners of her mouth stayed tightly in a frown. "As I tell you every year, Vivian is doing great in class. She is polite and well mannered. She has all high grades and she is clearly very intelligent for her age." She stopped and I almost wanted to ask her why I am here then? If she tells me the same thing every year, then why is it important for me to waste my time being here? But then the one word I wished not to hear, spoke out of her mouth. "But, she does seem a bit distracted by a feeling that she gets from home."

I lightly shake my head. "What do you mean? What is she feeling?"

Ms. Springfield folded her hands together and swallowed before smacking her lips open to speak. "I asked her what is going on at home and she said that it wasn't anything going on exactly, it was just she is worried that you and Mr. Forester are going to get a divorce."

I practically flinch at her sudden words. Why would she think of that? Has she noticed anything different with Dean and I? I pondered on her words before it suddenly hit me like a semi truck going ninety miles down a hill and plummeting into my Range Rover from the side. Fast and fiercely. Oh my god. She knows. How could she know though? Dean doesn't even know that I know what he's been up to. How in the hell would Vivian know?

Ms. Springfield narrowed her eyes on me. "Has there been issues going on between you and Mr. Forester?" I forced my gaze back to her as she tapped a pointy, polished nail on the clipboard waiting for my response. As if it is any of her damn business anyway. I clamped my mouth shut and inhaled shallow but calming breaths in through my nostrils. I plastered a fake smile and shook my head.

"Of course not. There hasn't been any issues between us two." I lie through my gritted teeth. "I'm not too sure why Vivian would be worried about that? Dean and I are doing great." We are far from great. We are as deep as the Pacific Ocean could go. In a pit of darkness in drowning water with not enough air in your lungs to reach the top in time. We are insufferable around each other. A *"normal couple"* would be getting a divorce. The wife wouldn't be keeping dark secrets from her husband and family, and the husband wouldn't be lying about work so he wouldn't have to be at home. If there was any other choice for me, I would indefinitely leave him and take my daughters with me. But I have no source of income. I have no career. I wouldn't make it out in the world on my own. I never could have made it if it weren't for the people who took me in and cared for me so I wouldn't be alone. They helped me survive and get me to where I am in life. But they also kept me from learning how to be independent and to not rely solely upon others to make decisions for me, and to simply live in this world on my own. I'm grateful for what I have, and I'm not grateful for what I need. I need Dean more than anything, and that makes me hate myself more than I already do. But I continue to think about how much the girls' need him in their life. Even though he's rarely been seen around them. They still need him the same way as I do. I will continue to lie for him, but it won't be for me. It will be for them. My girls...

Ms. Springfield continued to falter her gaze on me. She knows I'm lying, but it isn't any of her business as to why I am. "Well, for whatever reason she is feeling the way she is. I would try to reassure her that her feelings are valid but incorrect. You don't want her emotions disrupting her grades before the end of the year, do you?" Her dark eyes drilled into mine like an auger drilling deep into the earth's soil. I could feel the slight vibration and the sound of the auger boring into the ground from under me. I kept my smile on my face and narrowed my eyes.

"Of course not." I say, slowly enough for her to grasp onto my unappreciative tone of voice. "I will get this situated by tonight."

Ms. Springfield for once smiled fully at me but her eyes stayed narrowed and dark. A sarcastic expression. "That's wonderful to hear. That is all I have for you tonight. Thank you for coming, Mrs. Forester."

I thanked her for having me even though I am far from thankful, and I marched out the classroom door with vengeance on the tip of my tongue. I clenched my jaw tightly so words couldn't slip out from my mouth. I headed towards the green classroom where the parents chatted about god knows what to each other. I'm not in the chatting mood so I kept away from everyone and scanned my surroundings for the one person I hate the most. Dean. And as I figured where he would be, he was in the corner of the room with a woman beside him. Miranda Foux. The president of the parents school committee where she bosses people around and forces them into agreeing to participate in the school fundraisers and parties just so she wouldn't have to waste her hard earned cash on the events herself. I don't think she has ever bought anything for the fundraisers or class parties since... well, ever. She also happens to work at Dean's business selling cars. He talks fondly of her all the time about how many sales she made in the past week and how she helps him out with the paperwork for the company and so much more. She is also the reason why our marriage is sinking into the ocean. She smashed holes into our boat, making the water flood in and slowly but gradually sinking our boat deeper into the ocean with us chained inside. I can't blame Dean for falling for her. She's a couple years older than us, in her early to mid-thirties, I believe? Her hair is naturally curly with an ashy-blonde color that coils down to her tailbone in long layers. Her face is round and mature. With thick eyebrows and dark full lashes that flutter as she bats her sapphire-blue eyes at him. Her skin is as smooth as a porcelain doll and her body is tall and slender. She always wears her usual white button-down underneath a navy-blue blazer and flat ironed trousers with four gold buttons on the sides for a stylish look, and her pointy heels that makes her six-feet taller than she already is. She is also a single mother with twin sons, Jasper and Frankie. Vivian doesn't talk to them as she says "they are rude and selfish" and she doesn't want to be friends with anyone like that. She has morals and self respect for herself and I love her so deeply for that. The two things that I wished I had. If I had those traits, I wouldn't be searching the halls and rooms for my husband who is flirting with another woman right now. Instead, I would be lounging in a steamy bath with flower petals in my soapy water and only candles lighting up the space around me. It would be so much more enjoyable and relaxing than all of this. I watched silently in the doorway at Dean and Miranda chatting with bright smiles. I haven't seen Dean smile like that in what feels like ages. His eyes crinkled as he bellowed a deep laugh. Miranda reached her long hand out and touched his shoulder and lightly squeezed it in her fists. A playful gesture that I am sure she does to him often. I am sure they have done way more than just touching shoulders. Dean's eyes flicked to mine behind her and his smile slowly faded as he stared into my fiery gaze. I turned away from him and walked towards the school doorways and out into the humid evening air. The sun peeked behind the building and it slowly shrunk down to let the moon rise high above to get its spectacular appearance. It was a crescent moon that glowed with calming light. Moonbathing is so much more relaxing than sunbathing in my opinion. It doesn't burn your skin like a chicken nugget being deep fried in salty oil. And you could actually see the creases and craters of the rock, rather than being blinded by a burning star. The moon will always have my heart. Dean on the other hand will not...

He dashed out of the building doors and trotted behind me as I beelined for the black and white Range Rover that reflected the blue moonlight on its front shield.

"Morgan, wait up." Dean called out rather nonchalantly than he should be. "What did the teacher say about Vivian?"

I stomped a boot down on the cement ground and turned my body to face him. I could feel my cheeks burning as the rage built up inside me. "Wouldn't you know if you were even there." I seethed through my gritted teeth. Dean narrowed his eyes at me like I was some insane person that needed to be convicted into the ward. His expression only made me angrier than I already was. "Instead you were off flirting with the whore inside." I didn't mean to use such foul language. I don't agree with calling women a prostitute. But she knows she is flirting with a married man. She is old enough to take accountability for her own actions. I should see her differently if she didn't know that Dean was married at all. But she knows. She knows who I am. She can also tell by the silver band that is wrapped tightly around his ring finger. She knows better than I do. And yet, she was still flirting with him and knowing very well that I arrived with him into the school. I think she deserves that title more than the women back in the late eighteen-hundreds when women were just trying to get by in life on their own. This is a new century where women *can* make their own money and their own decisions in their life. Miranda still chooses to have sex for money with *my husband*. So yes, she is a whore. And he is *so much worse.*

Dean shook his head. "I wasn't flirting with her." A lie that I'm sure he tells himself when he feels guilty. *If* he ever does feel guilty for his behavior and actions. "We were just talking about work related stuff."

I scoffed and turned away, stomping towards the parking lot. I could hear Dean's shoes scuff behind me. "Morgan, wait."

I stopped and turned back to him. "I know what you have been doing with her." I say, my voice is smaller than I expected. A large stone was lodged into my throat, and I forced saliva to go through it with more effort than it should have been. "Wives know what their husbands are up to without even witnessing it." Dean opened his mouth ready to give out another lie but I turned away and stopped next to the passenger side door. I reached a shaky hand into my purse pouch and dug out the keys to the car, and tossed them with a bit of force into Dean's chest. He caught them without hesitation and stared at me with a blank expression. He knows he fucked up, and he knows there isn't any way to fix what he did. I let out a short sigh and opened the wide door. "You can do whatever you want with her, but you will forget that this argument ever happened. For *our daughters' sake.*"

* * *

The drive home was silent. Even with the girls' in the backseat singing loudly to the song that blasted through the speakers. I'm glad these two had a good evening. I informed Dean later about what Vivian's teacher had told me and he silently listened as I threatened him to keep the affair a better secret from everyone. Including from our family. He can break my heart all he wants, but he will *not* break my daughters' heart. As I got the girls ready for bed, I sat down on the edge of Vivian's bed and wrapped my finger around her blonde coils. Her eyelids sagged from exhaustion and she yawned widely as the tiredness crept up on her. I inhaled shortly before looking lovingly into her fresh river spring eyes.

"You know Daddy and I love you, right?" I waited until Vivian nodded to continue. "And Daddy and I love each other very much. Whatever way you're feeling between us, and your worries for us, isn't right. Your father and I are doing great. I promise you that there is nothing you should be worried about, alright?" Vivian didn't nod nor did she give me a confirming answer. She just stared at me with blankness as I bent down to peck her cheek with my lips. I pulled her floral blanket up to her neck and stood up to head for the door. Before I could walk through the doorway, a small voice stopped me in my tracks.

"You should leave him." Vivian said. I looked back at her with narrow eyes. I went to speak but she shook her head for me to listen. I clamped my mouth shut as she continued on. "A husband shouldn't be unfaithful to his wife, like dad is to you." Before I could retort with words, Vivian rolled her tired face away from my sight as she buried herself deeper into her covers. I stood there with my hand resting on the doorknob and with no thought in mind. I only listened as her breaths grew longer and fainter and she fell deeply asleep.

Chapter 32

The rest of the week was more mellow than usual. Everything went smoothly. The girls' got to school on time every morning. Vivian is acting like she had never spoken those surprising words that night and her teacher hasn't mentioned anything about her being distracted with her emotions which is good. I guess? Charlotte hasn't gone missing in the past week, which is a new record. I still glower at that damn monkey every time I see her sagging in Merritt's lanky arms. Dean has been coming home early every afternoon, trying to make up for his absence from home lately. But his silent demeanor just looming around the corner of the rooms makes it far more uncomfortable. I want him to *want* to be home, not forced to be...

Joel left four days ago for Carl and Jodis' funeral and he will be spending a few days at their home to decide what to do with the ranch. I haven't called him because I know how hard of a time he is having and I don't want to interrupt or seem like I'm nagging him for his time. He has gotten enough sympathy from everyone. So I keep to myself for the rest of the week, no matter how hard it is to ignore the landline that is perched on the kitchen island and to dial his number and to ask how he is doing.

As Monday approached, so did the farmers market downtown that I had planned for weeks to attend. It is the only exciting thing happening in this lonesome town. Of course, as I made plans to go down after dropping the girls off at school, a child had to randomly get sick over the weekend. Little Miss Merritt had brought home a head cold from a classmate at school. She spent the two days off resting, but the sickness is being too clingy and unfortunately for the both of us, it won't go away. I called her teacher and told her that she won't be in for a few days as she is fighting a stuffy head cold. Though I am not going to let some head cold stop me from my plans. Not unless Merritt was too sick to even be walking and should be staying in bed all day. But she is perfectly capable of walking and playing with Charlotte. Except for the few coughs and sneezes that she lets out here and there. Otherwise, she is perfectly fine. I also asked her if she would like to come with me and she simply said, "Okay". It will be good for her to get some fresh air anyway...

After we dropped off Vivian at school, Merritt and Charlotte sat buckled in their car seats and bobbing their heads to the thumping of the music. And what I mean by, *bobbing their heads,* was Merritt is moving her head back and forth while moving Charlotte's beady little head side to side with her right hand. She also added a bit of up and down arm movements with one of Charlotte's lanky arms. They're having a rave in the backseat. It looks like they were having a blast rather than the time Dean took me to a club to dance. It was so loud in there I could barely hear him speaking to me as the thumping of the music blared out of two large speakers behind the bar. A disco ball circled overhead of the dance floor, leaving a square light pattern across the walls and the black and white checkered dance floor. Dean danced like no one was watching as I felt more out of place. I just bent my knees and bobbed up and down with my arms pin-straight to my sides. Dean is the equivalent of an extrovert which is something that I am not. I'm glad he had fun because I sure as hell did not. Merritt's small voice shouted over the music and I turned it down and gave a little, "huh?".

"What is a farmers market?" Merritt asked, tilting her head to the side.

"It's a market where people sell things." I said as I flicked on the turn signal. The ticking sound blinked and I checked both ways before going in for the turn. "Like, freshly grown vegetables and fruit, some gardening supplies and farming equipment. They sell all sorts of things."

"Oh." Merritt pondered on the words I had said. She looked out the window and glanced up at the trees that were starting to blossom with pink and white flowers. The leaves were brightly green with the spring rain watering their soil. She looked back at me. "But we aren't farmers."

I nodded with agreement. We are far from farmers. We live in the city, in a community of small houses. There is no land except for an hour outside of the city where there are endless fields of green grass and hungry cattle ready to eat their days away. I haven't gardened in over thirteen years. The endless chores out in the fields and gardens in the excruciating summer heat made me exhausted, but the deep feeling of yearning to garden again has never left me since. Maybe someday I will garden again. And someday I will feel the same way about it. For now, the only gardening I will do is planting the basic flowers along our brick house.

"You're right, we're not." I agreed, slowly pulling into the parking space where the farmers market is held. A couple hundred cars were already parked along the grass as vendors were waiting up by the front entrance to the park. They are having the farmers market at the Crystal Park, which is snuggled in between a few buildings surrounding it with a small pond and a pathway around it. A patch of grass that's large enough to hold gatherings such as the farmers market is close by. The pond has a little fountain in the center that sprinkles out muggy water into the puddle where the geese land from traveling. I'm pretty sure the flock of geese are always in the water as you never see the pond empty. I parked the car and glanced up at Merritt from the tiny mirror above my dashboard. I pondered on whether I should say something I have never spoken about before. Whether I should even mention her to my daughter. But before I could change my mind, the words flooded out my mouth. Forever in the air and never being able to take them back. "My mother took me to a farmers market once."

Merritt flicked her eyes up at the mirror. Her emerald green eyes flashed with wonder. "Really?"

I nodded. "Yep. I thought it was a nice bonding moment between me and her. Maybe it will be for us too. Don't you think so?"

Merritt shrugged, glancing back out the window. "Maybe?"

With that, we unbuckled our seatbelts and climbed out the car. I talked Merritt into leaving Charlotte in the car as we don't want her to go hiding around a crowd of strangers. Thank god, she listened to me. We held hands as we weaved through people to get to the vendors. A fiery haired woman welcomed us from under her tent and preached about her freshly grown peaches. She even gave us a slice to taste. It was so sweet and juicy, so full of flavor and goodness. Of course, we had to take some home with us. The lady gave us a reusable linen bag to carry around our goodies in. I let Merritt carry the bag of peaches over her shoulder. The bag was almost the length of her and pretty soon *I* will be the one carrying the bag as it will become too heavy for her to. She trotted next to me with cheer and we walked down the dirt pathway to some more vendors. We began to purchase a whole grocery store of ingredients for some tasty meals. Fresh fruits for breakfast and vegetables for some soups for dinner. Merritt wanted to purchase some tulips for the center of the dining table as in her words, "it would look great on the table." I couldn't agree more.

When we reached the last vendor we took our time looking at the herbal remedies that a woman in a purple shawl was selling. Fresh tea packets were laid out in a wooden box for us to buy. I am more of a coffee drinker and Dean is a tea drinker. He only drinks tea throughout the day and I drink a cup or two of raw coffee every morning, or whenever I really have time to. Merritt is slowly following Dean. She drinks a cup of warm jasmine tea every night before bed as she said it's relaxing for her. She only drinks jasmine, nothing else. I knew once she saw the jasmine packets she would force me to buy it. And yes she did. As we made our way back up the pathway she skipped beside me, eagerness was biting at her back as she couldn't wait to get home to try her new jasmine tea. I glanced one last time at the vendors as we walked, my eyes scanning my surroundings before they suddenly stopped to stare at the sudden face. The face that looked identical to when I last saw her. I abruptly stopped in my trance to stare through the crowd as my eyes flickered up and down her appearance. She had the same caramel skin and large chocolate brown eyes. Her lips were a pinky shade when she smiled at a stranger. Her hair was dark and curly even though it was pinned up in a messy bun, two coiled strands fell out from the rest and swayed across her face in the soft spring breeze. She wore a black sleeved dress that went down to her ankles and some black ballerina flats on her feet. I watched her hold a plump peach in her soft hands and bring it up to her nose. She inhaled deeply and her eyes fluttered shut as she took in the juicy scent. She then bent down and faced an elderly man with thin white hair and a wrinkled face that sat in a wheelchair and brought it up to his nose for him to smell. She smiled sweetly at him as he spoke words that I couldn't hear. A sudden finger pressed against my rib cage, making me jump in my stance. I looked down at Merritt who narrowed her eyes peculiarly at me.

"What are you doing, Mommy?" She asked with a curious tone in her voice.

I opened my mouth but words didn't come out. I was too stunned, too shocked to even speak. To even think. I just stood there with a blank expression. I finally inhaled deeply and forced my brain to focus. "I-I was just looking at someone." I pointed a flimsy finger towards the direction where I saw the woman.

Merritt raised a thin eyebrow and cocked her head. "Staring is rude, Mommy."

I nodded my head. "I know that." I glanced back towards the vendor to see that the woman and the man were still there, minding their own business. I dropped my bags and reached inside my purse and pulled out a tablet of paper and a pen. I quickly jotted down a short sentence and ripped the note out of the tablet, folded it once and held it out for Merritt to take. "Can you take this note over to the lady in the black dress for me, please?" I pointed and gave her a weak smile.

Merritt slowly took the note without questioning why, and marched through the crowd in the pathway and over to the vendor. She tapped the woman on the shoulder with a kind smile. The woman looked wearily at Merritt, handed her the note without saying any words and walked away. I watched as the woman narrowed her eyes before opening the note. Her caramel eyes slowly moved side to side as she read each word carefully, her smile slowly fading from her lips and slightly parted open in a short gasp. Before she could finish the note and glance around her surroundings for me, I swung the linen bags over my shoulders and grabbed Merritt's hand and marched through the endless stream of people. Merritt towing beside me. I'm not sure *why* she is here. I'm not sure *how* she is here. But what I do know is that *we* have a lot of catching up to do.

Note;

Meet me at Cafe Blou, tomorrow afternoon at 2:00.
-Sincerely, Vi.

Chapter 33

I sat at a table in the back, away from the widely large windows in front of Cafe Blou. Joel took me to this cafe once before I moved into a place with Dean. It was our last lunch together. Just the two of us before life took a hold over me and made it so much harder to have lunch with him again. It was a relatively quiet cafe with good tasting coffee and snacks. Just good, not great. Nothing will ever compare to Carl's tasty coffee and Jodi's famous banana pecan and walnut bread. It was only famous at church whenever they had afternoon gatherings. Not a single crumb would be left over. What I would kill for another slice of her bread...

The little bell above the door jingled. I looked up from my table to only see a bald man walking towards the counter. I sighed and glanced down at my silver and brown band watch. It was only one-forty. I arrived at the cafe around one-twenty to get a quick coffee and secure a table before the afternoon rush began. The rush typically starts five minutes before two, but it seems like a mellow day. It is a Tuesday afternoon, most people are at work or school. Merritt felt better today and surprisingly she wanted to go to school. She was going either way but it seems like she's becoming quite responsible for her age. Quite different from Vivian, who I had to drag by her legs out of the house for school at Merritts' age. Now she loves it and she has a friend group that she didn't have before. Not sure what Merritts' reasons were, but at least I didn't have to play *bad mother* and force her to go.

I wrapped my icy hands around the warmth of the coffee cup. The cardboard cup penetrated warmth as hot steam rose from the top of the lid. I'm not sure why Cafe Blou decided to turn on the AC on a fifty degree day, but my peacoat and scarf can stay on for the remainder of my stay. The bell jingles again and I take my time looking away from my cup and up towards the door. A curly haired woman walked in with a peacoat overtop of a spring blue dress that went past her ankles, barely grazing the ground as she walked past. Her chocolate eyes scanned the room until they finally landed on mine. A smile arose on her face and her eyes lit up, the same as mine did. I stood up from my seat, not knowing why but my body felt too jittery to stay seated. As she approached my table I beckoned her, wrapping my arms tightly around her shoulders. She squeezed my ribs tightly and for a moment it felt like time had stopped. That everything was still, except for us. Like our hug would last forever. Unfortunately, reality kicked in too soon as Bonnie released her grasp and took a step back to take me in. I did too. I took in her floral scent, like a field of dandelions and buttercups with a soft breeze on a bright sunny day. Like the one we had, fourteen years ago. A dimple sank deep into her cheek as her smile grew bigger. Her round eyes glistened in the light from above. I took in her warm aura that always made me feel calm. Like a warm hug from a lost loved one. I haven't seen her since the night I left. Besides her being taller and her face a bit more structured as she is a matured woman now and not a young girl, she looks the same as I remembered her. She still does her hair in a tight bun that always looks messy as her curls refuse to be tamed. Her skin glowed like freshly melted caramel with a smooth complexion. I can go on about how beautiful she is but her soft tone of voice distracted me from her beauty...

"You look beautiful." She said with a slight gasp as she sucked in brisk air. "Still as I remembered."

I nodded in agreement. "Same with you." A warm sensation ran through my face, suddenly making me feel hot underneath the scarf and coat. I gestured for her to take a seat in front of me as I unraveled my scarf from my neck and draped it over my lap. The sudden coldness on my neck made chills slither down my spine. I forced my eyes away from hers and grabbed my cup of coffee. "Did you want me to order you something? Coffee or Tea?"

Bonnie shook her head with a polite smile. "No, thank you. I'm not much of a drinker. Besides water of course." She chuckles sweetly, if that's even possible. Anything's possible when Bonnie does it. A special touch that not many can do.

An uncontrollable wide smile appeared on my face. "I could get you some water then." I retort, ready to head over to the counter as soon as she accepts my offer.

Bonnie waved her hand dismissively with a giggle. "I'm good, honest."

We sat in silence, but it didn't feel awkward. With most people silence would feel uncomfortable. But with Bonnie, silence was never a problem for us. Her aura made it feel comfortable and warm like laying in the sun on a quiet beach with only the waves crashing down onto jagged rocks. Unlike the present humming that came from the overused AC in the cafe. Bonnie clasped her hands together on the table and narrowed her eyes.

"How have you been?" She asked, truly meaning it. Some people may ask that question without truly meaning it. Just a question to be nice but not caring at all. Bonnie means things when she says it. That's why, when we used to get into arguments with each other, some of the words we spoke would truly hurt. She knows me more than anyone else does. She knows what would hurt my feelings and I know hers. Our arguments weren't that intense. I've had worse with Dean. But it still breaks my heart when we do. Bonnie inhaled a short breath before continuing to speak. "What has happened since you left?" Since I left? I didn't leave, I ran away. Leaving would be me saying goodbye before walking out a door. Running away is me climbing out of my bedroom window and running as fast as I possibly could in a forest in the middle of the night to save myself from unwanted death. Bonnie knows I ran away, she helped me do so. Maybe she used poor wording, or maybe she truly believes that I did leave. That I left her behind. I shuddered those words out of my mind and gave her a soft smile before telling her everything that has happened to me since. I told her about the nail in my foot, about that man Patrick who took me into town shortly before meeting with the couple that took me in from under their wing and raised me until I had to run away once again because of the cult finding me. I told her about Carl's younger brother Joel and Dean and about how I am now a mother of two girls who I love from the depths of my heart. Bonnie didn't say much. She just nodded along as I spoke. I then take a moment to finally ask how she has been...

"I've been good." She smiled at me as her eyes roamed the room. She seems uncomfortable and I'm not sure why. "When you left I was sort of under surveillance for a few months." She gave a faint laugh that dissipated quickly. "Someone had to be with me at all times. I suppose they thought I would leave too since you had."

"Did you ever think about running away?" I asked, curiosity taking hold of me. I wanted to know if she ever considered searching for me. If she thought about me as much as I have thought about her from over the years I was gone. If I was ever on her mind.

Bonnie nodded, flicking her gaze back to me. "I had. Yes, but shortly after things started to go wrong with the group. The elders became sickly, some had died while others were bedridden for several months. I had to care for them, all of us girls had too." She took a moment to ponder on her next choice of words. Eagerness to know what she was thinking snipped at my tongue as I clamped my jaw shut, forcing myself to patiently wait for her to continue. Her face dropped as she glanced around the cafe and when she looked back at me I could see her eyes welling up with tears. I restrained myself from reaching out to her for support. I gripped my hands to my knees as I waited. Bonnie sniffed and opened her mouth to speak. "Martha was taking care of Elder Grimes when he grew ill from a virus. Shortly after, she grew sickly and Mother had to tend to her when she couldn't get out of bed. I don't know what was happening to her, but the last I saw her she was very pale and thin, her lungs were scratchy when she breathed." A tear escaped from her eye and trailed down her flushed cheek. She inhaled deeply and said, "Shortly after I saw her, she had passed away."

I stopped breathing as my ears started ringing. I couldn't move or speak. All I could do was replay her words over and over again in my brain. Martha's face flashed in front of my eyes. Her rosy cheeks grew chubby as she smiled up at me, her small eyes glistened with joy when she bellowed a laugh from something I had told her. How could she be dead? She was perfectly fine when I left. More importantly, why didn't they get her help? Why didn't they take her to the hospital? I know why, because if they go to the hospital then they are risking getting caught and arrested for what they are doing. It is simply too risky. I shook my head dismissively, I do not want to believe she is gone. I do not want to believe it at all.

"Wh- why didn't you get her he- help?" I stammered as I tried grasping the new information. "Why didn't you get her to a hospital,

Bonnie?" Bonnie looked at me stunned, like I had just asked her if she had murdered Martha herself. I know it was a dumb question as I already knew the truth, but I wanted to hear what she has to say about it. If she is still with them or not. When Bonnie didn't speak I said, "are you still with them?"

Bonnie narrowed her eyes on me. "Of course I am. They're family." My mouth gaped open wider than I had expected. I clamped it shut and scoffed.

"Bonnie, those people are not family." I pointed out the window. Metaphorically pointing at the group that was not there. There was only a Magnolia tree where the buds started blooming pinkish petals. "Those people are satanic. They murder young girls as a sacrifice, for Christ sake." Bonnie stared at me blankly. She didn't speak or shift in her seat, she just stared. For a moment I thought she hadn't heard me from over the obnoxious humming from the AC behind me. But I know she heard me by the subtle twitch of an eyebrow. I'm not sure what that means but I know for a fact that she had heard me. I shook my head in disbelief that she wasn't agreeing with me and I reached for my coffee, when I did so I noticed the shiny silver band that was wrapped snugly around Bonnie's ring finger. She gripped her hands clasped. I withdrew my hand and pointed to the ring, hoping that it wasn't what I thought it was. "What is that?" Bonnie finally looked away from me and looked down at her hands. I looked at her eyes. They were as dull as stones. What once was vibrant earthy covered irises were now black as night. At that moment I knew that the girl I once knew, the girl that was once my best friend, was now a woman that I didn't recognize. Someone that I no longer knew. A lot has changed over the years. It's impossible to not change with it. I just hoped that it hadn't changed so much. I kept quiet as I waited for her answer. Bonnie stared at the ring with a dull expression before she placed her hands on her lap...

"I was chosen to marry an Elder." Bonnie finally said after several minutes of silence. The picture of the old man in the wheelchair I saw with Bonnie at the farmers market, flashed into my mind. His thinning hair was so thin that you could see his speckled scalp. His pruned cheeks and saggy eyelids glistened with glee as Bonnie bent down for him to smell the freshly picked peach. I was so stunned by Bonnie's presence that I never thought about who the man even was. We girls didn't see the elders much because we were taught to never speak to them and to always stay out of their way. Especially when they worked in the fields. If I had seen him before then he would be a lot younger than he is now. His aging makes him unrecognizable. I couldn't imagine marrying him. Marrying an older man, old enough to be her great grandfather. Carl is a lot younger than he is and it sickens me to know that he *chose her* to *marry him*. Bonnie looked at me skeptical about my reaction. I must have looked like I just saw a ghost. All wide eyed and raised brows, mouth slightly gaping open. She rolled her eyes at me and sighed. "It's not what you think."

I sat back in my seat and narrowed my eyes. "Really? Because what I'm thinking is that an old perverted man chose to marry you like you're some object to use." Bonnie narrowed her eyes on me as well. "But please, tell me what *you* think."

"That's not why he chose me, Vi." Bonnie shook her head and straightened her posture. I sat there expectantly, waiting for her response to alleviate his excuse to be a pervert and marry a woman he knew since a child. Probably since she was born. "He chose me because he needed me. He needed a caretaker. He never forces me to do anything that I don't want to." Bonnie's eyes flashed sincerity as she spoke her next words. "He's a good man, Vi."

She was the only one to ever call me that. *Vi.* It was a nickname she chose for me. A way to describe her love to me. I didn't expect her to continue to call me that after all these years. It's nice to see that something's never changed. I pondered on her words for a while. Rearranging them in my mind until I could see what she sees. It's hard for me to believe that an elderly man could be a good man, especially after he married Bonnie who is so much younger than him. I could never be with a man like that. But better yet, Dean isn't any better than him. Bonnie fidgeted with her fingers as we sat in silence. The strong defensive presence surrounded us and kept us from looking in our direction. I just stared out the window behind her as she stared down at the wooden table. The wind picked up speed and forced past the magnolia tree that stood firmly in the ground, refusing to be swept away by the breeze. I looked back to her when she inhaled a deep ragged breath.

"The group isn't like that anymore, you know." Bonnie stated, looking back at me wearily. Probably worried I would scream in outrage from even mentioning them to me. But she continued on anyway. "They don't do rituals anymore. Not since you left. The other girls took their chances with leaving. Some made it out and some didn't."

"What happened to the girls that didn't make it out?" I asked. If they were generous enough they would just make them do endless amounts of chores as a punishment and maybe write a fifty page essay on why it is important to stay as a whole together. But if they were not so generous they would do far worse than that. Something more sinister than that.

Bonnie shrugged. "Not much. Just excessive amounts of chores around the pastures and cabins. If they had done something worse than that, I wouldn't have known. I was broken away from them and had to help with the Madems instead. I even had to sleep in the same cabin as them. I wasn't ever allowed to speak or even look at the other girls."

"Why?" I narrowed my eyes on her.

Bonnie shrugged again. "I guess they thought I would try to get the girls to leave, like you did. They didn't think leaving was my idea. They knew very well it was yours. But they knew I had agreed with you and helped you leave."

I guess that makes sense. But the girls still left anyway. I'm glad some of them chose to leave because of me. Maybe they saw what I saw, and hopefully some of them did make it out alive. Maybe they found their own path in their own life. But why are they still after me? Is it because I was the first to leave? Because I was the first to rebel against them?

"Do they believe that I was the reason for Martha's death?" I asked, somberly. I know the answer to my question. Of course they believe it was my fault. I didn't sacrifice myself like I was "chosen" to do and now they are paying for the consequences of my actions. Maybe they believe that killing me like they were supposed to do, will stop the death that's upon them. Or maybe they are finally paying the price for what they have done for decades. Either way I need to hear what Bonnie has to say, whether or not she believes them or me...

Bonnie slowly nodded. "They believe that the lord is out to take them as a sacrifice because you didn't die for them." She squinted at me with fondness in her dark eyes and shook her head ever so slightly. "But I don't believe that. I'm glad you left. I'm glad you found a loving husband to take care of you and your daughters. You made a life for yourself. I'm truly happy for you, Vi." Her expression softened and the corners of her lips turned into a gentle smile. The smile warmed me from inside as my face flushed. I didn't tell her about Dean cheating on me with his assistant. I didn't tell her about how the cult murdered Carl and Jodi just a week ago. I know they did and I don't need Bonnie to tell me otherwise. But not telling her about Dean was out of embarrassment for me. It's embarrassing knowing that your husband is having an affair behind your back and you can't do anything about it. I can't leave as I have nowhere else to go. I guess I'm still in the predicament I was back with the group. Feeling hopeless and lonely, not being able to take a hold of my life for more than two hours. Everyone has always told me how my life will go. But I could never tell myself how it would go. It's all so tiring really. Having to fight for my rights to find my own path. I don't know if I will be strong enough to fight for it again...

"Why are you here?" The words flooded out my mouth before I could even process it in my brain. They were words I had in my mind since I saw her at the market yesterday evening. I wonder if she's trying to help them find me. If so, then she found me. I know she came alone. I keep glancing out the window waiting to see familiar faces to take me back with them. Nothing but the Magnolia tree was present outside. Bonnie flinched back from my sudden harsh words. She drew in her eyebrows and tilted her head to the side, puzzled by my sudden remark.

"What do you mean? You asked me to come here."

"No," I shake my head. I clasped my hands on top of the table, my knuckles turning white, and leaned into them. My face is now just inches away from hers. I could feel her wavered breaths on my face as I stared coldly into her soiled colored eyes. "Why are you here in this city, Bonnie?"

Bonnie leaned away from my face and folded her arms across her chest. "I told you that the group changed. I told Finch I wanted to live in a house of my own with my husband. He generously agreed and now I live here."

I slowly leaned back while biting my lower lip. "But you said you are still with the group?"

Bonnie nodded. "I am. We no longer live in a convent together. Finch gave us a choice to live and be wherever we want. But we are still in the religious belief that we grew up in. He's letting us have our own freedom now."

"But only if you still believe in the gospel and savior." I add in. Bonnie gave me a simple nod and we grew silent again. It's easier to believe in something you were taught since birth, than learn to believe in something new to you. I understand the fear she feels when she thinks about leaving a place she has called home her whole life. I felt it myself. But once you push past that fear, you unlock warmth and comfort from within. Bonnie may not realize that to truly choose your own path, you must first create a home for yourself and the family you've created. Don't let anyone choose it for you...

My phone suddenly buzzed inside my jeans pocket. I pulled it out and saw the call was from Ms. Springfield, Vivian's teacher. My heart leaped out of my chest and my breath caught in my throat. I never get calls from her, especially when Vivian's in class. I can sense that it won't be good news but I still forced myself to hit the green cellphone button and put it up to my ear. I gave a strangled "Hello", and the immediate response came from the other end. It was rushed and winded, like after a pack of cats finished fighting to protect their property. Heavy breathing, rushed speaking, and the overwhelmed tone of voice. After Ms. Springfield finished speaking, I agreed to meet her at the school as soon as possible before she abruptly hung up on me. I quickly stood up from my seat, almost knocking the chair over behind me and wrapped my scarf around my neck. I'm too warm to be wearing it, but I put it on anyway.

"I have to go." I told Bonnie hastily. I avoided her puzzling gaze and dug out a five dollar bill from my wallet and tossed it on the table in front of her. "Buy yourself a cup of coffee. Trust me, you'll like it."

* * *

I marched into the school hallway with such force in my steps that I swore I could hear the walls rattling besides me. I entered Ms.Springfield's office and what waited for me in two seats was Vivian with a solemn gaze and eyes welling up with tears, and a boy with curly brown hair and olive skin beside her. He looked down and stared at the checkered flooring as he traced his sneakers along the black and white squares. He didn't acknowledge my presence nor did he glance up at me. He just sat there blankly slumped into his chair. I have never seen that boy before, nor has Vivian ever mentioned him. I assume he is new and might be the reason Vivian is in trouble. Ms. Springfield sat behind her desk displeased by them both. It's past three now and the other students have gone home for the day, except for these two. And of course one of them has to be mine.

"You two," Ms.Springfield snapped, pointing a lanky finger at them. They snapped their heads up to look at her as she moved her finger towards the open door behind me. "Out! While I speak to your mothers." I glanced out the door, half expecting the boy's mother to come striding into the hallway any second now. But she never showed. Not until five minutes later when she came through the door, interrupting Ms.Springfield's and my moment of silence and glares. When I glanced over to the opened door to see who was walking through it, my eyes widened and my jaw slackened in disbelief. The mother to the young boy was Bonnie. As she trailed in she stopped in the doorway when she saw me, her expression the same as mine. I'm not sure why she is surprised to see me. I told her I have two daughters, but I never told her their ages. Why didn't she tell me that she is a mother also? Was she ever going to tell me or did she think we would never see each other again after our meet up at Cafe Blou? Either way, I know now... Ms. Springfield looked at us both, analyzing our expressions in puzzlement. She drew in her brows and narrowed her eyes and made a *'click'* sound with her tongue when she opened her mouth to speak. "Do you two know each other?" We both nodded our heads and Bonnie moved away from the door to sit down in the chair beside me. Bonnie gave a courtesy smile to Ms. Springfield and glanced over at the both of us.

"We knew each other when we were children." I silently nodded and withdrew my attention from her and to Ms.Springfield who had a raised brow as she glared at the both of us. She rearranged some papers on her desk and shuffled them into a drawer before, once again clicking her tongue before she spoke. I braced myself for whatever she was going to say about what our children had gotten themselves into.

"Mrs.Forester," She glared at me. "Mrs. Whitmore," She glared at Bonnie. I noted Bonnie's full name in a notebook of a list of names that I have to miraculously memorize in the back of my brain. It's easier to remember them when you imagine yourself jotting them down with an imaginary pen and notebook. *Bonnie Whitmore*. Right underneath our dentist's name, *Steven Fitz.* Mrs.Springfield continued- "both of your children had started a fight with two students in their class."

I fought back the urge to bellow laughter out of shock. This has to be a joke. There is no way my daughter would start a fight with anyone. Not unless she's finishing one that had already been started by someone else. Even then, it is hard to imagine Vivian getting into a fight at all. Yes, she has specific abilities to tell someone to kindly *fuck off*. But to physically fight someone? Nah, there is no way. I glance over at Bonnie who is just as confused as how her son would react to a fight.

The cult is very keen on the no fighting rule. Unless it was verbally, then they wouldn't really care. The only time I had witnessed a physical confrontation was between two girls in the group who started yelling and pulling hair. Later one of them bodying the other to the ground before repeatedly slapping her in the face. I remember that day so vividly as it was the first time I had seen a verbal argument turning into a physical beating before. I remember the chunk of coarse blonde hair gripped tightly in the other girl's hands. The way she swept her ankle around the other girl's legs to sweep her from under her feet, like a rug abruptly being pulled out from underneath you. Fastly falling from thin air and cracking your spine on the wooden floorboards. The way that the brunette girl sprawled on top of her and wheeled her arm back to hit the other girl's face. The way that the blonde girl's cheeks turned bright red from the impact of the girl's swing meeting her face. I remember the rest of us girls' watching with fright because we have never seen such an interaction before. I also remember getting shoved into Bonnie beside me who also fell on top of another girl beside her and the Elders raced from behind to break up the fight. We all went tumbling down like a stack of dominoes that was meticulously put in a line before knocking the first one over. The girls got in trouble for fighting with another "sister". "We were chosen sisters and we shall not act as enemies for we shall always love and respect one another". That's what Reverend Finch preached to us that Sunday morning. It turned out that the cause for the abrasive interaction between them two was because the one girl allegedly stole the other girl's hair ties because the one girl kept accidentally breaking hers and needed more for her hairstyle. So, as a punishment for their actions, mother cut all of their hair off into a botched pixie-cut to keep them from ever needing hair ties again. Their hair didn't take long to grow back but the uneven layers took longer to grow and made their hair look thin and uneven for years. I wonder where they are now?

"I'm sorry?" Bonnie interjected, bringing me back to my senses. "But my son would never do such a thing. He wouldn't even hurt a pesky mosquito if it had landed on his arm." Her voice sounded in disbelief and she looked at Ms.Springfield wide eyed and gently shook her head dismissively.

"I agree," I say, nodding my head. "Vivian might be a fireball but she wouldn't harm anyone. She's all talk but no do, Ms.Springfield."

Ms.Springfield must've found our statements to be unnerving and untrue as she shot daggers in our eyes and snapped at us with annoyance. "I had already spoken to the students parents shortly before you two arrived and they said that your daughter and your son had started the interaction with them-"

"That's simply not true!" Vivian interrupted. She's now standing in the doorway, clenching her fists with frustration. She looked at me with pleading eyes and in that moment, I knew she was telling the truth. As her mother it's easy for me to spot a lie in her face. Her tone of voice wouldn't be so clear and shoutout. She would be more quiet and muffled. Her face would be blank and her eyes would never meet mine. I'm also aware of her fists clenching when she gets upset or angry. It's not in an aggressive manner but more in an emotional and desperate way to express her emotions. Everyone expresses their emotions differently and that is how she expresses hers...

Ms.Springfield shook her head and pointed to the door sharply. "I have already heard what you have said and I would not like to hear it again. Now please go sit back down in the-"

"No!" Vivian turned to me. "Jasper and Frankie were bullying Boyd and all I did was tell them to leave him alone. Then Jasper pushed me and Boyd went and pushed him back, and then Frankie tackled Boyd down to the floor and was pinning him down. All I did was push him off of him and that's when Ms. Springfield came in." Vivian inhaled a deep breath as she finished telling me her statement in only a few seconds. She was eager to tell me the truth before she got interrupted again. Bonnie and I stared at her as we comprehended her statement and then we turned to look at Ms. Springfield with narrowed eyes. Of course it had to be Miranda Faux's twins. It couldn't have been anyone else's.

Now Miranda will tell Dean whatever lies of her sons' story and then he will get pissed that our daughter got in a fight with them. Well, a semi fight...

Ms.Springfield sighed and clasped her hands together in front of her as she waited for our interjections. Only I spoke out. "So, what's the problem then? Our children didn't start the fight. Vivian isn't lying, the twins are."

Ms.Springfield expressed a stern look. "It doesn't matter who started it or not. Your two children," She pointed at me and Bonnie. "were still in a fight. We don't tread lightly on fighting here."

"And you shouldn't." Bonnie agreed. "Fighting is a serious matter. But I expect that the twins will be punished as our children will." She talked with gentleness in her voice. Like a warm breeze on a summer's night. She cocked her head and her gaze was as sharp as a serpent's tooth. Unfortunately, summer hasn't arrived yet.

Ms.Springfield leaned back in her seat and for the first time ever, she actually looked content with Bonnie's *kill them with kindness* act. "I wasn't going to punish anyone." Ms.Springfield said, crossing her arms across her chest in a big bear hug to herself. "I am warning you to get your children's act right as I will hate for them to bear some responsibility for their actions the next time they get into a physical encounter again. Does that sound right to you?" She raised her eyebrows and plastered a very fake smile. Bonnie and I nodded in agreement. Bonnie flashed her a kindhearted smile that was filled with sarcasm while I kept a stern face as we got up and walked out to the hallway to gather our children, and walked out the empty school doors...

The air was moist but the breeze was as cold as ice. My nose immediately started running and my hand felt like a frozen icicle against my skin when I wiped my nose with the back of my hand before stuffing it back into my peacoat pockets. *Spring equinox,* my ass. It still feels like the middle of January in April. At least the humidity from spring showers blossomed some warmth when the wind took a moment to regulate itself and blow stronger than before. It's like the spring goddess and the winter goddess are battling it out in who will last longer and who will start sooner. So far, both of them had equal chances to win, as one week would be sixty-degrees with light rain and the other week would be forty-degrees with icy wind. I just wished one of them could win already. Preferably the spring goddess...

Bonnie and I watched Vivian and Boyd race to their cars that were parked in the front row parking space, seeing who was the fastest. It turns out Boyd's the fastest. He turned around to face Vivian who stomped up to him and he stuck his tongue out at her. Vivian laughed and playfully punched his shoulder. I glanced at Bonnie as we descended the school stairs and walked sluggishly next to each other. A small smile arose onto her face and she looked fondly at her son and my daughter. Paying no mind to my stolen glance. She really has become so beautiful with her mature facial features and her long dark lashes, and fuller lips. It's strange how time can change you so much but make you look the same all at once. I'm finally an inch taller than her now than when we were kids. I was a late bloomer, I guess. I looked back at Boyd, now seeing the resemblance of Bonnie in him. His dark eyes, his full lips, his curly dark hair, and his bright smile that could light up a dark room, were identical to Bonnies'. But there was also a resemblance that I couldn't quite capture in him. One that I had seen before but not knowing when. I pictured the Elderly man that is Bonnie's husband in my mind like a photograph I mentally captured from afar. His facial features don't seem to match Boyd's at all. It made me wonder if he is truly his father. It's hard to believe that Bonnie would have wanted to have his child. I know her views have changed a lot since I've been gone, but I don't think she would change her mind on that. Unless, she never really had a choice...

"I thought you said your husband didn't force you to do anything that you didn't want to do?" The words flew out of my mouth before I could stop them. Honestly, I am not sure what is up with me today. I'm not a blunt person but my brain isn't functioning properly either. I half expected Bonnie to get snarky with me about my question, but she just stared at the kids as Vivian laughed at something Boyd had told her. Then she looked at me with no emotion on her face. Just blankly staring back at me. She pondered on my words, knowing very well that she knew what I had meant. But she still pondered them carefully. Then her lips parted and the words came out...

"He didn't. Finch did." My heart immediately sank deep into the pit of my stomach. Suddenly the world started spinning around me but I didn't feel dizzy or lethargic. I could feel the ground spinning from under my feet and making me stop in my tracks. Before I could proceed to say anything or to even think, Bonnie reached into her navy blue peacoat pocket and pulled out a folded green dollar bill. Then she held it out and waited for me to take it. My fingertips caressed the thin bill and unfolded it. A five dollar bill jittered in my shaky hands. I looked up from it to see Bonnie faintly smiling at me and gave me a single head nod. "Buy yourself a bottle of water." She said sweetly. "Trust me, you'll like it." Then she walked away and towards her car, leaving me standing there in the middle of the school's front entrance. I wasn't sure how long I stood there with my mind drawing a blank like an unused piece of paper. But when Vivian called out to me to unlock the car door, I was suddenly aware that the ground wasn't spinning from under me and the icy breeze had caused my hands to go stiff and numb, and that I wasn't breathing at all...

Chapter 34

I stared up at the cumulus clouds that drifted over me in the sweet breeze. The sun was close and warm with its harsh rays. I lay down in the pastures of yellow buttercups and dandelions. I felt a strong sense of calmness and peace as I listened to the buzzing bumblebees that worked hard for their pollen to take back to their queens. I closed my eyes and inhaled deeply. I took in the scents in the environment around me. The floral scent of pollen from the sweet dandelions and the buttery scent of buttercups. The earthy scent of thick grass and sweet maple cedar from the trees close by in the light cool breeze. The scent of smoke and burning wood... smoke?

I opened my eyes to suddenly see a small building in white with the peak at the top that now displayed an upside down cross on the tip of the spiked roof. The building was engulfed in flames that melted the white paint and burned into a crisp. I was once again standing in front of the little building and I once again couldn't move or speak. The crunching grass of footsteps walked up beside me. The small hand grasped mine and I interlock my fingers with theirs. My fingers seemed to be the only part of my body that could move. I could sense the panic from the person beside me and I squeezed their hand to know that I am here for them since my words came out silent. All I could do was watch as the raging flames climbed up the little building, when I blinked the building came crashing down with a sudden uproar as the flames bursted up into the air.... then I awakened.

I pulled myself up and leaned back onto the headboard on my bed. I placed a hand onto my chest and felt my heart pounding as I inhaled deeply and exhaled slowly, trying to steady it and bring it down to slower beats. I could hear Dean snoring next to me. I fought the urge to slap him across his charming face as he sleeps so soundly. Dean has always been a heavy sleeper. A tornado could rip our house apart and he still would be asleep. I don't know if I'm just jealous that he can get a whole night of sleep or if I'm mad that I keep waking up from the same dream for thirteen years while he gets an uninterrupted night's sleep. It could be a mix of both. I glanced at the alarm clock on the nightstand beside me. It read, **5:55 *am***. I sighed and pulled off my covers to get up. I headed to the bathroom to shower before I had to make breakfast for everyone. I brush out my damp hair and braid it down my spine. I let a coil hang down the side of my face. I am too tired to pin up my flyaways. I barely do any makeup, just light mascara, a tint of blush, and a pinky hue chapstick that gives the slightest tint of color. Jodi did her makeup like this every morning. I guess I learned that habit and I still do it now. I learned a lot of habits from Jodi such as overly cleaning the house, especially the kitchen. My god, I *hate* a dirty kitchen. Also the habit of never sitting down for just two minutes. I'm always finding things to do instead of just simply relaxing. I never understood why Jodi used to do it? Procrastinate from relaxing. I'm not sure why I do it now. I guess, I don't feel useful if I take a break for a few minutes. Maybe that was how she felt? I would never know anyway. Not anymore...

The eggs sizzled on the frying pan as I mixed them with a spatula. The girls love scrambled eggs and sausages for breakfast. I glaze the sausage in sweet honey and fry them to a crisp with one pan while I scramble the eggs with some rosemary and pepper with another pan. I've never been an eggs and sausage person but the girls get what they want. It is better than whipping up pancake mix and having to spend the next thirty minutes cooking them. It's a lot quicker and easier this way, so I really can't complain.

My body was still full of rage from yesterday. My mind kept flashing Finch's face like a projector that shined his features brightly in front of my eyes. No matter how hard I blinked, I couldn't get his silhouette out of my sight. I thought long and hard on what Bonnie had told me yesterday evening. "He didn't, Finch did."

The sadness that portrayed in her gaze. I could tell she was trying to hide it, but I could see through her like I have X-ray vision. I could tell what she is thinking and what she tries so hard on hiding. Knowing her has its benefits, while it also has its faults. I try not to picture how it happened. I quite frankly, don't want to know. Whatever happened had made her a mother to a kind boy. I could tell he is kind by the way he's close to Vivian. Vivian doesn't trust easily, so if she trusts him when she only knows him for like a day, then he must be special. I wonder if they could somehow sense that Bonnie and I were close back then? Maybe deep down they could feel the connection we had that they now have for each other. Their friendship is sweet. But I don't know if I'm supposed to be staying or running? Like I always do... I'm so tired of running...

"Yay, my favorite!" Merritt shouted as she climbed up onto the barstool. She rested her chin in her hands and leaned her elbows on the island countertop. I smiled and dished out some eggs and sausages on a plastic tiger plate with a matching fork and placed it in front of her. "Thank you, Mommy." She cheered and munched on a mouthful of eggs. I glanced back down the hallway and waited for Vivian to come rushing in, but she never showed.

"Vivian, breakfast!" I shouted, but there was no indication to let me know that she had heard me. I sighed and blew it off my shoulders. If she doesn't eat before school, then that is her problem.

Dean walked into the kitchen with a white button-down-top and brown trousers with his hair slicked back and dress shoes that clunked as he took steps on the wooden flooring. He always looks so neat and put together. While I never care to dress as fashionably as he does. Why should I if I just run errands and stay in the house all day? I don't have to charm people with my looks like he does. The problem with Dean though is that he charms too many people for all the wrong reasons. He can do whatever he wants with Miranda. As long as he keeps it out of *my house* and away from *my family*.

"Breakfast?" I ask him as he pours himself a flask of coffee from the coffee machine that I had brewed for him earlier. He filled his flask up to the brim, leaving no room for even a splash of milk. Just pure black coffee. As rich and dark as his soul.

Dean shook his head while he screwed on the lid to his flask. "Nah, I'm good." He simply said before turning around and facing me. He forced a polite smile. "But thank you, though."

I gave him a simple, "*mhm,*" and turned back to Merritt who nearly had her breakfast finished. "Got any school projects planned for school, Merritt?" Merritt looks like a chipmunk with her cheeks stuffed with food and pudged out. I stifled back a giggle as I don't want her to think I'm making fun of her. I waited for her response as she chewed some of the food and swallowed. She shook her head.

"No, but spring break is in four weeks." She mumbled, still with a mouthful. Her eyes lit up in excitement to be finally getting a break from school and to be a little girl again. Her excitement radiated into me and I couldn't help but smile the widest. I can't wait until I get to be with the girls' for longer than an hour in the morning and five hours in the evening. I enjoy the little times with my girls though...

"Don't talk with your mouth full, Merritt." Dean snapped at her as he carried his cup towards the garage door, already ready to leave for work. Dean didn't turn back to say goodbye. He only hollered over his shoulder, "it's rude." And then he slammed the door shut.

Merritt's eyes dulled and she placed down her fork. I took my finger and booped her petite nose to grasp her attention. When I had it, I leaned over the island with my elbows and gave her a warm smile.

"How about me and you stop by at Starbucks after school to get ourselves a little treat, does that sound good to you?" Merritt's smile came back and she nodded with excitement. Footsteps came down the staircase and Vivian emerged from the hallway. She slumped into a bar stool without saying a word and kept her gaze down at the counter. I looked at Merritt with drawn eyebrows, wondering if she knew what was wrong with her sister Vivian. She just shrugged and climbed off the bar stool to take her plate to the empty sink. I reached out and booped Vivian's nose too, but I got no reaction. I decided to quit wasting time and get to the point.

"What's wrong, Vivian?" I asked, while I dished out some eggs and sausages onto a plastic monkey plate. "Cats got your tongue?"

"No?" Vivian looked at me narrowly. She sighed and straightened her posture. "I'm just worried that Miranda will tell dad about what I did and he will yell at me for it."

I nearly rolled my eyes at her name, but I just did a long hard blink instead. I don't blame her for being upset. Dean will believe whatever Miranda says over the truth from his own daughter. Vivian has also never been in trouble since she was five when she decided to use her bedroom wall as a canvas for her stick figure portrait of all of us. Luckily the markers weren't sharpies, so it came off well. But Dean nearly threw out all of the markers just from that one instance. I talked him down and we never spoke about it again. We did keep the marker box up on the top shelf of a cabinet and only let the girls use them when they have supervision. Merritt may be five, but she is more responsible for her age. I know we won't have any marker instances anymore. You could never be too careful though…

"I don't think he will." I tell Vivian as I slide her plate closer to her. "And he will have to go through me first if he does." Vivian kept her gaze down at her monkey plate. She picked up the fork and pushed her sausages up and down. They rolled around the eyes of the monkey. I placed a firm hand on her forearm and cocked my head. "You did the right thing. You stood up for your friend who was getting bullied by other students." I nodded and her eyes flicked up to mine. The same river blue glistened in the light like the water flowing down the spring on a sunny day. "Don't let anyone tell you otherwise. Alright?" I waited until Vivian nodded to tell her to eat while I went to get her and Merritt's backpacks packed and ready to go.

On the drive to school it was quiet. Merritt played silently with Charlotte and Vivian just stared out the window in a certain type of daydream. I'm not sure if she's thinking about anything or if her mind is just blank. Like a black hole that leads to an abyss.

After I dropped off Merritt at her school, I parked in a lot in front of Vivian's school. She begrudgingly climbed out and slammed the door shut and I walked around the car and towards Bonnie who stood by the steps of the front entrance with her son Boyd in hand. When Boyd spotted Vivian a bright smile gleamed on his face and he ran up to her. Her mood immediately shifted and they walked together up the steps and inside the building. Bonnie turned towards me as if she recognized the heels of my boots clicking on the cement ground. A small smile flashed across her face but quickly fell when she noticed my demeanor.

"Hello Vi." Bonnie greeted me. "How are you today?" I shook my head at her question. I'm confused and in rage by her presence. Why exactly is she even here, and why is she acting like everything is fine and dandy when it is obviously not? I gently grab her elbow and guide her away from the group of mothers who are flocking the entrance. They're going to be asking us to chip in for some party they decided to have for the school later. I assume since they're all chatting like a flock of birds, that tweet and chipper early in the morning, in a haze that slightly gets on your nerves when you are trying to sleep for another five minutes before trudging throughout the day. Bonnie doesn't say anything nor is she trying to break her arm free from my grasp. She just lets me guide her towards the parking lot and I let her go when we are now standing in front of my black Range Rover. I lower my voice like I'm silently disciplining her like one of my children.

"First off, don't call me Vi." I raise my eyebrows. She blankly stares into my eyes as I practically scold her. She has always been unfazed by things. Especially, when you have been scolded for your entire existence. "My name is Morgan now."

Bonnie drew in her eyebrows and narrowed her eyes. She slightly shook her head, not understanding why. "Since when did you change your name?"

"Since your elder from the cult found where I lived and I had no other choice but to change it so they couldn't track me down." I snapped. I almost flinched at my own reaction. I never knew I could get this mad about anything, really. I glance away from Bonnie's searching gaze. "Obviously, it didn't work." I practically mumbled to myself.

Bonnie didn't say anything and she had that blank face again. I let my eyes venture into her face, gazing on her dark as soil eyes, her smooth caramel complexion, her soft lips. It's crazy how her face started becoming a blur in my mind after the years. Her features started to disappear and leave nothing but a smooth surface across them. I could never forget her, no matter how long it had been since I last saw her. But the moment I would reminisce on her it made her look different. It first started by forgetting her bright smile. Her mouth formed over a flat surface. Then it was her left eye. Eventually, she almost became nothing but a blank face in some of our memories that started drifting away from my mind. But now that she is here with me and I could see her face again. Those faces started flooding back into my sacred memories. I wonder if she feels the same way?

"Why did you truly bring me over here, Vi?" Bonnie asked rather calmly. Her eyes softened and the corners of her lips turned up. She could sense that something has been on my mind. It's been on my mind all morning.

"Why are you still with the group?" I blatantly asked. My voice wavered and I struggled to get the next words out. "Especially after what Finch did to you?" Bonnie glanced behind her. She eyed the school as she nibbled on her bottom lip. Then she looked back at me, now with tears welling up in her eyes.

"I am free, Vi. It may not look like it, but I am. My husband Rick, talked Finch into letting us move out from the cabins and into our own house. Finch wanted to change the group and this was one of his ways." She slightly nodded as a smile of happiness crept up on her cheeks. "I may still be *in* the group, but I *am* free. I mean, my son gets to live a normal life. He gets to go to school and just be a kid... you had your way of being free and I have mine."

I didn't know what to say. It may not be my way of thinking but I could see how happy Bonnie seems now. Of course there's still some regret and sadness about her that I could sense. She is still a part of the group and she is still married to an elder from the group, but at least she could get some sense of freedom that has been given to her...

"Hello ladies!" A high pitched voice came from beside us. I turn my head to see a woman with short black hair and green eyes that are so vibrant it could burn a hole into your irises if you stare long enough. Wendy Goode is her name, and not because I wanted to know but because she forces everyone she meets to know her name. It's almost like she wants to imbed herself into your brain for as long as you know her. Her noxious voice already does that for her though. Wendy turned to Bonnie, completely bypassing me. "I'm Wendy Goode, you must be new here." Told ya. Wendy extended her hand to shake Bonnie's but she didn't accept it. Bonnie just politely smiles.

"Bonnie Whitfield." She said with a nod.

Wendy clasped her hands with a cheerful grin. "Well, I'm Wendy Goode. I'm-"

"You already said that." Bonnie interjected, with an annoyance in her tone of voice. Wendy's smile lessened and her eyes dimmed. She glanced over at me and back at Bonnie. I wasn't sure if she wanted me to step in, but I just kept my mouth shut.

"Yeah well, I like to make sure my name sticks." Wendy laughed. She continued on when we didn't acknowledge her joke. "Anyway, I'm the woman you go to when there's an event happening here at the school. I was wondering if you two would like to chip in for the spring dance that is happening the weekend the kids are off for school."

Bonnie plastered a very fake smile to me, but a believable, flattering smile to Wendy. "Actually, you had just interrupted a conversation I was having with Morgan, but I will get back to you on that." Wendy just stared for a moment at Bonnie, contemplating if her way of speaking was being rude or a unique way of being nice. I knew it wasn't very nice. Then she finally nodded and walked off, back to the flock of tweety birds at the front entrance. She glanced back at Bonnie with discernment as she directed her attention back to the chatting mothers.

Bonnie dropped her smile and let out a heavy sigh. She narrowed her eyes on me. "What?"

I hadn't realized that I was smiling, but my satisfaction was taking a strong hold over me.

I shook my head. "I don't know how you can tell someone to politely *fuck off*. But you did."

Bonnie's corner lips curved up and she shrugged. "Kill 'em with kindness, I guess."

We stood in silence for a few minutes. I stared at Bonnie with squinted eyes, wondering what she was thinking about. Then she turned back to me and said, "Do you want to get out of here?"

I glanced around pretending to think it over. But I'm sure she already knew my answer.

"Hell yeah."

* * *

"Seriously, who taught you to drive?" Bonnie questioned as she bellowed a lighthearted laugh. On the way downtown there are pathways of buildings in a row of shopping centers and antique shops. A truck swerved into my lane which caused me to swerve off the side of the road and onto gravel and patchy grass. Could I have handled it better rather than swerving off the road? Yes, I could have. But was I in a daze of bewilderment and excitement about being with Bonnie again after so many years? Yes, I was...

I rolled my eyes and held the door open for Bonnie to walk through. We entered an antique shop called ***Antique Treasures***. It was small, and what I mean by small, I mean only one aisle long and with no place to stand if someone came back up it. The smell of dust and old wooden furniture permeated the air, making my nose tickle when I inhaled it. I wouldn't say it's treasured antiques as the items were newer and nothing from the vintage years. But it sure smells like it. Bonnie picked up a small glass elephant. She turned it over with her fingers before setting it back down on a dusty glass table. Her fingers were coated in a thick layer of gray dust and she wiped her hands together. She glanced back at me eagerly for my response to her question.

I inhaled deeply before responding, bracing myself for the inevitable emotions that will shortly arise in me. "The man that took me in along with his wife."

"Yeah, Carl?" Bonnie narrowed her eyes as she caressed an oak dining table. She has to touch everything like a greedy child. She rubbed her fingers together to clean the dust off of them and moved on down the aisle.

I nodded even though she wasn't looking at me. "Yeah, Carl. He taught me how to drive but I didn't get my license until I was with Dean." I never told her about Dean and his love affair with his coworker Miranda. I just told her the sad pathetic story where the wife lies about how well her husband treats her and how he is such a loving father to his daughters. No one always tells the truth, even when they should be.

Bonnie drew in her brows before pointing a long, skinny finger at me. "Didn't you say that something happened to him and his wife?"

"Carl and Jodi," I explained. I could feel my eyes starting to burn and a lump behind the sockets grew as I fought back the tears that wanted to escape. "They died recently from a gas leak in their home."

Bonnie spun around on her heels and placed a firm hand on her abdomen. Her eyes softened and she stared at me with sorrow. "I am so sorry, Vi. That's awful."

I wave a dismissive hand. "It wasn't your fault." It may not be hers but it sure as hell is *theirs*. I know it is. I can feel it so deeply inside me that the group is the reason for their deaths. But I could sense Bonnie didn't know that. She would never agree to such things. She isn't harmful by heart because it's not in her nature to be.

"But still." Bonnie says as she reaches her arms out to embrace me. She squeezed my shoulders and I rested my chin onto hers. A tear broke free and slithered down my cold cheek. "I am so sorry for your losses."

When she pulled away I wiped the escaped tear off my cheek with the back of my hand and sniffled back the rest. I shook my head. "I'm fine, I just don't like talking about it. It makes it too real, you know?"

Bonnie nodded before turning away and continued to scan the items in the aisles. "Yeah, I know what you mean." I know she's talking about Martha. I wished I could have seen her one last time before she passed. I wondered if she would have come with me if I had just simply asked. I didn't want to risk anyone ratting me out, except for Bonnie. I knew she never would have...

"How did they find me?" The question left my mouth long before I could even process it properly. The question has been on my mind for years. How did the group find me at Carl and Jodi's house?

Bonnie looked at me from over her shoulder and a crease appeared in the center of her eyebrows. "What do you mean? Who found you?"

I almost rolled my eyes at her question. Seriously, what have we been talking about since we reconnected a couple days ago? It's a dumb question, if you ask me. "The group. They had found me living at Carl and Jodi's ranch a few years ago. That's why I am here today." I tilt my head. "Why is that?"

I watched as Bonnie's eyes scanned the room, searching for an answer for me. I don't think she is going to find one here. Then she shrugged. "I have no idea? They never told me they had found you... I honestly never knew they were even searching for you." Bonnie looked forward and continued to slowly walk back down the aisle, leaving me with more questions than answers.

* * *

After I picked up the girls from school, I headed home to make a chicken casserole for dinner. It's something simple and easy I had planned for the week. The leftovers should last me another day so I won't have to be making anything special tomorrow evening. It will be Friday tomorrow and Dean will do the cooking for Saturday. Sunday we have dinner at his parents house, which is also my dreaded days. If I could skip any day of the week, it would be Sunday just so I won't be forced to go to dinner with his family. It's a time of day where Meredith can criticize me for literally anything and everything at once, and I can't say a single word about it. If I did, it would get so much worse, and pretty fast too.

I dished out some casserole on plates and handed them to Merritt to set the table while Vivian did some science homework for school. She hates science but she does very well on it. Science is one of her highest grades in school compared to all of the other classes. I tell her that she should go to college for a science degree since she's great at it. She always gives me a shrug and a, *mhmm*. She can't help but be a scientist by heart, no matter how hard she tries not to be. I carry the last two plates out to the table and set them down in their usual places. Vivian has papers laid out on the table and cluttered Merritt's and her space. Merritt slid into her seat and gently pushed the papers to the side and away from her space. Vivian grudgingly moved them back and Merritt shot me a look of annoyance as I took my seat across the table. "Vivian, why don't you clean up these papers so we can eat." I say, reaching across the table and pushing the papers away from Merritt again.

Vivian shot daggers at me and huffed. "I can't eat right now. I'm busy." She complained. "I have to get these done tonight so I can turn them in tomorrow morning."

I wave a dismissive hand at her. "Well, they can wait till after dinner. Now put them away."

Vivian angrily stacked the papers in her binder and slammed it shut. Then she stomped her way up the staircase to put her homework safely in her room. As she stomped back to her seat and pulled her plate closer to her chair, Dean came stomping into the dining room and sighed when he took his seat without saying a word. Merritt and I gave each other a look and we silently started eating.

I watched Dean unbutton his top halfway down and just stared at his plate of chicken casserole placed in front of him. I normally would have asked him what happened today at work, but that was before I found out what he was secretly doing behind my back. Now I just don't give a damn anymore.

Dean looked up at Vivian who pushed a piece of chicken around with her fork, and now I knew what he was upset about...

"So," Dean said rather loudly, catching the girls' off guard. They looked at him with wide, peculiar eyes. "Are you going to tell me what happened the other day at school?" Vivian looked away from him and lowered her head like a cowardly puppy. Merritt wasn't sure who he was talking to so she gave him a simple answer.

"I painted a butterfly and counted all the way up to one-hundred." Merritt chippered, pretty satisfied by her accomplishments. I flashed her a proud smile and paid my attention back to Dean.

Dean gave her a blank expression while he kept his eyes on Vivian. "That's great sweetie, but I wasn't asking you. I was asking your sister."

"Oh." Merritt's face dropped and she lowered her head.

I reached out and padded a hand on the table to grab her attention. When she glanced up at me I gave her a smile. "I'm proud of you, Merritt."

"Vivian!" Dean shouted across the table, making all of us jump in our seats from the sudden outburst. Now all of our attention is on him. "Why did I have to hear from Miranda that you beat up her son?!"

Vivian dropped her fork and shot him a look. A look of rage that boiled up inside her and is ready to overflow any minute now. "I didn't beat Frankie up! I pushed him off of my friend. Who by the way was getting bullied by her sons!" Now it's a shouting match. If there was a contest of who could yell the loudest, Dean and Vivian would be in a tie. Vivian definitely inherited her anger from her father. That's for damn sure.

"You do realize that Miranda works for me, right?" Said Dean. "You can't be going around and beating up the twins like you did!"

"No, but you can go around and fuck her!" Vivian said abruptly. I knew she didn't mean to, but her anger and frustration got the worst of her.

Dean looked at her in horror, like he had just seen a ghost child walking past him. I don't blame him, I probably looked the same.

Merritt looked ever more confused as she glanced back and forth at the three of us. "What does *fuck* mean?"

I dropped my fork and slammed my chair back against the wall when I stood up. "No one will be talking like that in my house, is that clear!" I couldn't hold in my anger anymore and I shouted at all of them. Now the attention is on me. I turned to Dean. "You can't be sticking up for Miranda's sons when you don't even know the full story!" I turned to Merritt who stared at me in disbelief by my sudden rage. She has never seen me this angry ever. I quite frankly haven't either. "Merritt you will never use that word again, is that clear?" She slowly nodded her head. Then I turned to Vivian. "I understand you are frustrated and angry but you will never talk to any of us like that again!" Then I glanced at each and every one of them, who faltered their gazes on me like children who just got in deep trouble for something they had done. Except, two of them are children and they did get in deep trouble for what they had done. "You all will stop with this nonsense and grow the hell up! Do I make myself clear?" I waited until all three of them reluctantly nodded their heads and I glared down at my plate. No longer feeling the urge of hunger. I snatched my plate from the table and stomped towards the kitchen sink. "Now I'm not hungry."

Chapter 35

Sunday arrived quicker than expected. One moment I was at the dinner table, shouting at my family for their outbursts while I had an outburst of my own, and now I'm walking up the pebble sidewalk to Dean's parents' manor with a carrot cake in hand. The girls followed suit as I led them and Dean to the large steel front door.

Dean trudged beside me with a roasted turkey in a tin tray with a plastic lid domed around it. The steam trickled down the sides of the lid as it was freshly cooked before our arrival. We climbed the stone staircase leading up to the steel front doors. Dean reached out and pushed the doorbell, a doomsday song chimed from inside and after waiting a couple of minutes, Meredith answered the door herself. She smiled brightly at Dean and the girls, while she kept her gaze from my direction. She was wearing an all white sundress with fringe sleeveless and tan wedges with ever so slightly pink lips. Today she chose something pinky, which isn't like her usual deep red or nude tan lipsticks.

I just plastered on a fake smile, knowing very well that Meredith can see through me. I try to keep the peace for the girls, and not because I am afraid of Meredith. That I am damn sure not! If it wasn't for Dean's parents being the girls's only grandparents, then I would have told them both to politely fuck off. But seeing how the girls absolutely adore their grandparents, then I can make an exception to bite my tongue everytime Meredith says something snarky towards me... I do wonder how she would feel knowing that her son is an unfaithful bastard of a husband that she birthed and raised? Who am I kidding? She would be delighted knowing that Dean was with another woman besides me. She would thank Miranda for helping Dean realize that he never truly loved me and that now he could live a happy fulfilling life. Like I am so hard to live with. I never snapped back at Dean for yelling at me or the girls, except for dinner that one night. But that was only because I had lost my respect for him. The same as he did for me. I kept my demeanor low so I wouldn't intrude on Dean's work life.

The girl I was then, isn't the woman I am now. I am done keeping the family together. I am done pretending that our marriage isn't over, and I am done letting people tell me what I should and shouldn't do with *my life!* I am taking back what is mine and I'm sure as hell am not going to apologize for it...

When I finally brought myself back to my senses, I noticed Meredith eyeing me with a hint of disgust. I cocked my head and narrowed my eyes at her. "What's the matter?"

Meredith slightly shook her head. "Oh, nothing." I sighed thinking maybe that was all she was going to say. But knowing Meredith for almost a decade now, she is certainly not done with speaking her mind. She gave the faintest smile, not wanting to waste her energy on me for a full one. "I'm just wondering how you can style your daughters' hair but not your own." I ran a hand over my signature braid that trailed along my spine. I did put in effort by pinning back the flyaways and using hairspray to prevent the frizz. But she means I always wear my hair in a braid and never anything else. I know how to do my daughters' hair almost professionally, mine not so much. I don't mind though, I was only taught how to braid or put my hair in a low bun. The low bun is more of Bonnie's signature look and the braid is mine. I gave her the same expression. Narrowed eyes and a faint smile.

"Well, not everyone can afford a hairstylist to come and do their hair daily, Meredith." I knew I should've stopped there but I couldn't help myself. My eyes flicked across the space we were in. The girls had run off into the backyard and Dean marched into the kitchen before he could hear our conversation. I knew at that moment I could finally get in a little jab at Meredith, since no one's here to stop me. "By the way, how can you afford to have a hairstylist, a makeup stylist, a housekeeper, a groundskeeper, and a butler? I sure as hell know it ain't with your money. Oh wait, it's with your *husband's* money. It seems to me that you and I both are the same." I knew she would find offense by the use of her husband making all the money and by saying that we were the same person. We kind of are though. We both live off of our husbands money while we take care of an entire household of our own. The only difference between her and I is that I don't hire caretakers to do all of my household duties and basic needs like she does. I work hard for what I have and I don't need an old witch telling me differently.

Before Meredith could retort with an insult, I marched past her and into the backyard to watch the girls play. They danced in their floral dresses with happiness in their steps. Their happiness makes me happy, that's why I stick around with a family that doesn't want me around. But my girls do, and that's all that matters to me...

We sat down at the dining table. Dean and I sat near the far end and the girls sat in between their grandparents in the center. Spencer had a far away look in his eyes as he took a bite out of the carrot cake that I made. I examined his face to see if there was a hint of enjoyment from the piece. But there was nothing but isolation in his eyes. I could tell that

Spencer hates family gatherings like this. At least he and I have something in common. Meredith looked at us, making sure that we enjoyed dinner with empty plates. Of course though, she didn't look at mine as she really didn't care if I had enjoyed dinner or not. She was probably wishing that I hated it. Have some undercooked turkey, maybe? Or a hair in my cheesy rice? Neither of those came true, but I wasn't a fan of the flan that their chef made. It wasn't as good as Jodi makes it. It wasn't as creamy nor as sweet as hers. It was rather slimy and sour, which is quite unusual for flan. But I never complained. I won't let Meredith get any satisfaction from it...

"I spoke with Tabitha over the phone the other day." Dean said, scooping a piece of flan *and* carrot cake on his fork. The audacity to mix my delicious cake with the vomit worthy flan that his parents didn't even make. If I hadn't known better, I would take my butter knife that rested beside my plate and stab him in the back with it. Just like he's been doing to me for years. When will it be my turn?

"Oh really?" Meredith tried to seem interested in Dean's choice of conversation. She does a terrible job at hiding it. "What did she say?"

Tabitha is Dean's cousin. The girl that was reading Dracula at the dinner table that one evening. It was the first time meeting his family. I'm pretty sure she was in college for a literature professor degree. I hadn't heard anything about her since. I haven't even seen her in any Christmas cards. I wonder why Dean didn't tell me the other day that he had spoken with her. Unless he just never had the chance to.

"Well, she just graduated with a masters degree and now she is going for her doctorate." Dean informed us as he continued to eat his mess of my dessert. Every time he stabs into my cake and scoops a piece of flan, it is like the hundredth stab into my heart. I should be immune to his inflicted pain no matter if he means it or not. But I'm really not.

"That's good to hear." Spencer finally spoke, snapping out of his abandoned stare. "I like that girl, she's smart."

"Well, her choice of degree says otherwise." Meredith murmured as she took a sip of her red wine.

The sound of a fork hitting a plate startled me. I looked over to see Merritt sitting there with eyes on me. I almost forgot that the girls were here. They were a certain kind of quiet that I had never heard before. Merritt looked at me expectantly.

"Can I go?" She asks me, pushing her plate away from her. It was mostly empty except for the strip of turkey and a few grains of rice. Turkey was never her favorite kind of meat. She prefers chicken except for the occasional steak, which I don't blame her. I prefer those choices too... "I'm finished eating."

Before I could respond, Meredith chimed in for me. "Of course sweetie. Go have fun."

Even though Meredith gave her the go, Merritt still looked at me for an answer. At least someone cares for my acceptance. I give her a nod with a faint smile. She immediately pushed back her chair and hopped off shortly before running off down the hallway and out towards the garden. The fireflies are out when the sun starts to dawn. Merritt and Vivian love to catch them in jars and watch them as they glow. They do eventually set them free. They wouldn't dare let them die on their watch.

Vivian watched as Merritt raced outside to the garden and she looked at me with excitement.

"Can I go too? The fireflies are out."

"Of course," Meredith yet again, answered for me. "Go ask for a jar in the kitchen, so you can catch them."

Vivian raced down the hallway and soon disappeared outside.Now the table is empty except for the four of us who occupied half of it with empty plates and short glances and glares at one another. The room was full of awkward silence until a loud ringing of a bell filled in the empty spaces of the room. Dean leaned his torso to the side and pulled out his cellphone from his pants pocket. I took a short glance at his phone. The caller was none other than Miranda Faux, in bold white lettering that popped up on his screen. I nearly rolled my eyes at it. I could feel my blood starting to simmer. Why the hell would she be calling? She knows Dean is occupied with his family on the weekends. Dean shuffled out of his seat and put a finger up before exiting the room to take the call. I was left for one excruciatingly long minute alone with Dean's parents. I swear to god, if this isn't a work related call then I'm going to lose my mind. I kept my gaze down until I heard heavy footsteps march back down the hall, and when I looked up to find Dean standing in the doorway, his face was stricken with anxiousness and fear. It looked like he had seen a ghost. He's all wide eyed and flushed face with a trembling lip and shaky hands. He didn't look like he was going to cry, but he trembled out of fear. But fear for what? I immediately stood up from my seat out of too much concern for someone like him. I may still look at him as the man I met before I married him, and sometimes all I want to see is him. Sometimes I pretend he didn't change and that he didn't have an affair. Sometimes I have to think past those feelings and actions just so I won't lose myself again. I just sometimes hate myself for caring too much about him than I should...

"What's wrong?" I ask him. "What happened?"

Dean grabbed Spencer and Meredith's full attention now and they also stood up in concern.

"What happened, son?" Spencer asked him after he didn't respond to me.

Dean inhaled deeply before saying, "Something happened with the dealership."

"What do you mean?" Meredith asked with eagerness in her tone.

Dean shrugged. "I'm not sure? The cops think it was a break-in but no one stole anything."

"Why didn't they call you first?" I said, narrowing my eyes. "Why did Miranda know before you?" It seems a little concerning that the woman he is having an affair with was called about a business that isn't even hers. Yes, she works for Dean as a saleswoman, but she isn't a beneficial owner of the company. Dean is. It just seems odd that he is now informed about what happened to his business.

Dean stared at me like he was pondering his next choice of words. Then he replied, "Because I put her down as my business partner. She gets the calls if anything happens when I'm off work."

"Wh- why would you do that?" I said before I could process it. I know it's not a, must know now, sort of question but I just can't believe he put Miranda down as a business partner. She gets all of the access to the company. Why would he be so stupid and stubborn to do such a thing?

"Nevermind that." Spencer interjected with a dismissive hand. Dissing me out from the conversation. "What happened to my dealership?" His tone became clear and angry with a boiling expression on his face. I could practically see the pot overflowing on the stovetop and ready to catch fire any second now.

Dean matched his expression and pointed a finger to his own chest. "That dealership is *mine* now. You had me sign for it, remember? *I own it.*"

Spencer raised a finger in the air, ready to pounce on his son if he speaks again. Meredith stood in between them both and shouted, "You both need to get your shit together and shut the fuck up!" After her outburst, there was nothing but fuming silence. She turned to Dean on the heels of her coastal wedges. "Should we go down to the dealership with you?"

I'm surprised she is even asking. Normally she would just march right out the front door and drive herself there with no questions asked.

But now she suddenly has a change of mindset and decides to ask for Dean's acceptance. Maybe she thinks it will calm him down knowing that he is in control to say yes or no? Either way, I already knew the answer, and I already knew how much of a pain in the ass she will be once we get down there... So god, please help me now.

* * *

We all climbed out of our Range Rovers and marched up the dealership parking lot that was filled with parked cars for sale, and entered the building's front entrance. The building was full of police officers and clerks, and now adding us. We headed towards the sheriff who was chatting with one of his deputies, and as I walked I felt a thick *crunch* from under my boots. I looked down to find pieces of glass spilled over the granite floors. I followed the shattered shards of glass trail and saw that the big window that overlooked the parking lot and highway was no longer there. Two men nailed up a blue tarp to substitute a wall for the meantime. The warm breeze rolled in and evaporated onto my skin. The warmer weather is finally coming in, officially saying goodbye to winter until the next eight months when it rolls back in again. I turned my attention to the sheriff who came over to Dean and pulled him over to the side. Spencer kept himself in the center of both of them to assert his authority over the dealership, even though he is no longer a part of the business. He never wanted to give it to his son. He knew he would make too many changes and risk losing the business. But all Dean ever did was turn it into something bigger and better and make it thrive again. Meredith talked Spencer into letting Dean take ownership over it. She told him how he is getting old and needs to retire and spend more time with his wife than with his coworkers. That must be hell for him to be around Meredith all day, everyday. You can tell on his face he isn't happy with his choice, but he is trying his hardest to support Dean and his decisions with the company. After this, I don't think he will trust and support Dean as the owner anymore.

I couldn't hear much of what they were saying or what the sheriff was telling them, but I followed suit with them as they walked towards a nearby Jeep that was parked inside the entranceway. It was a yellow Jeep with black rims and a soft top roof. Glass shards surrounded the Jeep and on the inside leather seats. The windows were smashed in and the side of the passenger door was dented in. I examined the damage as the sheriff spoke. I told the girls to stay with Meredith and away from the glass, which I knew she wasn't too thrilled to do so with the sigh she let out, but I didn't really care. I walked around the front of the Jeep to see the bumper was torn off and thrown onto the ground beside it. As I looked up at the front window I saw a red substance that wrote a word in rigged lines. **Repent**.

I knew then that the break-in wasn't for Dean but it was for me. I recognized the red substance as the red paint that was smeared on me the night of the ritual. The paint that tingled my face and left a tinted stain on my skin. No matter how hard I scrubbed at it, it would never really come off. Not until after the fifth bath when it had finally disappeared from under the warm water.

They must've found out about me and Dean. Where I lived and where he worked. It was all a huge sign that they are still coming for me. **Repent** for my sins and sacrifice myself to save us all. How are they always a step behind me whenever I think I lost them for good? Bonnie's sudden arrival here and now this? It all seems like a plan they are masterminding. Bonnie said she didn't know they were looking for me, even after all these years. But was she lying to me? Was everything she told me a lie? I need to stop this, for once and for all...

Chapter 36

I marched up to Bonnie with anger boiling inside me. The police couldn't figure out who did the break-in at the dealership, nor was the break-in really one. The cameras also were turned off, so it didn't record anything. Whoever did it never stole anything. No cash, no files or information. They took absolutely nothing. They just vandalized the building for whatever reason they didn't understand. I knew why. But I never told them I knew. I never spoke to Dean about my past, especially the group. I never thought it was relevant and I also wanted to forget about it. To move forward from my dark past and make a new life for me. But unfortunately, my past doesn't want to forget me like I do.

Bonnie was speaking with the flock of tweety birds about the spring dance that was arriving soon. The mothers will probably flock to me about chipping in for the party or to be a chaperone. But I have plans for today and talking to the snobby mothers is not one of them.

Bonnie turned around when she heard my boots thunking up behind her. Her eyes lit up when she saw me and a small smile appeared on her lips. She looked as elegant as usual wearing a long yellow sundress with frilled sleeves and white flats on her petite feet. I remembered when she had told me that the color yellow suits me. It seems that it also suits her. Her hair twisted up into a low bun with strands of coiled hair that wisped over her face as the breeze blew softly against her skin. Her hair was similar to mine, curly with frizz that refuses to be tamed. Only she lets it go however it likes rather than perfecting it. She somehow manages to always look so beautiful that way than when I let my hair do whatever it wants. It's a messy but elegant style for her. But a lioness mane on me.

Her smile falters when she senses my anger and she prepared to be excused from the other mothers before I even reached her. When I did I grabbed her by the elbow and practically pulled her away and behind my car to keep out of sight from the crowd. I release her arm and stand with my hands on my hips while I tapped an impatient boot on the cement ground.

"What's wrong, Vi?" Bonnie finally asked when I hadn't spoken. I'm not even sure how to speak to her right now, but I know I need to.

After I contemplated on what I was going to say, I let out a dragged sigh before I spoke. "Were you lying when you said you didn't know the group was searching for me?" I finally urged out. I tried to keep my words from pouring out with rage and frustration. But I wasn't sure if I did a good enough job on that, because Bonnie practically flinched like I just spat in her face instead. She looked at me like I was insane for even asking her that question. Her eyes flicked around our surroundings and she folded her arms tightly across her chest.

She shook her head. "I don't understand what you are saying?" She said, narrowing her eyes. "Why would I lie about something like that?"

I scoffed. "I don't know, why don't you tell me?" I shifted in my stance, starting to feel uneasy about this. Who am I kidding, I was already uneasy about all of this. "Or was that just your guy's plan? To use you to find me because they knew I would run if I saw them again."

Bonnie stared at me for a long moment before shaking her head again in disbelief. "Look Vi, I don't know what the group has done to you. But the last time I knew, they were back in the same ol' town that is five hours away from here." Her eyes flashed sincerity as she spoke. If she isn't telling me the truth, then she is a really good liar. And the last time I checked, Bonnie couldn't lie worth shit, even if her life depended on it. That might have changed since then and maybe now she grew her acting abilities? I do want to believe her but after everything that has happened I'm not so sure if I can anymore. Bonnie inhaled deeply before speaking again. "I told the group where I live, but I have *never* told them about you." She reached out and placed a soft hand on my forearm. Chills slithered down my spine as her touch penetrated a warm fuzzy feeling through my skin. I wanted to cave at that moment. I wanted to wrap my arms tightly around her shoulders and tell her how scared I am for me and my family's safety. I wanted to ask her for help to end all of this pain and suffering that the group had endured on me. I wanted to ask her to help me get rid of them for good, but I know she wouldn't agree to it. The group is all she knows and she still sees them as her family. She wouldn't ever betray them like I would. So I fought that urge before it got too much to handle. Bonnie fluttered her eyes at me before speaking in a low but soft voice. "You have to trust me."

I pulled my arm away from her touch and shook my head. "I don't think I can anymore."

I walked away from her and climbed into my car. The engine huffed as I switched the ignition on and stared at Bonnie through the rearview mirror. I watched her stand in disbelief that I would ever say such a thing. It caught her off balance and it did the same for me too. Never in my lifetime would I ever think I would speak such words to her. Bonnie has been my best friend since we were born. We would joke around about us being friends in another lifetime. Like being reincarnated into someone else but still being as close as ever. We got each other through so much and we were always by each other's side. Especially when we needed each other the most. We never knew our relationship would change and for the worse. Everything has changed and there is nothing we can do about it. Now we have to protect our families from each other. I just wished we could have stayed close after all these years. I suppose, not all things can be possible...

I waited until Bonnie moved away from my car before backing out of my parking space and exiting the school lot, and onto the main highway. Leaving my thoughts behind with her. I can't think about her anymore. I have bigger issues to deal with, and one of them is hopping on a train to the town I hoped to leave in the past, that I am now forced to face again.

* * *

I texted Dean to pick up the girls after school. I didn't tell him why and neither did he ask. He's probably busy putting the business back together to even check his messages. Or he's too busy sucking Miranda's face again. Either way, it is none of his business where I went and why. All he has to do is be a father for once in his damn life and take care of our daughters while I'm gone. Is that really too much to ask? Probably, but I don't give a damn. I'm too busy trying to save me and my children's life to worry about him.

The train was long but scenically beautiful. There was nothing but pastures of flowers and cows for hours. Some fields were full of yellow dandelions and wild flowers, and others had cows and sheep that roamed the green fields. The spring showers certainly brought spring flowers and vivid greenery from miles and miles away. It reminded me of the first time I rode on this train when I was fleeing from my past and moved in with Joel. I nearly tear up when I think about the farewell to Carl and Jodi before I stepped onto this train. Never realizing that would be my last time ever seeing them again. I wonder what would have happened if I never got on? Would Carl and Jodi still be alive, or would we all end up dead?

Fond memories of Vivian and Merritt flashed in front of my eyes. The first time I ever saw Vivian was when I gave birth to her. It was a long labor that made me regret all of my decisions that had gotten me there. But the moment she was brought up to my chest and I saw her perfect little face that wailed for me to soothe her, changed my whole mindset. I didn't regret it because now I have her. My perfect daughter. Another memory flashed from when Vivian was three and she was meeting Merritt for the first time in the hospital. I held them both onto my lap and watched in admiration as Vivian smiled and cooed at baby Merritt. I knew from then that they would be close. Another fond memory was Christmas, four years ago. Vivian jumped with excitement when she saw her first bicycle. It was purple with pink tinsel on the handles and flowers that were in the shape of her name on the sides, and white stabilizers hooked on the back tire. She was begging Santa for a bicycle to ride when we went on our afternoon strolls around the neighborhood. Something that we enjoyed doing as a family once, but now I can barely get Dean away from work and the girls to play outside. I can't even remember when we stopped hanging out as a whole. It might have been when Spencer signed over his business to Dean.

Dean worked for four years for his father while he was in college for business. After he graduated, Spencer finally gave up the dealership to his son. Everything was going great until Dean wasn't making enough sales to afford the business. So he had to work extra hours to get the dealership rates back up before it got too close to sign for bankruptcy, and had to shut it down. Luckily it never got to that point and after a few months of hard work, Dean got the dealership up and running again by making hundreds of sales each month. Turns out Spencer was charging too high for each vehicle and the coworkers weren't taking the job seriously enough to even make sales. "He had his workers slacking on the job." Dean had told me after a month of being owner of the dealership. "I have no choice but to let them go." After lowering the rates and rehiring new employees, the sales went through the roof and the business was back up and running again. It's great that Dean takes his job seriously and he is a good business owner. But he never learned how to manage his work life and his family life together.

He started coming home later than usual, sometimes even missing dinner, and started working on weekends as well. He eventually stopped spending time with his family all together and his job became his life. After years of arguments over him choosing his job over his family and that his children simply missed spending time with him, he finally made a change and started coming home for dinner everyday. Unless something important came up at work and he had to miss it. He did make up for his absence by spending the weekends with us annually. Everything was going well with him. Everything was going great for us. That was until he hired Miranda Faux. She slowly made her way into our life. She played the damsel in distress part really well, with being a single mom to twin boys and needing a job to afford to feed them. I actually supported her and became close friends with her since our kids were going to the same school and all. I would listen to all of her depressing stories about her ex husband leaving her and the boys for another woman and going cross country in a minivan together like some hippies in love. She loved calling her ex and his girlfriend hippies, but not in a good way. The way where they camp out to smoke marujuana everyday and basically just ditch their lives and families to get high and party with other people like them. The last time I was told that the boys haven't seen their father since they were two. I actually liked Miranda and thought that we were good friends. Of course, that was until she started getting close to Dean, and now they have sex in his office behind my back. Just because she thinks that she has Dean wrapped around her dainty little finger, she is some rich bitch that can be snobby to everyone including me. I hope she comes to the realization that just because Dean comes from a wealthy background doesn't necessarily mean that he's wealthy as well. Because he is far from rich, but he is far from poor...

The last memory that flashed in my mind was Merritt's first ballet recital. She was in ballet for only two years and she came to the realization that she didn't want to do it anymore. But her recital was special to her. Her entire family was there to support her. Dean's parents and his aunts and uncles and cousins came to cheer her on and the joy that showed brightly through her eyes when she was flooded with love and bouquets of her favorite flowers was my favorite memory of all time. Those memories made me realize that if I didn't get on this train fourteen years ago, then I wouldn't have these memories at all. And I don't think I could imagine my life without them...

A sudden noise directed my attention towards a woman that sat two rows down from me. I could only see the back of her head as she bent forward in her seat to sneeze into her cupped hands. Her hair was a silky blonde that trailed down her spine and disappeared behind her seat, but I could imagine how long it was. The different blonde hues and pin-straight hair reminded me of a special someone from decades ago. Someone who bullied me daily just because I wasn't like them. I didn't have the mindset that Finch had embedded into our brains since birth. I rebelled against them and their savior when I ran away that dark night. I wonder what she thought or had said about me when she found out I had left. She probably called me weak and disgraceful to our family and savior. Though I was weak by not sacrificing myself for them, I did have a strong will to live and discover a life that I could choose for myself. Not one that was already chosen for me.

The woman sat up straight and poised and she never scanned her surroundings. She just stared straight forward at an empty wall, barely moving as the train bumped on a shifting track. I decided to keep my attention to myself and rest my head against the large window. It was warm from the sun beating down on it in the humid afternoon. I closed my eyes and let all those memories replay in my mind as I let it soothe me into a deep sleep..

Then I woke to a high pitched squelch from under the train. A small building emerged from the window and a flat cement surface was in front of the tracks. The platform to the station to my past. Carl and Jodi appeared in a flash. They were standing together as they watched the train approach. They waited for me to come home. I waited for them too. But I'm not naive because I already know that they aren't really there. Just another fixation of my imagination. I squeezed my eyes shut as I stretched out my craned neck. When I opened them, they were gone... like I said, another fixation of my imagination.

The train came to a halt and the whistle blew a signal to exit if this is your stop. I sat impatiently watching the people in front of me come to a line as they exited through the cart doors and reunite with their loved ones that waited out on the station. As the line grew farther down the aisle the blonde woman stood up from her seat and joined in without a glance back. I scanned her silky hair that grew past her waist and the long white dress that brushed the ground as she took a step forward, slowly moving up the line. She looked unusual standing in the line dressed like that. Everyone wore basic clothes like jeans and a t-shirt with a light coat overtop. But she wore a handmade dress with long tight sleeves. Not only was her appearance peculiar, but her mannerisms were also. They were almost robotic with the way she clasped her hands together in front of her waist and bowed her head ever so slightly to make herself seem smaller than she actually was. That was a manner that us girls were taught to not bother the elders, and to keep small so they wouldn't notice us. As I watched her disappear through the door, I stood up and joined the line. When I was finally out of the train and into the thick air, I glanced around for the blonde woman. But she was nowhere to be seen. I shook her out of my mind and made my way to the station's parking lot where Joel stood in front of his truck. He leaned against the bumper with folded arms as he scanned his surroundings for me.

I called him this morning before taking the girls to school and told him that I was coming to town. He asked me if that would be a good idea with the cult and all, but I told him that I needed to get closure from Carl and Jodi's death. And that maybe I could help him pack up their belongings with him, so he's not doing all of it alone. He sold their house and pastures within a week of it being on the market. He got a good fortune from it but I do wonder if he might regret selling it since the property has been in his family for generations. I knew he wanted the property but I also knew how much he loved being in the city rather than in an isolated town. He would also have to close down the diner which I knew he would never do. It was a big decision for him and I would hate for him to do the rest of it alone. Besides, I need his truck.

When Joel spotted me walking out of the station, he plastered a weak smile on his solemn face. I can tell all of this is eating him alive. A twinge of guilt pained my stomach. I should have gone with him a long time ago to help with the funeral and everything else. He shouldn't have to do it all alone, and yet he did. I can tell how all of the stress has aged him with his dark circles and pale skin almost made him look sickly. His skin showed more wrinkles than he had before. It's hard for me to see him this way. When I stood inches away from him, I wrapped my arms tightly around his shoulders and embraced him tightly. I can hear Joel stifle back some tears as he squeezed me back. When our embrace was over we silently climbed inside the truck and pulled out of the station and down a dirt road.

After a few minutes of silence passed by. Joel glanced over to me and cleared his throat. "I assume you're only staying for a day since you didn't bring a bag."

I only planned to be here for a few hours before spending the night on the train ride back home. It was already the afternoon when the sun was the warmest out of the day. In a couple of hours the sun will dawn and that will be my cue to head back home before the girls wake for school in the morning. I didn't make it clear to Joel that was my plan, but yes to his question...

I nodded. "Mhmm." I stared out the side window at the valley of green grass and farm life that was around every corner. This town is known as farmland where many of the farmers work and live. A lot of the diners produce comes from this region of town and not from the city itself. Found that out when I had to order produce for the diner.

The town is a quiet, desolate place compared to the city. But it can be peaceful to visit once in a while to get away from the noise.

When I glanced over at Joel, he had an appreciative smile on his face. "Well I'm glad you're here. I have a lot of running around to do. It's great that you're here to help."

I reached out and placed a firm hand on his shoulder before turning my attention back outside the window. "What are you going to do with their stuff?" I asked, not needing to emphasize the *their* because he already knows who I meant.

Joel let out a heavy sigh and ran a hand through his silky hair. "I'm renting a storage unit until I know what to do with all of it."

"That's smart."

"Yeah, so feel free to take whatever you want." Joel flicked on the turning signal as we were making our way into town. "If you want any furniture for you or the girls, I can bring it with me when I drive back to the city."

"Okay, thanks." I smile at him. The sky is so vibrant and pretty today. The cumulus clouds were so fluffy like cotton being plucked right off of the trees. It reminded me of that dream I had a couple of nights ago. The dream where I was lying in the field of tall grass and wildflowers. All of the scents in my dream permeated my nostrils again. The fresh grass and flowers, and the pollen that was being collected by the singing bumblebees. It was right before I started to smell smoldering smoke and before I got transported back in front of that burning building. I still don't know what the dreams are telling me. But I can sense that it's trying to get through to me before something happens. I take it as a warning that something bad will happen. I just don't know when or how?

"Oh, how was the funeral?" I blurted out. My mind brings me back to the reality that was outside of my head.

Joel shrugged. "Oh you know, the same as every funeral. Depressing and expensive."

I giggle at his choice of words. He gave a faint smile before turning back to seriousness. "A woman named Mary wanted me to give you her condolences." Joel looked at me with raised brows and waved a hand in a sweeping motion. "That lady is a chatterbox, for sure."

I let out a lighthearted laugh while nodding my head. "She really is. Jodi never liked her very much."

"Well, I can see why." Joel blew out some air from his flat lips. Mary must've done a number or two on his patience scale. I forget that Joel doesn't know who the people at church are. I could imagine how awkward he must've felt being in a room with grieving strangers. It must've been awful.

"I knew her daughter Isabelle." I filled him in on what she was like before I had to leave. "I'm not sure where she is now, but hopefully she's doing what she feels passionate about." I remember her telling me that she wanted to be a travel journalist, but her mother wanted her to marry a boy from church just because his family had money. It reminded me of Dean and I, how I married him not because of his wealth. Because like I said before, he is not wealthy like his parents are, but because of the pregnancy. However we are now distant and lonely. I hope Isabelle didn't get a similar fate that I had...

"Yeah." said Joel, inhaling a deep breath. "She went on and on about how she chose to be some sort of journalist and how she isn't going to make it well in life because of her decision."

I looked at Joel wide eyed and a huge smile appeared on my face. I feel a sense of joy creeping up inside of me and I couldn't be happier for Isabelle. She actually stood up to her mother and chose what she is passionate about. "That's great." I practically cheer. "I'm happy for her."

Joel looked at me, puzzled. "What? That her mother had practically said that she is doomed in life?"

I shove a hand on Joel's shoulder in a playful manner. "Of course not. I'm just happy that she listened to herself, that is all."

"Ahh okay." Joel nodded and rested an elbow on the opened windowsill.

We drove the rest of the way in silence as we listened to the static noise that played through the radio. The road down to Carl and Jodi's property doesn't have any frequencies for the radio stations in the area. The ongoing popping of static is the only thing you will be listening to for several miles on. It can get less annoying when you hear it over and over again. Usually, I just turn the radio off. But in this instance we leave it on to fill in the gaps of silence that lingered in the air.

When we made it to the property and up the pebble stone driveway, I took in the home that I used to live in. It looked the same but the windows seemed darker than before. The house that was once occupied with love and care, is now isolated and nothing but an empty place. Everything seemed dreary and haunting. Though, It didn't help that the sky was gray with stormy clouds that clumped together and were almost ready to release the moisture that was trapped from within.

Joel turned off the engine and pulled out his keys from the ignition, and glanced over at me before exiting the vehicle. I watched him walk up towards the house and up the patio staircase. His keys still in hand, he rummaged through them until he found the correct key to the front door, and moments later he disappeared from inside.

I unclenched my jaw that bit hard on my cheek and climbed out of the truck, closing the door behind me. I trudged up the pathway and up the stairs. I shook out the weight that bore down my shoulders and entered through the ajar door. As I entered I got a whiff of gasoline in the air. Though I'm sure it was all in my head since the gas leak was several weeks ago. Maybe almost a month ago. I was never told how long Carl and Jodi had been dead for. It could have been days or even weeks before their bodies were discovered. I'm not even sure who had found them, nor do I want to know any more information about their deaths. I know enough to be sure that it was all Finch's fault. He's a psychopath. Of course, I know it was his fault...

"I already finished the kitchen and the mudroom." Joel entered the room with a cloth and a spray bottle in his hands. He glanced around at the empty space and pointed towards the windows. "I just need to wipe down the windows and then I can start with the living quarters." I reached my hand out and he knowingly gave me the cloth and spray bottle. "You can start packing the living room. I'll join you once I'm done." I gave him a courtesy smile and he nodded, and started for the trinkets on the fireplace mantle.

I sprayed a window and wiped it clean. Dust settled on the windowsill and I wiped it off with the rag and spray. Jodi would have a fit if she saw how dusty her house was. She cleaned daily to keep up with the southern dirt that blew in the wind. It always found a way through the crevices of the windowsills and settled somewhere in the house. That's the bad thing about living in the south. Red dirt and brown dust blows in from the doors and windows and coats a thick layer all over your house. That's the reason why Jodi didn't buy many trinkets or glass ornaments that sit on shelving and mantle tops. Because the dust hides in the clutter and makes it much harder to clean.

When I finished cleaning all of the windows in the house, including the upstairs windows, I set the cloth and bottle down on a small table in the hallway and I pushed open a creaky door to what once was my bedroom. Everything looked the same just as I left it. I glanced around looking at the bed that sat in the corner. A closet and a small wooden stepping stool were in the other corner. I walked over to the window and moved the lace curtains to the side. The barn rests abandoned in the pastures with no animals in sight. I suppose Joel sold off the horses and sheep and all the other critters Carl cared for, to other ranchers in town. I wonder if the people that bought this property will use it for the same reason Carl had? I tug the curtains back in front of the window and turn around for the door. I looked up to find the horseshoe that Carl hung up for "good luck", still hanging from above the door. A smile rises on my face and I reach down to move the stepping stool in front of the doorway. I stepped up on it and reached up, and grabbed the weighted horseshoe from off the wall. Once I got it, I moved the stool back up against the closet and I wiped the dust off of the shoe with a damp cloth, and soon closed the bedroom door behind me. I gathered my things and marched down the staircase to place them down onto the table. I slid the horseshoe into my bag and checked the time on my phone. **2:32** in the afternoon. Shit, I better get the keys to Joel's truck and run out before it gets too late. I'll come back of course, to help Joel pack up the rest of the house. But I need to make sure I get what I need done before dark...

"Hey, Joel?" I nonchalantly lean a shoulder upon the living room door frame. Joel placed a picture frame that was wrapped in bubble wrap into a box beside him. He glanced up at me with an expectant expression on his face. "Can I borrow the truck for a bit? I want to go to the graveyard to visit their gravestones." He just stared at me with squinted eyes. I add, "I had mentioned it this morning. From over the phone."

"No, I know." Joel nodded but his gaze stayed the same. "I'm just thinking about where I placed the keys. Have you seen them?"

I stood up and shook my head. "No. You may have misplaced them in the kitchen?" I started for the kitchen and like I had said, they were on the kitchen counter by the sink. I snatched them and dangled them by the key ring in front of Joel to see. "Found them."

"Oh, good." Joel slumped his shoulders. "My mind hasn't been right since everything that happened."

I wave a dismissive hand. "I don't blame you. It has been an odd couple of weeks, huh?"

Joel nodded, staring outside the window. He looked to be reminiscing on something then said, "Yeah, it has been." I waited until Joel looked back at me before telling him that I will be back soon to help with the rest of the packing. Then I marched towards the car and switched on the ignition shortly before driving off back down the dirt road.

* * *

The turning signal *tick tick ticked* as I turned into the Magnolia Cemetery. It's gotten its charming name from the acres of aging gravestones and flowery magnolia trees. Each twenty rows of gravestones had a pinky tree that stood tall and firmly in the dry soil. Its petals cupped around a tentacle bulb called the stamen as they started to blossom their light pink petals. I parked the truck on the side of the pathway and climbed out. I trudged through the graveyard in search of the grave that I had to see for a final goodbye. Joel said that Carl and Jodi reserved a spot for their future burial right in front of the third magnolia tree on the right. I thank the lord above for the trees that had been planted to help me navigate the one grave out of hundreds in the acres that goes back for miles. And thank heavens that Carl and Jodi reserved a spot that is easy to find. I spot their gravestone from a distance and I waver before I trudge my way up to them. I stare down at the bevel stone. Magnolia petals rested on top as two fell from the tree when the wind blew through. I bent down onto my knees and ran my hand over the stone to push the petals aside and onto the freshly cut grass that was greener than the grass throughout the entire town. I run my fingers along their names that were deeply carved into the limestone. A burning sensation smothered my throat and I blink back tears that wanted to escape from my eyes.

I promised myself I wouldn't cry. But I also know how I don't keep promises very well. I let the tears pour out of me. Tears that I have sealed tightly in a bottle until it bursts open from the overwhelming pressure. Like a piggy bank that is filled with penny's, dimes and quarters. I held the heavy bank in my hands when I suddenly slipped and the piggy came rushing down onto the ground. The ceramic cracks and shatters and the change flies everywhere. Some burst into thin air and land somewhere between the corners of the room, some rolling across the floor and spinning in circles until it finally collapses. Then everything becomes motionless, and now you have a mess to clean. That's how I feel.

When I finally compose myself, I wipe my hazy eyes clear and tuck the wavy strands of hair behind my ears before inhaling the thick spring air.

I place my hands on their gravestone and think about how I shouldn't have left them. I shouldn't have left them to handle the cult. I shouldn't have gone to their barn that stormy night, and if I did then I should've left before Carl got the chance to find me. I blame myself for their deaths because it is on me. If I had never even met them, then I wouldn't have led Finch and his demon army to them in the first place. Demon army is a nicer way of saying cult, but that is what they are. They worship the wrong lord and savior...

The wind blows heavily in the humid air. The loose strands of hair untucked from my braid and whirled in circles in the breeze. I closed my eyes and sat in silence, listening to the brushing and clacking of the Magnolia branches and petals. The faint sound of birds singing cheerfully in the distance of the field. The sound of crunching light footsteps under pebbled rocks from up ahead of me... wait, what?

I shot my eyes open and examined my surroundings, but no one was there. Maybe it was a figment of my imagination? Maybe it was a rabbit hopping along the field of graves? Either way, I redirected my attention back to Carl and Jodi. A smile crept up my lips and I finally said the words that will wretch deep inside of me. But the words that I needed to say the most to finally get some peace and closure in my heart.

"Goodbye." I kiss my fingers and sweep them over their engraved names. Then I stood up and started back down the aisle of gravestones and farther away from them.

As I trudged through the pebbled pathway down towards my car, a thin figure appeared from the corner of my eye. Startled, I looked at the figure and my eyes grew wide. It was the blonde woman from the train. All dressed in white with pin-straight golden hair that went down to her petite waist. I recognized her from her appearance. But her face reflected a girl I once knew before.

It was Sally, but only taller and older. Her face was the same as when I last remembered. Slender, pale with dark blue eyes like the depths of the ocean that gets darker the farther you swim down. She looked at me in shock. As if I had caught her in the act of deviance. Why is she here? Has she been watching me all this time? Why do I question myself when I can just go up to her and ask. But when I took a step forward, Sally took off.

She ran down the pebbled pathway in her off-white flats. She ran stiffly because those shoes aren't easy to wear nor to sprint in. In the past we usually just walked barefoot around the compound. It made us girls feel more grounded to earth. That, and the flats gave us blisters on our feet that would be too painful to walk in. Luckily, I'm wearing boots. I'll catch up to her. She will not be getting away.

I sprint down the pathway after her. My boots crunched on the small stones that kicked up from the ground and landed in other spots of the path. When I was inches away from her, I reached an outstretched hand out to her floaty hair that bounced behind her and gripped tightly to her golden locks. I don't mean to pull her hair back but it's not like I can grab anything else when her hair covers her entire backside. Her head whipped back and her feet kicked up from underneath her. Her flats practically flew off as her whole body fell backwards, knocking me down in the process. Sally sat up and was starting to stand but I wrapped an arm around her waist and tackled her back down. I turned her onto her back and climbed on top of her, pressing my knees into her waist to keep her from squirming away from me. She flailed her arms in front of her, smacking and pushing my upper body to get me off of her, but I grabbed her wrists and held them down to the sides of her head.

"Get off of me." Sally grumbled as she tried to move her waist up to loosen my grip against her. I squeezed my knees tighter to keep her firm against the ground.

"Who sent you?" I practically shouted at her. I inhaled short breaths to keep me from hyperventilating in the thick humid air. When you live in the south, you're used to dry air. The dry air that makes your eyes burn and your throat sore if you breathe out of your mouth long enough. But when the spring rain arrives, the humidity rises and it feels thicker than it actually is. Southerners are used to dry conditions, not humid conditions. It feels thick and heavy in my lungs, but it is bearable to breathe in.

Sally kept squirming and my patience started running low. "Did Finch send you to follow?"

Sally stopped squirming and lied slacked against the stones. She inhaled deep breaths, winded. Her eyes stared into mine, but I couldn't feel any emotion from her. They were like still water in the deepest part of the ocean. Dark and cold. Her silence told me everything I needed to know. Finch *did* send her to spy on me. But for what purpose? It's been a decade and he's still out to get me.

"Joanne died because of you." Sally sneered, her eyes glinting hatred towards me.

My grip loosened on her wrist and I looked at her puzzled. "What do you mean because of me?" My tone lowered and I could feel my heart pounding in my chest.

"She sacrificed herself because *you left*." Her tone raised with smoke. A fire is about to erupt from inside of her, but she keeps her breathing steady to compose herself. "We've been cursed because of you. Finch wants to stop us from dying."

I raise my brows. "Oh yeah? And the only way to do that is to kill me, right?" It wasn't a question but an assumption. I knew he wanted me dead the moment I left him. I'm just rather surprised by how persistent he is. Sally held her mouth firmly shut and I sighed. "Sally, everything he has told you is not true. You aren't cursed and certainly not because of me."

Sally tilted her head like a serial killer who found their next target. I wouldn't doubt if she tries to kill me herself. She would do something like that. "Of course, it's because of you. Since you left, people have been dying. Martha, Joanne, Elder Grimes. Though, he did deserve what came for him."

I glanced up at the sky and saw the moon reflecting brightly from the sun that started to dawn on the horizon. Pink and red clouds drifted over us and I knew that I had to get back to Joel to help with the rest of the packing and cleaning. Before I catch a train back to the city. I need to wrap this up.

"Look Sally, I don't have all afternoon. You tell Finch to leave me and my family alone." I let out a twinge of anger in my voice, before mirroring the psychotic expression on her face. "Is that clear?" A slight grin appeared on her face and she narrowed her eyes at me. But spoke no other words. She understands me, but she is also wondering what I will do if he doesn't listen. That, I haven't quite figured out yet. I do know that it won't end well for him and for the rest of them. If I go down, I'm taking all of them with me.

* * *

The train back home was tiring. I tried to shut my eyes for a bit but the blazing lights above me were too bright. I could only see my reflection in the window as I stared out into the dark abyss. It was midnight when I arrived home. Hopping out of the car and headed towards the house. As I locked the front door behind me I heard a voice calling out to me.

"Morgan?" The voice was deep but soft. He tried to be quieter than usual. The house was dark except for the kitchen island where Dean sat on a barstool with a beer bottle in hand. He isn't a big drinker. Except for stressful days at work. Then he would have two beers. In this case there are four empty bottles standing tall by the sink.

I placed my purse on the counter and started unraveling my braid and fluffed out my knotted waves. "How were the girls?" I asked, like nothing had happened. Like I totally didn't leave town for a few hours out of nowhere and without speaking to him about it. "Did they go to bed on time?"

Dean takes a swig of his cold beer. Sweat beads slithered down the brown bottle and droplets fell into a puddle on the island counter. He nodded without words. I nodded back and turned my back to him. I was about to leave the room before his sudden words came out, stopping me in my tracks. "Where did you go?"

I turned to face him and slowly walked up to the island. "I just went to see Joel for a while." I didn't say where because Dean doesn't know who Carl and Jodi are. Nor would he care to know anyway. He never asked me much about my past, and before we met. Why would I tell him? It's easier to never speak to him about them if he never even asks.

Dean stared at me blankly, his eyelids sagged and head tilted in a way that said, *I don't believe you*. He has no reason not to believe me. It's not like I'm having an affair behind his back. Maybe he thinks I was at some strange man's house? Either way, I have morals and he does not...

"So, we are now disappearing for hours on end out of nowhere?" Dean replied with a hint of sarcasm in his tone. I knew it wasn't a question that's why I didn't bother to respond. Dean took another swig and this time he slammed the bottle down. "Honestly Morgan. You didn't even inform me on where you were going. You just upped and left."

"So what, Dean?" I say louder than expected, but I don't dare dialing down. "I don't have a right to do whatever the fuck I want? Do I have to have your permission now?"

Dean narrowed his eyes in annoyance. "Of course not, don't be so rash." He took a swig of beer, swallowed, spun the bottle around in between his fingertips. "Just inform me next time when you're planning on ditching town and not arriving back until midnight again. Alright?"

I bit my tongue from saying something *rash* in his words, and forced a tight smile. "Well, you won't have to worry about me *"disappearing"* again."

Before he could react to my sarcasm, I walked out of the kitchen and down the hallway to our bedroom. It's small with white and red striped wallpaper that gives the room a circus flare. It was there when we bought the house and just never got around to tearing it off the walls. We probably never will. It grew on me. Even though it gives me a migraine from the bright, hypnotic stripes every time I enter the room. I learned to live with it...

I step into the bathroom and lean my hands on the countertop. I close my eyes and reminisce on the day I had. I yelled at Bonnie, which was something I never thought I would ever do to her. I met Joel since his older brother passed, and I got to say goodbye to Carl and Jodi forever. It might not have been the way that I wanted to say my forever goodbye. But it made me feel some sense of closure and relief that I needed for a long time. Then I got to meet Sally again. It has been over a decade since I've seen her. Not surprising that she's still the most brainwashed, psychotic person I have ever known. At least, she will get my message across to Finch and hopefully, he listens. But I know he won't. He never does. It's always his way or no way....

Then something caught my eye. A glimmer of light when I opened them and stared into the mirror. I turned my head towards where the light sparkled on the bathroom floor beside the shower. Something small was in the corner of the wall and shower step. I moved towards it, bent down and picked it up. I stared at it as it rolled in my palm. A small diamond earring that was in the shape of a Lily flower. Six petals that fanned out, and in the center where the pistil is located, was a diamond. It glistened and gleamed in the overhead light. At that moment, all I felt was numbness. I'm used to Dean sneaking around with his coworker

Miranda in his office, but to bring it into *my house* with *my children* here is messed up in so many ways. It's overly disrespectful. It's insulting and inappropriate.

Before I knew it, I was marching back into the kitchen and slammed the earring down in front of Dean's drink. It's a new bottle, his sixth drink now and all I want to do is smash that bottle right into his skull. Maybe I will hear the crack of his skull busting open? Maybe I will feel a sense of relief and peace from the overbearing weight that is dragging me further down into the sinking soil? Either way, I will not be letting him get away from this. I will not push it aside as I did for his *not so secret love affair.* I am finally getting *my life back.*

When Dean spotted the earring, his eyes grew wide. I was suddenly aware of his messy hair that is normally so perfect that it actually infuriates me how he can tame such a mane, and his unbuttoned collar and cuffs that were pushed up to his elbows. He normally changes into a t-shirt and checkered pajama pants right before going to bed. He never looks so haggard in his work uniform…

I nod at his surprised reaction. "I didn't care about you having an affair with her." Dean opened his mouth to interject but I raised a hand to silence him before he could make an excuse for his unfaithful actions. "But to bring it into my house, and while my daughters are here…" tears welled up in my eyes, but they were not from sadness but from exhaustion. Exhaustion from having to deal with everything all the while, trying to keep my family together and safe. It's overwhelmingly exhausting. "It's so fucked up, Dean."

"I know." Dean began while he rubbed his forehead with his palm. He's thinking hard about his excuses and how he is going to fix this. But all he can manage to say is, "I'm sorry."

I nod while taking slow steps back. I bit my lip to keep the urge from crying. But I know what I need to keep them away for good. "I want you out." I managed to say. "Tonight." I added in but he already knew what I meant. I turned away from his slacked eyelids and made my way towards the hallway.

"Where am I supposed to go?" Dean asked like it wasn't obvious already. I think he mainly wanted to break the ice that held us together.

"To your girlfriend's house." I say, letting the ice shatter around me. Now I can step away from him and let him go forever.

Chapter 37

I took off my wedding ring for the first time today. I never thought I would do such a thing like this. Yet here I was, staring at the thin gold band on my nightstand this morning. My hand actually feels lighter and weight started to lift off my shoulders, finally letting me relax a little. The band is plain with only a speck of a diamond in the center. It's so small that you can't even see it unless the light catches it just right.

This morning was a whirlwind though. I woke up alone for the first time in nine years. The other side of the bed is empty and cold. The sheets and pillows are still carefully in place like nobody else lives here. I also had to explain to the girls why they won't be seeing their father for a while. Perhaps, forever. If he wants to keep a relationship with his daughters then I won't stop him from doing so. But why would he care now if he never cared before. Why change now?

Vivian took the news well, a little too well. After I finished my speech that I replayed in my head all morning, Vivian pushed away her empty plate and shrugged a shoulder and said absentmindedly, "Well, it was only a matter of time." Before she hopped off the barstool and walked upstairs with a pip in her step. I'm sure she expected this would happen someday, but her nonchalant response is a little concerning.

Merritt's reaction was the opposite. Tears streamed down her cheeks, hoarse questioning and a quivering lip. After what felt like an hour of intense conversations and consoling later, she is now completely serene as she sits in the backseat with Charlotte the monkey laying snuggly in her arms while I drive them to school. Pulling into an empty parking space, I spot Bonnie and Boyd from the window. A stabbing pain wrenched in my stomach as I watched her talking to Boyd. She bent down to meet eye to eye and had a firm hand on his shoulder. He nodded to everything she said before waving to Vivian when she walked up towards the school entrance. I sighed and climbed out the door and managed myself to go up to her. Bonnie watched the kids enter the building, fondly. But her bright eyes dimmed when she turned to face me after I tapped her shoulder. She looked at me expectantly but when I looked into her eyes, I felt an odd sensation that ran down my spine. Tingling trailed down my back and the words I planned out to say for hours came out a jumbled mess.

"I-I just wanted to s-say," I inhaled deeply to keep my composure before I bursted out of rage. My patience meter is dwindling a lot lately. Not sure how much I can take before I just burst out into tears and anger all at once. But before I could finish my sentence, an obnoxious voice came from behind me.

"Why hello ladies!" Wendy Goode said in her usual high-pitched tone of voice. I nearly rolled my eyes at the sight of her. Why does she always show up when I least expect her to? She's like a pest that you can't get rid of. Like a cockroach. When you think you killed them all, they multiplied and now you're infested with babies. She just never goes away... Wendy looked at the both of us and frowned. "I can see I interrupted something, so I'm going to make this quick. The spring formal is coming up and we are in need of some chaperones to keep an eye on the littlies. If you two wouldn't mind joining our chaperone list, we would really appreciate it." She looked at us expectantly with wide eyes and raised brows.

I just nodded and said, "Of course, put us on the list." Bonnie nodded in agreement and I turned back to Bonnie in an indication that our conversation was over. But she still pestered me with more questions.

"That's great news! I also was wondering if you two could put some money towards-"

"Of course, whatever you need." I interjected, trying so hard to end this discussion. But Wendy just wouldn't bugger off. She began to say something else but I raised a hand to stop her from saying more.

"Wendy if you do not leave us alone, I swear to god I am going to lose my patience and freak the fuck out!" The words came out louder and harsher than expected but I have no time for nonsense anymore. The other mothers behind Wendy stopped their chatting to stare at me, completely stunned. Wendy looked horrified by my temper, but I don't care. She's starting to piss me off. Without saying any more words, Wendy angrily turned on the tip of her high heels and marched back towards the group of mothers. My eyes landed on Miranda who stared at me with a sly grin before I directed my attention back to Bonnie, who stared at me with narrowed eyes. Miranda must've thought she won whatever little game she had started. I'm sure Dean went to her place last night and I'm sure he is planning on staying for a while. I don't care anymore. She can continue to give me dirty looks and a devious grin and I won't give a shit. I'm done with assholes like them. Even if that makes me an asshole to them...

"Could you control your temper?" Bonnie snapped at me in a hushed tone, so the other mothers wouldn't hear. They snickered at us from a distance before walking off towards the parking lot like a flock of chickens. Annoying ass chickens. Bonnie crossed her arms across her chest and impatiently tapped her flat shoe on the cement.

I inhaled a deep breath and said, "I just wanted to apologize for yesterday. I shouldn't have yelled at you like I did." I rubbed my forehead with my hand. "I was just upset and I blamed you which I really shouldn't have an-"

Bonnie waved a hand to silence me from my anxious rambling. "Wait, why were you upset?" She cocked her head and softened her sharp gaze at me. "Did something happen to you?"

"Bonnie, someone broke into my husband's dealership the other day."

Bonnie frowned and reached a palm out to my arm. She squeezed my arm in a comforting way. "I'm sorry."

I stared at her hand on my arm, and for a moment it gave me a comfort of warmth that receded up my arm, up my neck and into my cheeks. They burned with uncontrollable heat. I nodded, "Can you guess who did it?" I looked into her soil colored eyes with instant fury. I'm angry with how she sticks up for that cult like it's her own skin and still be a part of it. She still believes they are her family. That they still care about her. That she still believes what they preach. I know she will try to defend them. Just like she always does. I just hope she will believe me for once in her life.... But by the surprised expression she showed, I don't think she will.

"No," Bonnie shook her head. "They wouldn't."

"But they did." I say assertively, pulling my arm away from her grasp. She took a step back. "They smashed the windows and painted *Repent* on a car in red. They also killed the two most important people in my life, Bonnie. I don't understand how you can defend them when they've been trying to kill me. I'm your best friend. Don't you remember?"

Bonnie pressed her lips tightly together and her eyes looked frantically around like she is trying to process everything that I have told her, and thoroughly thinking it through. Then she looked back at me and nodded. "You're right. You are my best friend, and if you say they are doing all of this. Then I believe you."

"Thank you." I say in relief. I could feel my blood pressure dropping and I finally felt some relief from this.

"But what are we supposed to do about this?" Bonnie questioned. "What are we supposed to do about them?"

I shrugged. What are we going to do about them? I'm sure as hell ain't going back to the village and giving them an advantage to murder me. "I saw Sally the other day."

"Oh?" Bonnie raised her brows. "She's still the bitch she has always been, huh?"

I stifled back a chuckle as it is not the time to make jokes. But of course I had to agree with her. "Yeah she is. I told her to let Finch know to leave us alone."

"Do you think he will listen?" Asked Bonnie. Her tone said everything she thought. She knows very well that he won't.

"Of course not, has he listened to anything we ever said before." It wasn't really a question, it was a statement. But Bonnie still shook her head in agreement. Whatever we do, I'm sure not going after him first. He can come to me, and I will be waiting...

Chapter 38

The rest of the week was quiet and actually quite peaceful. Without Dean around, I finally feel like I can breathe again. I never realized how much Dean had shoved me into a tiny box and I only had two air holes to breathe out of. Now I can feel free from that crammed box, and I can finally fill my lungs with a pack full of fresh air. I'm no longer contained for nine years. Bonnie and I haven't spoken much since our last discussion. We always do this when things get heated between us. We stop talking for a while until everything is sorted out on its own. In this case, I don't think it will ever be solved. Not until Finch and his minions are gone and completely out of our lives. Until then, short hellos and goodbyes will do.

I now sit in the gymnasium on a rickety chair and table from Vivian's school. Blowing up and tying balloons and tossing them onto the shiny cement floor. I have blown up fifty colorful balloons, as well as polka dot ones and clear confetti ones. Vivian's spring dance is just around the corner and I somehow managed to get myself into the preparation process. I have been here for two hours straight. I would know, I've been checking the large round clock above the gymnasium doors. I watched the minute hand slowly ticking around and around until it was now two-twenty in the afternoon. My lungs burn as I force air out of them and into the stretchy rubber, tying a knot with my pointer finger and thumb before bopping it up into the air with my palm, and watching it drift across Merritt's head. Her school goes on break two days before Vivian's does. She's enjoying herself. Running around the gym and bopping the balloons up into the air. She's playing the game where you see how long you can keep the balloon in the air without letting it touch the floor or else you lose. Normally, you play it outside because then it is far more terrifying to keep it from touching the prickly grass or else it will pop. This way is more fun because you don't have to worry about it erupting with a loud *bang* if you don't reach it in time. I watched as she hit the balloon like a volleyball and it drifted across the room. It went over the tables that stood in a row to the side of the center room. Merritt scrambled through the line of tables, squeezing herself past two that were close together and she unfortunately, didn't make it in time. She watches it in despair when the balloon bounced off the floor and settled itself in the corner of the room. She looked back at me with defeat.

"Aww man." I say, glancing up at the clock. "You lasted twenty-two minutes though." I watched as her face lit up in excitement over her new record and she proceeded on with her game. Working hard to accomplish her new goal. I looked ahead to the stage that stood a few inches up against the wall. Wendy, two other mothers and a few men, who I suspect to be some of the fathers that were forced to be here also. The two men stood on ladders on each side of the stage and stapled party streamers and banners onto the walls. The banners read enthusiastic quotes that make my nose crinkle when I read them. The party streamers reflected a rainbow beam, flickering across the room when the streamers swayed in the air. Wendy wordlessly pointed a lanky finger at the far right of the stage, directing the men where to staple the banners up. I'm glad I am across the room, or else I would have to listen to her constant bickering about something that isn't acceptable to her standards. Wendy takes her *"school president of the mothers committee"* seriously. *Very seriously.*

A *creak* and then a *bang* sound distracted me from the others and I thoughtlessly glanced over at the gymnasium door. Bonnie walked in and glanced around the gym, at the decorations, at Wendy who ordered people around, and at Merritt playing with the balloons. Finally to me. Our eyes met and we exchanged small smiles. She wrings her hands together as she approaches me. She probably thought I was still mad at her but really, I'm just glad to see her.

"Hey." Bonnie says, her eyes darted to me and then to the bag of rubber balloons that were yet to be blown and tied. As if she became consciously aware of her presence, she dropped her hands to her sides and cocked her head, looking at me with a soft gaze. "How long have you been here?" She looked over her shoulder to the fifty balloons I made scattered across the gym floor. "By the looks of it, you have been here for a while."

I giggled and nodded. "Two hours, actually."

"Two hours?" Her forehead creased and she looked flabbergasted. It really hasn't felt that long, but the clock says otherwise. "You have been here that long and this is all you have gotten done? A couple of balloons?"

My mouth fell open and I waved a finger around. "First off, I helped with making the banners an hour ago, and secondly, blowing up a hundred balloons by mouth is a lot harder than it seems."

Bonnie chuckled. "I guess so. Do you want any help with the other fifty balloons?"

I sighed, dropped my hands onto my lap and gave her a pleading look. "Yes, please." I put up my pointer finger and thumb, revealing the bruised flesh indents with redness that swelled around it. "My fingers are getting sore."

"Oh, poor baby." Bonnie gave me a playful smile as she pulled up a chair beside me and sat down with a short sigh. I roll my eyes and slide the plastic bag of rubber balloons in front of her. She takes a purple polka-dotted balloon and brings the end to her mouth. She takes a deep breath in through her nose and exhales through her mouth. I watched with amusement as she pushed the air out of her lungs as hard as she could, but the balloon remained deflated. Her eyebrows cinched together then she ripped the balloon out of her mouth, and stared at it with puzzlement. I waited until she looked at me for an explanation before I raised my brows and nodded.

"Do you see why I had only finished fifty?" A wide smile forced its way onto my lips. I grabbed a red balloon from the bag and held it out to show her. "The trick is you have to stretch out the rubber and it will be easier to blow up." I demonstrated for her to see as she followed along. Then she blew from her lungs again and the balloon effortlessly inflated. After it was filled completely with air, she tied it with her long, thin fingers without any problem. That's how I was until after ten balloons. Now my fingers are throbbing in pain. Bonnie watched the dotted balloon float down to the clusters of others in the center of the gym room floor, before reaching over and taking another one to fill.

Merritt stared up at an orange striped balloon that glided through the air like a feather in the summer breeze. It drifted down and she bopped it back up into the air. I looked over at Bonnie beside me and remembered back to when we were young. Back in the group...

Bonnie and I snuck around Sally's bed one early morning, in search of an item that we usually wouldn't be allowed to have. But because it was Sally and she got whatever she wanted due to *"good behavior"*, she kept hers hidden from the rest of us. Bonnie checked under the bed and

I checked under her mattress. Running my fingers along the creases of the mattress and bed frame. I checked both sides, but there was nothing there. I looked at Bonnie with anticipation and in hopes she had found it, but she just shook her head in defeat. I stared at Sally who slept like how she pretends to be around the adults. Like an angel. But only I can see the horns that protruded from the sides of her upper skull, short and stubby with pointy hooked ends. Only us girls know who she truly is. I stared at her face, her complexion white as snow, then it hit me. My gaze drifted down to the white pillow that she rested her head on as she slept. I silently poked Bonnie on the shoulder and when she looked at me, I pointed to the pillow. Bonnie's eyes grew wide out of fear. We never want to see who Sally becomes if one of us girls wakes her from her deep slumber. Someone ungodly, that's for sure.

Bonnie shook her head as she read my face. But I never really listen to her. I slip my fingers in the crease of the pillow and mattress. Carefully sliding my fingers around from under her head. Suddenly, Sally flinched but her eyes remained closed. Then she rolled over to lay on her left side. Bonnie squeezed my shoulder. I looked at her and she shook her head again and mouthed *"Don't do it."*

I tilted my head at her and my gaze read annoyance. *"It's fine."* I mouthed and I turned back to the pillow where my hand still remained underneath. I reached further in and caressed something familiar. Something that stuck to my fingers and felt tacky like warm, melted paint in the heat. I pinched it between my pointer finger and thumb, and then slowly slid my hand back out from under the pillow, and emerged the bright red rubbery balloon. I turned to Bonnie with it dangling between my fingers and gave her a snarky expression. I wanted to annoy her so badly about me retrieving the balloon without waking the beast that slumbered, but then Sally gave a grunt and stretched out her arms like she does before she wakes. Wide eyed in fear, Bonnie and I dashed out of the cabin door, into the misty morning air, and into the green pastures. There Bonnie and I played, bopping the balloon up into the windless air with the palms of our hands. We laughed and played for hours that morning. It was all fun and games until the wind swept the balloon away and we watched it levitate down into the spiky grass. We could never unhear the sound it made when it popped...

Watching Merritt play brings back fond memories, but also dreary ones too.

"Don't you remember playing that game in the pastures when we were young?" I blurted out as I reminisced on the special memory.

I could see the end of her lips twitch up and she stared at Merritt playing in front of us. Then she slowly nodded her head. "Of course I do. I also recall getting in deep trouble when the balloon popped." Because it was Sally's balloon, not ours. We popped ours from playing the same game the day after we received them. The punishment was to clean all of the cabin's floors with only a kitchen sponge and a bucket of soapy water. Our hands and knees got blistered from the raw wooden flooring and our backs ached for days as we scrubbed until midnight that day. The memories were worth the price for our sins though. "I never knew how Sally persuaded Mother into buying us useless things such as a balloon?" Bonnie questioned and tied the end of a red and white striped balloon. Then started on another one shortly after.

I sighed as my lungs ached in agony, begging for rest when I forced more air through them. Just forty-eight more to go. "Because Sally always got what she wanted. She is the devil in disguise."

"I'll say." Bonnie agreed.

We continued in silence until the gymnasium floor was flooded in colorful balloons, and the walls sparkled in streamers and glowy white lights. It looked as if a wild Christmas party was being thrown instead of a spring dance for a few dozen kids. I gathered Merritt to leave for the rest of the afternoon when Vivian skipped into the gymnasium with her backpack bouncing happily behind her. She complimented the hard work I and the others did to the gymnasium and how excited she is for the school dance tomorrow evening. I turned to say my farewell to Bonnie, but she had already left with Boyd. She must've been in a hurry to get home to her elderly husband. I wonder who takes care of him while she's gone? Doesn't he need her as much as I think he does? Perhaps so, but I don't ponder too much on that topic as it gives me flashes of heat that I can't shake from the thought of her and him together. Something simmers from inside of me, but it diminishes quickly as I march through the front door and into a house that I could live in forever. Now that Dean is gone. I used to feel suffocated in this house alone, knowing that Dean could arrive anytime of the day while I tried to relax for an hour before picking up the girls from school. Now all I feel is clean air that brings me a sense of peace and quiet that I never want to disturb again.

I continue my usual routine. Cook dinner, clean up the kitchen and tidying the house, help the girls with their homework that I am grateful they won't have to do for another four weeks after their spring break is over. Getting the girls cleaned up and into bed before I, myself, clean up and into bed...

Alone and exhausted, I stare up at the blank ceiling thinking about nothingness and everything all at once. I stare until my eyes slowly close and all that there is, is darkness. I exhale and prepare myself for the busy day ahead of me and what may come from it.

Chapter 39

I stood in front of the white building. Orange and white flames grew stronger as it engulfed the upside down cross. Soot sprinkled down on me and I stood firmly in place. The same place, the same time, just like every time I dreamt about this. Nothing has ever changed. Except for the flames that rage stronger and higher to the peak and almost all of the white paint is turned into soot, showing bare wood that became black charcoal as the flames burned the wood to a crisp.

I didn't try to move or speak because I knew I couldn't do either. I just stood there staring at the building that was being destroyed in front of my eyes. I listened intently for the footsteps that walk up beside me and when I did hear them, I didn't try to look. I knew I couldn't move. But, maybe I could? I mean, I wouldn't know if I didn't try. Right? I felt a small, soft hand clasp mine, and I could feel their pulse racing through their fingertips. It may be stupid but I need to know if it works.

My neck feels stiff but I force it to loosen and turn to my left. I was surprised that I actually looked away from the burning building and saw something different after all this time. I scan my surroundings. Grass, trees and a starry sky was all there was. Except there was someone there.

Three in fact. All with blank faces. All there was, was their dark silhouettes. Two short ones and one an inch shorter than me. The person looked to be female from the long coiled locks and the outline of a dress with a rippled skirt. The one that was holding my hand was another girl. Her height was past my waist and she looked to be wearing a dress too. The third silhouette was next to the tall woman and kept them out of view. All I could see was a small head with short hair and they seemed to be holding the woman's hand. They all stood still like stone statues in a museum. I always loved to see the magnificent artwork that was made with bare hands. I have only been to a museum twice, but everytime I see the statues I have to stop and admire their beauty before moving on. But these statues don't have any sculpted objects or texture like most statues. These ones are completely black with only an outline. Like in a drawing of nothing but a blob. But why can't I fully see them? Why can I see the color and texture of everything that surrounds me, but only them I can't? Matter of fact, why do I keep having this dream? What am I missing? Recurring dreams could have a significant meaning to them but what does this specific dream mean that I keep reliving almost every night? But before I could look further ahead of this nightmare, the whole building collapsed in on itself just like the last dream before... *and then, I woke up.*

* * *

I dropped Merritt off at Meredith's mansion like we had planned two weeks ago. Before Dean's separation. I'm not sure what we are going to do. Get a divorce? Perhaps. But I need to get a job and be stable enough before I do so. I'm sure Joel would accept me for waitressing again at the diner. He has talked about needing extra hands since I left. I'm sure he would be delighted for me to be back... Meredith didn't say anything to me when I dropped Merritt off at the door. I thought maybe she doesn't know about the feud between Dean and I since he doesn't really speak to her on a normal basis. But the death stare and side eye she gave me, told me otherwise. Normally, she doesn't even waste her energy on just glancing over at me. This time she was full of it. She wouldn't take her eyes off of me. It felt awkward, but I held my ground. My feet firmly planted and my chin high in the air, attempting to assert my dominance. But who am I kidding? Meredith is way more dominant than me. She would always win in an argument. She *has* won. But I don't let her get to me as much as she used to. She never liked me anyway. Not since the first time I set foot into her home...

Vivian sat down on a stool in front of my bathroom mirror. She painted her nails a soft shade of violet purple to match with her dress we bought a week before the dance at a small boutique near Joel's diner. Along the rows of vintage buildings filled with boutiques and antique shops galore. The dress is a violet purple with a glittery skirt and fringed trim, and puffy sleeves on the shoulders. She said it reminded her of the dress Repunzel wore in the Barbie movie. I have no idea what she was referring to as I never saw that movie before. I think it is one of Meredith's films that they've watched when they visited once. She has a whole movie theater in her mansion. I'm sure they watched all sorts of films there. But I just silently nodded along to Vivian's rant about the resemblance of the two dresses, not sure what I was agreeing too but she seemed excited about wearing the dress anyway.

I curled her hair and pinned up the sides with two flower bows and did her eyeshadow with purple sparkles, and pinky cheeks and lips. She looked as beautiful as a princess. After she finished getting ready, I got myself dressed in a silky, bright sapphire blue dress that had short sleeves and went past my calves. I rarely wear dresses anymore but Vivian picked it for me on our outing for some formal clothing that I did not have.

Luckily, Vivian has wonderful taste. Otherwise I would be wearing jeans and a floral top. I decided to curl my hair and pin it up into a loose bun with short curled pieces of hair that dangled over the updo, and did minimal makeup because I hate not being able to recognize myself from overdoing it. I'm very tedious with my makeup. Just plain mascara, blush and lipstick is all I do. Anything else makes me look like a completely different person than I already do in this dress and hair. Why would I want to look in the mirror and not recognize who is staring back at me?

When we are ready, I gather my purse and march out the door into the muggy afternoon fog. A mist of rain has been falling from the heavy grey clouds all day long. Vivian was worried that the dance would be canceled, but I consoled her and told her that spring is like this every year and it hasn't stopped anyone from leaving their house yet. We will be alright...

After we buckled our seatbelts, I pulled out of the driveway and into the foggy mist. I could see faint outlines of dark trees and the red brake lights from the car ahead. I keep my speed limit slow, just in case I can't see someone in front of me. As I drove down the housing street and towards the open intersection when a sudden dark minivan pulled out in front of me from the street over, nearly crashing into me if I didn't react fast enough. I stared at the vans blacked out windows and eyed the black silhouette from in the driver's seat. I could see their head turn away from my direction and continue to slowly drive past me and to the intersection. I exhaled the breath that caught in my lungs from the sudden fright and I shook out my hands. They were shaking uncontrollably and became moist and clammy.

"Is everything alright?" Vivian asked, nervously from behind me. I could see her peering over my shoulder at the empty street with eyebrows drawn in. "Who the hell was that?"

"Vivian." I say, not in the mindset of correcting her choice of language. I let my foot off the break and slightly pushed on the gas pedal so we're now cruising down the road. "Everything is fine. They probably didn't see me through the fog. It happens sometimes."

"Well," Vivian sat back and glanced out her window. "They need to be more cautious when driving." I silently nodded in agreement.

We continued on in silence until we made it to our destination. Vivian dashed up the staircase and through the open doorway, disappearing into the building. I entered the gymnasium with a couple dozen students filling the dance floor. The once large space looked so small when it's filled with students and adults. I immediately regretted signing up to be a chaperone as I watched some students dancing, bickering about nonsense, and spilling the punch out of the bowl, tinting the white table cloth red... *Sigh*. It's going to be a long evening...

My gaze soon fell on Bonnie who was standing by the snack table across the room. She handed a boy a plastic bowl of pretzel sticks with a soft smile. Her smile pinched as her gaze fell on me, watching me walk up to her through the crowd. When I reached her, I gave her a courtesy smile and a hello. She smiled back and continued with filling plastic bowls of pretzel sticks and cheese puffs, and placing them up in a straight line for children to grab. I make myself busy unstacking plastic cups and filling them up with fruit punch. Children come and they go. Bonnie and I refilled the cups and bowls without saying a word to each other. It feels like we're connecting without communicating. Like a red ribbon that ties us together and holds us firm in our hearts.

As the hour passed by and we chaperone the kids as they danced and played, I watched Vivian from a distance dancing around Boyd. He stood in the center of the floor with his arms pinned straight to his sides. Awkward is an understatement for how he seems. He's a child who probably never interacted with any other people his own age, whom also was born in a culture of satanic rituals and fucked up mind games. I honestly feel bad for the boy. I hope Vivian can show him how to actually be a child his age. As if two worlds collided, Boyd smiles shyly and Vivian bent her knees and straightens them, and repeats again in a bobbing motion. Boyd watches intently, then mirrors her moves. He stiffens his arms and slightly bent his knees and stiffens them again. Vivian laughs then holds his hands into hers and sways them to the rhythm of the music. They look like two Cockatoo birds synchronizing their movements to the rhythm of music. Not perfectly though...

"Vivian's very sweet." Bonnie appeared beside me with a roll of paper towels in her hands. A smile crept up her lips as she watched her son giggling. They now danced in a circle in a cheerful chant. Then she looked at me with a glint in her eye. "You did a good job with her."

A wave of heat ran up my spine and burned my cheeks. Her soil eyes sparkled under the fairy lights from above, and I could see a flint of our futures in them. A future with her and I, together with no one else but our children. A cheerful feeling ran through me as I gazed into our futures that are full of hope and joy. I knew at that moment, I was meant to always be with her. She's my forever companion, and I am hers. Does she feel the same way about me? Does she get a warm sensation when she looks into my eyes like I do? Or does her heart beat harder inside her chest when I'm around? All of these things never phased me because I didn't know what it meant. But now I do. And now I don't want to lose her again. Never again... I was brought back to reality from my mind of endless thoughts when a roll of paper towels were tossed into my arms.

"Could you clean up the punch mess on the floor by the stage for me?" Bonnie asked, but I really didn't have a choice. She slowly stepped backwards towards the main entrance to the gym with raised eyebrows. "I need to go to the restroom." I nodded.

"O-okay," I stuttered, my tongue suddenly feeling thicker in my mouth than before. I watched as she sashays away in her coral sundress and disappears around the corner. A pit in my stomach formed inside me and made me feel a sense of wonder and nervousness about what we could have... I need to know if she feels the same way. I set the paper towels down on a table and I sprinted up the entrance, and into the school hallway that was dimly lit by one LED bulb ahead of me. I walked down the line of lockers and towards a hallway to the right. As I turned the corner, two doors that read **Boys** on one door and **Girls** on the other beside it. I entered the girls room and there she was, in front of a mirror, aimlessly rinsing her hands under the running faucet. She looked up to the mirror and her gaze softened when she saw me standing in front of the doorway. We locked eyes for a moment and shared a desperation through them. We're desperate for a life together. To always be by our sides no matter what happens to us. I know that's what she's thinking. I can read her like an open book. The words are printed in thick letters and short spaces. I can read her better than she can read herself, which may not be saying much. But I know her better than anyone else in the world, and that says more than enough.

Bonnie reaches over to the paper towels, takes a piece off the roll and dried her hands, dropping it into the trash bin beside the sinks. She turned around to face me and cocks her head, narrowing her soil colored eyes at me. Her eyes put me in a trance of darkness. I'm standing in a dark room with only Bonnie and I, facing each other. We're no longer in a restroom with stalls and sinks and tiled flooring. Just the abyss of darkness that surrounds us. I take a small step forward to get closer to her. She just stands there, still looking at me with wonder.

What are you staring at? I could read on her face. But when I parted my lips to respond, the darkness suddenly vanished, and the tiled flooring, stalls and sinks appeared again. Then I was aware of how ridiculous I looked. Just standing in the middle of the girls restroom and staring at Bonnie without saying anything at all. But my thoughts were suddenly cleared when I heard a shrill scream coming from the gymnasium. Bonnie and I gave each other a peculiar look before storming out of the door and into the open hallways. Children's small voices came in a chant. So loud and clear as we rushed our way towards the gym entrance. What we saw when we entered were gathered children in a circle all shouting, *Fight! Fight! Fight!*, like in the movies when a group of children get into a fist fight in the school yard. Some of the chaperones tried shouting over the commotion and tried to break up the huddled crowd. But it was no use. They all stood firmly in their places, pushing into one another to get a better look at the fight in front of them. My eyes scan the crowd and try to spot Vivian's blonde hair. But I don't see her. Then I knew exactly where she was...

Bonnie and I shoved our way through the huddled crowd, pushing past small bodies as we made it to the center. And just as I thought, Vivian was in the center circle on top of a boy. She swung her arms back to fist the boy right in the face. Boyd was there too, on top of another boy, but he's not fisting him like Vivian is. He's recoiling a flat hand and smacking it into the other boy's face. Vivian recoiled her fist again and I reached out and grabbed her forearm, and yanked her back, off of the hidden boy who covered his face with his arms. Vivian quickly pounced up onto her feet and began to walk towards the boy again, but I wrapped my arms around her waist and lifted her off the ground. She squirmed in my arms but I kept my hands locked tightly together to keep her from breaking free...

"Vivian, stop!" I shout over the chattering crowd. They stopped their chanting but began to speak loudly to one another. It all sounded like chirping birds in the early morning. Singing all at once as the sun rose. Some mornings it can sound calming while other mornings it can sound like nails on a chalkboard. In this case, it's noxiously loud. Like biting my fingers off with my bare teeth, annoying. I fought the urge to scream just to stop the noise, while Vivian kicked and wiggled to break free from my hold on her. I could see Bonnie crouching beside Boyd as tears streamed down his puffy cheeks. I glanced back down at the two boys laying on the floor, when I realized who they were. They moved their arms away from their faces, red tinting their noses and mouths as they sniffled back tears.

"Oh my god!" A scream came from behind me. I could recognize her voice from anywhere. Miranda Faux pushed past me and bent down at her twin sons with a hand clasped to her mouth as she let out a muffled scream. Then she moved her hand away from her mouth and stood up stiffly. She turned around on the ball of her heels, her face reflected red as a tomato. She looked ready to burst into flames as she eyed Vivian and Boyd. "You two!" She pointed a lanky finger at each of them and she stomped her heel hard into the ground. "You two are fucking evil! Look at what you did to my boys!" She glanced back at her bleeding sons who slowly stood up onto their feet. They wiped their sleeves at their bloody noses with a devilish glare.

I hadn't realized that Vivian stopped wiggling and now she is a sack of potatoes in my arms. She panted as she sneered at the boys with a malicious grin. Meanwhile, Boyd cried into his shaky hands. Two very different children right here. I know for a fact that Vivian wouldn't attack anyone without a solid reason to. The twins probably laid their hands onto her and she gave them what they were asking for. I always taught her to *never start a fight but to always finish one*. She just took my advice and did so. I know she did…

Miranda took a step towards Vivian and I, but Bonnie stood in front of us. "Actually Miranda, your boys are the equivalent of evil. Their father must be the devil himself by the way it looks."

Miranda narrowed her eyes at her and the fire that simmered in her eyes was now raging with flames. "What did you say?" She seethed through her clenched teeth, her hand tightening into a fist. I let go of Vivian and stood beside Bonnie. I wouldn't doubt if Miranda would attack her. That is probably where her sons learned it from.

"It was their fault!" Vivian interjected, walking up to Miranda with her shoulders back and head held high. She showed a sort of dominance, despite her petite size. I grabbed her by the shoulder and held her back. "Frankie punched Boyd in the stomach! They deserved worse than what they fucking got!"

"Vivian, that's enough!" I shouted, letting the rage consume me. I tightened my grip on her shoulder and forced her around to face the entrance doors. Then I shoved her towards it. "Go wait out in the hallway now! We're leaving." I watched her reluctantly walking away but before she disappeared behind the wall, she turned around to face Miranda and the twins and gave them a devilish smile and slowly raised up her middle finger in the air for all to see. Then she disappeared out of sight. I inhaled deeply before turning back to Miranda who now held the twins in each arm, cradling their abnormally large heads for their lanky bodies.

She looked at me and Bonnie and said, "If your bastard children broke my boys' noses. I am suing both of you." She threatened. But I couldn't take her seriously enough to feel threatened.

A humorous smile rose on my lips as I took a step closer to her. "If you do that, then I'm taking you and my disloyal husband with me. Don't be so naive and think he wouldn't do the same to you as he did to me."

Miranda held her fiery gaze on mine and then on Bonnie who held her ground with her chin held high and then she marched away. Dragging her boys with her.

I let out a long sigh as I felt the fire inside me come down to a simmer. I turned to Boyd who wiped his bloodshot eyes with his palms. "Are you alright?"

Boyd sniffled and nodded. Bonnie placed a gentle hand on the small of his back and looked at me with a sincere smile. "He'll be alright, but yours might not be." She nodded towards the entrance.

I nodded and turned away without any other words. Once I'm out in the narrow hallway, I expected to see Vivian waiting beside the front door, but no one was there except for me. I looked behind me and down at the end of the hallway. But there was nothing other than some graffitied lockers in a row. Maybe she's in the restroom? But when I was there, it was empty. Each stall had just a single toilet and a roll of toilet paper. I could feel my pulse quickening and my breathing shorter with worry. Where has she gone? I dash outside and down the steps. I frantically looked around for any sign of a curly blonde haired girl, but I couldn't find her. My hands began to uncontrollably shake and I couldn't catch my breath. My mind began to race. Thinking about all of the worst possibilities of what might have happened to her, or what has happened to her. She's missing and I don't know what to do.

A soft hand touched my shoulder and made me flinch as I whipped my head around to see Bonnie and Boyd behind me. They both looked at me with worry as the pounding of my heartbeat thumped into my ears. I could see Bonnie open her mouth and began to speak, but her voice came out muffled over the drums that were beating into my ear canal.

"Is everything alright?" Bonnie asked with worry in her soft tone of voice. Then she suddenly realized that Vivian wasn't nearby when she scanned her eyes around the parking lot to the school. Then she drew in her eyebrows and gave me a puzzling look. "Where is Vivian?"

I shook my head. "I-I don't know." My throat started to burn and salty water welled up behind my eye sockets. I scanned the parking lot behind me, placing a flat hand on my chest that suddenly tightened up inside. "I don't know where she is."

"Okay, let's take a deep breath in and out." Bonnie grabbed my hand and squeezed it. The pressure slowly lifted from my chest and I filled my lungs with wet airdrops in the breeze. We exhaled together and repeated two more times. She looked at me as if I were a ticking-time-bomb that was ready to explode any minute now. But I'm not going to burst into flames. I'm going to burst into water that will flow out from my eyes. Like a dam that is filled to the brim with water. A couple more inches of water and the dam will burst, and water will flood everywhere. Soon flooding a town and their homes. That's how I feel... "Alright, now we need to stay calm." Bonnie exclaimed. "Do you know where she might have gone?"

"Other than the school? No." I said, feeling a little bit calmer than I did before, but my hands still uncontrollably shook when I unclenched them from a fist. I looked down at Boyd who aimlessly looked around in bewilderment.

"Do you know where she might have gone?" I ask him.

Boyd looked on the verge of tears, yet again. Then he just shook his head. I looked at Bonnie in hopes she would know. Why would she know? She didn't know Vivian very well. They haven't spoken much, other than a quick exchange before school. I expected her to shake her head and shrug, and continue to console me and tell me what I should do. But instead, she just looked away and slowly turned around to avoid my gaze. I no longer felt fearful or worried. All of those emotions vanished, and now I am full of rage. A simmering pot started to boil over inside me and my cheeks began to burn up with heat.

"Bonnie!" I said rather harshly than expected. But how else should I feel when she is acting like a child that just got caught doing something deviant. "Bonnie, what do you know?"

Bonnie turned back to face me and bit her bottom lip. Her eyes were soft and moist and she inhaled deeply before answering with a head shake. "Well, I'm not sure. But I recall Rick telling me that there was going to be a ceremony sometime soon. But I don't remember when exactly."

"I thought they don't do ceremonies anymore!"

"They don't." Bonnie said, bringing her fingers up to her lips then slowly said, "They don't, usually."

"What are you telling me?" I take a step forward to her, my body towering over hers.

Her eyes flickered across me, not wanting to look me in the eyes. "Finch might have taken her."

My eyes grew wide and the pot now overflowed with boiling liquid. "They might have!"

"Obviously, I'm not sure." Bonnie interjected. I turned away from her and marched towards my parked car. She continued to follow suit. Stumbling to keep up from behind me.

"But they wouldn't do that. They have changed."

"Oh, please just shut the hell up!" I turn back to face her. She flinched from my abrupt tone, but I don't care. She deserves to be yelled at by the way she keeps defending this cult like it owes her her life. They were going to take mine. Does she truly even care about me at all? Or am I just hoping she does like the way I do for her?

"Could you just stop defending them! They took my daughter!" I turned away and walked towards my car before she could say anything else to defend them again. I dug my keys out of my purse and unlocked the driver side door. Before I climbed in, I looked back at Bonnie. A single tear streamed down her cheek as she wrung her hands together. "If something happens to her. It's on you."

Chapter 40

The drive to the town I used to live in was quicker in the car than on the train. It could be because I drove eighty miles on the back roads, nearly popping my tires in potholes and plummeting my car into the ditches along the road. But I made it in one piece. I pulled into the driveway to the convent I grew up in. I could feel my pulse quickening through my fingertips as I tightly squeezed the steering wheel. My mind raced thinking about what might have happened to Vivian. What if they had already sacrificed her? I thought they wanted me. Why would they want her instead? I tried to push the endless thoughts out of my mind and trailed down the stone pathway towards the cabins and pastures. I rolled up to the center of the buildings that circled around. I expected to see the elders or madams walking out of the cabins from the sound of the engine and the gravel against the tires crunching and scraping the thick rubber. But nobody came. It was almost like a ghost town. No lights shining in through the windows. No doors opened wide to let the cool breeze in. No sign of living beings around or even lived here. But there was a dark minivan with blackened windows parked in front of the trail. The same van that almost hit me back at the house. A sign that they are here and the convent is not abandoned.

I parked the car and turned off the engine and stuffed the keys back into my purse and shoved it under my car seat, keeping it out of view if anyone came to look inside. I'm not carrying a heavy bag around. There's nothing important inside or nothing that I can use against them. I climbed out of the car and shut the door behind me.

I wearily walked around to the front of the hood. I glanced around my surroundings, listening intently for any sign of living beings in the convent. But only the sound of a chirping cricket in the tall grass in the distance was heard. The pastures looked underkept with the grass being several inches high. The elders would never allow this to get out of hand. They trimmed the pastures Sunday morning of every week, even when the grass didn't need to be trimmed. I walked up to the van and cupped my hands around my eyes to peer in the windows. Nothing but worn seats with no buckles and a thin steering wheel was inside. Nothing and no one was inside. I turned away from the dark van and marched towards the cabins ahead.

I walked up the staircase to the dining hall. Where the food was made by the madams and where it was served. I grip the doorknob and hesitated before twisting and swinging the door open, and stepping inside. It was dark with the only light source being the windows where the dawning sun shined through. The night was arriving and the sky would no longer be bright enough to guide me through. The air smelled of mildew and dust. The sun shone on a long wooden tabletop, showing a coated white cast. Dust balls floated in the sun rays and mold grew in the corner ceilings that were tinted a rustic orange over the once white walls from rain damage from a leak in the roof. I didn't care to continue on through the building as it's obviously clear that no one was there. But when I went to turn back a sound of metal clattered in the kitchen. I kept my footsteps light. I don't want to alert anyone that I am here. It's better to sneak up on whoever is around rather than giving them a chance to prepare to run or attack me. Especially if it's Finch. He's the last person I would want to fight. He's lean but there's some muscle built on him. He's stronger than the rest of them. Obviously, stronger than me too. When I reach the swinging door to the kitchen, I place my hand on its tacky wood and slowly push it open to a crack. I peek my eye through the crack, looking for any sign of a person inside. A shadow, perhaps? Or a shift of clothing? But there was no one there. No noise came from inside and when I pushed it all the way open. I came to the realization that the sound came from a tin bucket next to the mop right beside the sink on the far end of the room. It was lying on its side, but how did it get there? Who knocked it over? And as if I had said it aloud, a furry rat came from behind the bucket and scurried into a small hole underneath the cupboards. I let out a gasp of air and retreated back into the dining hall. Taking one final look around at the moldy ceiling, the dusty tables, and the empty space. It looked to be abandoned for years. Like this room had never seen a person before. But there is no time for questions...

I made my way back outside and decided to leave the other cabins alone. It's clear they no longer live here. I don't need to go to each one to know that. But where else are they living? Bonnie never mentioned moving territory. So where else would they be? Then it hit me like a lightbulb that flickered on. Clearing my mind from the haze I was in. Bonnie said there might be a ceremony tonight. All of our ceremonies and rituals always took place at the altar of the church. That has to be where they are... but I thought the church caught on fire? Bonnie did it when she was trying to distract the elders for us to escape. She was supposed to steal the dagger for the ceremony, but instead she caught the whole building on fire. A bit extreme, but it did its job. For the most part...

Then I saw something far off into the woods. From across the fields. A light flickered through the trees. A white speck disappeared behind a tree and reappeared through the cracks of the forest. And then I was off. Into the tall grass that slapped my face as I trampled through the field. The light grew smaller when I got closer, going across the trees and away into the night. The sun had set and the sky became dark and so did my sight. I let my mind guide me through.

Remembering back to the night of the ritual. Us girls in a single file line, trampling across the field and into the woods. The dirt pathway all lit up with torches to guide us to the church in the dark. It's now all dark with the only light source coming from the full moon that peeked through the branches as they swayed in the wind. It felt like a storm was approaching, but there were no clouds in the sky. Just the harsh, cold wind in the air. It felt good being out in the open. No humidity from the city air. It felt colder than the usual spring weather.

I stared down at the pathway. No light came from it. Whomever was there before is now gone. My steps felt loud. Dried dirt and rocks crunched from under my soles, and I thanked myself for choosing to wear boots over heels. I didn't thank myself for choosing to wear a dress instead of jeans and a t-shirt though. As I trampled down the dark path I was brought back to that night when I was chosen to be the next sacrifice. I felt small and weak, and afraid. Nerves punched my gut and I could feel myself slipping into the darkness. I prayed to never come back here. But they were never answered. Now I'm back, but not for me. The crunch of sticks, dirt, and prickly grown grass echoed through the air and into trees when I approached the church. I stood in front of its doors. Looking up at the upside down cross that stood tall. The little white building stood in place like nothing ever happened. It looked to be unscathed from the flames that were once there. They built it again. Fixed it from the fire. Why would they continue to fix the building if they left the cabins? If they moved the convent someplace else? But I can't stand here and continue to question things. I came here for my daughter.

I try to quietly walk up the steps, but my boots make that almost impossible on the thick wood. If anyone's inside, they sure had heard me approaching. I place a shaky hand on the doorknob and twist it until the door pops open. A small stream of light came through the cracks of the ajar door. I braced myself to come face to face with the man that terrorizes my mind as I swing the door open... nothing was there except for two candles on a gold candelabra that was placed on both ends of the altar. Only the altar stood in the entire building. No rows of pews were lined or any rugs to cover the bare wood. Thumping footsteps and thumping heartbeats when I approached the altar.

The life I once lived flashed in front of my eyes again. I was the frightened little girl walking up to the altar to slice my palm for my savior. *My savior is no longer mine*. I no longer want him. I left him behind when I left the gates of hell. *This place is hell*. I ran my fingers along the cracks of the wood. No rug was placed on the altar to hide the charred remains on the wood. White wax dripped off the lit candles and seeped through the cracks. They looked to be lit for a while, only a quarter of the candles were left still burning. I hold out my left hand and turn it over, palm facing upwards. I opened my clenched fist and stared at the white slice on my palm. A flash of me holding the silver dagger and running it against my skin, appeared in front of me. I pictured the dark red ooze that ran down my wrist and forearm, later dripping eleven droplets into the blessed water. Selling my soul to the devil himself. I can't take it back. I wish I could, but I can't. A rock formed in my throat and I clenched my fists, digging my nails into my palms. The despondency was quickly replaced with vexation. The simmering pot inside me overflowed with boiling water.

Where else could they be if they are not here? What am I missing?

I shove the toe of my boot into the thick wood. I did it again. Again. Again. Each time is harder and harder as I shove it deeper into the wood. Again. Again. Again. Then suddenly, it shifted. The altar moved an inch back and so did I. When I looked downwards there was a crack between the floorboards and the altar. The seam was too small to tell what was underneath. I placed my hands on the edge of the wood and pushed my entire body into it. At first it didn't budge, not until I shoved my shoulder into it. It scraped against the floorboards as I forced it to move until it was completely back and away from whatever's hidden underneath. A wide square hole was underneath there. It was dark except for the wooden plank that glowed from the candles above. I grabbed the closest candelabra and bent down to brighten my path. A staircase went down to a cellar of stoned walls and concrete floors. I carefully descended the staircase and emerged into the dark space...

It was chilly inside, and smelt of mildew and mold. I waved the candle along the cracks in the walls until the edges drew in and into a narrow hallway. I scuffed my way down the hallway until another narrow corner appeared. Turning the corner was a flicker of light that appeared at the end of the path. I set the candelabra on the floor to keep the hallway lit and left it behind. As I got closer to the light beam a faint murmur appeared from around the corner. I stopped in my tracks and tried to point out what was being said, but it was too quiet. Almost in a whisper. I peeked my head around the corner and into a small room. Candles flickered across the ceiling and illuminated twelve figures that stood in a row. They wore blood red cloaks that grazed the ground and their wide hoods pulled up, covering their faces and bodies. They all whispered and chanted words I couldn't make out in unison. Then I shortly realized that they weren't speaking English at all. They were speaking in tongues. A faint whisper of unknown words that almost sounded like a snake's hiss. The whole room sounded like snakes that slithered and hissed in unison. They encircled something I couldn't quite see. All I could see was blonde curly hair that draped over a wooden block, similar to the altar above. Red velvet cloth ran underneath her and draped over the speckled wood, and a candelabra placed above her head. I know that is her. But I still inch closer to peek over a person's shoulder. Then I saw her. Lying down on the altar, her eyes closed and her breathing faint. Her chest barely raised and for a moment, I thought she was already dead. They must've drugged her or something. Behind the altar stood a tall cloaked person. Their head hovering over her sleeping face. I impulsively took a step forward, nearly ready to run and grab her from right off the altar. But then something touched my left shoulder, nearly scaring me to death. Then it grabbed me and whirled me around the corner, and shoved my back against the cold, wet wall. Water droplets seeped into my dress and caused shivers to slither down my spine. A soft hand clasped over my mouth before I could comprehend what was happening. When I finally came to my senses, I saw Bonnie's wide soil eyes staring back at me.

Besides Finch, she is the last person I want to see right now. I pulled her hand off my mouth and stepped away from the wall.

"What are you doing here?" I whispered so low, even I could barely hear myself. But Bonnie either had read my lips or had some super hearing powers that I don't know about.

"What do you think is going to happen if you go in there?" She responded, not answering my question.

I glared at her and stepped towards her, forcing her to take a few steps back. "I'm going to save my daughter."

"If they see you coming, they will kill her before you even make it across the room." She spoke in a tone that I never heard before. It was filled with fear and anger for me to listen. It actually made me flinch a little. And so I listened. "You don't have anything to fight them off, but *he* does."

"Then what am I supposed to do, Bonnie?" But before she could respond, a voice shouted from inside. The voice sounded the same before I left. It was loud and clear with a hint of enthusiasm as he spoke. We inched around the corner and peered in.

The person behind the altar now stood with their arms out and palms raised. It seemed as if they were feeling the spirit of the lord casting down onto them. The others raised their heads and their arms, still hissing in tongues. Then they suddenly stopped and lowered their hands back down under their cloaks. Then the man behind the altar lowered his hood and revealed his face to them. He looked the exact same since the last time I saw him. Just older. His shaggy hair shined silver from the roots and his stippled chin grew white in small patches. There were deep set wrinkles around his eyes and forehead that only grew deeper when he squinted and raised his eyebrows to the crowd...

"We have been called here today by the Lord!" His voice rang through the room and the crowd hissed again. Raising their heads in rejoice. Finch silenced them with a flat hand in the air and continued on. "He has sent us a gift." They cheered...

"Almost fourteen years ago our savior claimed a sacrifice for him to feast upon, but she denied his graces, and now we have all paid for her actions." They hissed and growled like the demons they are...

"But we shall not suffer any more. Thy now we have the blessing that will save us all!" They cheered again but were quickly silenced by his dark and twisted glare, and the devilish grin that grew on his lips. "With her blood we shall live in peace knowing that we will be saved!"

This time no one cheered as Finch reached into his cloak and pulled out a silver dagger. The same one I sliced my palm with. The same one that would have sacrificed me to the lord, and is now being used to sacrifice my daughter instead. I don't care what Bonnie says. I can't just stand here and watch my daughter be killed by a satanist...

"Wait!" My voice echoed loudly in the air. I stepped out from behind the corner and raised my hands out towards Finch in a plea to surrender my daughter's life.

Finch looked at me with widened eyes. Clearly shocked by my sudden presence. The cloaked people turned around to face me, but only one of them pulled down their hood and revealed their face to me. It was Mother Renée. I haven't seen her since the afternoon before the ceremony. Before I ran away. She helped dress me and did my hair. She still looked the same. Except her face was worn and her hair thin with a white stripe that weaved through her twisted bun. Miserable and frail as ever. Wrinkles enhanced her peachy lips and green eyes. She looked me up and down as she examined my appearance. Then her eyes smiled at me. Like the way eyes softened and turned into crescent moons without actually smiling with her lips. She was always terrible at showing affection and she always seemed too depressed to even smile. Some things never change. But my attention was brought back to Finch who now displayed a devilish grin...

"Viola, what a nice surprise." He cheered, his fingers still tightly wrapped around the handle of the dagger. "I suppose the Lord gave us *two gifts* this fine evening." The crowd cheered, turning their attention back on Finch.

I ignored them and gave Finch a pleading look that truly felt right at this moment. Scared and hopeless. "It is me you want right? Just take me and let her live, Finch."

Finch's eyes crinkled with pleasure and he let out a bellowed laugh. "That's not how this works, Viola. If you hadn't run away from our savior. Then we wouldn't have to sacrifice her instead of you." He pointed the sharp dagger at Vivian's body. "You have to repay the trouble and death that you have caused all of us. Don't you understand?"

I glanced down at Vivian's resting face and noticed her eyes started to twitch open. Whatever drug they used on her is starting to wear off as we speak. Hopefully, there will be a way to get her before he does. But before I could say anything else, Finch's gaze flickered behind mine and his smile grew wider. "Nice of you to join us, Bonnie."

I glanced behind me and there stood Bonnie with a look of discomfort. Then she stepped out in front of me with her hands raised. Trying not to provoke Finch like he is a rabid dog. Might as well throw him a bone too.

"Don't you think all of this is getting out of hand?" Bonnie gave a strangled laugh, trying to lighten the mood. Or trying to get on his side. Either way, it seemed to be working by the way he tilted his head and softened his gaze on her. Bonnie took another step forward and forced a smile. "Don't you think that maybe, all of this isn't Vi's fault? People die from mysterious reasons everyday. It wasn't the Lord's punishment for us."

"Don't you remember what happened to Martha?" Finch said with remorse in his tone. "How upset and angry you felt towards Viola? How, *you* blamed her for her death?"

Bonnie looked back at me. Her eyes flickered on mine as I could see the guilt eating her from inside out. I know how she feels. Like a monster that lives inside your chest. Strangling you as it munches you apart until there is a gaping hole between your breasts. I could see the hole being formed from underneath her dress. The coral fabric sinking into a shallow pit. I don't blame her though. If all of this was reversed and Bonnie was the one who ran away. I would be as brainwashed as she was. But I am glad to see that she isn't brainwashed anymore, because her expression turned stern and she shook her head.

"That wasn't her fault." She pointed to me as her tone raised. "None of it was ever her fault!" She turned to the crowd and now she's pointing at Finch who looked amused by her lash out in front of his eyes. "Why do you all believe everything he says? He's a psychopath and—,"

I cut out her voice when I noticed movement from the corner of my eye. Vivian lied on the altar with her eyes wide open. She frantically looked around her surroundings, fear straining her face. I watched her eyes glance up at the cracked ceiling, then at Finch who paid no mind to her, and finally at the dagger clasped in his hands. I could see her shoulders tense and her breathing quicken. She slightly turned her head towards the crowd and stared at the hooded people that surrounded her. Their backs turned to her as they stared at Bonnie with hidden faces. Then she spotted me and she drew in her eyebrows. I slightly shook my head. Trying to communicate with my eyes to not move or else. Then she spotted the candelabra above her head and the red velvet cloth that was draped over the altar. I could see the lightbulb flicker on and the determination growing on her face...

Then it all happened so fast. Vivian quickly rolled over off the altar and pulled down the velvet cloth with her. Knocking over the candelabra onto the cloth, and the flames catching in seconds. It clinged onto the velvet with burning rage. The hidden crowd started to scream and frantically moved around in panic. The people ran into each other and bumped some into the burning altar, catching their cloaks in flames. Smoke absorbed the air and dried my lungs with heat, forcing me to cough.

I ran up to Vivian who was struggling to stand. Her body is still having effects from whatever they did to her. I wrapped my arm around her waist and held her up as we sprinted towards the hallway. I glanced behind me and looked for Bonnie in the panicked bodies that filled the room. Finch, still standing behind the altar, dropped the dagger onto the ground and raised his hands up towards the ceiling. He called unto the Lord to take him away and let him be saved from the wrath of the cruel world. Fire singed his long sleeved cloak, and grew along his body as he embraced the flames that slowly burned him alive. All I could hear was screaming and crying. All I could see was red cloaks hidden beneath the gray smoke, and yellow and orange flames that grew high upon the ceiling. I couldn't see Bonnie anywhere, and fear rose into my chest. As we rounded the corner and out into the dimly lit hallway, I stood Vivian against the stone wall and bent down to meet her frantic gaze.

"Are you alright?" I was strangled to speak from the dryness of the smoke in my lungs. I examined her body for any blood stains, scratches or any marks that showed they had harmed her in any way. "Are you hurt?"

Vivian coughed in her arm and shook her head. "I'm sorry. I shouldn't have left the school." Tears welled up in her eyes and I pulled her in for an embrace, wrapping my arms tightly around her petite body.

"I know. It's okay." I pulled away and cupped her face in my hands. "I'm not mad at you. But I need to go back in there and find Bonnie, alright?"

I waited until she nodded and then I rushed back into the smoke that started escaping into the hallway. Once I'm back inside the room, I scan the crowd for any sign of Bonnie. Pushing past bodies in the gray smoke, coughing from the fumes in my lungs. The smell was strong of burning flesh and ash, and the screams and crackling fire penetrated my eardrums. After seeing nothing but red robes and gray smoke, I finally spotted a bright coral dress lying on the floor by the altar. When I got closer to her, I realized that she was crouched down onto the stone ground. Hovering over a body in a red cloak. I reach out and touch her shoulder. She looks up at me with tears streaming down her cheeks. Renée lay in Bonnie's arms, her eyes open with a white glaze over her emerald green irises. Blood streaked down her chin as it pooled out of her mouth. The red handle of the dagger stuck out of her abdomen. For a moment, I felt a pain in my chest. I never liked her, but she was the only person who raised me since birth. She hated us girls. I knew that. But the way she looked at me earlier was a reflection of how much she was truly proud of me. Of how much she had grown. I might have never known it then, but I surely do now...

"Sh-she." Bonnie stammered, coughing from the smoke. "She sacrificed herself."

I pulled her shoulder back and away from Mother's body. "We don't have enough time, Bonnie. We've got to go!"

She nodded, wiping her eyes and grabbing my forearm for support to stand. An arm around her waist and an arm around my neck, we carried each other out of the smoke and into the wet hallway where we gathered Vivian and helped her walk through the candle-lit alley.

We went past the candelabra on the ground as the stairs were in sight. Thick smoke protruded from the hole above and then I remembered the second candelabra on the far right corner of the altar. It must have fallen down when I pushed the altar out of the way of the hidden hole underneath. But I never heard it fall, or I just never registered it because I was too occupied by the hidden cave that is underneath the church. I'm not sure if it has always been there or if it was created when they rebuilt the church. Either way, I'm pretty sure the church is on fire. But we still need to get out of here one way or another...

Bonnie gave me a weary look and I nodded towards the staircase. "I'll climb up first and help you guys. Then Vivian will go second so you can help her from behind, alright?"

Bonnie gave me a slow nod and I turned away, and started up the steps. When I emerged from the smoke that burned my eyes, I glanced around the church, but I could only see gray smoke and a blinding light that came from all directions. I could hear the crackling of the fire burning deep into the wooden walls and roof. A piece of singed wood fell down from the ceiling and landed on the ground in front of me. I gasped for fresh air but only got thick smoke that burned my lungs raw. I turned around, bent down and reached a shaky hand out for Vivian to take. Bonnie held her by the waist while she climbed up the steps. She grabbed my hand and I pulled her out of the hole, and guided her to stand beside me. Then I reached back down for Bonnie's hand. She took mine and started climbing out. Then suddenly, something pulled her back down from behind. I grip her hand tightly as I try to pull her up, but her foot keeps slipping while she's being dragged down and back into the thick smoke.

"Someone has my ankle!" Bonnie shouted over the raging fire around us. I gripped her hand as tightly as I could while she attempted to kick her ankle free. After four tries she finally managed to hit the person right in the face and they let go of her as they screamed in agony. I pulled her up and we stepped back to stare at the person that emerged from the smoke. They pulled their hood down and revealed a woman with silky blonde hair and a pretty complexion. Even with the blood that slithered out of her nose and down her porcelain chin. It was Sally. She held out her hand with frantic eyes...

"Please help me!" Sally pleaded. She looked hurt, but her expression remained neutral. She has no feelings, she's numb. Her act wasn't convincing enough to trick me. I went to take a step back when she suddenly revealed the bloody dagger from underneath her cloak, and swiped the sharp blade across my foreleg. I fell to the ground and cried out in pain. I watched Sally emerging from the hole in front of me with a sinister smile on her red tinted lips. She let out a small giggle and raised the dagger above her head. But before she could drive it through my thigh, Vivian drove the end of a candelabra down onto the top of her head, and knocked her out in seconds. Her body slid down the staircase and disappeared into the thick smoke and ash...

"Move out of the way!" Bonnie shouted from behind the altar. Vivian wrapped my arm over her shoulders and pulled me up to stand. My right foreleg seared in pain as I applied my weight onto it. My blood ran down my boot and slushed inside when we trudged away from the hole. Bonnie pushed the altar back over the hole, before she rushed to my aide and gripped my waist tightly. She and Vivian guided me through the hot flames and smoke that engulfed the building that surrounded us, and out of the church doors.

The air felt like a wave of cold water that soothes my lungs as I inhaled the spring breeze through my nostrils. I have never smelt anything better than the air right now. I squeezed my eyes shut to relieve the burning sensation that seared through them before opening them to find myself now in front of the burning church. Bonnie and Vivian coughed and gasped for air as they stood beside me.

Exhausted and dizzy, we stared up at the building engulfed in flames. It felt familiar, like déjà vu. I had been here before, watching the flames tear the building apart. It had been a recurring nightmare in my dreams for years. As if I had predicted it before it even happened. Maybe it was a sign all along—that this would always come to an end. That my past had finally become just that: the past.

The white paint peeling off the walls and the wood charring in the heat. Flames grew high into the sky and engulfed the upside down cross that peaked on the night sky. Stars twinkling above and ashes raining down on us. Grass crunched from the distance and grew louder to my left. A small hand intertwined their little fingers between mine and gripped my hand firmly. That sense of worry ran through me as I knew how they felt. Just like in my dream. I squeezed them back to give them a sense of comfort that everything will be alright...

This time, I knew I could turn my head, and I looked around my surroundings. The sky was dark with twinkling stars from above. The trees swayed in the fresh breeze that brushed my hot face in a cool coating. Beside me was Vivian. Soot covered her face with streaks around her eyes from where she wiped them with her fingertips. She held my hand beside me as she stared up at the building in a daze. A lot has happened to her. She didn't know about *them* before. I never had told her anything about my past life. I'm sure she will have loads of questions for me to answer on the long drive back home. Bonnie stood beside her holding her son, Boyd's hand as they also stared up at the church in a daze. He must have been in the car and gotten curious as to why smoke was coming from above the trees from afar. I may still be mad at her for a lot of things right now. But she did come back to the place she wanted to leave behind, just to help save my daughter from this cult that we were born in. It couldn't have been easy for her as it was for me. Maybe because I mentally prepared myself for this moment. Subconsciously, knowing that I would always come back. But not for the reasons I thought...

The trees swayed in the wind and the tall grass waved like the ocean in a current. But something in the grass caught my eye. Right in front of the church stood a small white flower that poked out from the ground. A single dandelion had grown in the thickness of the grass between me and the church. A small speck of ash landed on the tip of the white pappi and ignited a tiny flame on the soft puffball. Forever being a symbol for this day and this moment for the rest of my life. My life is reborn and I'm finally letting go of the past that carried me through half of it. I broke the curse that they prayed upon me. New beginnings are along my pathway through life now, and I for once get to choose them for myself...

Footsteps crunched from behind me and a soft hand touched my right shoulder. I could sense it was Bonnie by the shallow breaths that brushed my ear from between her lips.

"This is a sign." She said in a shallow tone of voice. "Listen to it."

I looked back at the church and prepared myself for what I knew was about to happen. Suddenly, the church collapsed entirely, and for the first time in my life, I felt the burdens lifting off my shoulders. It was as if I was floating, even though my feet remained firmly on the ground. In an instant, everything vanished. The dying dandelion and the dying past, torching in flames and becoming nothing but a memory...

The End

Acknowledgments

Dear Reader,

Thank you so much for reading my debut novel!

I worked so hard on it, and I hope that it exceeded your expectations and more.

If you want to read more stories written by me, follow me on my social media accounts, where I will announce new novels and events.
Instagram: @megangraceauthor
Facebook: @megangraceauthor
LinkedIn: @megangraceauthor

Thank you again for choosing and supporting my novel!
– With Love, Megan Grace.

About the Author

Megan Grace is an excited new Author with her debut novel being, The Altar. She treasures her family and pets, and is driven by her love of reading and writing.

https://www.instagram.com/megangraceauthor
https://www.facebook.com/MeganGraceAuthor26
https://www.linkedin.com/in/megan-grace-author-762550396/